Corrupted Crimson

PAINTING THE MISTS, BOOK 5

PATRICK G. LAPLANTE

Published by:
Patrick G. Laplante

First edition, 2019
ISBN: 978-1-9994447-8-5

Other Painting the Mists Books

Clear Sky
Blood Moon
Light in the Darkness
Pure Jade

Dedication

To those who forgive.

Author's Note

At the time of writing this note, there are five hours remaining until the new year. I can't help but look back at the past year in satisfaction. With the release of my books *Clear Sky* through *Pure Jade*, readership for *Painting the Mists* has soared. My writing skills have improved, and everyone's impatience for the next book lets me go to bed with a smile every night. You, the readers, are what makes this all worthwhile.

But enough of that—let's talk about *Corrupted Crimson*. As the tittle suggests, nothing can remain the same forever. Slowly but surely, even the most resplendent gold will become tarnished. The sharpest blade will dull, and the brightest silver will tarnish.

The same applies to people, to groups, and to nations. Chains of karma hold us down one by one, until choice is nothing more than an illusion. Can anyone be truly unfettered, a golden soul with freedom of choice? Or will everyone be forever tainted with a modicum of corruption, a crimson stain that will forever mar an otherwise perfect existence?

Most of us will never know, but one thing is certain: Nothing can remain unchanged. Time affects all things, and even the purest gold must be dusted and polished.

Prologue

The way forward was dark. The ever-present blackness sought to devour the small group of adventurers as they wandered through the underground tomb. A sphere of light traveled in front of them. It was a warm, soothing brightness that banished away the cold shadows that bit them. The artifact shone with unfettered gold, banishing the traces of corruption wherever they passed.

"Why would they build such an extensive labyrinth?" a man said. He was bald and wore an orange kasaya. Unlike Master Zhen, he looked to be in his midtwenties. His qi cultivation was practically nonexistent, but his soul shone brightly, banishing the mortal world's corruption wherever he walked.

The middle-aged Master Zhen had spent fifty years establishing his resplendent soul. He was now one hundred years old, the oldest of the World Tree Master's direct disciples.

"Patience is a virtue, Sibi," Master Zhen said. "The battle we Buddhists fight is an eternal one, and impatience invites corruption and fetters one's heart."

"My apologies, Master," Sibi said, regaining his usual composure. "It has been so long since we've seen the sun, and the shadows eat away at one's very soul."

"You are right," Master Zhen said. "These shadows aren't natural. They are the reason we've wandered so far and so long. Our order was wrong to ignore this tomb until now." He caught a glint of gold at the end of the dark corridor. Seeing this speck of brightness, the impatient monk beside him quickened his steps. "Hold your ground, Sibi," Master Zhen said, stopping him with a gentle palm. "You must not let temptation corrupt your innocent heart."

"But I'm not tempted by worldly possessions," Sibi protested. "This gold means nothing to me." Nevertheless, he slowed down and allowed his teacher to take the lead.

"You were not tempted by gold, but by time," Master Zhen said. "You were tempted by hope, by an end to the dreary scenery. But you must remember that these are all illusions that shackle us to the mortal realm. Only by shedding these attachments can we transcend and become a buddha. The only surefire way to Buddhahood is diligence, perseverance, and purposeful avoidance of these temptations. If you do not shield your heart…"

"… it will be corrupted by karma and sow seeds of evil in your spirit," Sibi finished. "Don't worry, I always remember your teachings."

Master Zhen smiled at his disciple's quick response and continued his slow pace toward what was now a golden glow. The rough stone walls eventually transitioned to marble inlaid with golden runes. They preserved the resting souls of the ancient emperors so they could guard the dynasty for all eternity.

"What a foolish ancient practice," Master Zhen muttered, shaking his head. The bodies of the ancient kings rested on marble slabs, which were adorned with a golden plate inscribed with protective runes.

"Why foolish?" Sibi said. "Do the Bodhisattvas not teach to protect those who cannot fend for themselves? In my opinion, these are honorable men. Despite their empire fading into ruins, they still protect their descendants without fail."

Master Zhen shook his head and walked over to one of the marble slabs. A gentle wind blew the dust off the gold formation plate, revealing a blurry name he couldn't quite make out.

"It isn't their purpose that is foolish, Sibi, but their methods.

Souls who transcend using the Buddhist path and the Evil Spirit path are expelled from the plane because their transcendent souls are eternal. Even without transcending, a soul will survive for fifty thousand years. Mortals, on the other hand, have a much shorter lifespan. A mortal human can live for up to one hundred years, while a demon monarch can live for five thousand. This is the natural order of things."

"That is naturally why they sought this path, Master," Sibi said. "It is the only way in which they could extend their protection through the generations."

Master Zhen sighed. "How long have you been alive, Sibi?"

"Twenty-five years," Sibi said.

"And how has age affected your perception of the world and your perception of time?" Master Zhen asked him.

"I can barely remember my younger years," Sibi replied. "They are gone like a ripple in the water. I can only live in the present, for fear of being confused by the dull image of a once-sharp past."

"And that is the problem," Master Zhen said, gesturing to the corpse. "This man died ten thousand years ago. How does his spirit see the world now? Does it still see the nation as something to protect? You need to realize that we Buddhists do not become spirit entities until we transcend to a higher plane, where we can continue our good work. That is because a mortal soul is far too vulnerable to outside influences. It is better that we enter the cycle of reincarnation rather than bare our souls to the material plane's corruption.

"Conversely, these kings have mimicked the path of evil spirits. They have bound themselves to their nation's karma and the will of their people. They will remain as spirit protectors for 50,000 years. Will they remain unaffected by the ravages of time?"

Sibi nodded slowly as he absorbed this useful knowledge.

The pair soon left the protector's marble slab behind and continued deeper into the mausoleum. The narrow hallway opened up into a large gold-covered room. In the center stood a gold dais which held a small jade object surrounded by twelve golden sarcophaguses.

Master Zhen gestured for them to halt and took out his exorcist's staff, which he waved back and forth while chanting mantras. His resplendent soul shone with a golden light that resonated with the runes on the walls. The dais and the walls shattered like a thin sheet of glass, dispersing the wondrous illusion and showing the tomb's true colors.

What remained was a scene from a nightmare. Crimson lines covered the once-pure golden walls like spider webs. On the broken dais lay a crimson seal. Only a single speck of green jade remained on its corrupted surface.

"And that is why this method is foolish, Sibi," Master Zhen said gravely. "The emperors bound their souls to the karma of the nation using their imperial jade seal. They thought that by doing so, they could protect the destiny of their nation for eternity.

"But look at it now. The descendants of their once-prosperous nation have been through multiple civil wars, plagues, and famines. Devil cults sow chaos and panic, and civil strife is rampant through the competing kingdoms that once formed their empire. The nation's destiny is corrupted, and as a result, their holy spirits have now become evil spirits.

"They now haunt and curse the nation in their bitterness, the opposite of what they had hoped to achieve." He sighed, shaking his head. "Only the Grand Master can take care of this. It will cost him dearly, but he will do it for the sake of mankind. The corrupted artifact will soon sow discord throughout the empire, causing friends to kill each over paltry matters and children to turn on their parents. Millions will die in the process."

"Is there truly nothing we can do?" Sibi asked, his eyes downcast. "There is still a speck of purity on the crimson seal. If we act quickly, we can propagate it."

Master Zhen patted Sibi on the shoulder. The boy was far too young, and this was only the first of many setbacks he would encounter.

"We are helpless," Master Zhen said. "If we approach the seal, the brightness within our souls will conflict with the corrupting aura within it. Either the seal will be unfettered, or we will be corrupted."

"So it's possible?" Sibi asked.

"For me, there is a one in three chance of purifying it," Master Zhen replied. "For you, it's a one in five chance. You must consider that losing one of us will grant the evil spirits a powerful new recruit. We would turn against mankind and sow misery amongst the countless mortals. The damage we cause could be much worse than the corruption of the seal itself."

"But if we do nothing, millions will suffer," Sibi said. "I became a monk to save the innocent. How can I possibly give up on my calling?" He moved toward the seal.

"Stop!" Master Zhen yelled.

As he spoke, the golden characters of the Mantra of Restraint surrounded the young monk and pushed him backward. Sibi remained calm. His resplendent soul shot out and expanded around his body. It glowed golden, and the vestment was covered in Buddhist scriptures. The Mantra of Restraint could only bow in obedience and shoot back to their originator. Master Zhen was now the one bound by his own mantra.

"When did you achieve the Soul-Like Scripture Realm?" he asked in shock. Only the Masters had achieved such a thing.

"I'm sorry, Master," Sibi said. "This is something that I must do. If there is a chance to alleviate the people's suffering, I will do my utmost to help them. Even at the cost of my soul."

Master Zhen could no longer stop him. Therefore he silently supported Sibi and hoped for his success. Sibi grasped the seal, and the battle between buddhas and evil spirits began—unfettered gold and corrupted crimson ate away at each other like swarms of ravenous insects. Slowly but surely, the seal's crimson aura receded. The small speck of jade became one percent of the seal and soon expanded to thirty percent.

Since he achieved the Soul-Like Scripture Realm, he still has a chance, Master Zhen thought.

He calmed his mind and held out his exorcist's staff. He chanted the Mantra of Support as he poured out his soul energy into the struggling youth. Little by little, the crimson aura receded to fifty percent. It continued slowly until it ultimately reached seventy percent before stopping. At this point, Sibi's golden soul suddenly underwent a drastic change.

The corruption in the seal shot out and sent eighty-one crimson chains that began digging into his spiritual flesh. Master Zhen looked on tensely as one by one, these chains were unfettered. They poured into Sibi's soul, brightening its golden color as they disappeared. This continued until only a single chain remained. This chain was far thicker than the rest.

Seeing the young man's struggle, Master Zhen ignited his remaining vitality to aid the young monk. He burned away his life and soul until only ten years of life remained. To his relief, a light golden glow returned to Sibi's rapidly fading soul. The last chain disappeared and fused to his body.

Master Zhen sighed in relief. "Are you all right?" he asked.

"I'm fine," Sibi said.

Master Zhen realized with a cold shudder that the young monk's voice seemed off.

"Turn around and greet your master," Master Zhen said. His sweat-covered body barely had any strength remaining. He could only despair as little by little, Sibi turned around and revealed a drastically changed appearance. His golden face was covered with crimson veins of corruption that crawled across his body like evil runic lines.

"Greetings, Master," Sibi said, giving the older man an awkward bow.

Master Zhen sighed. "Why did you fail? How could you fail when you'd clearly resolved the corruption?"

Sibi shook his head. "If only the final trial were so easy. But it wasn't a complete loss—by fighting against the corruption, I realized the truth."

"And what truth was that?" Master Zhen asked as he ignited a tattoo that rapidly replenished his soul. It was a gift from the World Tree, a blessing only given to potential World Tree Master candidates.

"That this country is terrible, and it must be annihilated," Sibi explained. "They ignored their origins and murdered their countrymen for the sake of profits. Tens of millions have died in the process. The only way to resolve the karma of this nation is to destroy it." The man's gentleness and compassion were gone. They had been replaced by the malice and resentment of the Song Empire.

"Hate only begets hate," Master Zhen said firmly. "With mercy, even an evil spirit can be saved and reenter the cycle of reincarnation. Will you follow your master to obtain the World Tree's blessing and unfetter your soul?"

He didn't know if this was possible, but it was worth a try.

"I'm sorry, Master," Sibi said. "You monks show no mercy toward evil spirits, so I dare not follow. I cannot obtain vengeance for the Song Empire if I die."

The man's hands came together in a teaching pose. A crimson glow appeared around Sibi as he uttered corrupted Buddhist mantras. They shot out from his mouth and struck the aged monk one after another.

Master Zhen shot out 108 talismans, which turned into 108 golden lights. They purified the corrupted runes, buying him time to jump back and evade a hidden assault. Having avoided the lethal strike, he pulled out a large rosary. Ten thousand and eighty golden pearls shone with unfettered gold light as they came together in an exquisite formation that banished Sibi's crimson light.

But Sibi's glow fought back. It intensified as his scripture-covered vestment unraveled and shot out toward the 10,080 rosary. They clashed together, granting Sibi an opening to charge at Master Zhen. The old and young monks exchanged gentle fist strikes in the monastery's traditional style as their artifacts fought in midair. As they fought, Sibi's style changed little by little. He shed his gentle fighting style and transformed it into an insidious and tricky one. Soon, Sibi found an opening. He struck Master Zhen in the chest and threw the older man into a crimson-colored wall.

"It pains me to do this," Master Zhen said, tears flowing down his cheeks. He had severed most attachments, and his apprentice was one of the few that remained. "Ten Thousand and Eighty Spirit-Banishing Pearls," Master Zhen said in a commanding voice. "Using my life force as a selfless medium, grant me the power to banish evil spirits from the realm. Grant me the strength to fight corruption and cleanse this man's soul. Ignite my own soul to grant him eternal peace."

Master Zhen's golden soul dulled, and with this sacrifice, the golden glow inside the pearls grew in power and tore apart Sibi's scripture-like vestment. Sibi howled in anguish as he quickened his offensive. He slashed at Master Zhen's weak body with claws coated in crimson corruption. It invaded the older man's soul and eroded it one piece at a time.

"Ksitigarbha, grant me your blessing," Master Zhen intoned as he ignored the pain. "Let your unfettered goodness send this evil spirit back to the cycle of reincarnation where it belongs." The 10,080 pearls flew out toward Sibi's crimson body and burned into his corrupted flesh. Sibi could only stop his offensive to defend against the golden rosary.

Master Zhen coughed up a mouthful of blood and tightened his fist, causing the pearls to dig into Sibi's crimson skin. They ate away at his body until all that remained was a golden skeleton and a weak crimson soul.

"Congratulations on destroying this useless body," the crimson soul said. It sounded nothing like Sibi. "Your lifespan has been significantly weakened. Meanwhile, I will enjoy the next fifty thousand years of existence. If I accumulate enough karma, I could even transcend and enjoy eternity."

"You won't live that long," Master Zhen said weakly. "The World Tree Master won't let you live."

"That old fart?" the evil spirit said. "By the time he gets here, I'll be long gone. Any last words?" The golden skeleton's fist clenched. Sibi's evil spirit could control the remnant body like a corpse puppet.

"One of us will kill you," Master Zhen said. "If not me, then someone else will take up the mantle."

Crimson tendrils shot out toward the older monk, who activated the teleportation sigil that had been branded onto his inner arm. The evil spirit, sensing the fluctuations in the surrounding space, rushed out to land a killing blow. A crimson talon slashed out toward Master Zhen, leaving a deep gash on his chest as space lurched and brought him back to the temple.

Master Zhen woke up in a cold sweat. *It's all in the past,* he thought, reaching out to the 10,080 beads around his neck. The lustrous golden pearls were blessed by the will of his predecessors. He too would bless it before reentering the cycle of reincarnation.

He rose from his bed and walked outside. It was hours before dawn, but most of the monks had already woken to perform their daily tasks. Both monks and animals bowed their heads in respect as he walked across the bridge and arrived at the Bodhi Tree.

"My old friend," Master Zhen muttered to the ancient tree. "It's time."

Yama, the Lord of the Underworld, was seated at a small golden table in the middle of a large temple. He didn't like it here—the monks were preachy and insufferable. Which was why, a few aeons ago, he'd placed a ban on door-to-door preaching. Ksitigarbha had been less than pleased, but his ire was a small price to pay for never having to hear the famous words, "May I please come in to discuss our lord and savior, Ksitigarbha?"

Speaking of which, this particular buddha was seated before him serving tea. He poured gently and without a word, using tea grown in his own backyard. Yama recognized this as a recent fad—meditation through tea drinking. They had been at it for ten Underworld days, and even Yama was beginning to lose patience.

As though sensing the man's volcanic temper, Ksitigarbha banished the tea set. "How do you feel? Are you one step closer to enlightenment? Has a small bit of karma faded?"

"My karma binds me to the universe for all eternity," Yama said wryly. "I doubt a few cups of tea will make a difference. Besides, you're making us sound estranged, like a preacher and his clergy. Why, it only seems like yesterday that we last spoke."

Ksitigarbha raised his eyebrow. "We haven't spoken in aeons."

"Which passed by in the blink of an eye," Yama said. "Surely you can forgive a man for his moment of foolishness?"

Ksitigarbha sighed. "What do you want? You are never this pleasant unless you want something."

"Well, you see, I'm in a very difficult position," Yama explained. "The Yellow River is overflowing, and I'm very shorthanded. Heaven and hell have been poaching my talent, and I've been left scrambling as I try to salvage the cycle of reincarnation. Therefore, I am supporting a candidate for mayor to push for tax reforms."

"You know I don't involve myself in politics," Ksitigarbha said dismissively. "Politics breed more attachment than sweets and loving promises. Political discussions have ruined more friendships than all other causes combined."

"I understand that," Yama said. "However, I have no choice. I need supporters, and the monks in your church live forever. You have so many of them."

"And why would I have them perform such senseless actions like voting?" Ksitigarbha said. "We all know it's a money game in the end."

"I..." Yama said, gritting his teeth, almost vomiting in the process. "I can end the ban." The ancient man's croak was barely audible in the quiet monastery.

"What?" Ksitigarbha said, his face finally showing a trace of emotion. "The ban that you should never have instated in the first place? The ban that us benevolent monks could only passively accept? Meanwhile, you allowed those petty door-to-door preachers with pocket scriptures to move unhindered in the Underworld, converting countless souls in the process."

"That's different!" Yama said. "All they're trying to do is tell people to be nice to each other so that they go to Heaven when they pass away. It's rather harmless if you think about it."

"And how exactly is it different?" Ksitigarbha asked. "We tell our people to be nice, and they actually do it with no karma attached."

"It's very different," Yama said solemnly. "Your followers were swelling out of control. Their preaching was emptying out the Underworld. Every soul that comes here is precious and rare. They stay for as long as their destiny allows it. However, you were convincing them to forcibly sever their karma with the Underworld and reincarnate. My workforce was getting decimated, and I was at my wit's end!"

"And now you're willing to reconsider," Ksitigarbha said. "All for the sake of winning an election."

"All for the sake of the cycle of reincarnation!" Yama yelled. "I do what must be done for our universe, without fail. In return for the votes of your clergy, I will allow you to preach door to door once more. *However,* it must be within reason. I won't have preachers visiting the same door dozens of times every day like last time. In addition, your clergy cannot exceed more than ten percent of the Underworld's population at any point in time."

"It's a start," Ksitigarbha said. "I imagine you'll have to allow evil spirits to start preaching again as well?"

"Don't remind me," Yama said, massaging his temples. "Truth be told, I would decimate the lot of them if I could do it without being punished by the cosmos."

"Might I make a suggestion?" Ksitigarbha said. "Now, I would *never* encourage you to do something dishonest, but I recall the Underworld's bureaucracy being notoriously slow. If their application for a preaching permit was to be delayed by ten thousand Underworld years, it would save us both quite a few headaches."

Yama's eyes lit up. "In fact, I've heard that some permits require up to 100,000 or a million years to get approved. Applications get lost, and trivial paperwork errors get made. Better yet, there is nothing they can do about it."

"Then we are in agreement," Ksitigarbha said while escorting Yama out of the premises. The faces of his followers were burning with fervent passion—it was obvious that Ksitigarbha had already informed them of the deal. Seeing that unmistakable gleam in their eyes, Yama secretly contacted Cerberus and sent him an employment offer. If there was anything a preacher hated, it was a vicious guard dog standing between him and a heathen's door.

"By the way, I've noticed some strange movements in the mortal realms," Ksitigarbha said. "It seems the evil spirits are making a play. Meanwhile, there have been some anomalies in your cycle of reincarnation. You should look into the reincarnation edicts you've issued recently."

Yama paused thoughtfully. "I think I'll do just that."

Then, eyeing the leaflet that had suddenly appeared in his pushy friend's hands, he promptly vanished.

Chapter 1: Value

Songjing City's walls cast a large shadow outside the gates. For centuries, these walls had defended the city from enemy invasions and beast tides. Although their robust military and well-placed fortresses had rendered these walls useless, their symbolism remained. The kingdom would never fall so long as they stood strong.

To Cha Ming, it was a godsend, but for a different reason than fortification. His furred and feathered companions now spoke in hushed whispers. They couldn't help but occasionally glance at the large structure and quiet down whenever they got too loud.

"Why are you so afraid of walls?" Cha Ming asked as they waited for Wang Jun to return.

"We do not speak their names aloud," Huxian whispered. "They are only mentioned in bedtime stories to scare newborn cubs. Every beast inherits memories of these atrocities. We remember millions of corpses and rivers of blood. Hordes of beasts collapsing under a flood of arrows as they pawed helplessly against unbreachable structures." Huxian shook his head mournfully. "We are fully aware that we have the strength to break them, but when we attempt to do so, we can't help but be paralyzed with fear. We are helpless against them."

Cha Ming looked up at the gate thoughtfully. "Will you be all right?

"We'll stomach it," Huxian said. "It's not so bad in smaller courtyards and buildings. It only gets out of hand with the more massive structures." He eyed the gatehouse cautiously.

Cha Ming scratched the tiny fox's ears to alleviate his worries. They spotted a blond-haired figure walking out of the city gates.

"They are so well behaved compared to the journey over," Wang Jun said cheerfully as he approached them. He handed Cha Ming three golden collars covered in black runes. "They shouldn't feel like anything more than regular collars," Wang Jun said. "They are purely cosmetic, with functions that falsely identify the wearer as a tamed beast."

Huxian walked up and stuck his head inside the first collar, which shrunk until the runes turned crimson. "Any change?" Cha Ming asked.

"Nope," Huxian replied. "And it comes with a built-in portable meat locker. Come on, guys, put these on so we can get out of this atrocious shadow."

His companions followed with uncharacteristic haste. They led the way toward the gates, making Cha Ming wonder if they knew even what tamed beasts were.

"The collars can grow up to a width of fifty feet if required," Wang Jun said as they walked. "Any bigger, and they'll fall off. The cost was outrageous since they had to mimic core treasures."

"Add it to my tab," Cha Ming said. "I'll find a way to earn money quickly."

"Ah, what's money between us?" Wang Jun said. "Besides, you don't need to worry about finding odd jobs. I already have a list of formations I need you to build. Soon, I'll be the one owing *you* money."

The registration process went smoothly. The guards collected a qi imprint and registered the beast's abilities—the ones they chose to reveal, at least—before sending them on their way. Cha Ming would be liable for any damages they caused in the city. His heart cringed in anticipation of a gigantic bill.

"It's been a long time since we've had a decent meal," Wang Jun said as he led them to the center of the city. "Let's make our first stop the Dragon's Claws. It's the best restaurant with private rooms in the city."

The oppressive heat baked the four road-weary travelers as they passed unfamiliar buildings. There were similarities between Songjing and Quicksilver—the Jade Bamboo Auction House kept its plain decoration and bamboo garden while the commodity exchange maintained its massive stone construction. The Blacksmith Association and the Alchemists Association shared a common look with their Quicksilver counterparts, though unlike Quicksilver, the stores here were unusually cluttered with high- and low-leveled cultivators alike.

There was no Geomancer Guild. The Spirit Doctor Association was also very different than Cha Ming remembered from his short stay in Quicksilver. A small group of commoners were lined up to receive treatment along with the cultivators. The building was also far less opulent than Quicksilver's.

"There's no Talisman Artist Guild?" Cha Ming asked.

"There is, but they aren't located in Central Square," Wang Jun replied. "They are too small, and their members are lacking. Plus they don't have any qualified instructors, which greatly limits their potential. I've always wondered what the Talisman Artist Guild's top brass is thinking by allowing it to exist."

After passing a few more buildings, they entered a large marble building where they were greeted by a gust of cool air.

"A legitimate use of refrigeration runes," Cha Ming commented. "The heat out there is unbearable."

"Air cooling is a must in this city," Wang Jun said. "The weather here makes me wonder whether the royal family descended from dragons."

"The royalty is naturally descended from dragons," a soft voice said. The speaker was a pale, skinny man in black robes with a cheerful demeanor. He accompanied a well-dressed man wearing black armor and a black-and-gold cape. Dozens of figures in red-and-gold cloaks were also present.

Both Zhou Li's and the black-and-gold-caped man's souls were excessively strong; they repelled the light probing from Cha Ming's resplendent soul, something only possible if they were core-formation cultivators.

"The royal family's crest is that of a five-clawed dragon," Zhou Li continued. "The national history books teach that the Song Dynasty's first emperor, Song Di, could partially transform his body and manifest claws and scales."

Wang Jun stepped up and bowed at the man beside Zhou Li. Cha Ming followed his lead.

"Crown Prince," Wang Jun said. "It is always a pleasure meeting you. How fares His Majesty? And has your favorite dog, Zhou Li, been behaving?" He had completely ignored Zhou Li's presence and chosen to address the more important person in the room.

The crown prince's face twitched. "Unfortunately, my royal father's condition worsens with each passing day. As his health declines, I find myself increasingly busy. I imagine it's only a matter of time until I'm no longer allowed to leave the palace."

"I wish His Majesty all the best," Wang Jun replied. "Both for the kingdom and your quality of life."

"My freedom and quality of life come secondary," the crown prince said. "Both the kingdom and I would be overjoyed if my father's condition improved." He then glanced at Cha Ming and gave him a short nod. "I am pleased to make your acquaintance, Master Du. Your reputation as the youngest mid-grade formation master on the continent precedes you."

Cha Ming bowed to the prince with clasped hands. "This one's talents are not worth mentioning. I can only affect a few people, while your own work impacts the lives of everyone in the Song Kingdom."

"If I become half the man my father has been, the kingdom will be in good hands," the crown prince said. "Now if you will excuse me, we must head back to attend an important council meeting."

As his group moved to leave, Zhou Li walked up to Huxian. The black-and-white fox bared his teeth and held his ears back, the universal sign of displeasure among animals.

"Be a good dog and eat this," Zhou Li said as he suddenly tossed a small string of gristly meat." Before Cha Ming could warn him, Huxian ate it on reflex. Zhou Li smirked. "I might be a dog, but at least I behave myself in front of my master. This one just does whatever he wants."

Cha Ming glared at Zhou Li's retreating figure and walked up to Huxian; he looked at him worriedly for any abnormal signs.

You can't just eat anything he gives you, Cha Ming said. *What if it's poison?*

Relax, Huxian sent back. *I can eat anything under the sun. What's a little poison to a Godbeast like me? Even the Geomantic Boa couldn't poison me if it tried.*

Cha Ming sighed in relief. "It should be fine," he said to Wang Jun, who nodded and led them to a private room.

A short while later, Huxian and Silverwing were fighting over large pieces of meat while Lei Jiang ate seeds and magical herbs. Cha Ming ate his vegetables while Wang Jun ate a bit of everything. Cha Ming let out a satisfied burp at the end of the meal. It had been weeks since he'd last eaten, and while eating was optional at this point, it had psychological benefits to a cultivator who had once required three meals a day.

Following their meal, Wang Jun had the restaurant staff bring a tea set and three large bowls. He poured three small pouches of red powder inside each bowl before the waitstaff poured buckets of hot water inside them.

"These small pouches contain an herbal blend that demon beasts appreciate in the same way humans appreciate tea," Wang Jun explained. "I call it Demon Soothing Tea." True to its name, Huxian and his two friends mellowed down considerably as they lapped it up.

"Just this peace and quiet is worth it," Cha Ming said with a sigh.

"Please order some for me in bulk once you get a chance."

"Not a problem," Wang Jun said. "You might not know this, but formation masters are a hot commodity in large cities. It's a rare occupation, and unlike talismans, formations have prolonged effects that can affect an entire clan's prosperity."

"Regrettably, I only studied offensive formations in Quicksilver," Cha Ming said. "Permanent formations aren't my forte."

"That's easy to resolve," Wang Jun said. "A few days ago, I had Elder Bai procure some single-use formation scrolls and mid-grade formation flags."

Cha Ming nodded. "That would be the cheapest way of obtaining the techniques. With any luck, I'll find duplicates when I return to Quicksilver."

"I'll give them to you back at the auction house," Wang Jun said. "For now, I have a promise to fulfill." He placed six small jade boxes on the table. "The immortal jade must be sealed like medicinal ingredients. Otherwise the energy contained within them will dissipate with time."

Cha Ming let out a sigh of relief. "Thank you. I need these ingredients to cultivate my body."

"Then you have an extremely overbearing body-cultivation art," Wang Jun said. "Even demon beasts wouldn't need such expensive natural treasures to break through to core formation."

"Except for dragons," Huxian said between sips of Demon Soothing Tea. "Those guys could eat a kingdom out of house and home."

One hour later, they entered the Jade Bamboo Auction House. Dozens of staff members were busy selling weapons to hurried customers while clerks were running around with thick stacks of paper. "I noticed the alchemists and blacksmiths associations were very busy," Cha Ming said. "Much busier than Quicksilver."

"It's because of the political unrest," Wang Jun explained. "Everything is now thirty percent more expensive than it was a week prior. It won't be long before there aren't any weapons or pills to buy. The blacksmiths and alchemists don't even bother with custom jobs anymore since it's so profitable to pump out large quantities of generic wares."

"Would it be the same for talismans?" Cha Ming asked, the wheels in his mind turning.

"Now you're starting to think like a businessman," Wang Jun said. "But that can wait until you've laid down enough formations for me."

For some reason, a twinge of irritation crossed Cha Ming's usually calm mind.

They walked through a few doors that led to a veritable war room. Maps were laid out everywhere and peppered with colored figurines. There were maps of the Song Kingdom, maps of the individual cities that composed it, and several maps of Songjing City. Some displayed economic influence and others market share or political influence. Each map had three colors—green, red, and blue.

"We are the green faction, and the crown prince's faction is blue," Wang Jun explained. "The red faction, which is rapidly dwindling, are loyalists or those who haven't yet chosen a side."

A door opened softly, and Elder Bai walked in with an armful of golden scrolls.

Wang Jun frowned. "Elder Bai, you could have put them in a storage ring or something."

The older man shrugged as he placed them on the table. "Money is tight, and I've sold our extra storage rings. You said it yourself that cash is king in these turbulent times."

"Fair enough," Wang Jun said, seating himself at the large wooden desk beside a fireplace. It was the same desk as in Green Leaf City, and the same fireplace. Elder Bai sat down and poured tea for three. Then, glancing at the three nervous beasts, he let out a sharp whistle. A small white cat dashed into the room.

"You called?" the small cat asked. It was an early-purification demon beast.

"Can you take these three friends to the gardens?" Elder Bai asked kindly while scratching his ears. "The war room is no place for them."

The cat's ears perked up when it saw Huxian and his two friends. "This way, esteemed sovereigns," it said, cheerfully guiding them out a door to the side.

Cha Ming let out a sigh of relief. "I didn't know what to do with them," he said. "A city isn't exactly the best place for a beast."

"The gardens have been beastproofed," Elder Bai said. He then gestured to the pile of scrolls. "As instructed by the young master, I've purchased a standard mid-grade energy-gathering formation package as well as a few defensive formations."

Cha Ming picked up one of the golden scrolls and inspected the writing on the carefully inscribed runic seal. It was a Mid-Grade Flame-Gathering Formation. He thumbed through the other scrolls and found that all five elements as well as wind and lightning were included. There was also a scroll for light- and shadow-gathering formations.

"A full set of energy-gathering scrolls costs about the same as five scrolls," Wang Jun said. "It made sense to buy the bundle, even though you can't set up light and shadow formations. I plan on selling them."

"No need," Cha Ming said. "I've recently discovered a way to make light-based and shadow-based formations. I am new at them, but it shouldn't be an issue given enough time."

Wang Jun grinned. "Then I'll add them to the list. Elder Bai, why don't you give us the rundown?"

"The capital is in turmoil, and so are the major cities," Elder Bai began. "The price of food has shot up by fifty percent, weapons by thirty percent, and pills by thirty-five percent. This is due to the shortage of these resources and the increased use of spirit stones as cultivation resources. Everyone is using every means possible to increase their strength during these turbulent times.

"Meanwhile, real-estate prices are at their lowest in fifty years. Many smaller noble families are looking to liquidate their assets, as they are reluctant to involve themselves in the struggle for power."

Wang Jun nodded. "This is only the beginning. It might seem like a good idea to dump our inventory of weapons, but the time is not yet ripe. Wait one week to begin trickling the weapons into the market. Sell to allied forces when considering equal offers. I don't want you selling all of them, however. Leave me ten percent to play with. And for heaven's sake, don't give in to the temptation and buy real estate. The prices have yet to hit rock bottom, mark my words."

Elder Bai bowed. "I'll get right on it." He then left the war room to give out multiple orders.

"Being the boss is that easy?" Cha Ming said.

"You've only seen the results of thousands of calculations based on tens of thousands of pages of information," Wang Jun said. "Being the boss is very troublesome and very risky. I'm afraid I won't be getting much sleep now that I'm back in the city."

"Neither will I," Cha Ming said while standing up to leave. "There are far too many formations to learn. Which should I prioritize?"

"Prioritize the Mid-Grade Flame-Gathering Formation," Wang Jun said. "There are five noble families whose descendants cultivate fire qi and body refining in the city. They don't like the Zhou family or the crown prince very much but are still sitting on the fence."

"I'll get right to it," Cha Ming said before heading to the residential quarters. As he walked, he couldn't help but feel annoyed at his recent orders.

Chapter 2: Gold Bone Forging

Cha Ming sat cross-legged in his residence, which was situated near the gardens where Huxian, his friends, and the small white cat were playing. His generous accommodations were much like the auction house itself—plain and simple on the outside with a pleasant-looking bamboo garden.

The luxury was in the details. There was hot and cold running water, an imported technology from Quicksilver. The heating and cooling elements were powered by runes, but the pump was mechanical. A tube in the washroom contained luxury scented soaps from a faraway kingdom. Finally, an exquisite tea set was carefully stowed in a cupboard, along with an unlimited pitcher of boiling water and dozens of high-quality teas.

Cha Ming hesitated as he pondered his next course of action. While he knew he should get to work straightaway, a nagging thought distracted him as soon as he got to work.

What's a few days? he thought. *Surely Wang Jun can wait a bit while I start my bone forging. After all, personal strength is paramount.*

After a half hour of indecision, he opted to follow the voice in his mind. He set aside the formation scrolls and withdrew a one-jin chunk of gold immortal jade; it emanated a sharp and incisive aura. He chose gold bone forging because it focused on the spine, the basis of the entire skeleton. The tricky part was using the solid immortal jade as ink, something he couldn't quite fathom.

As though answering his doubts, the Clear Sky Brush darted out without Cha Ming's consent and devoured the large chunk of immortal jade. The gold character on the brush lit up brightly, and inside the Clear Sky World he saw a small golden puddle of melted jade. It reminded Cha Ming of gold evanescence, but in a much stronger and purer form. He observed it more closely and noticed that it was laced with black and white threads. The Clear Sky Brush had likely infused it with creation and destruction qi.

He took a deep breath and visualized the pattern etched in his mind. There were 206 bones in an adult body, and the Seventy-Two Transformations Technique had a runic pattern for each one. Cha Ming drew thin runic lines in the air like he would a sigil. Unlike previous times, they didn't shake or quiver. It was as though they were inherently stable and at no risk of collapsing or self-destructing. He painted until his gold qi was exhausted, leaving the faint outline of his forearm bone floating in midair. He exhausted his qi one more time before completing the bone-forging sigil, which instantly burst apart upon completion and darted into his forearm.

He screamed in pain as the runes burned through his nerves, his muscles, and his tendons on their way to the smaller bone. But this pain was only an appetizer—he nearly blacked out when the runes entered the bone itself.

Gold energy poured into the bone while simultaneously breaking and rearranging its structure. He felt the pounding of ten thousand golden hammers as it was deformed tens of thousands of times. With each strike, the structure of the bone shifted increasingly closer to perfection. The process felt like it took hours, but only an incense time had passed.

When the pain ended, he noticed that the burned muscles, tendons, and nerves had completely recovered. They were much stronger and more sensitive than before.

He adjusted his condition before continuing. He forged his left arm and hand in half a day, and his right arm and hand in the other half. His legs came next, followed by the peripheral bones in his torso and chest. The skull came next. Each individual bone had its own unique pattern that linked it back toward the key bone in the gold-aligned bone forging: the spine.

Cha Ming began forging his spine on the fourth day; its runic diagram was much more complicated than any of the other bone-forging sigils. Gold bone forging placed great emphasis on the spine, where the force in the body was originally generated. His brush poured out the remainder of the gold immortal jade as he started from the bottom, incorporating intricate runes into each spine bone. He painted it in thirty-three installments, one for each bone in his body.

The spine sigil took an entire day to paint, and once the last rune was completed, it burst apart and seared its way into his spine. The transformation was ten times more painful than with the other bones. He twitched involuntarily as pain suffused his entire body. He remained lucid, for it was a requirement of the technique that he remain aware of the changes taking place.

A hundred thousand golden hammers beat down on his spine, shattering it and remaking it. Cha Ming was paralyzed during this process; his resplendent soul could only look on in amazement as the tiny imperfections and fractures that had accumulated during his martial journey were removed one at a time. The structure of his bones was rearranged into a three-dimensional runic array. In the gaps within the array, he noticed a peculiar phenomenon: the appearance of tiny gray dots.

The miniscule dots materialized at key points in Cha Ming's bones. At first, they appeared like nothing more than imperfections marring an otherwise perfect rune. He soon realized that they were much more than that. Tiny eddies formed around each dot and greedily sucked in the ambient energy. They were like voids, and the world itself fed them with a portion of its essence. The more they drank, the more Cha Ming felt his body crush down on the floor below. He realized that as they drank in energy, they used it to manipulate his weight. His body became increasingly heavy and only halted once it matched his current fist strength: 6,480 jin.

Not only were his bones forged, but so were the nerves, muscles, and ligaments supporting his skeletal structure. Those in the spine were evidently stronger than those in his arms and legs. Unlike the gold-wrought ligaments that now linked his bones together, his spine was joined together with titanium. The nerves were platinum, the best metal for conducting electrical signals.

Finally, the hammers stopped pounding. The eddies in his bones ceased drinking one after another, and as they did, his weight decreased. With but a thought, Cha Ming activated these voids and summoned their weight once more; his bones creaked but didn't break, as his entire skeleton was akin to a magic treasure.

His ligaments and muscles had perfectly adapted to his new weight during their reconstruction in the bone-forging process.

A carriage rolled up to the palace gates, revealing Wang Jun's humbly dressed figure. He was welcomed by green-clothed guards, who ushered him into the third prince's study. The prince was already waiting before the fireplace. He looked gaunt and weary.

Wang Jun, noting his condition, sat in front of him quietly. "It's about time you came to see me," Prince Lei said. He looked less than pleased.

His father is dying, Wang Jun reminded himself. *It is best to be forbearing and compassionate.*

"My apologies for not coming sooner," Wang Jun said. "There were some important matters to deal with, and I wasn't able to extricate myself until now. I arrived in the city only yesterday."

"What could possibly be more important than my father's condition?" the third prince said sharply, lashing out. His angry expression was immediately replaced with an apologetic one. "I'm sorry. It's been a very stressful situation. My sister and I have been taking turns watching over my royal father. The only one who *isn't* affected by all of this is my second brother."

"I understand your suspicions," Wang Jun said, "but the crown prince can always make up excuses like needing to be strong for the country. You know that."

Lei shook his head. "He's always been like this. I have no idea why Father favored him in the first place. He's an unfilial prick, and there's nothing I can do about it."

"Perhaps there is," Wang Jun said. "If the crown prince is responsible, he will leave traces. We need to be patient and expose him when he makes a mistake."

The third prince nodded. He picked up a jug of wine from the shelf. "Would you care for a drink?"

Wang Jun shook his head. "I don't drink. It affects my state of mind, so I'll make tea instead. You would do well to note that your brother is clever enough to poison your father, he's also clever enough to frame you."

Prince Lei hesitated before setting down the flask. His eyes were bloodshot.

"What was it that kept you preoccupied?" Prince Lei asked. He sat down and accepted a cup of freshly brewed tea. It was a recovery tonic, and color instantly returned to the man's pale face.

"A friend of mine, a citizen of the Song Kingdom, accompanied me back to the city," Wang Jun said. "He's a mid-grade formation master, one who is capable of setting up all nine energy-gathering formations."

"Is that even possible?" the third prince asked doubtfully. "Not that I'm complaining, but I thought the human body was limited to five elements."

Wang Jun shrugged. "That doesn't really matter, does it? Formation masters are extremely difficult to recruit, and many noble families in the city can't afford such an extravagance. With his help, we can recruit many undecided members."

Prince Lei visibly relaxed. "The sooner we rope them in, the better. That way, Prince Tian won't be able to sleep comfortably, either."

"On another note, we'll be trickling our large stockpile of

weapons into the market shortly," Wang Jun said. "This will net us a tidy sum, and we'll sell to allies where possible."

"And the properties of the nobles who wish to escape the city?" Prince Lei asked.

"Hold off from purchasing real estate," Wang Jun said decisively. "The prices are low, but not as low as they could be. Our allies and enemies have large cash reserves, and it's important to deplete them. We'll swoop in and snatch choice properties when the time is ripe."

The third prince nodded. "Anything else?"

"There's one more thing," Wang Jun said. "The friend I invited has dabbled in medicine. Although he is not a spirit doctor, he *is* a formation and talisman master. He might be able to see something the others couldn't."

"I'm not against such a thing, but my sister listens to the spirit doctors unfailingly," Prince Lei said. "She cares about Father just as much as I do. She almost never leaves his side. It will take some time to arrange for your friend to examine my father in secret."

"Please look into it," Wang Jun said. "Every day matters."

The door to Feng Ming's dark cell opened, revealing his father's burly figure. As a one of the Song Kingdom's four marshals, both his cultivation and presence were imposing. Decades of fighting in the southern battlefield had tempered his will to the point that he could make the average man faint with a single glance.

Despite his overpowering status, the large man walked over calmly, sitting on the wooden bench located in front of Feng Ming's bed. "Why did you refuse to come back when I summoned you?" Feng Chuan asked. His face contained no anger, only concern.

Feng Ming, who was seated on the ground, looked up to his father's figure. "I finally found something worth fighting for out there, and now you want to pull me away due to petty politics. How could I leave my life-and-death brothers behind for the protection of Songjing's walls?"

Feng Chuan sighed. "Civil war is a frightening thing. You weren't there during the last king's passing, but I was. The streets flowed with blood, and the poor starved. Fathers were forced to push their own parents out onto the streets to save their children. Your perspective is limited, my son."

"Why can't people set aside their differences and fight for the good of the country?" Feng Ming asked, his voice laced with anger.

Feng Chuan sighed once more. "This is something I've wondered my entire life," he said. "But my thoughts can't change human nature. There is a struggle for the throne, and we must take sides. I've taken the crown prince's side because his claim to the throne is the most legitimate. He also has a higher chance of winning a civil war, should such a thing occur."

Feng Ming remained silent for a moment. "If you want me to come to Songjing, you'll have to tie me up and carry me over like a sack of rice." He looked at his father with a firm gaze and a tempered will. Despite his father's abundant experience, Feng Ming's resolve didn't waver in the slightest.

Feng Chuan chuckled. "That's my boy," he said. Then he struck his son across the face with a gauntleted fist.

He picked up the unconscious Feng Ming and slung him across his shoulder. He took off his black-and-gold marshal's cape and used it to cover his son's body.

"It's a long flight to Songjing. Can't have you catching a cold."

Chapter 3: Fire Gathering

Dazzling red lights flickered out as Cha Ming failed to properly connect the fire sigils. While the Dao sigils weren't suitable for establishing a permanent formation, they were ideal for practice. The only alternative would be to waste countless precious resources as he scrambled to improve his technique a little at a time.

Despite his recent failure, Cha Ming sent out tendrils from the thirty-six sigils once more. This time, the 200 lines connected without any issues. The formation hummed to life and hovered above his hands in the shape of a two-dimensional disc. The energy in his surroundings gravitated toward the formation, which converted and purified it.

As an experiment, he threw a mid-grade spirit stone into the prototype. It was slowly converted to the purest fire energy, which he directed toward his Dantian and incorporated into one of his qi pillars. The instant he did so, however, he felt a rumbling sound that threatened to tear his foundation apart.

This development wasn't unexpected. He converted the dense fire energy to the other four elements until they reached a fragile equilibrium. While converting the energy caused substantial losses, it was far better than the alternative. Unfortunately, this also meant that using raw ore to cultivate was just as effective as using a single energy-gathering formation for Cha Ming.

Cha Ming willed the small formation to break apart, retrieving his qi and thirty-six gray sigils in the process. The Dao sigils reminded him that perhaps it would be possible to make a multi-element formation that could accommodate his unique cultivation needs.

He dusted himself off before walking to Wang Jun's office. The young master was busy poring over documents while discussing something with Elder Bai. "I miscalculated the market's appetite for weapons," Wang Jun said. "You can start reselling them as soon as it's convenient."

Elder Bai bowed and retreated from the room, nodding to Cha Ming on his way out.

"How is it going?" Wang Jun asked. "Can you succeed in forming a Mid-Grade Flame-Gathering Formation?"

"I can form a preliminary version using sigils," Cha Ming said. "Given the formation's grade, I give myself fifty-fifty odds of success."

"Fifty-fifty odds are pretty good," Wang Jun said, his expression brightening. "And it only took you a week and a half to learn it."

"Thanks for the sarcasm," Cha Ming snapped, rolling his eyes.

Wang Jun frowned. "I know you spent some time cultivating, but your personal strength is very important. It didn't mean what I said sarcastically. Is everything all right, Cha Ming? You seem more irritable than usual."

"Sorry," Cha Ming said. The guilty feeling that should have come didn't make even a slight appearance. "Regardless, by the time I've made ten, my odds should increase to nine tenths, if not ten tenths. I suggest we make some permanent formations in this building so I can practice making them using focus crystals. I've used flags and sigils before, but both materials are inappropriate for permanent installations."

Wang Jun nodded. He rang a bell, and one of the managers ran in and greeted Cha Ming. To his surprise, it was Hong Ling. The silence between them was palpable as they walked.

"How are your parents?" Cha Ming asked.

"I'm... not sure," Hong Ling answered as they walked. "I haven't seen them in years. Not since Xin Er ran away."

They passed by dozens of sealed cultivation rooms until they arrived at one of the larger premium cultivation rooms. It was a ten-by-ten-foot room built with an insulating material that could withstand the self-detonation of a peak foundation-establishment cultivator.

"Why are you still here, then?" Cha Ming asked Hong Ling.

"I'm still here because I've seen a side of the young master that they haven't," Hong Ling said. "I saw him lose weight when Xin Er disappeared. I saw him waste his precious time to look high and low for her. I've counted every penny he's spent to find information on her—a king wouldn't spend as much to find their only child. How can I hold a grudge against the man after all that?" He shook his head and left Cha Ming alone inside the cultivation room.

Is he really doing it for Xin Er, or is he doing it to recruit loyal subordinates? a voice whispered in Cha Ming's mind. Cha Ming rapidly pushed this preposterous thought out of his mind. *What's wrong with me lately? Why am I putting such a negative spin on everything?*

He sat down in meditation to calm himself before proceeding. Then he took out a ruby-colored crystal, which he painted with an exquisite formation using flame essence. It flashed and glowed with a warm light upon completion. Satisfied, he moved onto the next one. He continued until twenty-four crystal focuses were completed. Two of the focuses he attempted shattered due to slight mistakes in his brushwork.

Next, he took out twelve clear focuses. He used pure liquified elemental essence this time. He painted them with gathering and conversion formations—utility formations that were useless on their own. His success rate for these was abysmal. He broke half of them in the process, as he didn't have a suitable technique for using a sterilized ink like liquified elemental essence.

After recuperating his mental energy and fire qi, he proceeded to the next step. He summoned the Clear Sky Brush in its large form and threw out the thirty-six crystals simultaneously, and they floated in place with the aid of his resplendent force. He painted thick red lines on the floor between the crystals.

He didn't paint as quickly as he would mid-combat. Instead he took his time and paid great attention to detail. The types of lines used in utility formations varied greatly in both thickness and curvature. Thanks to his prior practice, he finished each one with ease, the lines snapping together once the last one was drawn, and the formation rapidly began absorbing the ambient energy and converting it to concentrated flame energy. Even if no one cultivated here, the formation would constantly create flame-energy crystals that a fire cultivator could use to cultivate for twice the result with half the effort.

Satisfied with his work, Cha Ming approached each formation eye one after another. He laid down a least-grade protective formation to prevent tampering and disruption by the formation's users. They weren't strong enough to prevent malicious actions but would still protect cultivators from their own stupidity. He nodded in satisfaction after inspecting his work one final time and headed upstairs. Only an hour had passed.

"You succeeded?" Wang Jun asked in surprise.

"I got lucky," Cha Ming said. "Though I'm apparently terrible at programming unaligned focus crystals. You'll need to order more."

"A small thing," Wang Jun said. "Ling Shao!" he called out.

A lanky cultivator in green robes walked in. He was one of the foundation-establishment guards at the Jade Bamboo Auction House. Wang Jun tossed him one hundred mid-grade spirit stones. "Go to practice room seven and test out the new energy-gathering formation. It should be quite effective. Make sure to note down the amount of time it takes you to fully process these stones. Use a standardized time-measuring incense."

Cha Ming sat down in meditation as Wang Jun worked. However, he couldn't focus on cultivation. He couldn't help but mull over negative thoughts in his mind.

Why couldn't he take the time to inspect the work himself? Is his time so precious? Besides, what's a man like Wang Jun doing in a small city like Songjing? What's his real purpose? And what's this favor I owe him?

His train of thought was interrupted by the man's return. "The hundred stones took one and a quarter hour to process," he reported.

"Excellent," Wang Jun said, dismissing the man. "That means the formation is operating at eighty-percent efficiency."

"Sorry," Cha Ming said.

"No, that's quite good," Wang Jun said. "A run-of-the-mill flame-gathering formation operates between sixty to seventy-percent efficiency, which means I can rent out the formation for a higher rate. It also increases my bargaining position with the noble families. I think I can rent out the formation you made for ten mid-grade spirit stones per hour due to the time savings. I expect I can rent it out at least twenty hours per day, so we're bound to make a tidy profit."

"Should I make another one?" Cha Ming asked.

Wang Jun pondered for a moment and nodded. "The market can take four more without a reduction in price. I want to keep the prices high to exaggerate the benefit of having a clan formation. Once you're done, we'll head straight to the Huang family."

"I'm starting to feel like a servant," Cha Ming said bitterly.

"Are you sure everything is all right?" Wang Jun asked with concern. "Maybe you should have a rest and relax a little."

"I'm fine," Cha Ming said as he shut the door just a little bit too hard.

The Huang family's residence was much larger than the Jade Bamboo Auction House. The architectural style reminded Cha Ming of Earth's Tang Dynasty. Its brick and stone buildings sported curved rooftops while golden decorations and paintings of landscapes adorned the walls. He recognized one of landscapes as the Silverwing Mountain Range.

A servant ushered both Cha Ming and Wang Jun through a quiet garden. They soon arrived at a small pavilion surrounded by a shallow lake. Red fish swam within it, giving life to the dark colors reflected off its surface.

"Have these young friends come see me?" an aged voice said from the pavilion.

Cha Ming followed Wang Jun across a thin bridge. They were greeted by two old men seated before an *Angels and Devils* board. One of the older men shook his head. "I concede, old friend. After all these years, I still can't match you."

"It's only two and a half points," the other man pointed out. "Why don't you try again next week?" The loser of the match bowed to the other and left without greeting Wang Jun and Cha Ming.

That's one of the ministers allied to the crown prince, Wang Jun explained mentally. *He's been trying to rally the old man to his faction for weeks with little to no success.*

"To what do I owe the pleasure, Second Young Master Jun?" the old man asked. With a swish of his sleeve, he sorted out the black and white stones to their appropriate containers beside the kaya-wood board.

"I've naturally come to continue our conversation," Wang Jun said pleasantly. "Would you care for another game?"

"I don't dare," the old man said, shaking his head. "I know my limits, and I don't like embarrassing myself."

"How about I play?" Cha Ming interjected. The man looked him up and down before glancing at Wang Jun.

"This is my friend Du Cha Ming," Wang Jun explained. "No relation to the Du Clan. Cha Ming, this is Huang Taishan, the grand elder of the Huang aristocratic clan. All decisions must pass through him."

"You're exaggerating things a bit," Huang Taishan said, motioning toward the mat in front of him. "I only advise, and my advice is highly respected. Young man, would you like a teaching game or a competitive match?"

"A teaching game, please," Cha Ming said. "The board position from your previous game was extremely complex. My skill is obviously lacking."

"Honesty is a good trait," the man said, nodding. Cha Ming played his first stone, and the man casually responded to his opening. "Second Young Master Wang, it's not that I want to rebuff your every advance, but I am truly helpless. I may seem like I have all the power, but I need sufficient benefits to convince the council of elders to take any action."

As they spoke, Cha Ming frowned, realizing that he'd already fallen into a disadvantageous position. The man was playing with the intent of forcing out everything he had. If he played too aggressively, he would be slaughtered, and if he was too passive, he would constantly lose ground. He chose to play an intermediate position, regaining a little of what he had lost.

"I have come today to offer you these benefits," Wang Jun said. "You are already aware that joining our faction will give you a steep discount when purchasing weapons. I know that you've been unable to adequately arm your promising juniors."

"But if we remain neutral, we can preserve much of what we have," Huang Taishan said, playing another aggressive move against Cha Ming.

Cha Ming sensed an opportunity and pounced on it. He was rewarded for his efforts by Huang Taishan's retreat. It was all for show, of course. This was an opening intentionally left by the older, more experienced man. It was a dance, and there would be no winner or loser in this game.

"Have you considered our proposition on guaranteed slots for spiritual blacksmith and spirit-doctor apprenticeships?" Wang Jun asked.

"The Zhou family has offered an equivalent guarantee on slots for alchemist apprenticeships and foreign spiritual-blacksmith apprenticeships," the man countered.

"You and I both know that you don't want those juniors leaving the city," Wang Jun said.

"And you and I both know that I have alternatives," Huang Taishan said.

Sparks flew as the young master and the grand elder faced off. The old man was a tough nut to crack, as Cha Ming could tell by the man's robust teaching game.

"I've come to sweeten up the deal," Wang Jun said.

"Do tell," the old man said casually. The intense conversation hadn't affected his game in the slightest.

"My friend here is a mid-grade formation master," Wang Jun said. "Just recently, he set up a few Mid-Grade Flame-Gathering Formations at eighty-percent efficiency."

"Then I'll be glad to have my family's juniors pay your auction house a visit," the man said. "You wouldn't let the allegiance of a neutral party stand in the way of making money, would you?"

"Naturally," Wang Jun said. "But I'm offering to have him build you one in your estate. This is all in addition to the previous promises."

The man's bony fingers paused as he was placing a stone. It was clear that he was performing some intense mental arithmetic.

"I doubt that you would allow us to be competitors," the shrewd man said, finally playing the stone.

"There would naturally be usage restrictions," Wang Jun said. "Only your family and sworn retainers could use it, not just anyone you hire off the streets."

"I must admit that your offer is very tempting," Huang Taishan said. "But I could also pay the Obsidian Syndicate 200 high-grade spirit stones and set myself up as a competitor."

"You can't," Wang Jun said, shaking his head. "Guo Jia is dead, so they are down a formation master. Cha Ming killed him in a formation battle."

Cha Ming could now feel the man's resplendent force lightly probing his cultivation base. He condensed his own resplendent force and easily repelled the older man's aura, causing the latter's eyes to narrow.

"Besides," said Wang Jun, "if you had this sort of cash available, you would have done so already. You know far better than me that raising a family's juniors isn't cheap. Only the Obsidian Syndicate would bother coming to this backwater country to set up a few formations. Now that they no longer have this ability, good luck securing an alternate supplier."

The man thought for a bit before placing an inconspicuous white stone. Cha Ming blinked a few times before realizing that this stone had completely crushed him.

"Thank you very much for the teaching game," Cha Ming said, bowing his head slightly.

"You need to remember that there are two parts to the game of *Angels and Devils*," Huang Taishan said. "There is a momentum you must follow to win, but your opponent will resist this momentum. You like to switch between attack and defense, but you must remember that *Angels and Devils* is more than just that. You need to combine momentum and resistance and develop your own flow in each game."

Something about these wise words resonated with Cha Ming's soul. As he was deep in thought, Huang Taishan turned to Wang Jun. "Three of them, and you've got yourself a deal. Bring me a contract when you have time."

"What about the council of elders?" Wang Jun asked.

"You and I both know I was lying through my teeth," Huang Taishan said.

Wang Jun smiled. "And I've taken the liberty of preparing a contract for you in advance," Wang Jun said, handing the man a golden scroll.

The older man read the document, which contained exactly what they had agreed to. He signed it with a drop of his blood infused with his resplendent force. Wang Jun did the same.

"Out of curiosity, how many of those documents did you prepare?" Huang Taishan asked.

"Just three," Wang Jun said. "You're harder to read than most people."

The duo left the Huang residence a half day later. Cha Ming had failed in creating the formation twice but succeeded the next three times. As soon as the first formation was active, one of the clan's juniors entered it with mid-grade spirit stones and began cultivating. He looked to be around eighteen years old, but he already had a cultivation base at initial foundation establishment.

"How many of the families do you expect to accept?" Cha Ming asked Wang Jun as they walked to their next destination.

"Only two or three, including the one we just visited," Wang Jun replied. "The ones that reject our offer, however, will have substantially elevated expectations. They will think twice before accepting an offer from the Zhou Clan and the crown prince."

"Then is it even worth the effort?" Cha Ming asked bitterly.

"Seriously, what's gotten into you?" Wang Jun said, stopping. "And Huxian as well. He's been causing much more trouble than he did on the way to Songjing."

"Maybe he just feels constricted in this city," Cha Ming said. "Have you thought about asking him what he wants?"

He continued to their destination while Wang Jun followed, brooding.

Chapter 4: Meeting a Friend

"I already broke through!" an overjoyed young man said as he exited the newly installed gold-gathering formation. The boy, Cha Ming observed, was barely twenty years old, a prodigy in his family. Unfortunately, they had not been able to provide for him as well as they had liked. The gold-gathering formation would allow him and his talented cousins to reach unprecedented heights.

Cha Ming gently probed his cultivation. His foundation was solid, which was impressive given his cultivation speed. "By the looks of it, you'll only need a few days before your qi sea clears up and you can begin cultivating once more," Cha Ming said. "I confess myself impressed."

"It's not surprising," the boy's father said. "He's been trapped at initial foundation establishment for two years. Unfortunately, our family offended the Zhou family long ago. We been unable to provide him with as many medicinal pills as we'd like. This gold-gathering formation is a godsend."

"I'm glad I could help," Cha Ming said. Then he pulled out three mid-grade talismans from his spatial ring. "Here are the three Mid-Grade Gold-Rending Talismans, as promised in your agreement with the Wang family."

"So fast," the man said. "We have three promising juniors that are the hope of our family. These lifesaving treasures will greatly reduce my worries. I, Jin Hao, owe you a favor."

Cha Ming shook his head. "It will only even up the odds for them if they encounter someone at early foundation establishment. These won't help them much against stronger opponents."

"That's enough for me feel relieved, and yet not enough for them to grow arrogant," Jin Hao said. "Don't be a stranger."

At least they know how to show appreciation, Cha Ming thought. *Unlike Wang Jun.*

Just as he was about to leave the Jin Clan, he spotted a green glow out of the corner of his eye. To his surprise, it was a fifteen-year-old boy.

So young to have condensed a merit halo, Cha Ming thought. "Who is that?" he asked Jin Hao.

"He is my adopted son," Jin Hao said. "There are so many orphans out there, but for some reason, I felt compelled to take him in as my own. He is a kind soul, and he has been a wonderful addition to our family."

"Have you evaluated his talent?" Cha Ming asked.

"He's a lucky one," Jin Hao said. "Jin Huang is a grade-four talent with an innate soul force of seven. What's most amazing is that he has an affinity for all five elements. Unfortunately, our family only has gold-element cultivation methods and dual-element cultivation methods related to gold." He shook his head self-deprecatingly.

"A pity," Cha Ming muttered. "It would be a pity for such a kind young man to have his options limited." He looked at Jin Hao. "Once he turns sixteen, if he is interested, I can teach him five-element cultivation. If he is willing, I can also teach him talisman arts. He is qualified."

Jin Hao's eyes widened. "Would you?"

"Only if he wants to," Cha Ming said. "There is still one year until he reaches the proper age for cultivation. I suggest letting him do whatever he likes."

Cha Ming left the Jin Clan shortly after. He was joined by Wang Jun, who appeared out of the shadows. Huxian trotted out beside him.

"How did it go?" Wang Jun asked.

"Very well," Cha Ming said. "And there was a pleasant surprise. I want you to keep an eye out for a young boy named Jin Huang. He's a talent with much potential. More importantly, he has already condensed a merit halo at his young age."

"You want me to recruit him?" Wang Jun asked. "Fifteen is a little young, but the good fortune provided by merit is nothing to scoff at."

"No, I just want you to have someone keeping tabs on him," Cha Ming said. "I'll be looking for students one day. This one is a perfect match."

Wang Jun nodded.

"Where to now?" Cha Ming asked. Although it was gratifying to see many neutral families flock over to the third prince's side, he was getting tired of the ceaseless running about.

"I've booked a great restaurant," Wang Jun said. "You've been working hard. Let's have a little fun."

Cha Ming eyed Wang Jun suspiciously and looked at Huxian, who was grinning ear to ear.

No wonder you came, Cha Ming sent mentally. *The only thing that interests you is food.*

He never lets me out, Huxian said. *So what if I broke a few things? So what if I ate a few rare plants and hurt Elder Bai's cat? Besides, isn't it about time he shows you some appreciation?*

Cha Ming rolled his eyes.

"Why are we walking so slowly?" Huxian asked a half hour later. "We could have gotten there a quarter hour ago."

"Patience, young friend," Wang Jun said. "A special guest will be joining us, but he hasn't arrived yet."

Huxian looked to Cha Ming for clarity, but he just shrugged in response. The guest's identity was a mystery to him.

They entered the restaurant and were immediately escorted to a private room. Wang Jun waited calmly for a few moments before forming multiple hand seals. His shadow stretched out toward the wall and formed a shadowy door.

"Shadow Road," he whispered.

Cha Ming's resplendent force noticed a long shade pulling away from the building and toward a black-armored soldier with a red cloak.

"Heavens, I'm bored," Feng Ming mumbled as he wandered aimlessly through the back alleys. He was hoping he'd find someone getting mugged to rescue so that he could lighten up his day, but luck wasn't on his side. Although he had money to spend—his stipend as a colonel—he wasn't in the mood for shopping.

Maybe I can go gambling, he thought. *Yeah, criminals and thieves hang out at casinos all the time.*

Suddenly, out of the corner of his eye, he spotted a black door that was cleverly concealed in the shade of a building. A black figure with familiar features stood next to the door—it was a friend he hadn't seen in a long time. Feng Ming didn't hesitate to walk through the door. His surroundings turned black for a moment before he walked into a room filled with familiar faces.

"Cha Ming, Wang Jun, Huxian!" he said before walking over and giving Cha Ming a firm hug. They hadn't spoken since his disappearance, and Feng Ming had only heard about his survival from Wang Jun a short while ago.

"It's good to see you, my friend," Cha Ming said. His features had filled out considerably since the last time Feng Ming saw him. Looks aside, he could tell that his friend's cultivation had improved substantially. His incandescent force couldn't pierce his friend's passive defense.

"Resplendent soul?" Feng Ming asked casually.

"Yes," Cha Ming replied. "Though by the looks of it, you're much stronger than me."

Feng Ming's cultivation level was at the peak of foundation establishment.

Feng Ming shrugged. "I got lucky. It's what I do."

The waiters brought in tray upon tray of dishes into their private room. Huxian and his two friends were busy gorging themselves like their lives depended on it. Meanwhile, the human trio drank tea as they waited for their dishes.

"I heard a funny story the other day," Wang Jun said. "It was about a witless colonel who told his father he'd have to tie him up to bring him to the capital. They say half the country saw him by the time he was tossed through the city gates and prohibited from leaving the city."

"Who knew Father would take my words so literally," Feng Ming lamented. "Especially after all the military merit I've accrued. You'd think he'd be proud or something."

"I think it might have something to do with you being his only son," Cha Ming noted. "Plus, there's no rule saying overprotective fathers can't discipline their sons. You're lucky he didn't beat you black and blue before dumping you into the street naked."

Feng Ming sighed. "I just wish I had something to do. While I'm technically here on a military assignment, I don't have any actual duties to speak of. All I have is my rank and people occasionally saluting me."

"Then it's not much different than many of the noble clans I've visited," Cha Ming said. "Many of their descendants get honorary military positions and the like, and all they do is go to some training and then lounge around for the rest of their days, telling each other stories. Speaking of which, they tell a lot of stories about you."

A waitress arrived with six dishes balanced precariously in her arms. She accidentally tripped, but the dishes flew perfectly on the table in front of their intended recipients. Feng Ming didn't miss a beat. "What's your favorite one so far?" he asked after swallowing down a few mouthfuls.

"Definitely the one about the Yin Gathering Cult," Cha Ming said. Feng Ming's face darkened at the mention. "I heard you and twelve of your best dressed up as freshly trained courtesans on their way to a brothel. Fortunately, it was a dark night, and the cultists who found you were as blind as bats. That or they had atrocious taste. After leading you straight to their base, you caught them just as they were starting a ceremony that prohibited weapons from being carried on their persons due to an odd quirk from their leader."

"It's not that they were blind as bats," Wang Jun chimed in, "but rather that they were far too stupid to attend the ceremony in the first place. He just happened to be in the right place at the right time."

"Look, it's not the most honorable idea I've had, but it worked," Feng Ming said indignantly. "Besides, I think they had good taste. Who could resist a dashing man like me in a pretty dress?"

Cha Ming erupted in violent fit of coughing. "My apologies, tea ran down the wrong hole. Either way, I'm relieved to see that you haven't sworn yourself to the crown prince like your father. Filial piety doesn't extend to damning yourself for all eternity."

"He can't be that bad," Feng Ming said. "The crown prince seems genial and hardworking. I'm sure my father wouldn't swear his loyalty to a bad man."

"Then you haven't met Zhou Li yet," Wang Jun said.

Huxian, who was eating off to the side, scowled at the name drop.

"I haven't, but I've heard a few scattered rumors. They all seemed baseless," Feng Ming said.

"I can confirm that he has consorted with devils. And that his brother was responsible for the Fairweather incident," Cha Ming said. He also tried to have me and Huxian killed shortly afterward. Finally, either he or the crown prince hired around fifty devil cultivators from the Obsidian Syndicate to participate in the struggle for the Silverwing Mountain Range. Wang Jun, Huxian, and I directly participated in that battle."

Feng Ming frowned. "Do you have any proof of the crown prince's involvement?"

Cha Ming shook his head. "I only know about Zhou Li being involved. While it's possible that this is Zhou Li's independent scheme, I find it highly unlikely. Especially given the coincidental timing of the king's collapse and the benefit that his father's death would grant him."

"Unfortunately, Zhou Li is good at erasing his tracks," Wang Jun added as he poured tea. "He is an expert in burning karma—even an inquisitor would have trouble pinning anything on him."

Feng Ming shook his head. "I can only continue to remain neutral until I have something solid. One's first duty is to their parents. It would take some pretty damning evidence to make me move against my own father."

"It's your life," Cha Ming said.

"It will all work out fine," Feng Ming said. "I'm lucky, remember?"

"Do let us know if you happen to luckily stumble across some of that damning evidence," Wang Jun said. "Anyway, that's enough dark talk for the day." He held up a small glass of hot baiju, which had just been delivered. "I never drink, but today I'll make an exception. I propose a toast to friendship. Don't be a stranger."

"To friendship," Cha Ming said, downing his own glass.

"To friendship," Feng Ming repeated. Both he and Wang Jun gulped it simultaneously.

A few rounds later, Wang Jun had tapped out, leaving only Feng Ming, who was used to such drinks, and Cha Ming, whose body refining made him almost immune to mortal liquor.

"So what will you do with all this free time on your hands?" Cha Ming asked.

Feng Ming shrugged. "Maybe I'll pay those nobles a visit and have a drink or two. For some reason, I feel like going gambling, of all things. Do you want to tag along?

"I'm game," Cha Ming said immediately. He was a notoriously unlucky gambler, which was why he usually avoided it. However, a lucky star had just offered his services free of charge. How could he refuse?

"Good," Feng Ming said. "I'll let you know when."

Their feast continued for an hour, after which they parted ways.

As Cha Ming returned home with Huxian and Wang Jun in tow, his jovial mood rapidly dissipated. He became sullen once more, and so did Huxian. It was as though Feng Ming was a bright light that banished the gloomy atmosphere that surrounded them lately. The negative thoughts returned with his absence.

"So much for pulling him to our side," Wang Jun said as they walked back to the Jade Bamboo Auction House.

"What is it with all the sides and fighting?" Cha Ming said. "There's no need to pull him to our side. He's got a merit halo a mile wide. With his luck, a warning is enough. I'm actually looking forward to what kind of chaos he'll cause in the city."

Wang Jun chuckled uncomfortably. "I suppose you're right. I bet you one hundred high-grade spirit stones he'll get kicked out of the city within a month."

"Why is it always about money with you?" Cha Ming said. "And have you scheduled an appointment with the king yet?"

"What's gotten into you?" Wang Jun said.

As he reached out to Cha Ming's shoulder, Huxian growled and darted between them. His pseudo-core-formation cultivation immediately repelled Wang Jun, who could only back away in disbelief. The usually kind fox's teeth were bared and his ears pulled back.

"Soon," Wang Jun said coldly. "The king's condition is degrading very slowly as the spirit doctors are doing a good job keeping him alive. I hear the crown prince is holding a banquet sometime soon. The princess should be distracted for the entire evening. Although, I really wonder if you're fit to examine anyone in this state."

Wang Jun frowned and pulled a jade orb from his robes. Elder Bai's jade projection immediately appeared. "What's the urgent matter?" he asked the older man.

"Regulatory problems," Elder Bai said seriously. "The crown prince is using his position as intermittent leader to push forward price controls and choke out our potential profits."

Wang Jun's expression turned grim. "I'll be right there." The usually calm man walked toward a shadowy door that appeared on the wall. "Would you like to come along, or will you be heading back yourself?"

Cha Ming waved him off. "We'll take a walk and enjoy the scenery."

Wang Jun departed immediately, leaving Cha Ming and Huxian with two innocent-looking small animals. Huxian looked up at Cha Ming with teary eyes.

"You guys are still hungry?" Cha Ming asked incredulously. "Fine, but I'd like to visit the Talisman Artist Guild before they close."

A few hours later, Cha Ming and Huxian walked out of a shabby-looking building, their faces full of disappointment. Instead of a guild, it was better to call it a personal workshop for a single talisman artist. The lone man wasn't even a master artist, and the few students he kept were disappointing at best.

When asked where the branch leader was, the man said there wasn't one and shooed them off.

"It's too bad I don't have time to take over," Cha Ming said to Huxian. "This place is terrible. Do you think Feng Huoshan would even be interested?"

The "guild" was in a run-down alley where various shops were located. Cha Ming saw a pawn shop, a moneylender, and other less-savory businesses. Here and there, he saw red lights beckoning to their depraved customers."

"What's that?" Huxian said, perking up his ears.

A hooded figure stood in the distance, its black garment blending in with the nearby shadows.

Huxian sniffed. "That person smells familiar." He sniffed once more, and his eyes turned crimson. Shadows surrounded Huxian as he disappeared.

Cha Ming followed suit, wreathing himself in shadows and entering a surreal dimension. They were now walking in a space that seemed to defy physical laws. Pieces of ground and buildings littered this new landscape, which was divided by a sea of bright light.

Just jump from shadow to shadow like I do, Huxian said, darting from one piece of "land" to another.

You mean these are shadows? Cha Ming asked, looking at the perfectly visible pieces of road and building. He now realized they were a partial picture of their surroundings, the pieces that were originally obscured by darkness.

Of course, Huxian replied. *Those who dwell in the shadows see things differently.*

Cha suspended his disbelief and followed the small fox from one landmass to the next. In the distance, he saw a cloaked figure growing clearer and clearer in the ocean of light. He was walking at a leisurely pace, changing directions every so often. The process of tailing someone in the shadows was disorienting.

Why would he go there? Huxian sent mentally.

Before Cha Ming could wonder where "there" was, he noticed that they'd arrived in an alley. It was perfectly lit in their world of shadows, meaning that it was completely obscured in reality. However, the figure wasn't there. Instead, they saw a few inconspicuous scraps of meat.

They both emerged in the alley, and Cha Ming looked away with disinterest as Huxian ate up the scraps of meat.

"Who was that?" Cha Ming asked.

"Beats me," Huxian said.

"Should you really be eating something if you don't know where it comes from?" Cha Ming said.

"Who made you my boss?" Huxian growled. His pressure sent Cha Ming back a few feet, but he ultimately remained unharmed.

"Fine," Cha Ming said. "Have it your way."

They hid their bitterness in their hearts as they headed back to the Jade Bamboo Auction House.

Chapter 5: Regulation

A flash of light blinded Cha Ming as the Lightning-Gathering Formation collapsed. It was his fourth failure today, which was surprising given that he'd successfully built the formation five times over the past week. He couldn't help but stress over the mounting costs of production.

It's just money, Cha Ming thought. *The only one who'll worry about it is Wang Jun.*

Yeah, who asked him to be so cheap? a voice said in his mind.

"Another failure?" a worried elder said as he walked in. "Perhaps it would be best if you came back tomorrow?"

Cha Ming nodded. "Tomorrow would be best. Luck just isn't with me today." As he walked away, he couldn't help but complain inwardly about the extra stress he'd been feeling these days.

I'd feel a lot better if he shared more with me, Cha Ming thought. *He won't even tell me why he's in Songjing to begin with. Shouldn't a bigshot like him be lording it over in Gold Leaf City?*

What else isn't he telling you? the same voice whispered.

He was joined by Huxian as he exited the Lei family premises. "How was your day?" he asked Huxian.

"It would have been a lot better if Wang Jun didn't freak out when I broke a few things," Huxian said. "Why does he have to be so stingy? It's like he doesn't trust us."

Cha Ming couldn't help but be indignant at his brother's treatment.

Who does he think he is, treating you both like that? the voice whispered. *Isn't it just money?*

A soft pulsing alerted him of an incoming call, which he promptly ignored. It was likely Wang Jun and his usual demands.

Cha Ming and Huxian wandered aimlessly for a few hours before returning. He was greeted at the front door by none other than the second young master of the Wang family.

"We need to talk," Wang Jun said.

"We don't," Cha Ming replied, making his way toward the guest quarters.

An invisible force reached out and restrained both him and Huxian. "I'm afraid I have to insist," Wang Jun said.

Cha Ming rolled his eyes. "If it pleases His Royal Highness."

Wang Jun frowned but released his bindings. He brought both Cha Ming and Huxian to his office, where he looked at them with concern.

"Did anything happen to you since we came to Songjing?" Wang Jun asked.

"How is it any of your business?" Cha Ming snapped.

"With how much your personalities have changed, how can it not be my business?" Wang Jun said. "Your performance has been slipping with each formation you make. That's not like you. Your material costs are rising exponentially."

"So it's all about money." Cha Ming smirked. "The mighty Wang Jun, pinching every penny."

"You know that's not it," Wang Jun said.

"Do I?" Cha Ming asked. "What's the real reason you're in this backwater country? It can't be about money. You and your bigshot family have more than enough of it."

"It's complicated," Wang Jun said. "But I'll explain it to you once we figure out what's wrong with you."

"Always orders and never answers," Cha Ming barked. His temper was soaring, and so was Huxian's.

"Protector Ren, please restrain them," Wang Jun said. At his command, a cloaked figure appeared out of nowhere. Dozens of gold chains shot out and entangled both Cha Ming and Huxian, sealing their qi and physical strength.

Cha Ming panicked as his strength left him, and so did Huxian. Countless thoughts flitted through their minds as they tried to process what was happening. It wasn't long before they were both overwhelmed with anxiety and fear and could hear nothing but constant whispers that brought them closer and closer to the edge of their sanity.

Wang Jun is greedy. Why should you trust him? You need to relax. It's okay to make mistakes. Everything would be fine if it wasn't for that greedy fool. What are his goals?

The voices echoed endlessly as they entered a semi-conscious state.

"Protector Ren... Church of Justice..." said a voice that sounded like Wang Jun's. "I'm not welcome... Only you..."

Cha Ming felt a faint wind rustle his robes as the blurry scenery around him changed.

"Who...?" he heard. The voice was distorted and barely intelligible.

"Protector Ren... Conglomerate," another voice said. "... Inflicted... treated... possible."

Cha Ming felt weightless as he was carried through a massive opening in the blurry building.

"... beyond my ability," another voice said. "... chaplain."

"... hurry," the first voice urged.

Cha Ming fell onto a soft surface. Huxian, who was shivering, was nuzzled up against him and whimpering. He was the only other creature that Cha Ming could still make out clearly. Suddenly, a small light appeared up above. It looked like a lantern, but it was bright like the sun.

"... state of mind," a gentle voice said. "... confuses karma... drive a person to madness."

Cha Ming shivered at these words, recalling the seeds of doubt that had been growing inside him since they'd arrived in the city. His surroundings grew colder with each passing second.

With a gesture from a blurry figure, the warm light enveloped him. His mind relaxed as invisible threads collapsed and burned away. Slowly, his obscured surroundings became clearer. He and Huxian were lying on a bed in a small room, and a man with golden robes and a golden lantern appeared before them. He was a core-formation cultivator, and the lamp was a core treasure. Little by little, the voices in their minds faded away into nothing.

The golden-robed man's realm was much higher than his. He didn't even have to probe out with his resplendent soul—it was as though the man wanted to announce his late-core-formation cultivation to the world. A thick jade merit halo surrounded him, one that that was several times thicker than most in the Alabaster Group.

"How are you feeling?" the man asked gently. He wore his black hair in a topknot and bore the appearance of a Confucian scholar.

"Much better now," Cha Ming said, orienting himself. "Many thanks. I've not been myself lately."

"It's not a problem," the man said. "As a chaplain of the Church of Justice, it is my duty to fight against these spiteful things that should not exist in this world."

Cha Ming sat up and adjusted his robes. "My name is Du Cha Ming, and this is my brother, Huxian," he said, motioning to the sleeping fox. "How many I address you?"

"Just call me Chaplain Chen," the man said. "Would you mind telling me how you landed in such a miserable state?"

Cha Ming thought for a while as he processed his memories over the past week. "This is just speculation, but Huxian ate some scraps of meat dropped by Zhou Li, and our behavior gradually worsened over a period of two weeks. Our condition deteriorated once Huxian ate some more of this meat in an alley. What happened to us?"

"A curse," Chaplain Chen said. "This Zhou Li is the crown prince's advisor?"

Cha Ming nodded, causing the man's frown to deepen.

"As an oracle, he should know better than to dabble in such dark arts. I'll have to look into this."

"I doubt it's dabbling, and it's not like he hasn't done worse things," Cha Ming said. "It's a known fact that either he or the crown prince hired forces from the Obsidian Syndicate to fight in the north."

The chaplain grimaced. "I sense your words are true. The Obsidian Syndicate is a vile group. It's filled with evil creatures that think wrong is right and the heavens are hell."

"I've seen these devils myself," Cha Ming said, pointing toward his own eyes, which glowed with a faint jade light.

"Interesting," Chaplain Chen whispered. "Please follow me. I wish to verify something."

Cha Ming grabbed the unconscious Huxian and followed the man as they wandered through a hall filled with pews. Commoners and cultivators alike kneeled in prayer to the tall statue of a goddess. The smell of incense wafted through the large building, which was filled with tinted windows and glass art. Each piece was manipulated and refracted light, making the church a symphony of iridescent lighting.

"To which god do you pray?" Cha Ming asked as they walked.

"We worship Goddess Xihe, the ancient mother of the ten suns," the man explained. "She bathes the world in her protective light, and through her illumination, we see the truth and banish darkness."

They passed by a smaller chapel where armored men were kneeling in adoration before the statue of a woman surrounded by ten globes of light.

"This way," Chaplain Chen said as he led them through a door to the side. They entered a small library, which was filled to the brim with books. A middle-aged librarian woke up with a start as they walked to his desk.

"Exalted Chaplain, how may I be of service?" the librarian asked with a guilty expression.

"Where can I find the book on unconventional eye techniques?" the chaplain asked.

The librarian thought for a moment before leading them to a

dusty corner of the library. He pulled out a thick book with tattered pages and handed it to the chaplain.

"That will be all," the chaplain said. The man bowed and retreated.

The chaplain flipped through many pages before arriving at an entry entitled "Eyes of Pure Jade."

"A technique created by the Jade Emperor, who fought valiantly against the devils. He created 108,000,000 inheritances, ten for each lesser realm. They can detect both merit and sin, angelic and devil characteristics. They can also develop Devil-Sealing Intent and awaken a deeper inheritance. A pity."

"A pity?" Cha Ming asked.

"Your eyes have share traits with our inquisitor abilities, but they aren't what I'm looking for," the chaplain explained.

"Which is?" Cha Ming said.

"I am looking for spirit detection abilities," the chaplain said. "Inquisitors can detect aggregate sin and differentiate truth and lies. Given sufficient talent, they can detect devilized humans and angelic endowment. However, this only applies to living beings. Evil spirits are exempt.

"Unfortunately, there have been strange happenings in the city that can only be caused by ghosts and their impure ilk. Things like hauntings or possessions have become commonplace. If we were on good terms with the Buddhists, we could ask for their help. Alas, we were estranged centuries ago, and we rarely collaborate. We foolishly decimated nine tenths of their numbers a few decades ago for the sake of the 'common good.'"

The chaplain shook his head and led them back to a room where Protector Ren stood.

"I owe you two favors," Cha Ming said to the chaplain, "one for saving my life, and another for saving my brother's."

"You owe me nothing," Chaplain Chen said. "I was doing my duty."

"Regardless, if you find yourself in need of formations or talismans, you can find me at the Jade Bamboo Auction House," Cha Ming said.

Huxian followed him, still trembling slightly from the

experience. Protector Ren escorted them back to the auction house and immediately left for the palace.

How did it go? Wang Jun sent to Protector Ren mentally. The man had just walked into the assembly hall where the ministers were currently deliberating.

Full recovery, he said. *And it seems like Cha Ming and the Church of Justice hit it off well.*

Wang Jun nodded. *Good. They aren't people that can be drawn in with money alone. They want truth and trust. Unfortunately, the questions they ask are insensitive. It's like they believe they are entitled to complete and unfalsified information.*

In all fairness, they aren't hypocrites, Protector Ren said. *They don't lock their doors, and they answer any question asked, even if they are uncomfortable with the answer. They'll even talk about the inquisition a few centuries ago. They will tell you the whole, unabridged truth and express their sincere regrets about their order's actions.*

Wang Jun sighed. *The complete truth doesn't belong in polite society. Few people have the mental fortitude to handle it. They are fickle and prefer to remain ignorant.*

And what about your friend Cha Ming? Protector Ren asked. *Can he handle it?*

Wang Jun pondered how to bring up the sensitive topic. The cat was out of the bag, and even if his friend wasn't himself, everything had a source. Wang Jun's goals in the Song Kingdom were definitely in the back of Cha Ming's mind.

Sighing, he turned his attention back to the proceedings. They began the final hearing on an issue that had been beaten to death over the past week.

"I would like to call forward Minister Gong to offer testimony," Sima Liang said toward the throne.

The king was conspicuously absent, and so was his loyal servant. The crown prince sat on a small chair beside the throne.

"Minister Gong, if you please." The crown prince motioned.

The middle-aged minister bowed before speaking. He was a foundation-establishment cultivator, and his voice easily projected across the entire court.

"My prince, the people are suffering," Minister Gong said. "They feel unsafe in these turbulent times. Despite your best efforts to stabilize the nation during your father's ill health, the people cannot understand how hard you toil. Therefore, they seek to arm themselves to prepare for the unlikely event of a conflict. They seek lifesaving medicines and treasures to protect their family members.

"Unfortunately, the price of food and weapons has become increasingly steep. At first, it was only a premium of thirty percent over the list price, a reasonable number when facing uncertain times. However, supply has dwindled. Greedy merchants have been trickling their wares into overcrowded shops. They are taking advantage of the common people. Now only the rich can afford to protect their families. I beseech the crown prince to take charge of the situation for the good of the nation."

The crown prince, who was seated on the throne, frowned. "I have stated before that this is a very serious issue. Prices increases are normal, but there are limits. What are the latest figures?"

"Sometimes *double* the list price!" Minister Gong said in an exaggerated tone.

Wang Jun rolled his eyes. This price was likely obtained from one of the minister's own shops. He knew for a fact that they hadn't grown to that extent."

"That's very serious," the crown prince said gravely. "Is there anyone else who would like to testify on this matter?"

As though by prior agreement, half the ministers looked toward Wang Jun.

"Since the aim is to target me, I will naturally give my opinion," Wang Jun said.

"Our aim is not to target, only to protect the people," one of the ministers said indignantly.

"Yes, I'm sure that is your aim," Wang Jun said. "This is why you have all unloaded your personal holdings at an average of 1.45 times the market price before trying to institute a price ceiling at 1.3 times. Oh wait, in your case it was 1.67 times, Minister Bing. Am I mistaken?"

The minister blushed, not knowing how to reply.

"Need I also remind the ministers that those purchasing weapons so readily are those with the least faith in the kingdom's stability? Why should you enable these troublemakers? My humble Wang family only seeks to make profit by supplying what the people demand at a reasonable price. Right now, the reasonable price is much higher than historical figures. I am sure that most of the ministers here can attest to this."

The crown prince frowned. "I do not wish for the common people to become implicated in your money-making schemes. Is there anything else you would like to add?"

"Certainly, Your Highness," Wang Jun said. "But to do this I need to tell you a story. Have you ever heard of the Huangfu Kingdom?"

"Of course," the crown prince said. "It was a kingdom that suffered economic collapse 265 years ago. To my knowledge, their political situation was entirely different from ours. How is this case relevant?"

"Our Wang family has found this case to be useful when educating our family members," Wang Jun said. "I will share our family's analysis with you, as it may shed some light on the current situation."

He looked over all the ministers in attendance, evaluating their expressions before continuing. "The Huangfu Kingdom was peaceful and widespread. It occupied a fifth of the continent, and its ruler was benevolent but forceful. One day, he decided that he'd had enough of unstable prices. After all, his kingdom was ordained by the heavens; shouldn't everyone be happy under his reign?

"Therefore, the king stated that no goods could sell at what he called usurious prices. He capped maximum prices at 1.2 times their historical average, which became known as the list price. The merchants readily agreed—after all, such a move would choke out their smaller competitors. It was very favorable for large-scale sellers who could purchase goods more cheaply than their competitors."

Wang Jun sighed. "The peaceful times didn't last. One year, there was a drought. Food became extremely scarce. To balance supply and demand and line their pockets in the process, the merchants applied for an exemption to the price sealings. But the king was steadfast. He prevented them from selling at greater than 1.2 times the list price. In response, many merchants turned to the black market to offload their dwindling stockpiles. The king had these merchants executed as an example and distributed their goods amongst the people.

"The famine intensified. People were starving, despite there being enough food to go around. The king, in his benevolence, imported massive quantities of food, which he distributed throughout the nation. Yet despite these efforts, people still starved. As a side note, the merchants who'd had enough with the situation left the kingdom for better pastures. They went to the other four fifths of the continent. Due to this, the empire was faced with a distribution problem."

One of the ministers let out a loud snort.

"Is there something you would like to add, Minister Sima?" Wang Jun asked.

"I just find it amusing that you are threatening to pull the Wang family out of the Song Kingdom," Sima Jiang said. "I suggest you just get on with it and save us all from this boring speech."

"You misunderstand," Wang Jun said. "The issue with the merchants is hardly worth mentioning, which is why I mentioned it as a side issue. Would you please allow me to continue?"

The crown prince nodded.

"After the merchants left, there was naturally a distribution issue. But it wasn't something the nation couldn't remedy. The greater problem was that, at one point, there was ten years' worth of food stockpiled while half the kingdom went to bed hungry.

"The king wasn't sure what to do, but he remained adamant

about pricing. He investigated and discovered that due to the price ceilings, the black market had grown so large that it eclipsed the normal market. Tax revenues plummeted as people began trading food and other resources using unofficial channels. The issue had nothing to do with merchants. Instead, it was the people themselves that were selling their food at three times the list price. Eventually, food got so expensive that people were forced to shoulder usurious loans for the sake of feeding their children.

"Meanwhile, the ministers and nobles hoarded food. Once they had ten times the food they needed, they began using it to control their subjects. Prices spiraled upward as people starved. Food became the new currency, rendering the kingdom's fiat money system worthless.

"Soon, influential noble clans used their stockpiles to purchase entire cities. Before the king knew it, his kingdom had been taken over by a handful of noble houses. His coffers were full of worthless money, and he was helpless to prevent the black-market transactions. Eventually, the noble houses banded together and overthrew him. They used their chokehold over the food supplies to continue extorting the people.

"The situation continued for a full year. As the famine passed, the people remained hungry. Eventually, the peasants had enough, and they rebelled against their rulers. The noble families were overthrown, and the kingdom shattered into thirteen pieces, which are now known as the Desperate Lands, the most impoverished places on the continent. They are devoid of morality and think little of laws. Naturally, my Wang family was one of the early merchants that sold their stock and left before the true crisis began."

The court was silent. Wang Jun could hear the heavy breathing of the officials as they pondered their future actions. The crown prince's expression was cold. A man of his intelligence understood that Wang Jun had just sown mutinous seeds among his loyal ministers.

"Things as they are," the crown prince said, "I still move to instate a price ceiling at 1.3 times the list price. Are there any objections?"

"I naturally object, Your Highness," Wang Jun said. "If the

price cap is any lower than 1.7 times the list price, I will refuse to sell. I would rather use them to recruit able-bodied men into our Wang family. In this way, I can better protect our assets in the Song Kingdom."

"Anyone else?" the crown prince said coldly.

"If I might add," said Prime Minister Rong, who had remained silent this whole time. "I believe that Second Young Master Wang's story is worth considering. But I understand that you wish to comfort the people in these trying times. Why do we do things this way? Let's meet halfway at 1.5 times the market price. At the same time, let us exempt magic and core treasures, which are only important to noble families. If they want to arm themselves to the teeth, they should pay a sufficient price.

"At the same time, let us also institute gruel stations in the various prefectures to maintain public order and prevent the common people from starving. This benevolence will be well remembered by the masses. What are your thoughts, Second Young Master Wang?"

Wang Jun hesitated before nodding. "That is marginally acceptable. I would continue selling lower-level weapons and other commodities at this price."

The crown prince visibly relaxed with this suggestion. It wasn't for nothing that the prime minister had kept his role for twenty years.

"Then it's settled," the crown prince said. "Please ensure that these controls are implemented as soon as possible, and make sure that no one goes hungry. A kingdom must serve its people before anything else."

Chapter 6: Hidden Opponents

"What are your thoughts, Elder Bai?" Wang Jun asked as they sipped tea.

The years had not been kind to the older man, and fatigue wore away at him like rust did an iron bar—slowly, surely, and irreparably.

"My thoughts?" Elder Bai said. "Surely you know more about the situation than I do. I just find it odd that, despite the obvious machinations of the court, and despite your persuasive arguments against the price ceilings, he would still insist on them. He is affecting his own power in the long run."

Wang Jun nodded. "This play is far too incisive and targeted against me. He is minimizing our gains at the cost of consolidating his power. This behavior is at odds with his play for the throne. Therefore, I think there is someone in the shadows guiding his actions. That person is pushing the crown prince to act against me."

Elder Bai nodded but didn't add anything. There was only one possibility—the first young master's agent was now making bolder moves, hiding his true motives by using the political struggle.

"It looks like there won't be as great of a windfall as you predicted," Elder Bai observed.

"That's fine," Wang Jun said. "We will recover our capital and consolidate our profits much faster this way. In addition, we'll make the crown prince realize the unintended consequences of his actions."

"Which are?" Elder Bai said.

"If the price is capped, then I no longer have to sell to the highest bidder," Wang Jun replied. "Since a higher bid is impossible, I will only sell to our faction. I will milk their coffers dry while simultaneously bolstering their forces for the upcoming struggle. Meanwhile, the crown prince's forces will have much unsatiated demand for weapons. They will offer exorbitant prices on the black market."

"Isn't that against the Wang family rules?" Elder Bai asked, raising an eyebrow.

"Please quote the rule for me," Wang Jun said.

"Being caught committing a criminal commercial act is a punishable offense in the Wang family," Elder Bai said. Then, as though just realizing the implications, he rolled his eyes. "I'm sure you have a way of hiding your traces."

"Always," Wang Jun replied.

Suddenly, the door opened. A middle-aged man walked in unbidden.

Wang Jun frowned. "This had better be important," he said coldly.

"Of course," the middle-aged man said without batting an eyelash. "Though I suggest that the young master should lock the door and use a dampening device in the future when discussing such conversations. Otherwise you might find yourself suffering a loss."

"I'll take that into consideration," Wang Jun said. "What news have you brought us?" He observed the black-cloaked man carefully. While he couldn't tell what it was, something felt out of place about him.

"This servant has just made preliminary contact with some hidden forces in the city," the man said. "I thought it would be best to inform you immediately."

The man handed him a folio, which Wang Jun carefully opened. He nodded as he looked through the information. Looking up, he saw that the man hadn't left yet. "You are dismissed," he said. The man bowed and exited the room.

"Who is that man?" Wang Jun asked to Elder Bai.

"His name is Hei Ling, and he joined us two months ago," Elder Bai said. "He's been vetted by the family and specializes in dealing with more... *unsavory* businesses."

"If only I could trust the family," Wang Jun said. "Please find someone within the group who has been with us at least two years. And have Hei Ling tailed. There is something off about him, something I can't put my finger on."

"I'll put Li Ming on the job," Elder Bai said. "He's been excellent at covert operations like tracking people and remaining unseen. Truth be told, I once offered him a job as an assassin. He refused and said that it was a troublesome profession."

Wang Jun grimaced as he drank some tea, only to realize that it had grown cold. He chucked it out and brewed a new pot. While he might be busy, he wasn't *that* busy.

Cha Ming slept deeply that night and woke with Huxian still snoozing on his belly. The small fox was no longer shivering, and on his foxy muzzle was a contented smile. He carefully moved Huxian to the bed.

The Jade Bamboo's staff greeted him as he walked past. He nodded to them apologetically as he made his way to Wang Jun's office. The door opened automatically, revealing Wang Jun and a pot of tea. A larger bowl of Demon Soothing Tea was waiting off to the side.

"How are you feeling?" Wang Jun said as he gestured to the tea set.

"Much better," Cha Ming said. "I'm sorry for all the harsh words and the terrible attitude."

"I know that wasn't the real you," Wang Jun said, sighing. "I speculate it had something to do with Zhou Li. His curses are difficult for me to detect, let alone unravel."

They drank in silence for a half hour, with Wang Jun pouring. During this time, Cha Ming mulled over the many questions he had for his friend.

"Why are you here in the Song Kingdom?" Cha Ming finally asked. Wang Jun poured another cup and reached out to a device on his desk. He activated the opaque orb, and an invisible field permeated the room. It isolated Cha Ming's spiritual force and any sounds they made; no one outside would be able to hear them.

"I'm here because of a mission issued by my family," Wang Jun said. "It's an enormously difficult mission that's meant to test my ability to compete for the family's leadership. The other runner-up is my eldest brother, Wang Ling."

Cha Ming thought for a moment before asking his next question. "Why do you want to compete against you brother?"

"Because he killed my sister," Wang Jun said softly as his hands clenched around his delicate teacup, threatening to shatter it with the slightest additional pressure. "It's something I can't forgive him for. She was just an innocent, talented girl who wanted nothing to do with the leadership. She wouldn't have bothered to compete with him, but he saw her as a threat. My goal is to take over as the Wang family patriarch and kill him."

"And is the favor I owe you related to that?" Cha Ming asked. He felt his heart clench as he awaited the dreaded answer.

"Yes and no," Wang Jun said. "Wang Ling is backed by my family's transcendent. I see great potential in you, and I want you to block him when I make a move against my brother."

Cha Ming shut his eyes. "You know that's basically the same thing as killing him. I'll kill evildoers from time to time, but I'm not an assassin."

Wang Jun sighed. "I won't force you to do anything you're not comfortable with. Just relax and help me out however you can. If push comes to shove, I'll just change the favor."

It was a simple exchange, but it resolved the growing knot in

Cha Ming's heart. He now felt much more relaxed about helping his friend's business in Songjing.

A soft knock on the door interrupted their conversation. Wang Jun disabled the device on his desk and walked over to open the door. A man clothed in a golden robe walked inside.

"We meet again," Cha Ming said, recognizing Chaplain Chen.

The man smiled. "I received an invitation from the second young master as soon as you left. The contents of his letter were intriguing, so I thought I'd pay a visit."

"I'm sure Brother Jun will help you out if it's within his capacity," Cha Ming said.

"I'm not happy to see you, but we both have things each other needs," the chaplain said, nodding curtly to Wang Jun.

"You know full well that I can't help my own physical situation," Wang Jun said awkwardly. He summoned a teapot, and he dropped ten golden leaves in. The gold in the leaves infused with the water, which soon glowed with a golden light. Wang Jun poured it into three cups. To Cha Ming's surprise, Wang Jun's own cup was considerably larger, something that would normally be considered rude.

"How luxurious," Chaplain Chen said. "Luminescent Sunflower Tea. Its brewing process was dictated by the Holy Mother aeons ago. I am surprised that you know of it, given your condition. Do you understand its uses?"

"I study all tea traditions and customs," Wang Jun said. "This is a tea of cooperation. It is meant to be served as an expression of good will and honesty." He took a large gulp from his own cup. "It is also a truth serum. Those who drink it cannot utter a lie."

Cha Ming followed his lead and took a sip, along with Chaplain Chen.

"I must confess that I would like nothing more than to win your support, Chaplain Chen," Wang Jun said. "But I understand how the Church of Justice operates. You will not change the way you behave for the sake of money.

"I'm happy that you understand," Chaplain Chen said. "I confess: I believe that your physique and shadow cultivation are an aberration. A man should not be able to hide from the light as you do. The powers of an inquisitor are useless against you. However, if I'm not mistaken, willingly drinking this tea means that your ability to lie has been inhibited. You drank this tea to reassure me. Am I right?"

"Quite right," Wang Jun said. "I have the larger cup because of my constitution, but for the next hour, I can tell no lies. Feel free to ask away."

"Very well, I confess myself intrigued," Chaplain Chen said. "You have offered me the services of a formation master who can set up a light-gathering formation. However, according to my assessment of this young man, I only see five-element cultivation. How is this possible?"

"I can best answer this question," Cha Ming said. He summoned five balls of colored light, one for each of the five elements. "The five elements are linked to creation and destruction."

A thick black star appeared, and so did a white circle, then another white stream flowed out. It turned azure and iridescent. Lightning crackled and wind blew.

"As a result, I can also control wind and lightning."

"This alone cannot create light," the chaplain said firmly.

"Quite right," Cha Ming said. "However, you saw my brother the other day. Huxian controls light and shadow simultaneously. Through our bond of brotherhood, I can make use of his demonic qi." Two additional balls appeared, one a glowing white and another a subdued black. They were very different from the black star and the white circle. They fed off themselves as soon as they appeared.

"Impressive," the chaplain said. "While others might think that the simultaneous presence of light and shadow is heresy, I know better. Nothing that bears the power of light can stray too far into the shadows, and only those who have touched the shadows can truly see the splendor of light. This is clear in the goddess's teachings: 'For no one who walks in the light will ever be alone in the darkness. The slightest speck will always be his guide.'"

"I think you're taking things a little too literally," Cha Ming blurted unintentionally. However, instead of getting offended, the chaplain simply smiled.

"Honesty is a virtue, so there is no need to be offended," the chaplain said as if reading Cha Ming's thoughts. "You are skeptical, but I believe this scripture from the bottom of my heart. Therefore your words can never lead me astray."

Wang Jun, who had kept silent during their exchange, finally butted into the conversation. "I take it that you wish to have a light-gathering formation?"

"I want three, and I will pay for them at the fair market price, adjusted for the remoteness of our location," the chaplain said firmly. "I will not owe you for it. However, what intrigues me more is his ability to create other light formations. There are two specific formations that I would like him to install. I will provide him single-use scrolls on both formations, and in exchange for their installation, I will gift your friend single-use scrolls on five light-based talismans and five light-based formations. What are your thoughts?"

"This seems overly generous," Wang Jun said. "The market value of these items far exceeds the value of two mid-grade formations."

"One of them is a grand formation," the chaplain explained. "It is extremely difficult to set up, and the material cost for it is much higher than for a normal project. However, desperate times call for desperate measures."

"What kind of formation are we talking about?" Cha Ming asked.

"The first is a Mid-Grade Spiritual-Detection Grand Formation," the chaplain explained. "It needs to encompass the entire church grounds. With it, we will be able to passively detect evil spirits. In addition, I need you to set up a Mid-Grade Exorcist Formation. Both would best be installed by a Buddhist monk, but no thanks to our order, they are in very short supply on the continent."

Cha Ming looked to Wang Jun, who nodded.

"Very well," said Wang Jun. "Cha Ming will first set up a light-gathering formation and then help you with both other formations. However, you will supply spirit stones for the activation and maintenance of each project."

"And you have no problem with me not owing you anything?" the chaplain asked doubtfully.

"The church being prolific in the Song Kingdom is to our advantage," Wang Jun said. "As Cha Ming has explained to you previously, devils are running rampant in the Song Kingdom. This must stop, or my businesses will suffer. The enemy of my enemy is my friend."

A few days later, Huxian was lazily lounging in the Church of Justice. He felt drained, and reasonably so. In a corner of the church, Cha Ming was steadily syphoning out his light qi into complex sub-formations. They were fixed to the floor via formation crystals, which had been secretly installed behind screens of light energy.

Huxian, please go get the chaplain and tell him the preparations are ready, Cha Ming said.

Huxian yawned and stretched out and trotted through the church unimpeded. The inquisitors and guards on duty had all come to know him. In fact, the pastors had preached the lesson of light and darkness, causing much of their initial apprehension to fade away. Now, only three of them disliked Huxian. They had told him straight to his face and then refused to speak with him further.

Huxian walked up to the chaplain's prayer room and scratched on the door with his tiny paw. The door soon opened and allowed him inside.

"Brother Cha Ming's preparations are ready," he said. "The formation needs one thousand high-grade spirit stones to activate. You should all get into position prior to its activation."

"Excellent," the chaplain said cheerfully while handing Huxian a bag of holding. "Please give these high-grade spirit stones to your brother and tell him to await the signal for activation."

As Huxian walked toward Cha Ming's location, he noticed many inquisitors swarming to the entrance and channeling their qi into shields of light. Many parishioners, who were kneeling at pews, began muttering amongst themselves.

"Do not panic," the pastor said in a soothing voice. "The chaplain will be holding a demonstration soon. It will be very beneficial to our church if you stay." The parishioners began speaking in excited whispers.

Huxian walked through a door toward the screen of light where Cha Ming was located. He dropped the bag of holding to the floor and cuddled up to his brother's leg for petting. Cha Ming scratched the back of his ears as they waited. The pleasant sound of a gong prompted him into action, and he immediately directed the high-grade spirit-stone energy through the nearby light-gathering formation. The formation roared to life and sent out beams of light as thick as an arm through the walls.

One by one, the pieces of the complex formation lit up. The light-gathering formation creaked and groaned under the strain of converting all thousand high-grade spirit stones in a short instant. It was a sacrificial formation, and it would break apart after the initial activation of the grand formation. By the time the last spirit stone was consumed, it collapsed into motes of light that were also absorbed by the larger one. Each node thrummed, and a light golden sheen spread out throughout the church.

A bloodcurdling scream caused Cha Ming to dart out into the hallway. An old servant who had been cleaning nearby was surprised by the sudden appearance of a ghostly figure. It was transparent, and its pitch-black eyes were filled with malice. Crimson veins completely covered the apparition.

Cha Ming sent out a lightning-based combat formation, instantly disintegrating the evil spirit. He continued along the outskirts with Huxian in tow. Nearby, a group of inquisitors brandished blades of light to banish the apparitions as they found them. They moved in a sweeping pattern that led them to the center of the church, where the pews were located.

"Reporting to the chaplain: We've slain three evil spirits!" an inquisitor yelled.

"Reporting to the chaplain: We've slain two evil spirits!" another yelled.

The reporting continued. When the chaplain looked to Cha Ming, the latter only held up a single finger. The man nodded and continued the tallying. It wasn't long before another scream sounded out. This time, it came from the pews.

"What is happening to you, honey?" a woman yelled.

Cha Ming looked toward an aged man who was covered in crimson veins from head to toe.

"It will be all right," the chaplain said reassuringly. He walked toward the man, who was struggling to free himself. The chaplain summoned the man against his will. "Miss Ji, your husband will return safe and sound. I promise."

Red-eyed, the woman nodded and bit back her tears.

After a full hour, the reports ceased to trickle in after six possessed individuals had been apprehended. The chaplain looked over to Cha Ming.

"You may begin," he said.

Cha Ming nodded and withdrew thirty-six white crystals, which he placed on the floor inside a nine-foot circle. He leafed through his memories and reviewed the information one last time before summoning the Clear Sky Brush.

The brush glowed with white demonic light as he painted two hundred complex lines with light essence. Painting the lines took a full incense time, and as soon as the last one was completed, the formation glowed as a single unit and rumbled to life.

Cha Ming bowed to the chaplain. "The Mid-Grade Exorcism Formation is ready."

The chaplain nodded. "Master inquisitors, with me," he said.

Nine figures in golden armor walked up to nine key points in a rehearsed manner. The men followed his instructions and began pouring qi into the formation. The chaplain waved his hand and summoned the older man he had captured before. He placed him in the center of the circle and bound him with his resplendent force.

"And the Blessed Mother did say, do not suffer the presence of remnants," the chaplain intoned. "For they are children of the shadows, and they do not belong in this world.

"Let not karma bind you with vengeance. Pass into the light and leave behind no regrets, for I am the light and will guide you to justice.

"Do not be tempted by corruption, whose crimson color blinds your eyes and binds your soul. Keep free from fetters that incite you to stray, for I am the sight that will lead you to glory.

"Do not doubt in your fellow man. If they be wrong, I will judge them accordingly. Trust in me, for I am the truth and will lead you to salvation."

The evil spirit screamed as the chaplain's incisive words wore away at its corrupting influence. Once the final word was completed, the crimson on the old man's body vanished. He prostrated himself weakly before the golden-robed man.

"Thank you, Chaplain," he said tearfully.

"Do not thank me," the chaplain said. "The goddess, in her mysterious ways, has saved you."

It didn't take long for the six possessed victims to undergo the same treatment. The chaplain allowed everyone to leave after their exorcism was completed. As they departed, the chaplain instructed them to guide their friends to the church for protection.

It was night by the time Cha Ming left with the payment of ten scrolls. To his surprise, it wasn't ten least-grade scrolls but one for each grade. He guessed that in the chaplain's opinion, having more light-based formations and talismans in the world could only be a good thing.

"Huxian, can I get a little light?" Cha Ming asked.

The fox cast a small white globe, which floated above them and illuminated the streets. They had stayed in the brightly lit church for three days. After so much time in the light, it was difficult to adjust to the darkness.

Chapter 7: Gambling

"So why exactly is *now* the best time to gamble?" Cha Ming said as they walked toward the entertainment district. The morning sun had just crept over the horizon. Its soothing light seeped into the cold paving stones that could only be found in this remote part of Songjing City.

"I'm not sure," Feng Ming said. "I just woke up at an ungodly hour with an itch to go gambling. You can't just ignore feelings like that—you need to go with the flow. Unless you had something better to do?"

Cha Ming thought of his gigantic backlog of formations but pushed them to the back of his mind—a single day of gambling would greatly improve his dire financial situation. More to the point, Feng Ming attracted trouble like honey did flies. Cha Ming needed to blow off some steam, and now was the perfect chance to do it.

Ten paces away from them, a restaurant was preparing for the busy day. Men and women folded dough and created tiny dumplings and buns for steaming. A little farther on, kitchen staff members were busy preparing ingredients: They precut vegetables and deboned meat while the chefs busily organized the menu for the morning rush. There were no customers to be seen, and most establishments were closed.

They traveled a little further before arriving near the inns and taverns. These, too, were closed. The tavern staff had not yet begun preparing like the restaurants, while the hotels ran on skeleton crews that awaited any impromptu orders from needy clients. This was also where Feng Ming veered them off to a nearby alley. The dim morning sunlight didn't reach these narrow streets; instead, they were brightly lit with spirit lamps.

Everywhere they looked, taverns were still brimming with rowdy customers. Pawn shops, money lenders, and other unsavory establishments waited for the constant trickle of desperate customers that came their way. They were situated right by the casinos, which rapidly gobbled up the small fortunes their clients accrued. The brothels were also there; their red spirit lamps beckoned invitingly to both the lonely and the depraved.

They soon entered a seedy tavern, which was brimming with customers despite the early hour. Dozens of sweaty gamblers were busy tossing away their fortunes while barmaids served them one drink after another. A customer would occasionally grope one of the barmaids, and her response to this lewd behavior depended less on the quality of the groper and more on the size of their wallet.

"Not again!" a man shouted. He and three men stood opposite a dealer. The pale man looked to the side of the room nervously. A cloaked figure beckoned, and the man hobbled to the table and began explaining himself in hushed whispers.

"I can win it back, I swear!" the man said. "Just give me another loan. I'm good for it. I still have my house and my business."

"And a wife and kids, and a healthy young body," the man said calmly. "I know your entire financial situation. I can give you a loan, but this time the interest will be double. You need to give me fifty percent every week, or I'll take you to the cleaners. Even your wife and two children won't be able to escape." A menacing light flickered from the man's eyes.

"Thank you," the pale man said, accepting a small pouch.

Cha Ming wasn't sure how much it contained, but it was likely enough to push the man to the brink.

"Let's go play Dragons," Feng Ming suddenly said, pulling Cha

Ming's attention to a long table in the back. The table's dealer tossed him a chit, on which he placed a mid-grade spirit stone. Cha Ming followed his lead.

"In this game, you hope the guy keeps rolling the same numbers," Feng Ming explained. "If he rolls dragons, they eat up everything on the table."

"Shut up," an aged man said. He was half bald, and a long, thin scar ran down the side of his face. Despite his unkempt appearance, Cha Ming determined that the man had reached the peak of qi condensation and was only a single step away from establishing his foundation. This single step was also a monumental one that the man wouldn't take for the rest of his life.

"My apologies," Feng Ming said. *It's rude to explain the rules at the table,* Feng Ming sent. *It's considered bad luck.*

The same man tossed two dice that bounced off a soft board at the back of the table. They landed on a pair of threes. Their bet was shifted by the dealer, and while Feng Ming seemed to know what was going on, Cha Ming was completely lost. Spirit stones trickled to their side of the table as he placed the same bets as Feng Ming did. It wasn't long before everyone started copying Feng Ming.

"All right, time to switch tables," Feng Ming said when the dealer glared at them. They picked up their money and moved on to another game. It was a simple card game that reminded Cha Ming of blackjack. Like the dice before, the cards were built from a material that repelled soul force and qi.

Excited murmurs surrounded their table as their bets doubled continuously. Soon they were the only active table in the tavern, and some of the dealers stood nearby with their arms crossed while others were busy chatting with the moneylender.

This one's less a game of chance and more a game of strategy, Feng Ming sent as they approached a table with twelve players. The crowd followed them and sat down to join the excitement.

Each man had three hidden cards, and four additional cards were exposed in the middle over time. The game was remarkably like poker, and Cha Ming used his strong soul and sharp mind to quickly adapt what he knew to this new game. He used these superior skills in combination with Feng Ming's freakish luck to quintuple his holdings.

At first, the dealers didn't make a big deal when they moved over since they made money on the rake. Unfortunately, many dissatisfied customers left the tavern with accusations of cheating. Before long, a well-dressed foundation-establishment cultivator headed their way.

"Gentlemen, my name is Hu Fa," the man said. "Senior Ba wishes to meet with you. Would you be so kind as to follow?"

Seeing that the hand had just finished, Cha Ming shrugged. Feng Ming nodded, and they followed Hu Fa to a small table in the back. It was none other than the moneylender's table.

"Let me introduce myself," the black-robed man at the table said. "You may call me Senior Ba, and I am the manager of this establishment."

The fact that the moneylender was also the owner was very telling.

"Can we help you with something?" Cha Ming said.

"Most certainly," Senior Ba said. "It's a pleasure to meet both Master Du and Colonel Feng. I must say that the rumors of Colonel Feng's good luck aren't the least bit exaggerated. Therefore, I'll have to remind you both that there are limits on how lucky one can get in my tavern. Do you understand?"

"Perfectly," Feng Ming said.

"Excellent," Senior Ba said. "Then please continue enjoying the free refreshments. Do let me know if there's anything else you need."

They soon left the premises with their winnings. "Well, that ended fast," Cha Ming said. "Thanks for the quick cash."

Feng Ming chuckled. "You thought I brought you here to make a small amount of money? Surely you know me better than that."

Cha Ming pondered for a bit before taking a stab at it. "Who's the owner of the casino?"

"Smart," Feng Ming said. "The owner, at least indirectly, is the crown prince. I trust my instincts, so if fate is willing to let me bleed him dry, he mustn't be up to any good."

"Then what next?" Cha Ming said.

"You'll see," Feng Ming replied with an impish smile. They soon arrived at another casino. This one was significantly better furnished than the last one, and each of the tables was managed by a beautiful female dealer. The drinks here were served by gorgeous foundation-establishment cultivators with low-cut dresses. They spoke with the customers and laughed at their jokes, all for the sake of keeping them and their money in the building for a few more guests.

We had to stop by the other casino because here, there is a minimum bet of fifty high-grade spirit stones, Feng Ming explained.

Cha Ming's eyes nearly popped out of their sockets. *Exactly how much money does this place make in a year?*

Now that he looked at them, the walls were adorned with exquisite paintings that resonated with the heaven and earth qi in the room. Each one was worth thousands of mid-grade spirit stones and served to stabilize one's cultivation and temper one's soul.

It's difficult to say, Feng Ming said. *It depends on foot traffic, and the casino's edge is small. This makes them especially susceptible to losses, thus the man's reaction in the other tavern.*

Cha Ming nodded as Feng Ming guided him through another cycle of games. They never stayed at a single table for too long, but regardless of the game, their funds increased by leaps and bounds. They'd made a combined total of 10,000 high-grade spirit stones before getting kicked out.

"Now what?" Cha Ming asked, addicted to the feeling of ripping off casinos.

"Now we head to the arenas," Feng Ming said.

Intense yelling drowned out vicious roars as a large crowd of cultivators rooted for their favorite sprit beasts. In the arena, a large dire wolf was fighting against a slightly larger spirit bear. The odds in this fight were three to one in favor of the larger bear. The were both covered in deadly gashes, but it was clear that the bear's endurance was winning out. The spirit wolf would soon join the pile of corpses at the base of the arena.

Cha Ming's stomach churned as he made his way to a desk at the back. He'd originally refused to place bets, but Feng Ming convinced him that the best way to stop such places was to shut them down. Cha Ming jumped at the chance.

"Can I help you?" a clerk said from behind the desk. He was busy scribbling in a black ledger. Some words he wrote, but others appeared on their own.

"I'd like to take out a loan," Cha Ming said. "As big as you can give me." The mere thought of borrowing money from such an establishment had Cha Ming sweating bullets.

The man adjusted his spectacles and looked him up and down. "Master Du, Dual Formation and Talisman Master. Age: Early twenties. Suddenly appeared out of nowhere in Quicksilver City and arrived in Songjing only recently. Has connections with the Wang family." The man paused for a moment. "You're good for 10,000 high-grade spirit stones at a twenty-five-percent interest rate due every week. You're also not allowed to bring your friend Feng Ming on the premises—that guy was banned three days ago. If you want the loan, you can sign here." He handed Cha Ming a black paper with golden writing. It was a certificate of debt with extremely harsh repayment clauses. He sighed before ultimately signing it.

The man reviewed the document before stowing it in a spatial ring and placing a crystal card on the table. Cha Ming inspected it before proceeding to a second desk. He looked at the next three fights—a seventh-level spirit fox against a seventh-level soul-screeching owl. The payout was 5:1 if the fox won, so Cha Ming placed a 20,000-stone bet on it. Then he placed a linked bet on the next fight. He would receive a 2:1 payout if a seventh-level dire badger won out against an eighth-level spirit wolf.

Finally, he placed a third linked bet. It was a preposterous round with a 10:1 payout. In this round, a sixth-level spirit bat would face off against a seventh-level dire badger.

"Are you sure you wish to place these three bets?" the attendant confirmed. Although such large bets were quite common, it was rare to see one linked to so many outcomes. "Please sign this contract if you accept."

Another black-and-gold document was placed in front of him. Unlike the last one, this one placed a large obligation on the upper echelons of the arena to pay him should he win. After reviewing it, Cha Ming signed and forked over his 20,000 high-grade spirit stones.

Are you sure this is a good idea? Cha Ming asked Feng Ming through his core-transmission jade.

Mostly, Feng Ming replied. *Win or lose, it'll all work out in the end. Just trust me.*

Cha Ming groaned. Could losing on borrowed money really be considered good luck? Unable to calm his nerves, he took a seat near the arena. An ordinary orange spirit fox was forced into the caged grounds where a fierce-looking owl was already waiting.

A gong sounded. The owl flapped its small wings and hovered midair while the cautious fox circled him from the outside. It mixed in feints with actual swipes as it tried to wear down its heavily armored foe. Small lacerations appeared on the owl's metallic wings as the fox's attacks became increasingly frantic.

Soon the orange beast's stamina gave out, leaving an opening for its feathered opponent. The owl let out a piercing screech that hit the fox point blank. It faltered as it let out a plume of fox-fire to escape.

The fox's movements became clumsy and lethargic. The owl flapped its tiny wings and raked the fox's exposed back with its glistening talons. Blood sprayed as the fox howled in pain. The crowd cheered at the sight of fresh blood while Cha Ming winced at the exchange. He hoped the little fox would win and live a little longer. Unfortunately, the odds didn't seem to be in its favor. The owl repeatedly used the same tactic, adding one wound after another to the fox's back.

Just let it end, Cha Ming thought. At that moment, a small fluctuation appeared in the arena. The fox gained a second wind as the energy of heaven and earth rushed into him from all sides. He howled fiercely at the owl, who suddenly shook in fear. Out of nowhere, a second tail popped out beside the first one. Everyone's eyes practically popped out of their sockets—the odds of something like a bloodline evolution happening mid-match were less than one in a million.

The owl retreated in a panic as the fox slashed away with its deadly paws. Two hurried swipes caused it to bleed while a third one pushed it to the arena's cage. It roared before finally biting down on the spirit screeching owl's tiny body, leaving nothing but a tiny puddle of blood where the spirit beast used to lay.

"And we have a winner!" the announcer yelled. The tired two-tailed fox was ushered off the stage by an excited tamer. A many-tailed fox was a rare existence, and he would likely get a hefty bonus for managing to raise it to this level. The fox was now in no danger of being killed in the arena—rather, it would be sold to the highest bidder.

"Next up, we have a neck-and-neck match between a seventh-level dire badger and an eighth-level spirit wolf!" the announcer said. "Don't let their level disparity deceive you—badgers are known for their tremendous endurance and their rage-based techniques."

A large wolf was released into the arena simultaneously with a much larger badger. Crimson streaks highlighted the dire badger's black-and-white fur. It held its hands defensively as the wolf circled around its weaker prey. From the stands, Cha Ming could see a green aura of vitality surrounding the badger while a frosty aura surrounded the fire spirit wolf and restrained the badger's movements.

Slash.

A bloody gash appeared in the badger's thick fur. The crowd roared in excitement as their favored spirit beast took the initiative. Their excitement increased as this gash was followed up with a dozen others. The dire badger was a bloody mess, but Cha Ming could tell that the fight had just begun.

The wolf darted in for another quick strike, only to be interrupted by the dire badger's sharp claws. It struggled to break lose as the badger closed in with its sharp teeth and began mauling the agile creature. The badger's wounds healed before the crowd's eyes as the wolf howled in pain. The previously subdued crowd erupted in cheers as the underdog bled the wolf dry.

Cha Ming loathed these people, but he wondered if he was any better. He, too, had bet money on this fight and made it happen. He could only hope that his swipe at the arena would make a difference. Although his earnings had increased to 200,000 spirit stones, the large amount of money felt hollow in comparison to the suffering in the arena.

"We have a problem," a man said as he approached a masked figure. "A 20,000-spirit-stone bet has gotten through two successive fights and has now been placed on a fight with 10:1 payout."

"And why is that a problem?" the owner asked. "Aren't the odds stacked against him?"

"Normally I wouldn't worry about it and let the odds take care of everything," the man said. "However, after doing a little digging, I realized that he's friends with that guy we kicked out a few days ago."

"You mean Colonel Feng, the welp who won ten straight bets and walked out of here with 200,000?" the owner exclaimed.

"That's the one," the man said. "While we can't detect his presence, who knows if that guy's freakish good luck will affect his friends. It's better to be safe than sorry."

The masked man pondered for a moment before issuing a rare order. "Poison the bat and try to make it as discreet as possible. I'll handle the negative karma from violating the bet contracts. Since we're at, increase the odds to 20:1 to try and rope in any stragglers and hedge bets."

The man bowed and disappeared, leaving the masked owner to

watch from his elevated platform as red threads of karma trickled into him.

"Now let's hope this karma doesn't come back to bite me all at once," he mumbled.

Cha Ming paced nervously as a short intermission was called just before the remaining match. An ordinary spirit bat wouldn't stand a chance against a higher-level dire badger. The 10:1 odds were actually quite generous toward the larger animal, making it a terrible bet to take. Sure as rain, the large black board by the betting tables flickered. The odds flashed to 20:1 in favor of the spirit bat in a last-ditch attempt to capture more wagers. Unfortunately, his bet was already locked in.

The crowd calmed after a half hour as they waited patiently for the fight that shouldn't have held much suspense. When the gates opened, a fierce-looking dire badger charged out and let out loud roar.

On the other side, a sluggish-looking bat exited a small pen. Cha Ming frowned when he saw its lethargic state. Spirit bats were usually energetic beasts and fought using their superior speed.

They wouldn't do anything to rig the match, would they? Cha Ming thought. Although his resplendent force couldn't pierce the match's cage, his sharp eyesight inspected every inch of the bat. He saw a green liquid dripping out of the corner of its mouth. It had clearly been poisoned.

The dire badger charged out immediately after the gong sounded. The dire badger looked at the bat with disdain as it lazily swiped its paw. To the crowd's surprise, it missed!

The distance between both creatures rapidly closed, allowing the bat to somehow latch on to its neck. Surprisingly, the dire badger did something unexpected; it didn't swat the bat but merely sat down subserviently, allowing it to drain its blood one liter at a time. The more blood it drank, the less lethargic it became.

The bat grew to twice its size before the weak badger finally managed to throw it off. It swiped defensively as the bat began its usual attack pattern. It attacked with its razor-sharp wings in the badger's blind spots. The enraged badger could do nothing but passively accept its defeat as cuts accumulated over his weakened body.

The crowds booed as the badger finally collapsed. The crowd was shocked, and so were the match organizers. The only one who wasn't surprised was Cha Ming, whose eyes were shining with a purple light. He'd activated the main ability of his Demon-Subduing Eyes to force the badger into submission.

Although he loathed what he had done, he reminded himself that a loss of two million high-grade spirit stones could very well shut down the arena and deter future investment. This thought did little to ease the pain in his heart.

Chapter 8:
Lucky General

Feng Ming hated the darkness. It was an irrational fear, one that he often ignored. But every so often, he couldn't help but glance into the empty nothingness to see if it would glance back. This time, it did. The glance was a prerecorded signal from Cha Ming through the arena walls via transmission jade.

Feng Ming pushed off the wall, making his way to the rooftop in a single bound. The light of the moon reflected off his obsidian armor; he wasn't wearing his red colonel's cape, which was far too flashy for a covert operation. His feet bounced lightly off the stone roof tiles as he executed his movement technique, Fire General's Steps. It wasn't ideal for sneaking around, but it was much better than nothing.

Forty more rooftops, Feng Ming thought. *If I'm lucky, we'll snag a big fish.* He felt a little guilty about using Cha Ming as bait, but sometimes you had to gamble big to win big.

As he ran, his foot caught on a poorly placed roof tile, which caused him to tumble down to the ground below. He watched it fall with concern, only to see it land on a thief's head. The man, who was just about to steal a woman's purse, was knocked out cold. Meanwhile, this movement distracted the nearby guards as he passed overhead.

It wasn't long before he arrived at his destination: an inconspicuous alley in the eastern quarter of the city. The shadows loomed over a group of men who escorted a blue-robed cultivator. He resembled a naïve nouveau riche following the butchers to his own slaughter. He chuckled as his friend inconspicuously dropped a formation he'd prepared beforehand.

In an incense time, Feng Ming would have the opening he needed.

"I don't understand why all these precautions are necessary," Cha Ming said as they walked into a run-down entrance. "Couldn't you have just paid me in the arena?"

"While we would have liked to, the amount you bet was far too large for us to disburse on the premises," a well-dressed man said. "The maximum bet for any single round is capped at 20,000, and the odds are typically balanced in such a way that we make a small profit. We aim to even out the odds so that all we collect is one to ten percent of all wagers.

"Unfortunately for us, your bet was able to bypass our bet limitations as it was chained bet. We don't carry two million high-grade spirit stones on hand for fear of being robbed. Therefore, any large winnings must be awarded off-premises. It was the same for your friend Colonel Feng."

The explanation was obviously full of holes, but Cha Ming didn't bother to argue against it. He only nodded in muted acceptance as they took him deeper and deeper into their lair. Taverns and whorehouses sprouted everywhere while the more sinister establishments in the city came into view. Cha Ming saw a building with a bloody knife welcoming discreet customers; it stood side by side with a hole in the wall that sold weapons and pills in small quantities at prices far exceeding the current market price.

The farther they moved the worse it got. Knife fights weren't uncommon, and neither was the sight of people making love out in the open. The place became a den of hedonism, but fortunately there were limits. He hadn't yet seen anything that crossed the Song Kingdom's bottom line like human trafficking or murder in the streets.

They soon approached a large three-story building. It was noticeably better built than the buildings surrounding it and was defended by guards that were armed to the teeth. As they passed through the black doors at the entrance, Cha Ming's resplendent force was cut off from the outside world. The only person he could communicate with now was Huxian. As his last avenues of communication had seemingly disappeared, his escort's reserved nature finally disappeared. They violently shoved him up the stairs and through a door that was twice as tall as a grown man.

Cha Ming tumbled to the floor in front of a large chair where an abnormally large man was seated. He wore a mask, and unlike the cultivators beside him, his body was bursting with energy. His arms were the size of a large man's legs, while his legs were the size of a normal man's body. An ochre aura with a familiar tinge of vitality identified the man as a wood-aligned devil.

To Cha Ming's surprise, the man tossed a bag of holding to him. He rapidly scanned the contents and discovered 199 crystal cards and a small pile of high-grade spirit stones.

"After your loan is repaid, we owe you two million, less twenty thousand spirit stones," the large man said. "The karma is settled, and I owe you nothing."

Cha Ming felt an invisible thread evaporating as two of his existing contracts were resolved simultaneously.

"How did you do it?" the masked man said. "Was it that damnable man's luck again, or is it some other ability? There's no way that dire badger would just stand by and wait for the bat to bleed him to death."

Cha Ming stood up and dusted off his blue robes. "I wouldn't have needed to do anything if you hadn't poisoned it."

"So you admit that you cheated?" the man said.

"Is there a need to play these games?" Cha Ming retorted. The two stood at an awkward stalemate. Cha Ming waited for a few breaths before continuing. "I came to propose a trade. I'll let you know about my ability, which is very useful for match rigging, and you will let me live and keep the two million. We'll consider it a deposit for future business."

The large man looked toward a smaller man seated beside him. "How do the numbers work out?"

"If he can succeed 100% of the time, we can rake in an extra 50,000 high-grade spirit stones per day," an older man said. "It's worth looking into. You know my cultivation eats up money like nobody's business. As do both of yours, for that matter. However, I think that giving someone two million spirit stones up front is ludicrous and risky. We'd need a life-binding oath to facilitate an agreement."

"What are your thoughts, my dear?" the large man said to a woman by his side.

"I think he's lying, my dear," she said with a voice that was soft as silk. "He can hide his soul fluctuations, so I can't trust him. I also don't like his eyes. I feel like he's stripping me naked, and not in an enjoyable way."

The woman was beautiful beyond all reason. Her long blue hair was soothing, like a trickling spring, while her soft white skin would put alabaster to shame. Like the large man, she, too, had a strong ochre coloring.

The older man shrugged. "The financial risks of cooperation are high, while simply taking the two million from him along with all his possessions is an extremely profitable move. I'm all right with it either way."

This older man's ochre aura was tinged with gold, and he possessed the distinguished poise of a scholar. As far as Cha Ming could see, all three of them were initial core-formation experts. He didn't regret his choice to call for backup just before entering.

"Then it's settled," the large man said. "I'll take his strong body, while you'll respectively take his money and his soul." He turned to Cha Ming. "Any last words, little mortal?"

"I hope you like fireworks," Cha Ming said.

They hadn't noticed that nine golden globes had dropped from his robes and tumbled to the ground in front of them. Their intricate runic patterns lit up, and the single-use formations flooded the entire room with a blinding light. Then the window shattered. The explosive formation he'd laid out earlier finally burst. The three devils, who had been distracted by the combined assault of the nine least-grade blinding formations, were caught flat-footed by the sudden turn of events.

Cha Ming slapped a Hardening Talisman and over a dozen myriad ice-shield talismans on his body as the aged golden man dashed toward him and struck him with a single fist. It tore through the many ice shields and caused him to fly back through five walls before being stopped by one of the pillars stabilizing the building.

I'm all right, he sent to Huxian. *Take out the water devil first.*

Feng Ming, who had been waiting patiently on the roof just above, summoned a fiery whip, which he fastened to a small chimney.

Three, two, one, go!

The blast destroyed the entire wall but stopped short at the roof. Feng Ming jumped off the building and swung in a short arc. Although a blinding light made it unclear who he would be striking, he thrust out with his strongest move: Ash Annihilation. It was an attack that consumed six tenths of his entire qi reserve.

His blind fighting was rewarded with a shrieking howl. A beautiful woman with blue hair appeared before him; his spear had created a foot-wide hole just beneath her collar bone. She didn't have a chance to send out the slightest attack before dissolving into a puddle of water. A rush of merit confirmed her demise.

At the same time, a bird's cry rang through the skies above. A vicious blade of wind slammed into the room, cutting half the men apart and slightly injuring the rest.

"The cavalry has arrived!" a small voice yipped.

A two-tailed fox, a small bird, and a tiny mouse appeared where the blade of wind had landed. The mighty Silverwing directed his attention to the large wood devil while the weaker two-tailed fox and Lei Jiang jointly attacked the gold devil in a burst of light, shadow, and iridescent lightning.

Feng Ming quickly joined them and ignored the small fries escaping the shock waves of their battle. Someone else would handle them.

Cha Ming woke with a splitting headache. He winced as he moved the various muscles in his body. Torn ligaments rapidly regenerated around his unharmed bones.

"I never would have thought they'd have three core-formation cultivators in the same place," he muttered. He'd only seen a few dozen core-formation cultivators to date, and their increasing numbers made him realize he was just a frog in a well.

Thirty-six green sigils appeared around Cha Ming. The combat formation solidified around him, causing his wounds to heal even faster. Meanwhile, he sent out his resplendent force and located twenty smaller targets. Thirty-six sigils formed a cloud around his feet while the thirty-six remaining Dao sigils glowed golden and formed a long needle. It quickly shot through a nearby cultivator, leaving only a tiny hole behind as evidence.

Cha Ming slapped another three Myriad Ice Shield Talismans on his robe and followed up with a Sharp Talisman and a Quickening Talisman, which drastically increased his speed for thirty breaths. He rushed from room to room, swinging his Clear Sky Staff in a wide arc. It grew to twenty feet in length as Cha Ming struck out with all his strength. Plumes of fire and ice rained down on him, burning the exposed skin on his arms and face. The Clear Sky Staff, whose offensive powers were greatly boosted by the Sharp Talisman, cut through five men before returning to its normal length.

The floors creaked as Cha Ming rushed toward his next target. He reduced his weight and jumped at another group of three. Dozens of blades shot up toward him. He quickly manipulated the gold needle to deflect them and swung out toward a body-cultivating devil. The large abomination grasped his Clear Sky Staff while the others closed in on him. Cha Ming swiftly increased his weight and smashed both his feet down onto the two other devilish cultivators, shattering their ribcages. The golden needle finished them before taking care of the one holding his staff.

Seeing that he was fully healed, he retrieved his thirty-six Dao sigils and cast out a Mid-Grade Conflagration Combat Formation, which exploded around the next three targets and caused massive collateral damage to the building. He also threw out one Mid-Grade Conflagration Talisman after another, each of which struck supporting pillars in the building and caused it to collapse. The ceiling crushed down on the remaining cultivators in all three floors, leaving only the core-formation cultivators fighting in midair.

The battle above was progressing smoothly, so he summoned thirty-six of his Dao sigils into an icy shield. Then he cleared away rubble using his Clear Sky Staff and exposed a camouflaged stairwell. At the bottom of the stairwell was a small wooden door covered in mysterious devilish runes he couldn't understand. After a moment of hesitation, he pushed it open. It slammed shut behind him as he entered the basement, where dozens of cultivators were trapped. Their souls and vital energies were being syphoned off into strange devices.

His blood boiled when he saw these humans being treated like cattle. In his rage, he walked forward and tripped a silver thread that lay across the entrance. A small click sounded, barely discernable, and a feeling of panic flared in him.

"Quick, we need to use our consumption ability before it's too late," a wood devil roared as the devouring pool beside him expanded by ten times.

Feng Ming didn't panic. Huxian's devouring ability quickly grew to the same size and counterdevoured it, leaving the strengthened but still-pitiable devil to fight against the early-core-formation falcon. His entire body was covered in lacerations despite his insane regenerative abilities.

While the others were fighting, Feng Ming sent his lucky aura out to support them. His spear strikes focused on defense and entanglement while Huxian's impressive physical strength and Lei Jiang's terrifying lightning strikes whittled down the gold devil's body. Black runes lit up on the thinner devil, and as they appeared, a frightening power surged out from his body.

"It won't last long," Feng Ming said to the others. "The black runes are shrinking."

Feng Ming observed the gold devil carefully as Huxian and Lei Jiang continued their assault. He popped a pill that rapidly regenerated his depleted qi as he waited for the right moment. Under the pressure of the strong, half-step core-formation demon beasts, the gold devil unwillingly twitched its hand in an involuntary tell.

Now! Feng Ming shouted mentally.

The gold devil, who had been biding its time earlier, burnt a quarter of its body as it struggled to escape its encirclement. Under Feng Ming's direction, Huxian's devouring and purifying power retreated and formed a bagua symbol around the golden man. Time stood still within the eight trigrams. Lei Jiang, who had been waiting for this very moment, unleashed nine-colored lightning from the exposed sky while Feng Ming struck out with yet another Ash Annihilation. Huxian's spacetime trap broke down as the two techniques struck the golden devil within. It burst into gold dust as it was overwhelmed by their dual attack and its own self-ignition.

The wood devil let out an angry roar as it transformed into a bundle of vines. "You think you can escape after the trouble you've caused?" it said. "You're all doomed to die!"

The vines wrapped around the three small animals and Feng Ming, who didn't panic in the slightest.

"It'll be all right, guys," he said to the struggling demons. The earth shook as a large explosion came from beneath the building, sending large chunks of rock up toward their small group. "Just relax and move around a little," Feng Ming said. Boulders and shrapnel that should have struck them bounced off each other. The three panicking demon beasts looked on in awe as every last piece of rock that could have damaged them struck the large vines instead. After being propelled upward by the shock wave, they fell onto unusually soft ground that cushioned their fall.

Powerful cultivators swarmed around them as they found their footing. Feng Ming spotted several generals and his father approaching from the surrounding alleyways.

"You are under arrest for causing havoc in the city of Songjing," a nervous-looking captain yelled through a voice-amplifying device. "Stand down and surrender yourself for investigation, or we will be forced to use lethal countermeasures."

Feng Ming calmly stowed his spear and put his hands behind his head. He knew the drill. Meanwhile, the three beasts ignored the forces surrounding them. They began digging like their life depended on it.

"Just a second," Huxian yelled. "My boss is down there. I need to dig him up!"

Feng Ming rolled his eyes as a large crater rapidly formed beneath the building's remnants. Soon, it uncovered a thirty-foot, three-colored dome. The lights comprising the dome faded, revealing Cha Ming and eighty people who were little more than skin and bones.

A half hour later, Cha Ming and his three companions lay shackled in four separate cells. They were to remain captive until the city guards completed their investigation and determined their level of responsibility in the entire debacle. Fortunately, half of the rescued captives were able to testify against their jailors. Regrettably, the other half had already lost significant portions of their souls and would remain in comas indefinitely.

"How nice. You even have your own personal cell," Cha Ming said as he looked to Feng Ming's velvet-draped accommodations.

Feng Ming, who was sitting cross-legged, ignored him. Seeing that his friend's aura was unstable, Cha Ming felt around with his resplendent force before his jaw slacked. After all they'd been through, Feng Ming was finally breaking through.

As Feng Ming sat in meditation, he noticed a new rune in his spiritual sea. Like the other eight, it hummed with one of the runes on his qi pillars and caused them to grow while his qi sea thickened. The process was smooth and effortless. Meanwhile, the nine golden runes scrunched together like a crumpled sheet of golden paper.

Feng Ming braced himself for his imminent breakthrough. The crumpled runes morphed and transformed before condensing into an entirely new rune. It was a jade rune, and it was the first of nine steps in cultivating the second volume of the Good Fortune Scripture, Lucky General.

His earthen-fire foundation seas surged into his nine qi pillars, providing them with a final nourishment before their combination into a core. They grew unstable as they drank in the liquid qi, but with this instability came an opportunity for change.

The nine pillars floated to the middle of his Dantian and aligned themselves perpendicularly to the center. Little by little, they melted into a reddish-brown substance that pooled into the singular point. Drop by drop, it accumulated in the center like a mass of molten lava. The nine runes which were previously imprinted on his pillars floated together and merged into the same jade symbol he had just condensed in his mental space.

The rune's appearance was followed by the appearance of a jade runic line. They covered the surface of the spherical blob and tightened around it like a net. Feng Ming shuddered as the lines compressed and condensed the liquid, causing it to shrink to one tenth of its original size. Then, it shrank once more for good measure. The only thing that remained was a tiny reddish-brown core that contained the entirety of the qi he'd accumulated in his lifetime. It was made of a solid that was much harder and more stable than his foundation pillars.

He felt the qi of heaven and earth rush into the small core in his Dantian, nourishing it until it was filled with a thick mist. It was purer and more condensed than the viscous liquid that had previously occupied his qi seas. Feng Ming finally opened his eyes and gazed around they jail where he'd begun his cultivation. He unintentionally released his core-formation pressure, causing the many soldiers in their prison to collapse. He looked around to his devastated surroundings—the furniture in the prison had clearly not been built to withstand the might of a formation cultivator.

"Sergeant Zhou?" Feng Ming said to one of the few remaining officers. The middle-foundation-establishment cultivator was shaking uncontrollably. "Please send a message to my father and inform him that I've broken through."

Interlude: Ten Thousand and Eighty

Gong Lan ascended the steps to the monastery with a calm and steady poise. She did not see visions, nor did she misjudge the number of steps. She saw things exactly as they were, a stark contrast to years ago when she had first arrived.

Monks went about their daily chores in their orange kasayas. They dutifully fulfilled their mundane tasks like sweeping and fetching water. In the distance, she saw the Bodhi Tree. Dozens of cultivators, animals, and monks sat in meditation beneath its enormous branches. All creatures in the world could find peace within its shadow. Even an evil spirit could find enlightenment and reenter samsara.

Many monks greeted her as she walked to the temple. She entered her teacher's sanctum, where the man sat in meditation like he always did; she joined him in reciting mantras. The mantra of peace flowed naturally, calming her weary body and soul. They spoke this mantra 108 times before changing to a complementary mantra, which they recited with alternating rhythms. It was the mantra of cooperation.

As they chanted, Gong Lan imagined the monks in the World Tree Monastery as they performed chores hand in hand and provided for everyone to the best of their ability. She then imagined the city life, where everyone did their own thing but somehow ended up serving others in some way or another. This too was cooperation, unintentional as it might be. However, within this fragile peace was competition.

A merchant sold rice for a cheaper price than the others, angering the neighboring businessmen. They argued and fought until one of them was run out of town. Elsewhere, a person with better skills was hired while another was fired. To feed his family, the older man became a beggar and eventually resorted to theft.

Theft ran rampant throughout the city, and before long, the thefts turned to robberies. Murders followed. The family members of the victims, in their mourning, took up arms against the perpetrators and hunted them down. The images disappeared, and Gong Lan was shocked to discover that they were now reciting the Mantra of Retribution. It reminded her of the concept of righteous indignation, which fueled her Buddhist powers and strengthened them in her fight against evil spirits. It was at odds with the Buddhist path yet somehow existed within it. It was a point that confused her and caused her much anguish.

The chanting stopped, and the older monk sighed. "My time in this world is drawing to a close, Gong Lan," he said softly. "Today, my body will die, and my soul will move on."

The news was shocking and unexpected. "Surely you jest, Master Zhen," she said. "Don't core-formation cultivators live for five hundred years? You are barely three hundred and have two centuries of life ahead of you."

The man chuckled. "Five hundred years is the maximum allowable by the heavens for a human body in a mortal realm. Unfortunately, my body and soul were both wounded many years ago. It is only with the Bodhi Tree's help that I've managed to live until now."

Gong Lan frowned but remained silent.

The older man sighed once more. "Before I pass on, however, I have some unfinished business I must leave to you."

"Please instruct me, Master," Gong Lan said respectfully.

"I once had a student named Sibi," Master Zhen said. "He was my brightest student, the kind that only appeared every thousand years.

His skill in mantras was unparalleled, and he had reached a higher realm in Buddhist techniques in ten years than I had in ninety. He was the perfect successor.

"One hundred and sixty years ago, we explored an emperor's tomb to exorcise evil spirits. Together, we braved many dangers and eventually arrived at the Song Emperor's Seal of Pure Jade, only to discover that it was too late. The corruption had seeped deep within the seal, and the nation's destiny was almost entirely corrupted.

"I told Sibi that it was best to seek out the old master and have him unfetter the seal." He shook his head. "The boy was young and brash. He decided to brave the corruption himself, and I couldn't react in time to stop him. In the end, he failed. He became an evil spirit, and we fought. I managed to destroy his body but not his soul.

"What became of him?" Gong Lan asked. A mere evil spirit should have been easy to exterminate for a powerful Buddhist monk like Master Zhen.

"I couldn't capture him due to my injuries," Master Zhen said. "I hunted him across the continent and encountered him three times. He used his corrupted Buddhist methods to evade me time and time again. After fifty years, I could no longer find him. Yet I know that he still lurks in the shadows. Once he senses I have died, he will surely try to finish what he started. He will accelerate the corruption of the Song Empire and use this to achieve a higher realm. He must be stopped, but now that my time has come to an end, this duty falls to you."

The old monk stood up. He didn't seem feeble in the least, and his nimble movements made Gong Lan doubt his condition. He walked over to the golden statue of Buddha in the room, which held a large rosary in one hand. He lifted it off and reverently walked back to Gong Lan.

"This is the 10,080 rosary of our monastery," Master Zhen said, emotion filling his eyes. "I had originally meant to pass it on to Sibi, but now I will pass it on to you. Should you accept this duty, you must remain leader of the convent until you find a successor. You must protect these lands against evil, and above all else, you must protect the Bodhi Tree from their influence."

Gong Lan's eyes teared up. She bowed deeply to her master, who had shown her nothing but kindness in her darkest days. "I accept. In this lifetime, I will bring Sibi to justice. I will protect the Bodhi Tree, and I will find a successor for the monastery."

A warm sensation filled her as the rosary was placed around her neck. It was coiled multiple times—uncoiled, it would easily reach the floor and back several times. She looked up to see her master glowing with a golden light.

"The 10,080 rosary is blessed by all previous masters who have passed away in this mortal plane," Master Zhen said with gentle smile on his face. "My teacher left a mark on this rosary, and I will now join him in helping you carry out your mission. Before I go, I only have one last word of advice: Trust and believe in yourself. The Bodhi Tree will guide you as he has guided me all this time." He glanced at the small seed that floated above her shoulder and nodded.

Master Zhen's golden glow intensified, and then his body disintegrated, leaving behind a white soul and 10,080 golden motes of light. Each golden speck floated to one of the 10,080 pearls of the golden rosary and merged with it. The golden sheen on it brightened ever so slightly. As Gong Lan grasped the rosary, she felt the warm presence of her master and the combined resolve of over five hundred senior monks. Her master's white soul smiled and was quickly whisked away by the illusion of a yellow river.

Gong Lan wiped away her tears and turned to the bodhi seed with a determined expression. "Where do we go next?"

"To get reinforcements," the seed said. "Our past failure has highlighted the futility of going to such a place alone. It is important to purify the corruption, but it is far more important to preserve your life. It is worth far more than you know."

Chapter 9: The Kings Condition

"A promotion to *general*?" Prince Tian yelled as he smashed a small table across the room. "After causing such a ruckus in the city, he gets a slap on the wrist and a promotion?" A large vein on his forehead was bulging as he vented his frustration.

"The investigation has already shown that he was not at fault," Feng Chuan said calmly. "At most, he caused some chaos in the city that reflects badly on the military. However, his rescue of the civilians has more than made up for this small loss of face. More to the point, it's a strict military rule that any officer who achieves core formation will be promoted to general, regardless of his achievements. While this has only occurred half a dozen times in the past hundred years, it is a rule that has been in place since the inception of the Song Empire that came before us."

"Of course, Marshal Feng," Prince Tian said as he regained his composure. "You must pardon me. I was just upset about his recent activities that cleaned out several years of profits from some casinos I own."

"To be fair, it's your own fault for engaging in such risky ventures," Feng Chuan said. "The person I really pity is whoever was behind that human trafficking scheme. From the investigation, we've determined that the same man owns the underground arena, and he recently suffered a loss of two million high-grade spirit stones. That's got to sting."

Feng Chuan noticed a slight twitch on the crown prince's face. The jab was a probe—he had strong grounds to believe that Prince Tian was the owner of the establishment.

"You're right," Prince Tian said with a chuckle. "There's always someone in a worse position. Many thanks for reminding me. Since Colonel Feng has reached core formation, please gift him with a red-and-gold cloak and handle his promotion immediately."

"Good," Feng Chuan said. "Now that the small things have been taken care of, there's something we need to discuss. The troop movements you've arranged recently have been... worrisome."

"How so?" Prince Tian said.

"I've noticed that they cross all the supply routes in the kingdom," Feng Chuan said. "Meanwhile, we've been receiving many complaints of intercepted cargoes and confiscated goods. Most of these complaints come from either neutral members or members from your brother's faction."

Prince Tian shrugged. "If there's something wrong with their shipments, there's something wrong with their shipments. I'm not my brother's keeper; I can't control how he conducts his business."

"I've been through a succession before, and you're not doing anything I haven't seen," Feng Chuan said. "However, the economics of a kingdom are in a precarious state. Whatever you do, you *must not* jeopardize the stability of the nation."

"I thank Marshal Feng for his kind words of advice," Prince Tian said. "Now if you'll excuse me, I have much work to do."

"It's not good to keep him around the city," Zhou Li said shortly after Marshal Feng left.

"I know that, but I'd like to avoid fighting against him if I can avoid it," Prince Tian said. "He has way too much military and political clout. It's best to keep him on my side, if possible."

"Not him," Zhou Li said. "His son. General Feng is a wildcard, a variable that has the potential to destroy all our plans. A conflict with Marshal Feng is the least of your worries."

Prince Tian massaged his brow. "Let's keep him around for a while longer. I'd need a very good reason to chase him out. His father is extremely overprotective, and he might even rebel if I push him too far." He sighed. "I don't know what my father was thinking, keeping such a strong adversary within his borders."

"Marshal Feng fought many battles alongside His Majesty," Zhou Li said. "They trusted each other like brothers. It's only natural that he supported the brother who helped him solidify his crumbling kingdom."

The prince nodded and turned his attention to a thick pile of papers on his desk. "It's getting late, and I have a mountain of paperwork to take care of."

Zhou Li nodded and walked toward the door. "You know, my sister is excellent in performing clerical duties such as these. It wouldn't kill you to use her when you're overwhelmed." The door closed shut, leaving only the crown prince in his study.

"Like I'll ever trust that snake," Prince Tian muttered.

Cha Ming was waiting in a lobby with Wang Jun when footsteps interrupted their conversation. A young man in green-and-gold robes approached them. The third prince looked amiable and approachable but lacked the powerful demeanor of his older brother.

"Please follow me inside," the third prince said. "My name is Song Lei, and I'm happy to finally meet you."

"The pleasure is all mine," Cha Ming replied as they entered his study. It was filled with beautiful paintings and a welcoming fireplace.

The room smelled like smoky oak and aged wine.

"Would you like anything to drink?" Prince Lei asked.

"Tea would be nice," Cha Ming said.

"I see you've taken up our mutual friend's habit," Prince Lei said as he brought a gilded green tea set from a cupboard to the marble table. He glanced at a timepiece before pouring them each a cup. "We still have some time before my sister leaves my father's side. Why don't you ask me some questions? Brother Wang has told me there are some things troubling you that I might be able to address."

Cha Ming glanced at Wang Jun, who nodded. "I'm definitely troubled by the matter of the succession war. If I might be so blunt, why are you fighting with your elder brother for the throne? I have my reasons for helping you, but it would reassure me to know your own reasons."

Prince Lei chuckled. "Until a few years ago, I would have gladly let him take the throne. Such a duty is tiring and thankless—no one truly knows the troubles of a monarch."

"What sort of earth-shattering news changed your mind?" Cha Ming asked.

Prince Lei sighed and poured them another cup. "Many people would kill you for knowing such a story, so please don't share it with others."

"My lips are sealed," Cha Ming said.

"The crown prince, Song Tian, was born thirty-six years ago," Prince Lei said. "That same year, my second brother, Song Chuan, was born from a concubine in the king's harem. He was named after Marshal Feng in honor of his illustrious military service. The two brothers were close in their childhood. That is, until it became apparent that Song Chuan was far more talented than his brother Tian.

"Not only was Chuan more intelligent, courageous, and benevolent, he also excelled in any topic you could think of. Archery, swordplay, politics, and commerce—he only had strong points and no weaknesses. He was a veritable genius. Tian, on the other hand, worked harder than any prince in history. He was ruthless to everyone, including himself.

"Upon reaching sixteen years of age, their cultivation talents were evaluated. Both Tian and Chuan were identified as cultivation geniuses. However, Chuan was ultimately appointed as crown prince due to his diverse skillset and outstanding temperament. From then on, they were kept separate and groomed for different paths. All this was done to prevent them from killing each other and vying for the throne.

"Therefore, no one suspected a thing when Prince Chuan was killed in the line of duty during their traditional military assignment. He and Tian were both posted in different regiments. They were also low in the military hierarchy, so it was deemed impossible that Tian could have gathered sufficient influence to orchestrate his brother's demise."

Prince Lei sighed and poured them another cup. He also pushed a bowl of what looked like a cross between nuts and figs of a magical nature. Thick heaven and earth energy surrounded each of the odd fruits, which Cha Ming nibbled on curiously.

"The incident was forgotten, and Tian became the new crown prince," Prince Lei continued. "I had been born when he was fourteen, and my fourth brother and fifth sister were born one year after that—fraternal twins. Song Tian was very close to the them. He always spent much time with them and lavished them with gifts. I was the odd one out—I always argued with my brother, so he never paid much attention to me."

Prince Lei sighed. "One day, a dreadful explosion occurred in the palace. Tian rushed into the smoldering wreck that was the room shared by the twins and discovered my little sister, Song Guo. He saved Guo Guo and looked for Wudi. He never found him, but he returned with severely burned hands. The court physicians healed his right hand, but he refused to remove the scars from the left."

Cha Ming frowned as he sipped his green tea. "It sounds like your brother is worthy of respect and cares very much for his family. I assume there is more to this story than meets the eye."

Prince Lei nodded. "Five years ago, a senior minister lay dying. He had served the country faithfully for fifty years. One by one, people filed into his room to pay their respects. As a prince of the Song Kingdom, I did the same.

"When I stood at his feet, he burst into tears and asked me to come close, so he could share his life's greatest regret. He told the story of how, twenty-four years ago, he was advised by the late court oracle that Prince Tian was the only suitable ruler for the Song Kingdom, and that he should support him wholeheartedly. He contacted the then-twelve-year-old prince, who was very eager for the additional support.

"The prince mostly requested introductions in military circles. After all, he was bound to serve there for his princely duties. Connections would pave him a smooth path for advancement within the army. It was only once the prince reached eighteen years of age, and Prince Chuan was murdered, that the minister realized the consequences of his actions. Most of the kingdom thought it was impossible for Prince Tian to engineer Prince Chuan's death. The minister thought otherwise.

"He spent the next three years poring over military documents and gathering information before concluding that Prince Tian was responsible for Prince Chuan's death. The discovery shook him to his very core, and his health began to decline. He continued to serve the kingdom, but one thing still bothered him: Was it just the second prince, or was the fourth prince also a victim of Prince Tian's machinations?

"He searched for the answer for the next decade before halting his investigation. Desperate to discover the truth, he consulted with the Obsidian Syndicate."

Cha Ming hissed between his teeth when he heard the familiar name.

"He discovered that, a decade prior, a twice-removed subordinate of the crown prince had hired the Obsidian Syndicate to assassinate the fourth prince. But he had not purchased anonymity. The minister speculated that they were assassinated since his own mother had fallen out of favor in the harem, and the king's new favorite was the fourth prince and the princess's mother."

Prince Lei sighed. "This story of a man on his deathbed wasn't enough to warrant my change of heart. People can talk and instigate, and even a dying man's words can't be trusted. It could have been a plot to upset the stability of the kingdom. Therefore I retrieved the information the man entrusted to me and began my own investigation. What I discovered shocked me.

"Out of seventy-nine men the minister had originally introduced my brother to, sixty-three had already died, and sixteen had left the military. Of those sixteen, seven of them had joined rebel factions that caused unrest in the kingdom. I spent almost all my savings and assets to validate the information. I bought information from four different companies, and I even purchased information from the Obsidian Syndicate. I spent extra to guarantee the information wasn't tampered with by a third party. The information was delivered under the life oath of a junior partner.

"I was financially destitute by the time I confirmed everything, but the truth was unsettling. The brother I admired so deeply had caused the death of two of my siblings. I couldn't live under the same sky as him anymore. That is why I have been contesting the throne, despite the upheaval I have caused in the process."

Cha Ming, unsure of what to say, could only shake his head in sorrow. He wondered what he would do in a similar situation. Would he drive the kingdom in a civil war and vie for the throne, or would he let his brother take over to preserve peace in the kingdom? Assassinating the crown prince, while the most direct approach, would leave the kingdom heirless.

An incense time passed before Wang Jun cleared his throat. "It's time," he said.

A shadowy door appeared in the room. Wang Jun led the three of them through a shadowy corridor, which led them to a second door. It opened into a large bedroom, where they saw an old man lying in a silk-draped bed. Cha Ming noticed many basic medical instruments. They were all low level, the type that Li Yin would use to treat villagers. Cha Ming was perplexed.

Why would a spirit doctor need to use such mundane items to treat a king?

He peered at the king's body, which was little more than a desiccated husk. Brown blotches covered his yellowish skin, and little hair was left on his head. He was unconscious and barely breathing.

"How long has he been like this?" Cha Ming asked.

"Ever since the contest ended," Prince Lei replied. "He had been ill for quite some time, but it came as a surprise when he suddenly collapsed. He hasn't woken since."

Cha Ming nodded. "May I please touch your royal father?"

Seeing Prince Lei nod, Cha Ming walked up to the aged man. Just before reaching him, an unseen pressure stopped his movements.

"Who is this?" a voice said from above.

"This is Master Du, a dual formation and talisman master," Prince Lei replied. "I brought him to get a second opinion."

"There has already been a second opinion, and even a third," the voice said.

"Then a fourth or fifth won't hurt," Prince Lei replied.

The room was quiet for a moment before the figure spoke up once more. "Fine. But if he does anything slightly suspicious, I'll take his head."

The pressure on Cha Ming's body disappeared, but his sensitive resplendent force concluded he was still being closely monitored.

Cha Ming approached the king and touched his wrist. He sent his resplendent force into the man's body. "Pulse is weak," he muttered. "Breath shallow. Blood pollution high. Kidneys failing. Liver failing." He frowned. "Despite all these things, everything seems normal. Bone age indicates 160 years of age, still young for a core-formation cultivator." He looked to the third prince. "His condition is completely incongruent with expectations. There should be something wrong with him for such severe symptoms to appear. What has the chief physician said?"

"He said it makes no sense, of course," the Prince Lei said helplessly. "He and his colleagues have tried all methods at their disposal. They even invited an expert from the Quicksilver Empire for a hefty sum. They consulted with alchemists because they suspected poisoning, but they were unable to conclude anything."

Cha Ming frowned. He threw out thirty-six blue and green flags around the king's bed. Then he withdrew his Clear Sky Brush and painted blue and green runic lines to link the flags. They glowed brightly as the ink activated and displayed their inscribed formations.

Seeing that the formation required more energy, Cha Ming withdrew five hundred mid-grade spirit stones, which crumbled to dust. A green and blue haze filled the area immediately surrounding the king's bed. Cha Ming guided the formation, which amplified his spiritual force and granted him the power to apply healing runes to anyone within its boundaries.

Where to start? Cha Ming thought. *His blood toxicity is the greatest threat, so the kidneys should be a primary focus.*

Cha Ming's consciousness traveled to the kidneys, which were barely functioning. He used the formation to channel a large amount of healing qi in a precise fashion. It formed runes of healing that rushed toward key points in the organ. But the moment the runes contacted it, they crumbled and dimmed. The healing energy that should have treated the malfunctioning kidney disappeared as though being sucked inside a black hole. Cha Ming frowned and tried again, but to no avail.

Seeing this strange situation, Cha Ming looked to the Dantian, where he saw a small core. However, the core was dim; it exchanged no energy with the remainder of the body. Therefore Cha Ming inserted the purest creation qi inside the man's Dantian. It was violently sucked inside the dim core, which didn't change in the slightest.

Cha Ming's expression turned grim. He probed the man's heart, liver, and other organs in turn. He probed the man's bone marrow as well. Each piece of his body caused the healing runes to disintegrate on contact.

"You said the investigation didn't detect poison?" Cha Ming asked the third prince.

"Nothing traditional and nothing alchemical, according to the alchemists," Prince Lei said.

"Wang Jun," Cha Ming said, "did you try reading his story?"

"I can't," Wang Jun said helplessly. "He doesn't respond to fate qi. Which is curious given that fate qi is impervious to most tampering. I scoured the information networks and the alchemist workshops for an explanation, but to no avail."

"Hm…" Cha Ming examined the king once more. This time, he activated his Eyes of Pure Jade.

Nothing. Then, to be thorough, he activated his Demon-Subduing Eyes. He felt drained as he activated both eye techniques simultaneously. His gray surroundings instantly lit up with a faint purple light.

"What in the world," he whispered.

"What did you find?" Prince Lei asked anxiously. Cha Ming held his hand up and probed the king's body once more with his resplendent force. He noticed the tissues in the king's body were suffused with a dull purple glow.

"I found something, but I need to confirm it with my contracted beast," Cha Ming explained. "I possess an eye technique that can detect demonic energies, and they happen to be present on your royal father's body. However, I know next to nothing about demons."

Meanwhile, he reached out to Huxian. *I need your help, brother. How soon can you get here?*

I just remembered a transportation technique, so it won't take long, Huxian replied. *Just say the word.*

"May I please invite him over?" Cha Ming said to Prince Lei. The young man hesitated for a while before giving his permission.

Cha Ming sent a message to Huxian, and to his surprise, his shadow began to grow. Wang Jun looked on with interest as Cha Ming's shadow transformed to that of a many-tailed beast. Prince Lei gasped. A two-foot-long black-and-white fox suddenly jumped out of the shadow.

"Man, that was fun," Huxian said. "Can I do it again?"

"This might not be the best time," Cha Ming said while massaging his temple. "Can you please activate your Demon-Subduing Eyes and examine the king? There is something wrong with him.

"Sounds good!" Huxian said excitedly. The little fox had been bored out of his mind since they had arrived inside the city. He hopped into Cha Ming's outstretched arms, and they walked closer to the king, the purple ring around both Cha Ming and Huxian's jade irises glowed brightly.

"Oh. *Oh*. This is bad," Huxian said.

"It's of demonic origin, right?" Cha Ming asked Huxian. They spoke openly to avoid any suspicion.

"Yes, and if my guess is correct, it's a venom of some kind," Huxian said. "The venom has permeated his flesh. What are the symptoms?"

"His body is failing," Cha Ming said. "Any qi used to treat his body disintegrates on contact."

The small fox pondered for a moment before shaking his head. "I'm not sure which beast's venom it is, but it's definitely a snake. I suggest we bring back a sample of blood back to the geomantic boa."

Cha Ming turned to the third prince.

"This..." Prince Lei said. "The physicians often need to draw blood. However, since my father's body does not heal properly, it is always drawn from the same place on his arm." The prince walked over to the bed and pulled the king's frail arm from under the blanket. It was tightly wrapped in white bandages stained with blood, which dripped from the king's exposed arm as soon as the prince unwrapped the bandages.

"Be quick about it," Prince Lei said.

Cha Ming withdrew a jade bottle and directed the blood into it. Once it was full, he used his spiritual force to temporarily stem the bleeding and rewrapped the bandage the same way as before.

"I will leave for the Silverwing Mountain Range tonight to inquire about the venom," Cha Ming said to the third prince. "Huxian is a sovereign of the mountain range and will request the aid of another sovereign who specializes in such matters. In addition, I know someone who can heal people without using qi or traditional spirit-doctor methods. Perhaps he can buy us time."

"Many thanks for all your efforts," Prince Lei said. "I only have one father. Please save him."

Chapter 10:
Foreign Aid

A black door opened inside the Jade Bamboo Auction House. Despite the late hour, Wang Jun's staff was still hard at work.

"It looks like you'll have another sleepless night," Cha Ming said when he saw the papers stacked on his friend's desk.

"It never ends," Wang Jun said, shrugging. He passed the desk and retrieved a folder from his cabinet. After leafing through a few pages, he pulled out a small bundle and handed it to Cha Ming. "I need you to deliver these papers to the Alchemists Association in Quicksilver. I've obtained permission to set up a competing branch guild in the Song Kingdom due to their lack of performance. I'd like to request Quicksilver's help in establishing this branch."

"Won't Quicksilver be uncooperative, given our past experience with them?" Cha Ming said as he stowed away the envelope.

Wang Jun shook his head. "Things change quickly in the business world. It wasn't wise for Wang Chen to antagonize a powerful transcendent being. The connections Lu Tianhao established in his lifetime couldn't be fathomed by a mere branch manager like him. There should be no problems with the branch under new management."

Cha Ming whistled through his teeth in amazement. "What a

quick response. No wonder Teacher Tianhao told me not to worry about it."

"Wang Bing is the new manager there," Wang Jun said. "Fortunately for her, she was quite neutral in the whole affair, and punishing her would have been a huge loss to the family. You'll find her quite helpful should you need anything."

Cha Ming pondered for a bit. "While I'm at it, the Talisman Artist Guild here is in deplorable condition. I'll ask the branch leader in Quicksilver if anyone is interested in taking it over. There must be at *someone* with ambition in Quicksilver."

"Do what you can, but don't waste time," Wang Jun said. "The Song Kingdom is considered a backwater location with no potential. People prefer to stay near their homes whenever possible."

"It doesn't hurt to ask," Cha Ming said before leaving Wang Jun's office.

He quickly exited the city with Huxian in tow. The guards at the gate were already familiar with him, so they didn't cause any trouble. "Are you sure this will be all right?" Cha Ming asked Huxian after they were a thousand feet out.

"It should be fine," Huxian said. "Silverwing, can you come out for a bit?" One of his two tails glowed before a small bird flew out from another dimension.

"What are you bothering this sovereign for?" Silverwing said. "It's not polite to wake a napping bird."

"It's not polite, but we were left with no other options," Huxian replied. "Lives are at stake, and we need to get to the Silverwing Mountain Range as quickly as possible."

"What does that have to do with me?" the Silverwing asked them suspiciously. Then, noticing Huxian's pleading expression, he rolled his eyes. "You know that it's demeaning for this sovereign to serve as a mount."

Huxian's eyes began to water when he heard this response. "I see... Yes, you're right. That's fine. You can go back now."

The bird ruffled his feathers. "You're not going to ask again?"

"No, you're completely right," Huxian said. "My brother and I will run as swiftly as we can. I just hope we're not too late. However, it's much better than inconveniencing a mighty bird like yourself."

"It's really not that inconvenient..." Silverwing said hesitantly. "But I don't want to be seen with a *human* on my back. Even a nice one like your brother. I would lose a lot of face among the sovereigns."

Huxian's ears perked up. "You mean it's fine as long as no one sees? No problem! Come on, let me see your biggest form!"

The silver falcon rolled his eyes before growing to a wingspan of eighty feet.

"I'm a small bird, so this is as big as I get," Silverwing said. Then he glared at Cha Ming. "Don't you dare ruin my beautiful feathers."

Cha Ming hopped onto his back while Huxian jumped onto his head.

"I've been wanting to fly for ages!" Huxian said. "But Brother Silverwing is always napping."

"Be nice to him," Cha Ming said as he shifted on the bird's back. The metallic feathers were extremely uncomfortable. A stray feather bit deep into his flesh as he moved.

Silverwing cleared his throat, and on cue, Huxian spewed out a cloud of darkness. It spanned two hundred feet and appeared like a gray storm cloud. Despite its outer appearance, they could see perfectly well from the inside. "Are you sure we won't be seen?" Silverwing asked.

"Absolutely sure," Huxian assured him.

"Then hold on tight!" Silverwing said. He flapped his wings once, instantly bringing them thousands of feet into the air. He flapped them a second time, propelling them a few thousand feet toward the Silverwing Mountain Range.

Cha Ming screamed as they accelerated. His hands bled as he grabbed fistfuls of metallic feathers to prevent himself from falling.

"Sorry about that," Silverwing said, creating a bubble of wind qi around Cha Ming. Several strands of wind also materialized and lashed Cha Ming onto the large bird. "I've never carried anyone around before, so I never bothered to look into any of these basic techniques."

Huxian was in a very sorry state. His paws weren't bleeding, but he'd slipped down from Silverwing's head and was now gripping his neck tightly. His fur was in disarray, and his tails were flapping uncontrollably behind him.

"Are you all right?" Cha Ming yelled to the small fox.

"Better than ever!" Huxian yelled. "This is the way I like it. I love the feeling of the wind on my fur!"

Silverwing flapped once more, almost throwing him off. Cha Ming could feel emotions of misery and determination through their soul link. He could tell exactly what was going through Huxian's mind—he would rather die than lose face to Silverwing.

Cha Ming chuckled as he saw Silverwing grin. The large bird dove down toward the land below, causing the antlike people and animals to grow at a rapid pace. Now that he didn't need to worry about holding on, Cha Ming felt at ease as they flew beneath the clear sky. He relished the freedom and the open scenery. Instead of just seeing the edge of forests, he could see it blanket over the entire continent. Instead of seeing a dozen fields in the distance, he could see the entire agricultural area of the Song Kingdom.

As they flew toward the Silverwing Mountain Range, Cha Ming looked back toward Green Leaf City. It had been so long since he'd visited that small dot in the distance. Would he ever get a chance to return in the future?

It only took three hours for them to arrive at the edge of the mountains. Huxian crawled off the mighty falcon looking thoroughly defeated after the harrowing experience. He dispelled the cloud of darkness before collapsing onto the grassy ground.

"How was it?" Cha Ming asked. "Was it just like you'd hoped?"

"That and more," Huxian said, his voice filled with pain. He was covered in cuts, and his fur was sheared in many places. Instead of going for a leisurely flight, an external observer might think he'd fought a vicious life-and-death battle. Fortunately, he was a half-step core-formation Godbeast. His wounds regenerated within an incense time, after which he strutted around proud as a peacock.

"Did you see how this sovereign flew through the clouds?" he asked Silverwing. "Did you see how I didn't need your help to stay mounted? I'm a natural flyer, a king of the skies."

"Oh? You want me to fly at my top speed next time, then?" Silverwing asked innocently.

"Perhaps it's best that you don't," Huxian said. "For Cha Ming's sake. Even with your protection, he wouldn't be able to hold on."

"Right." Cha Ming coughed. "For my sake." Both he and Silverwing exchanged a meaningful glance.

They walked to the jade boundary that separated the mountain range from the Song Kingdom. Cha Ming touched it with his hand, and it responded to its master by forming a door covered in runic lines. Cha Ming, Huxian, and Silverwing walked through together. Lei Jiang appeared out of thin air and bolted out toward a faraway mountain once they crossed the transparent shield.

"He's was very bored in the city," Huxian said. "He didn't like Elder Bai's cat, and I told him he couldn't steal cheese from the mousetraps. Then I had to ground him when he tried to set traps for the local cultivators."

Cha Ming chuckled. They walked at a leisurely pace toward Huxian's old mountain, where the geomantic boa resided. A multitude of venomous creatures watched them, and poison-related herbs grew out of every nook and cranny. The forest leading to the peak seemed to span endlessly.

As they walked, a swallow flew past them and rushed into a nearby tree. A snake slithered between their feet as they passed a tiny hole in a rocky mound. One thousand feet turned to three thousand, and three thousand turned to ten thousand. It wasn't long before they arrived near a peculiar tree. A swallow flew past them and rushed into it. As if to highlight the peculiarity, a snake slithered through their feet and entered a tiny hole in a rocky mound.

Cha Ming sighed as he activated his Demon-Subduing Eyes. Intricate purple lines displayed clever runic patterns. He activated his resplendent force and probed around his surroundings. He quickly uncovered several formations under their combined inspection.

"Geomantic Monarch," he shouted, "would you like to dispel your formation, or would you like me to break it?"

His question was answered by the gentle chirping of a tiny bird. Hearing no reply, he quickly sent out thirty-six sigils to a nearby formation eye, which rapidly broke under their onslaught. Its destruction restored a bit of reality to their illusory surroundings.

Their group continued forward at a leisurely pace. Whenever they saw a formation eye, Cha Ming broke it. Whenever they encountered beasts, both Huxian and Silverwing scared them away. Little by little, the mountain's illusion was disrupted. It wasn't long before they arrived at a barren peak.

"Who dares intrude on this monarch's mountain?" a voice said from the mountain itself. They suddenly noticed that a gigantic serpent was coiled around it. Its body surely measured several miles in length.

Cha Ming sighed. "Would you like to dispel your own illusory formation, or would you like me to do it?"

The boa's eyes narrowed. "Whatever do you mean?" Its aura was fierce and imposing, and its gaze mesmerizing. If not for his Demon-Subduing Eyes, Cha Ming would have been fooled by it.

"Have it your way," he said, sending out thirty-six sigils to key points on the mountain. His qi manifested runic lines, and the illusion shattered like a pane of glass. A forty-foot snake appeared where the giant one once stood, looking shaken and embarrassed.

"Where's your mother?" Huxian said, trotting up to the snake. "Does she know what mischief you've been up to?" The small snake trembled in fear but didn't dare move as Huxian walked toward him. The small fox grew with every step until he was eighty feet long.

"M-m-mother should be near the center of the mountain range," the small snake said. "Please don't hurt me, Sovereign Two Tails!"

"Right, near the center of the mountain range," Huxian said.

"That makes sense. It's too bad I'm so hungry. Oh, wait, I have an idea! Why don't we feast on roast snake before she arrives?"

Silverwing flapped his wings in anticipation as the fox summoned a plume of fire using Cha Ming's qi. He bound the small snake in shackles of darkness and held him above the open flame.

"Mother!" the little snake yelled. A loud snort extinguished the flame as a large snake appeared. It was coiled around the mountain and hidden from even Cha Ming's superior vision.

"How did you know I was here?" the geomantic boa slithered.

"A good guess," Huxian said nonchalantly.

"You aren't the type to let your children roam unsupervised," Cha Ming added. He deactivated his Demon-Subduing Eyes and wiped a trickle of blood from the corner of his eyes. His blurry vision focused as the taxing technique returned to its passive state.

The giant snake nodded. "This is true. They are my three purest offspring, and I never let them out of my sight. Now tell me, what is your purpose here? It isn't yet time to trade."

Cha Ming flicked out a jade vial full of blood. "This blood is contaminated with a poison. Huxian swears it's a snake venom. I was hoping you could identify it."

"And why should I do that?" the snake said. "I care not for the plight of poisoned humans."

Cha Min shrugged. "You don't have to do anything, but it is truly in your best interest to treat the man. He is the king of the Song Kingdom, and he is dying. Delaying his death will have a huge impact on the battle for succession."

"And the battle for the throne matters to me because...?" the boa said.

"The three signatories on the contract are the third prince, a minister, and my friend Wang Jun. The crown prince will likely have the third prince killed if he takes over the throne—which he likely will if the king dies as planned. The crown prince also hates Wang Jun. That means the treaty will be at risk if the crown prince, especially since he is willing to sacrifice a single minister's life. Wouldn't it be better to have the signatory take over the throne?"

The snake frowned. "That means you tricked us."

"Not at all," Cha Ming said. "Politics shift all the time. It just so happens that the king was poisoned after the treaty was signed. Like it or not, we're in the same boat."

The snaked snorted and willed the bottle over. It shattered, and the liquid inside separated into two substances—one small purple drop and one red blob. The snake directed a mass of demonic qi into the small purple blob. It immediately disintegrated on contact. As though expecting this development, the geomantic boa hissed. Hundreds of drops of venom flew out from its fangs. The purple drop split into hundreds of parts and flew into the other small drops. Two hundred drops instantly disintegrated while fifty or so took a little longer to evaporate. Only five venoms managed to coexist for a short while before eventually dissipating.

"This is a fourth-grade venom," the boa slithered. "And if my guess is correct, it's qi-binding venom, a rare innate venom obtained from a qi-binding serpent. It will destroy any qi it encounters, and it will seep into the flesh and blood of living organisms. While it won't waste a person's cultivation, it will render them incapable of cultivating. The same applies to demonic qi."

"Is there a cure?" Cha Ming said.

The boa shook its head. "Not that I'm aware of. The snake is extremely rare. There are perhaps two or three on the entire continent. They don't reproduce by normal means, and they are reclusive and antisocial." A cunning gleam appeared in its eyes. "However, given enough time, I might be able to duplicate it so that it can be studied. That is, if I could obtain the complete geomantic python inheritance from Lord Two Tails."

The small fox bared its teeth. "Even if I had it, aren't you asking for a bit much? These secrets are heavily guarded by the Geomantic Python Clan. Change your request."

"It's not that I don't want to, it's that I'm truly helpless," the Geomantic Monarch said, moaning like a wounded animal. "I need a higher-tier venom-manufacturing technique to reproduce it."

"Do you think the geomantic python inheritance is a venom

technique I can casually toss out?" Huxian said.

"I'll have it, or I'm not budging," the Geomantic Monarch said indignantly.

"Cha Ming, help me teach this snake a lesson," Huxian said.

Cha Ming rolled his eyes. He held out his hand and manipulated the Silverwing Mountain Range's protective formation. Huxian's power broke through to core formation, while the geomantic boa, who should have been the controller of the formation, was left with nothing.

"You... you left a back way in!" the Geomantic Monarch yelled. "Fine, I'll—"

She was interrupted by Huxian pouncing, biting deep into her scaly neck. She thrashed about in pain as he scratched and bit her. Scales scattered throughout the mountain as she was mauled in the presence of her three children, who cowered in fear as they saw their all-powerful mother being dominated by a small fox.

Huxian returned a short while later covered in blue serpentine blood. His powers of purification quickly eliminated any venoms that he had contracted in their exchange. The black and white colors drained from his fur and materialized into a black-and-white ball, which he tossed to the agonizing snake.

"This is a fourth-grade venom technique," Huxian barked at the barely living snake on the mountaintop. "And you're not getting any more out of me. Act up again, and I'll find another monarch to replace you."

Chapter 11: The Price of Power

*B*ang. *Crash. Bang.*

Trees fell one after another as Cha Ming brandished his Clear Sky Staff against a king-level frost wolf. Cha Ming didn't use formations, nor did the frost wolf use its innate abilities. They faced off in a contest of brute force, and there was no clear winner in the process.

Let's try this again, Cha Ming thought. He grasped the staff and slammed it down with all his strength, channeling as much earth qi as he could to execute a Quake Staff. His qi spread out into thirty-six qi points to mimic a combat formation. Unfortunately, it didn't work very well. The part near his hands vibrated slightly, but none of it transferred across to the wolf, who simply shrugged it off as he swung his massive paw at Cha Ming's small body.

Cha Ming flew back one hundred feet before crashing into a large rock. Its surface shattered as he plunged two feet into the solid granite. Fortunately, his bones were as strong as magic treasures, and his regenerative abilities quickly healed the lacerations his body had suffered upon impact.

"Are you sure you want to continue, pitiful human?" the frost wolf said. His voice was laced with disdain.

"I naturally need to continue," Cha Ming said. His staff lengthened to twelve feet as he lunged toward the wolf. He manipulated his weight and increased the thin staff's weight drastically while executing another makeshift technique using gold qi. The staff bit into the wolf's flesh like a dull blade but was ultimately ignored. Cha Ming swiftly manipulated his weight once more, using it and his heavy staff to redirect the wolf's massive body and push off against it. It was a crude manifestation of his Gentle Staff Art.

Then his staff expanded until it was twelve feet long and six inches thick. The ground sank under his feet as his weight increased to twelve thousand jin. The added weight enabled him to easily manipulate the 1,080-jin pillar in his arms.

As the wolf approached, he blocked its movements using the heavy pillar and interrupted its movements. He used wood and water qi to slightly trap and constrict the wolf before swinging it in a horizontal arc that easily struck the wolf's enormous body. It coughed up blood but stood strong and counterattacked with a vicious bite.

Cha Ming didn't panic. He kicked back in midair using his Stormchaser Boots, avoiding the wolf's bite by a fraction of a second. Then he bounced in midair several times before striking down once more while activating his Demon-Subduing Eyes and freezing the wolf in place. This time, he expanded the Clear Sky Staff to forty feet in length. The 4,000-jin pillar crashed down on the wolf's head and rendered it unconscious. It woke up after five seconds and lowered its head in shame.

"Sovereign, I have failed you," the wolf said mournfully.

Huxian's tiny frame jumped out of Cha Ming's shadow and into his arms.

"It's only natural that you'd lose against my big brother," Huxian said. "How was it, brother?"

"This physical strength is far too difficult to handle," Cha Ming said. "I originally thought I could use my old techniques, but I was wrong. I've made some embryonic techniques using my old qi-condensation techniques and combat formations as templates, but they are extremely lacking."

Huxian shrugged. "Worst case, you can use your staff as a big stick and combine it with your combat formations. Your Stormchaser formation is good for close combat, and you can work heavy staff strikes into your combat formation attacks without sacrificing anything. Not just that, you can take hits head-on without affecting your performance. You should be able to hold your own against late-foundation-establishment cultivators."

Cha Ming agreed with this assessment. He had reached early bone forging as they waited for the Geomantic Monarch.

"It's ready," a powerful voice said from the peak of the mountain.

Cha Ming and Huxian disappeared from the shamed wolf's side and reappeared on the barren peak. The Geomantic Monarch waved its tail and threw out a large jade bottle.

"Many thanks," Cha Ming said as he caught the bottle. Huxian frowned and let out a soft cough. The Geomantic Monarch slithered and threw out another two hundred jade vials, which Cha Ming caught with a look of surprise.

"Who knows, those venoms might come in handy when finding a cure," Huxian said to clear up the confusion. "I *convinced* the monarch to kindly help us. Silverwing lent a hand to make it happen."

Only then did Cha Ming see several large scars on the Geomantic Monarch's body.

"It's been hard on you," Cha Ming said apologetically.

"It has," she said. "In return, I'd appreciate it if you left my mountain as soon as possible."

Huxian shrugged. "Silverwing!"

A flash of silver leapt over from a nearby mountain. The large silver falcon impatiently gestured for them to hop on. Cha Ming gave Huxian a perplexed look.

He got over it, and now he enjoys carrying people around in the skies, Huxian said. A small protective bubble covered them and lashed them to Silverwing's back before the large bird leaped into the skies.

"Awwwoooooo," Huxian yelled as they exited the protective dome. "We made off like bandits. She'll never catch us now!"

"Boss is definitely the smartest," Silverwing said, chuckling.

"Is there something I don't know about?" Cha Ming asked.

Huxian responded by summoning a large assortment of roots, herbs, and fruits. Cha Ming quickly swept them into his Clear Sky World. "Where did you get these?"

Huxian chuckled. "While that old snake was busy making venoms, Silverwing and I pilfered the whole mountain range. Specifically, we took a bunch of herbs relating to poisons and the like. It just happens that most of them were on the Geomantic Monarch's mountain peak."

"Two Tails!" A loud roar of indignation carried from the mountain range to their small group, which was now dozens of miles away. "I'll have your hide for this!"

Cha Ming massaged his brow for what seemed like the thousandth time this week.

"By the way, where's Lei Jiang?" Cha Ming asked. As he spoke, an iridescent bolt of lightning darted over to them and landed atop Silverwing's broad back. He dropped a small bag of holding in front of Cha Ming.

"Can you keep these for me?" the small mouse said. "I brought some snacks for the trip."

Cha Ming peeked into the bag and saw dozens of strange objects. Fruits, stones, roots, bamboo shoots, and other lightning-based materials were stored inside.

"Well, at least they feed themselves," Cha Ming muttered. He set his sights on Quicksilver's mighty walls, which were rapidly growing in the distance.

The large city's hustle and bustle lightened Cha Ming's sullen mood as he walked out of the guard office. He'd just signed a guarantee on Huxian, Silverwing, and Lei Jiang's behavior. Given their prior escapades, it was possible that he'd lose his shirt before their time was up.

"It's just three days," Cha Ming said. "You can be a good Huxian during that time, can't you?"

"I'm always a good Huxian, even if you don't always notice," the small fox said, pouting.

The quartet flew above the rail tracks that led to the center of the city. It wasn't long before they arrived at Central Square. They passed several buildings before arriving at the northeast corner, where the Obsidian Syndicate and the Alabaster Group stood opposite each other.

Cha Ming ignored the dark building and made his way to the Alabaster Group's living quarters. He crossed the large garden of medicinal ingredients before arriving at a wooden door. A muffled boom sounded just as he rapped his knuckles on it.

"Who's there?" an aged voice called out.

"It's me," Cha Ming said. The door opened after a few moments.

"Well, you're back a lot quicker than I imagined," Mo Tianshen said. "Come in, come in. I have some good news to share with you."

He led Cha Ming to the table and poured him a cup of tea. Thankfully, Mo Tianshen paid more attention to standard laboratory rules than his apprentice, the leader of the Quicksilver Alchemist Guild.

"Where to begin," Mo Tianshen said, stroking his white beard. "Firstly, there have been some promising trials. I estimate that we can begin mass production of the ninth-generation pills within a half month. Those whelps Jun Xiezi sent have all learned the necessary runes, so we're only waiting for batches of raw ingredients."

"Congratulations," Cha Ming said, happy that his efforts had borne fruit. "I'm sure there will soon be a tenth iteration, followed by an eleventh and a twelfth."

"We're still a long way off from that," Mo Tianshen said. "Now tell me, boy, why are you here? You usually don't visit me without a reason."

Cha Ming looked at him sheepishly. "I want you to make me late-grade and peak-grade pills, as well as core-formation pills," Cha Ming said. With the old alchemist, it was best to be straightforward.

Mo Tianshen frowned. "I can tell that you haven't even broken through to late foundation establishment. What's the rush? Don't you know that cultivating too quickly will destabilize your foundation? Come back again in three months."

"I know it's best to wait to stabilize my foundation," Cha Ming said. "However, there's a war brewing in the Song Kingdom, where I was born. I want to be prepared in case of any unforeseen circumstances. Surely you can do that for me?"

He tossed a bag containing a multitude of rare ingredients from the Silverwing Mountain Range. These included the items on the list Mo Tianshen had given him earlier.

The alchemist briefly glanced inside the bag before giving Cha Ming a concerned look. "I'm very busy, and if I give you more pills, it means you'll be able to stay away for longer. What if I don't see you again for half a decade?"

Cha Ming chuckled. "So that's what's worrying you. How about this, I'll be back within three years, and not a minute later."

"No longer than a year," Mo Tianshen said. "And when you come back, you'll have to slave away for me for a whole year before regaining your freedom."

Cha Ming hesitated for a moment. For all he knew, the conflict could last longer. However, without these pills, he might quickly find himself outmatched.

"Two years," Cha Ming said. "And I'll work for you for six months."

"I'm not budging on the year," Mo Tianshen said.

Cha Ming hesitating once more before nodding. "Fine. Two years and one year of hard labor." The old alchemist sighed as he grabbed the bag of medicinal ingredients.

"You really need to be careful with your cultivation," the old alchemist said. "Your qi seas still need a couple more weeks to stabilize. Don't be in such rush to reach the peak, or you'll soon find it impossible to reach."

After speaking to the old alchemist, Cha Ming walked up the white marble stairs to a plain wooden door. Before he could even knock, he heard a gentle voice whisper for him to enter. He opened the creaking door and entered Lu Tianhao's library. The man was garbed in white like always, looking pensive as he stared at a doll on his desk.

"I heard from Xuehua that your trip to the mountain range was successful," Lu Tianhao said with a light smile.

"We only barely succeeded, despite the seniors you sent," Cha Ming said grimly. "It's unfortunate that so many of them couldn't return."

Lu Tianhao sighed. "It's always been that way, and it will never stop. The universe was built that way."

Cha Ming frowned as he sat. "How can you be so sure it was designed?"

"There is an old story passed down from the realms up above," Lu Tianhao said. "It tells of the first painter, who painted the mists at the dawn of time. He created a world of black and white, good and evil. We don't know who he is or what his goal was. All we know is that the world was created balanced. Whether it was his mood at the time, or his indecision, we all suffer from this first mistake. Both devils and angels have cursed him since the world's inception."

"How are the forces of good and evil balanced?" Cha Ming said. "It seems to me that devilish cultivators are overpowered, and their cultivation progress smooth and unhindered."

"That's one way of looking at it," Lu Tianhao said. "But have you ever wondered why the forces of good always happen to stumble upon the forces of evil at the most opportune time? How fortune favors them at the last second, enabling key individuals to undergo breakthroughs at critical moments?

"The world is balanced. Good fortune favors the benevolent,

who thus enjoy better resources that contribute to their growth. That's why there are so many good-aligned cultivators in this realm. Devil cultivators need to sacrifice thousands of lives to advance, so their numbers are limited. In compensation, they have been granted greater strength. How else would the war between good and evil continue throughout the aeons?

"Mortal worlds are in a constant state of flux. They change ownership between the forces of good and evil. Devilish cultivators seek to be unrestrained and pursue their personal desires. They believe that the will of this world is unfair. It punishes them for being selfish, and it benefits those with good hearts. They are fighting to reverse the scales. They seek a world where everyone can pursue their desires without fear of repercussion, and if they succeed, cultivating their devilish ways will become much easier. Instead of sacrificing thousands of lives, they will only sacrifice hundreds, and the world will soon be overrun with their devilish ways. Conversely, angelic ways will become much harder to cultivate, and the trials and tribulations of good men will increase exponentially. However, this greater difficulty will better temper their souls, and they will be stronger for it."

"Why would anyone ever design the world in such a way?" Cha Ming asked.

"Who knows," Lu Tianhao said. "But enough talk about things we can't change. How are your formation arts coming along?"

"They've reached a bottleneck," Cha Ming said. "I can't progress until I increase my cultivation. Sometimes, I think that it's best to abandon the path of stability and just forge ahead."

Lu Tianhao nodded. "It's a difficult decision, one that I also faced in the past. Patience is a virtue, but so is selflessness. No one can make this decision for you." Then he waved his hand, and an image of Huxian appeared. "Is this the beast brother you spoke of? I've never seen a fox like this."

"He's an enigma," Cha Ming agreed. "Something curious happened between us in the Silverwing Mountain Range. Have you ever heard of people transferring qi through a bond with a demon?"

"It happens sometimes in transcendent realms," Lu Tianhao said. "The Inky Sea Sect is well known for it. They can channel demonic qi to form new talismans. It's also useful to paint in elements that wouldn't normally be available. Tell me, which ones did you gain through your bond?"

"Light and darkness," Cha Ming replied. "Though I find it difficult to paint with light and dark-demonic qi. My success rate is abysmal."

"Demonic qi is attuned with nature," Lu Tianhao said. "It resembles a diluted form of elemental evanescence. When it fuses with liquified elemental essence, it becomes useable as a natural ink."

The man flicked his sleeve, bringing two thin books out from the shelf. "Here are two books on suitable brush techniques for light and dark qi." Then he summoned two thick books. "I'll also lend these two books to you; they contain dark-aligned formations and talismans. I acquired them by chance, but I've never used them. I don't have any light-aligned manuals, however, so you're on your own there."

"Many thanks, Teacher," Cha Ming said. "I've already obtained some from the Church of Justice."

Lu Tianhao wrinkled his nose. "Insufferable fellows, but very honest. Is there anything else causing you doubts?"

"I was wondering about condensing light and dark sigils," Cha Ming said. "Do you have any books on those?"

Lu Tianhao shook his head. "I don't, but weren't you very confident in those Dao sigils of yours? Why don't you incorporate runes into them?"

Cha Ming pondered for a moment before nodding. "I'll try it," Cha Ming said before standing up. "I'm sorry, Teacher, but I can't stay and chat for very long. I have a poisoned king to treat and an infestation of devils and evil spirits to deal with."

"Don't bother accompanying this old man," Lu Tianhao said. "Just holler if you need any help." He shot Cha Ming a lonely smile as the younger man flew out from his office.

Chapter 12: Changes in Quicksilver

The flicker of a black cloak caught Cha Ming's eye as he left the Alabaster Group. He normally would have paid it no heed, but its intense ochre coloring was difficult to ignore.

What is he up to? Cha Ming thought. He probed the man's cultivation before continuing his pursuit; peak foundation establishment was hardly a threat to Cha Ming's companions.

He followed the figure for several blocks before it vanished into a side street filled with various disreputable businesses. Then it ducked into a dark alley.

Huxian, are you ready? Cha Ming asked as he followed the figure.

Born ready, his shadow replied. Cha Ming steeled himself and entered the alley. To his surprise, his resplendent force could no longer detect anyone. The alley was completely quiet, save for a few rats that were aggressively nibbling at a large bag of waste. Yet he couldn't shake the feeling of being watched.

Dodge! Huxian yelled.

A sword whizzed past Cha Ming's chest, cutting a two-inch gash and glancing off his ribcage as he rapidly laid down a Stormwalker Formation. He ran up the alley's wall as nine figures in black cloaks rushed toward him. He hadn't realized that the black-cloaked man was bait.

Is it time yet? Huxian asked.

Not yet, Cha Ming replied. He winced in pain as the flesh in his chest slowly recovered. Flying swords and sabers left the nine men's hands and shot toward him. In response, Cha Ming threw down the Clear Sky Staff and poured his resplendent force into it. Instead of becoming longer, it became three feet thick. The swords and sabers bounced off the heavy object as Cha Ming sent out thirty-six blue sigils, encasing the entire alley in a frigid atmosphere.

"Now!" Cha Ming yelled.

The three initial-core-formation cultivators and six peak-foundation-establishment cultivators slowed down for a fraction of a second before shattering his rapid combat formation. That partial second was more than enough, however. Huxian appeared from the darkness, and Lei Jiang and Silverwing burst out from his two tails and pounced onto the shocked cultivators. Huxian summoned a bagua to trap them as lightning burned them and sharp blades of wind lacerated them. Nine sizzling corpses soon dropped to the ground.

Huxian landed on Cha Ming's shoulder. "Who would have thought they'd underestimate us so much?" Huxian said.

Cha Ming shrugged. "I don't think it will work more than once. We'll have to be careful until I finish forging my bones."

They quickly made their way to the Talisman Artist Guild. They entered through the back entrance, which was reserved for members to bypass the storefront. Cha Ming immediately proceeded up the stairs to Jun Xiezi's office, who let him in right away.

"You're back so fast," Jun Xiezi said. "To what do I owe the pleasure of your visit?"

"Two reasons," Cha Ming replied. He flicked a golden Sharp Talisman to Jun Xiezi. "First, I owe you a debt. This is the first installment. This talisman contains my insights on the sharpness of gold. People sharpen their skills in much the same way they do swords."

Jun Xiezi grinned. "Painting is the same way. I'd never thought of creating a painting about painting itself before, but I think I'll give it a try. What else can I help you with?"

A flower was already steeping in a clear teapot. He used his mastery over wood and water to accelerate the brewing process and poured the tea into two clear cups.

"I paid a visit to the Song Kingdom's Talisman Artist Guild," Cha Ming said as he sipped. "Are you aware of its current state?"

"A truly deplorable branch guild," Jun Xiezi said, pursing his lips. "The only reason it hasn't been shut down is because it wasn't worth the effort to send someone out there to do it. Why? Are you interested in taking it over?"

"If only I had so much time to spare," Cha Ming said. "There's a civil war brewing in the kingdom, and you know how these things work."

"I take it you've already picked a side?" Jun Xiezi asked.

"Yes, I've thrown support behind the third prince, who is backed by the Wang family," Cha Ming said.

Jun Xiezi raised an eyebrow.

"The *second* young master of the Wang family."

"That explains it," Jun Xiezi said. "But why are you talking to me about this? I don't have the time or energy to oversee yet another branch guild."

"But what if it was just a subsidiary branch? One that funneled a portion of its profits to the Quicksilver branch?" Cha Ming said. "In return, the Quicksilver branch could provide support through a vice branch head and some teaching support. It would be an easy way to increase your branch's profitability. You could also satisfy the ambitions of some of your senior members."

"But setting up distribution channels and a reputation is a huge pain," Jun Xiezi said, massaging his brow. "It's just not worth it."

"You do have a point," Cha Ming said. "Give me one second." He withdrew his core-transmission jade and placed it on the table. It pulsed slightly before revealing a miniature jade Wang Jun.

"Brother Cha Ming, to what do I owe the pleasure?" Wang Jun's figure asked.

"It's like this," Cha Ming replied. "Quicksilver's Talisman Artist Guild is considering setting up roots in the Song Kingdom, but they don't want to deal with marketing and establishing distribution channels. Can you deal with this side of the business? Say, in exchange for a sole-sourcing agreement with the Jade Bamboo Conglomerate in the Song Kingdom?"

Wang Jun thought for a moment before answering. "For a thirty-percent list-price discount on all talismans, we could definitely do this."

"That's too much," Jun Xiezi interjected. "No more than ten percent, or it isn't worth it."

"Come now, this agreement is worry free," Wang Jun said. "I'll tell you what, since distribution costs are much lower for magic-grade talismans, I can agree to ten percent on those. However, I'd like to meet in the middle at twenty percent for mortal-grade ones. That way, you can just worry about production and training. What are your thoughts?"

"That's reasonable, but I want an additional provision," Jun Xiezi said. "I want to begin negotiating a non-sole-sourced distribution agreement with the Jade Bamboo branch in Quicksilver. I don't need an agreement now, only an introduction."

"Done," Wang Jun said. "I'll have a preliminary contract sent to you in three hours. Cha Ming, you're familiar with Wang Bing, are you not? Would you mind setting up an appointment?"

"Not at all," Cha Ming replied.

Wang Jun's figure winked out, leaving the two men and their tea.

"I figured it would be easier if we just skipped the process. Bureaucracies can be excruciatingly slow."

"Tell me about it," Jun Xiezi said. "My business development team and legal department would take three months trying to resolve a deal before letting me know about it. By then, any potential client would be too annoyed to offer us a favorable deal. All I want to do is relax and paint, but I always spend my precious time cleaning up their messes. I can't wait until I finish repaying this favor, and then I can continue my permanent vacation. By the way, what are your thoughts on who should take over the Song Kingdom sub-branch?"

"Let me talk to someone first," Cha Ming said.

"The concept is definitely intriguing," Feng Huoshan said as he leafed through a book on high-grade talismans. "But I'm worried about the teaching load and the distribution aspect. I'm all for moving up in the world; if I do well, I might end up in headquarters where I can access the more advanced study materials."

"You won't need to worry about distribution," Cha Ming assured. "My friend Wang Jun and the Jade Bamboo Conglomerate will take care of it. As for the teaching load, why don't you bring a friend along? Perhaps Hua Dong or Luo Ming?"

"Hua Dong might," Feng Huoshan said. "There are many people who don't want to be alchemists or glorified gardeners in the Song Kingdom. His brand of talisman artistry might prove to be quite popular. Luo Ming, on the other hand, is far too lazy. I doubt he'd be willing to move his mountainous rump."

"Who has a mountainous body?" a voice transmitted through the walls. "You're a mountain. Your whole family are mountains!"

"My name literally means 'fire mountain,' so you're technically correct," Feng Huoshan said.

"That's the best kind of correct," the fat Luo Ming said as he barged in and took a seat. "Besides, I've been eating Quicksilver's food for quite a while. A change would be nice."

Cha Ming laughed. "You can't all take off at once. Jun Xiezi will have my head."

Luo Ming shrugged. "What can he say if I leave for a year?"

"That's fair," Cha Ming said. "I'd really like to stay for longer, but I must be on my way. Duty calls."

"Can't you at least stay for dinner?" Luo Ming asked. The man liked any excuse to go out for an extravagant meal.

"I still have many stops to make," Cha Ming said helplessly. "We need to leave in three days, and I need to leave town for a while."

"Go on, then," Feng Huoshan said. "There will be plenty of time to eat together in the Song Kingdom."

Cha Ming nodded and tossed a pouch on the table. "Can you do me a favor in the meantime? I want to purchase all the excess talismans in the guild. Can you do that for me?"

After a brief discussion, he flew off to his next destination: the Alchemists Association.

"What are your thoughts on the proposed terms, Grandmaster Yao?" Cha Ming asked the short balding man in front of him. The man was drinking a pungent liquid from a laboratory flask on his desk. Cha Ming held a similar flask. He sipped from it gingerly, hoping that his strong constitution would neutralize any laboratory chemicals he might accidentally ingest.

"The terms are good," the grandmaster Yao said. "My most senior apprentice is looking to move up in the world, and I'm just not ready to give up my spot. This might be just the challenge he's looking for. When do you need a team by?"

"We'll leave in three days," Cha Ming said. "On another note, I have a request of a more… sensitive nature."

The grandmaster frowned before rotating a device on his desk. An intangible ten-foot-wide barrier formed around them.

"What's this?" Cha Ming asked.

"It's a nulling device," Grandmaster Yao said. "You might be surprised to hear that there are ears everywhere. I activate this whenever I want to hide specific things."

"Why not use it all the time?" Cha Ming asked.

"Because the energy consumption is rather alarming," Grandmaster Yao said. "Now, please hurry up with whatever you want to say. Spirit stones are literally burning away."

Cha Ming immediately summoned a vial containing a purple

liquid and placed it on the alchemist's desk. "The venom of a qi-binding serpent," he said. "An important figure in the Song Kingdom has been poisoned with this venom. I was only able to identify it by seeking the aid of a serpentine beast monarch."

Grandmaster Yao frowned. "Does this have anything to do with the recent investigation into the king's health?"

"Yes, it's the same case," Cha Ming said. "The third prince informed me that your association has already performed exhaustive tests."

"Our poison master did perform some tests, but he was unable to isolate a specific poison," Grandmaster Yao said. "Given the nature of the venom, it's not surprising that he failed. Most conventional techniques extract poisons using qi. That's because virtually all alchemical compounds can be extracted in this manner; the same applies to most non-alchemical ones."

"Do you think he'd be able to determine an antidote with this isolated compound?" Cha Ming asked.

"It's difficult to say," Grandmaster Yao said. "Let's ask him."

With a wave of his hand, the nulling field retracted, and the orb it came from flew into his empty palm. Cha Ming followed him out of the lab and past the front desk, where Yao Ling stood at her usual post. They entered a large corridor that led to the master-alchemist laboratories.

Cha Ming recognized the many doors he'd failed to enter during his embargo. They passed these doors and proceeded to the end of the hallway, where a shabby brown door Cha Ming had always assumed was the janitor's closet was located.

Grandmaster Yao knocked on the door and sent a message through a jade slip. The door creaked open a few moments later and revealed a spiraling stone staircase. They walked down several floors before entering a dungeonlike room.

"What brings you here today?" a voice said softly. It came from a man with a young face whose black hair was filled with streaks of white. The unkempt man was manipulating a green ball in the open with his spiritual force. With a wave of his hand, the ball jumped into a bottle, which he rapidly stoppered.

Grandmaster Yao threw out the small nulling sphere once more. "Do you remember the recent case in the Song Kingdom?"

The man frowned. "A frustrating case. One of the few failures in my three-hundred-year career."

"Which is why you didn't accept payment for performing the work," Grandmaster Yao said. "Have you ever wondered why you failed?"

"Every day," the man said. "I've narrowed it down to three possibilities. The first explanation is that it's a transcendent poison. I find this unlikely because it would be prohibitively expensive. The second possibility is that it's not a poison but rather an injury or curse. An injury is unlikely because the medical examination revealed no such trauma. The damage would need to take place on the cellular level. Curses, on the other hand, would be much easier to apply. However, the curse would need to exceed the capabilities of the Church of Justice."

"And the third one?" Grandmaster Yao asked.

"The poison would need antidetection properties that exceed the techniques in this realm," the man said. "The world is a vast place. This possibility is the most likely explanation, but I won't discount the second one. After all, the Church of Justice is not all-knowing in the field of curses."

Grandmaster Yao nodded. "Take a look at this," he said, placing the vial of violet liquid in front of the man, who opened the vial and dipped his finger inside it.

"Why would you—" Cha Ming started. He was interrupted by a harsh gesture from Grandmaster Yao.

He has an innate poison constitution, making him immune to most poisons, Grandmaster Yao explained mentally. *He's able to identify poisons like no one else. His obsession in life is to reach the pinnacle in his craft. He loathes interacting with others and prefers to seclude himself down here, where he runs no risk of accidentally hurting anyone.*

"What's your name, boy?" the man said as he licked the residual poison from his finger. "And where did you get this venom?"

Cha Ming noticed that he had a pair of familiar red pupils.

"Du Cha Ming greets senior," Cha Ming said, bowing lightly. "I had this poison manufactured by the Geomantic Sovereign in the Silverwing Mountain Range. After analyzing the king's blood sample, she determined that the source of the poison was the venom of a qi-binding serpent, a rare creature in this realm. Fortunately, she was able to duplicate a large quantity of the venom."

The man sighed. "It will take some time to research an antidote. The venom is far too rare, and natural ingredients must typically be counteracted with other natural ingredients. I'll need to go traveling."

Cha Ming waved his hand, depositing a pile of poison-related medicinal ingredients onto the floor. He also placed two hundred vials of various venoms on the table. "Feel free to use any of these in your research."

The man's eyes widened. "Then it's settled. I'll come find you in the Song Kingdom once I've made sufficient headway." He gestured once more, summoning the purple orb of venom and manipulating it in strange ways.

"May I know how to address senior?" Cha Ming asked before leaving.

"You may call me Zhou Bei," the man replied. "The traitorous ancestor of the Zhou Clan."

It was dusk before Cha Ming finally arrived at the Jade Bamboo Auction House. The moment he entered, he was ushered to a bamboo garden several times larger than the one he'd seen in Green Leaf City. A tea time later, Wang Bing's familiar figure walked in from the opposite direction.

"Would you like wine, or has my cousin's obsession with tea corrupted you as well?" she asked.

"Tea will be fine," Cha Ming said as he sat before her. "I hear the embargo has been lifted on the Alabaster Group?"

"My uncle made a silly decision," Wang Bing said, tucking a strand of blonde hair behind her ear. "I advised him against such meddling, but he was too keen on currying favor with the first young master. He didn't know the second young master like I did."

"I heard it was Lu Tianhao's connections that made the difference," Cha Ming said.

"Is that what he told you?" Wang Bing said, shrugging. "Regardless, I'm happy to assist you in any way possible. I am not like my foolish uncle. As a token of our branch's apology for the prior matter, I've prepared a gift for you."

"I don't believe that's necessary," Cha Ming said. "I came here for a simple matter, nothing more. I don't care about past grudges."

"But *I* care," Wang Bing said. "Bad karma should be cleared as soon as possible. Please indulge me as I bring it out. I'm sure you'll like it." She withdrew a small bag of holding from within her green cultivation robes and inverted it onto the table. A small pile of crisp white flags with gray poles poured onto the top. In addition, there was a pile of 108 clear blobs—unaligned sigil focuses. "You may not need these now, but I'm sure they'll be useful in the future."

Cha Ming was tempted. The pile of unaligned high-grade and top-grade formation flags would be extremely useful in these difficult times. Ultimately, he pushed them back toward her. "This is far too large a gift."

She pushed them back. "I've investigated your purchases and your dealings with Mo Tianshen. I estimate your losses at roughly 20,000 high-grade spirit stones. The number is hardly exact, but I believe that compensating your losses is the best way of settling the karma between us."

Cha Ming looked long and hard at the pile before drawing it into the Clear Sky World.

"Fine. We owe each other nothing now, but I'm hoping that you'll do me a small favor," Cha Ming said. "The branch leader of the Talisman Artist Guild would like to negotiate a nonexclusive supply agreement with the Jade Bamboo Conglomerate in Quicksilver. I'm hoping you'll treat them fairly."

"I don't mind being owed a favor," Wang Bing said. "It's your karma, not mine."

Cha Ming shook his head. "I still don't understand anything about karma. Is it really such a big deal?"

"More than you know," Wang Bing said. "Second Young Master Jun would be the best person to explain it you. Will you be requiring anything else?"

"Yes, I'd like your help in completing a large transaction," Cha Ming said, dumping a sack on the table. It contained 800,000 high-grade spirit stones, the remainder of his half of the profits from ripping off the arena. "I need this converted to as many generic pills, weapons, and talismans you can get your hands on. Mortal, magic, and core-grade treasures are all acceptable."

"Aren't you a big spender," Wang Bing said. "It seems I'm the one who owes you a favor."

"Not at all," Cha Ming said. "It's just business."

A tea time later, Cha Ming walked out of the Jade Bamboo Auction House with a significantly lighter purse. "See, I told you she wouldn't cause any problems," he said to the empty air.

A small figured jumped out from his shadow and onto his shoulder. Huxian licked Cha Ming's ear as the latter scratched his small head. "It's better to be safe than sorry," Huxian said.

Cha Ming smiled. "Thanks for worrying about me. By the way, is Silverwing up for flying again soon?"

"Where are we headed?" Huxian asked.

"A small town not far from here called Crystal Falls," Cha Ming replied.

The sun was rising in in the small mist-covered village. A reddish-orange glow refracted through thin clouds as they landed nearby. The farmers had just risen with the dawn, and they were feeding and watering their oxen in preparation for a hard day's work while their children fed the chickens and their wives prepared breakfast.

Cha Ming hopped off Silverwing's back and walked toward the village. He took his time as he walked down the well-built path in the woods. Soon he passed a small guard shack where an elderly man was napping.

"Cha Ming, Cha Ming!" a couple of children yelled and grabbed on to him as soon as he reached the main street.

"Xiao Bao, Mei Guo, you've grown up," he said as he ruffled their hair. "How are your parents?"

"Tired but happy," Xiao Bao said. "We need to run, or we'll be late for school!" The two children rushed off and joined their friends, who were filing toward a small building. A young woman he didn't recognize herded them in and began teaching them to read. Such a thing hadn't existed back when the village remained in isolation.

Cha Ming soon found Li Yin's office. He smiled as he opened the door but was surprised to discover a middle-aged man seated at a desk, waiting for his first patient. A spirit-doctor emblem was pinned to his chest.

"Can I help you?" the man asked.

"Where is Dr. Li?" Cha Ming asked. The office looked nothing like the unorganized mess it usually was. There were no bandages or splint materials. Now it only contained an examination bench and a shelf full of herbs and beakers.

"Ah, you're looking for Elder Li," the middle-aged man said. "My name is Yong Bai. Pleased to make your acquaintance." He held his hand out in a peculiar fashion. Cha Ming shook it awkwardly.

"Does the doctor still live here?" Cha Ming asked.

"Of course, he does," Yong Bai said. "I just help him take care of patients while he conducts his research. It's fascinating that he's managed to accomplish so much without being an actual doctor."

Cha Ming supressed a fit of anger. "I take it this door leads to his house just like before?"

"Of course," Yong Bai said. He opened the door before yelling out, "Elder Li, you have a visitor." Hearing no response, he waved Cha Ming inside. "Just wander down the hall to his study. He often doesn't hear me when I holler."

Cha Ming walked into a newly built dining room, which resembled Li Yin's old accommodations. The hall contained new pictures; he passed these and lightly pushed open the door to the old man's study.

He sighed in relief when he saw Li Yin sleeping on his desk, as he usually did after a night's hard work.

The kitchen was different than Cha Ming remembered. For one, it contained more cooking equipment than it used to. For another, he noticed a lot more vegetables on the man's shelves. Cha Ming lit a fire before thinly slicing potatoes into tiny sticks. He washed them with water to remove the starch. After this, he heated a wok and added oil, peppers, and leeks to the pan, letting their fragrance seep into the oil. Then he threw in the thin potato sticks and stir-fried them until they became slightly translucent. He added salt and vinegar before throwing the dish onto a plate and moving on to the next one.

This time, Cha Ming cut tomatoes into chunks and heated them over a low fire. He cooked them until they broke down before throwing in small pieces of cauliflower. He finished this simple dish off with salt and pepper. Then, after washing the wok, he threw in some leftover rice and water, stirring until it formed a thick rice congee.

"Miss Xiao, why does the food smell different today?" Li Yin called suddenly from the dining room.

Cha Ming chuckled and brought a tray of dishes out to the dining table to the shocked Li Yin. He set a place for himself and the old doctor while Li Yin rubbed his eyes in disbelief. "Is it really you, my boy?"

"What, I can't visit my teacher?" Cha Ming asked.

The older man smiled and helped himself to the dishes. "You're always welcome to visit this old man. What brings you in today?"

Cha Ming looked toward the door to the doctor's office. "This Yong Bai doesn't bully you, does he?"

"Heavens, no," Li Yin said. "I ran into him a month ago. He was a middle-aged man with minor achievements as a spirit doctor. Since he'd reached a dead-end in his career, he was looking to settle down somewhere peaceful with his family. I invited him to stay in the village. He's been treating people here ever since, and they've never been healthier."

"But what about your medical practice?" Cha Ming asked.

The man had made phenomenal breakthroughs in mortal medicine. The thought of him being displaced by a lesser man boiled Cha Ming's blood.

"My boy, I've always known that my greatest contribution to medicine is my research," Li Yin said. "Through that, I can forge a better path for mortal doctors and improve the well-being of millions of people. If this man is more capable than me at treating the people, shouldn't I let him do it?"

At these words, Cha Ming calmed down. They ate in silence, and Cha Ming quickly washed the dishes as Li Yin brewed a terrible blend of tea. Cha Ming drank it like it was the best in the world, for the person you drank with mattered far more than the contents of the cup.

"I need your help with something, Teacher," Cha Ming said as they drank.

"You always need my help with something," Li Yin said. "What silly thing is it this time? Did you stub your toe and lose your will to live?"

"I returned to my home in the Song Kingdom," Cha Ming said slowly. "Things are less than peaceful, and the king has fallen ill. The country is on the brink of civil war."

"Ah," Li Yin said. "Well, I can't help you much in the field of politics. I've always avoided aristocrats like the plague."

"I need your help with the king's illness," Cha Ming said. "I've discovered that he's been poisoned with the venom of a qi-binding serpent. Any qi used to treat him breaks down upon entering his body. Spirit-doctor methods are useless to him."

Li Yin frowned. "What are his symptoms, and at what point does the qi break down?" The focused look of a researcher returned to his eyes.

"Slow organ failure," Cha Ming said. "Blood poisoning, faint heartbeat, lack of blood coagulation. The brain is fine, but the king is unconscious. His qi pathways are dry, and his core-formation cultivation is restricted but not destroyed. As soon as healing qi symbols contact his organs, they deteriorate. The venom has permeated every bit of his flesh."

Li Yin shook his head. "I might be all right at preliminary medicine, but I know nothing about poisons. This is a job for an alchemist, not an old man like me."

"The venom is being analyzed by the best poison master in Quicksilver," Cha Ming said. "We're just trying to keep him alive for as long as possible. Can you at least help with that?"

"It's difficult," Li Yin said, "but I can try. However, I doubt that the spirit doctors there will let me anywhere near him. They disdain people like me, and their words carry much weight."

"I can help you take care of that," Cha Ming said. "Can you help me? There are many lives on the line, and things will get bad very fast if the king dies."

Li Yin sighed. "I can try. Truth be told, I've always wanted to try my hand at treating a king. Let's see if he's any different than the rest of us."

Chapter 13: Surprise

Hundreds of raucous voices filled the shop, inundating Wang Jun's extraordinary senses with a plethora of information. The torrent of data didn't faze him. He analyzed as he received it, throwing out the insignificant details before storing the rest for future use.

Guards inspected jade permission slips as customers filed into the store in an orderly line. The limit of one weapon per customer, while infuriating, was a necessary precaution in dealing with forgeries. Guards were only so effective in such a heated market, and fake permission slips were found every quarter hour. It was foolish to think that they'd caught them all.

"What's this?" a man said at the front desk. "Not only did I need the permission slip, but I need to swear an oath not to sell it? What kind of scam is this?"

"You don't need to buy it if you aren't interested," a woman said coldly. She'd seen far too many of these customers today; her answer hadn't deviated in the slightest. Ultimately, the man chose to swear the oath and buy a grade-eight sword.

"We're doing so much, but it's only a matter of time before they find a way to make these weapons change hands," Wang Jun muttered. His eyes suddenly darted to an inconspicuous man standing in line. He looked closely as the man's jade slip, which was inspected before he was allowed into the shop.

"Everyone stop," Wang Jun said in a commanding tone.

The customers, the attendants, and the guards all paused what they were doing. The young master of the Wang family walked up to the newly admitted customer. "How daring. You forged a jade slip issued by my Wang family. Did you not think about the consequences of your actions before walking through that door? I don't even need to see the jade slip to verify it."

He took out a thin jade card from within his robes and poured his core-formation qi into it. It resonated with the authentic jade slips in the room—the man's slip was not one of them.

"Zhao Lishou, subordinate of the Tou family," Wang Jun continued. "I can read you like a book. You came in with this forgery at the command of the Tou family, thinking that at worst, you'd be caught and kicked out of the store. Well, I'm afraid it isn't that simple."

"What could you possibly do to me?" the man said, scoffing. "There are laws in this country. You can't hurt a hair on my head."

"Oh, I won't do anything to you," Wang Jun said. "You're just a grunt, and you'll surely be punished when you return to the Tou family. They won't be pleased to hear that from now on, the Tou family and its subordinates will forever be barred from doing business with the Jade Bamboo Conglomerate and its affiliates." The man paled and dropped the jade slip, which shattered on the wooden floor. "Guards, please see this man out. He isn't welcome here."

In the distance, Wang Jun saw a fifth of the people in line scramble off to nearby alleys.

"Killing the chicken to warn the monkey, I see," a man said from behind Wang Jun. To his surprise, it was Hei Ling, his employee with the black-market connection. The man had breached his personal bubble and appeared a single foot away from him. At this range, assassinating him would be a simple matter.

"You really ought to keep your awareness up at all times," Hei Ling said. "Others might not be as friendly as me. If I were an assassin, wouldn't you already be dead?"

"Shouldn't you be out performing your duties?" Wang Jun asked.

The man smiled and took one more step forward. He clasped

Wang Jun's hand and passed him a piece of paper.

It's done, the man said mentally. *Make sure to show up at this address, alone and with no subordinates. The Black King sets the rules in this city's underground, and he hates it when people break them.* Hei Ling then left as though nothing had happened, leaving Wang Jun shivering from the close call.

Elder Bai, didn't I ask for Hei Ling to be tailed? Wang Jun sent.

The one who was dealing with the black market? Elder Bai sent back.

Exactly, Wang Jun replied. *I don't appreciate it when a man we should be keeping tabs on catches me unaware and makes physical contact with me.*

Are you all right? Elder Bai asked.

I'm fine, Wang Jun said. *But I need to go out on an excursion for the next two hours. Don't contact me during that period of time, regardless of what happens.*

Aren't you taking Protector Ren? Elder Bai asked.

No need, Wang Jun said. *I can take care of this myself.*

He walked out from back door and blended into the shadows. The landscape changed to a patchwork of locations in the city, where he could walk at his leisure. Here and there, harmless denizens of the shadows roamed out in the open—only people like him could see their splendor.

In a nearby alley, a resplendent white rat walked out. It was the size of a dog, but it was quickly snatched up by the fleeting figure of a crow half its size. The bright shades merged together into a slightly larger crow. It flapped its wings and plunged into a piece of landscape, disappearing forever. Such a scene wasn't unusual in the world of shadows, where imaginary creatures were birthed every few moments.

Wang Jun glanced at the piece of paper in his palm, where he saw an address and instructions. The paper burned as soon as he read it. He willed himself toward a shade of darkness near the location and popped back to reality. His protective wreath of shadows blended in with the black alley near an inconspicuous door. He knocked three times.

"It is a fine day for a parade. What shall we wear?" a voice asked.

"I don't know about you, but I will wear the garb of a king," Wang Jun answered. He heard a door bolt unlatch, and a formation sizzled as it was deactivated. A man in a black cloak welcomed him inside and led him down a spiraling staircase. Wang Jun noted when they passed the elevation of the sewers and entered uncharted territory he didn't know existed. After a quarter hour of walking and several narrow corridors, they arrived in a simple room containing a desk and a man in a black cloak with a deep cowl. A wreath of shadows covered the mysterious man. He also noticed the shimmer of a dampening device, which would protect them from eavesdropping.

"Second Young Master Wang. How may I be of service today?" the man asked.

"Black King, it's so nice to finally meet you," Wang Jun said. "I have some goods I'd like to sell. The price cap on mortal-grade weapons has left me no alternative but to sell a portion of these goods on the black market. Is this a service you can provide?"

"Naturally," the Black King said. "But the cost isn't low. I'll require a commission equal to fifty percent of the markup between the current market price and the final selling price. You can choose to set the selling price yourself or leave this at my discretion."

"Half of the additional profits seems a bit steep," Wang Jun said. "How about twenty-five percent?"

The Black King chuckled ominously. Even Wang Jun, with his extraordinary mental resilience, couldn't help but shiver.

"There is no negotiating when you sell through me," the Black King said. "By all means, sell them yourself. However, the risks you run may outweigh the rewards. I am aware of your family rules and have plenty of contacts that could inform them."

Wang Jun's eyes narrowed. "That sounds like a threat."

"That's because it is one," the Black King said. "Do you accept or refuse?"

Wang Jun thought for a moment before throwing three bags on

the table. "These three bags each contain ten thousand high-grade spirit stones' worth of goods at the current market price. I want you to sell one at two times the list price, and one at 2.25 times the list price. The other bag's pricing is up to your discretion."

"How prudent," the Black King said, sweeping them up. A black page materialized on his desk. "Here is the service contract. I trust you'll find it adequate."

Wang Jun inspected the sheet, which was written in gold. His eyes widened when he realized the severity of the contract. "No wonder you've been able to maintain your secrecy since you started your operations."

"There is nothing better to maintain secrecy than a life-binding oath of nondisclosure," the Black King said. "Should I ever spill any details of our dealings, I will die. The same applies to you. The only way for either of us to avoid this is to transcend. Even then, the backlash will be quite severe."

Wang Jun sent a drop of his blood and signed the page. The Black King did the same.

"Pleasure doing business with you," Wang Jun said.

"The pleasure is all mine," the Black King replied in a mocking tone. "By the way, as your newest business partner, I'm very interested in your well-being. Therefore, I'll give you a word of caution and advise you to be careful on your way home. Things are not what they seem, and your intelligence may be your downfall."

The Black King's figure shimmered and disappeared, leaving Wang Jun alone in the dark cellar.

I'm on my way back, Wang Jun sent to Elder Bai as he exited the meeting place.

Hearing no response, he tried again, but to no avail. A cold shiver ran down his spine as he sensed life-threatening danger. His figure distorted instinctively as he barely dodged three long needles. He barely noticed five talismans heading toward him through the gaps in the needle's offense. Four of them bore frightening energies he wasn't confident in resisting. He shifted his body and collided with the fifth talisman, which covered him in a layer of invisible suppression. It was a dampening talisman, which would render him unable to communicate for a period of time.

A dagger suddenly burst out from a nearby shadow, threatening to pierce his heart. Wang Jun used his superior control, condensing the shadow into binding chains that bought him the split second he needed to evade. He then entered the shadows, where he was greeted by a white-cloaked man. Wang Jun's own cloak had turned white and his hair black. In the shadow world, everything was inverted and surreal.

They exchanged no words. Wang Jun flitted from landmass to landmass, and the assassin did the same. Daggers of light condensed and attacked Wang Jun, and as he dodged, he sent chains of light to bind his faster and more powerful opponent. Wang Jun was surprised at the man's strength and skill, but his mind was calm. His only option was to bide his time until he could contact Protector Ren.

Was it Hei Ling who leaked my position? Wang Jun thought. He had no proof, only speculations. The man was suspicious and sneaky, and the more he thought about it, the more he felt the man was hiding deep secrets. It was even possible that Hei Ling himself was the cloaked assassin.

A blade of light shaved off a strand of Wang Jun's hair, jolting him back to the present.

I can't afford to be distracted, he thought. A door of light appeared in front of him. As he reached out to climb through it, a fiery explosion caused it to collapse. Wang Jun coughed out a mouthful of blood as the backlash ravaged his organs. He wasn't a body cultivator, so his physical durability was rather low. To make matters worse, his opponent had at least reached the middle of core formation, two subrealms higher than his.

Wang Jun decisively jumped out from the shadow world beside a guard barracks. Thinking fast, he activated an expensive Flicker-Form Talisman, which allowed him to teleport five hundred meters away in the blink of an eye.

His timely reaction saved his life—a blade that was meant for his heart only pierced a quarter inch of his skin. Blood blossomed on his black cultivation robes as he continued flickering in a confusing pattern. Once twenty-eight seconds were up, he teleported to a nearby Wang family safe house.

Wang Jun panted as he tore open his robes to reveal the gash that was spurting blood. While the dagger hadn't pierced his heart, it had cut some significant blood vessels. He pulled out a pill, which he crushed into a powder and mixed with the blood on his wound. Pain wracked his chest as the flesh knitted and the blood scabbed and peeled away.

No time to stay put, Wang Jun thought. He stowed away his black robes and changed them out for bright-blue ones. He then retrieved a thin mask from his bag of holding and placed it on his face, which wriggled and contorted as his features became fine and subdued. His skin darkened slightly, as did his hair. His qi fluctuations were hidden to some extent.

After removing any traces of his short stay, he walked out onto the street and blended in with the crowd.

Chapter 14:
Concealment

In Central Square, a young lady walked through the crowds with a sense of purpose. The people parted slightly as she bravely approached a small establishment with an intricate wood construction. She attracted awkward glances and disdainful stares on her way to the front desk. Pretty girls with bright complexions and refined expressions evaluated her as she walked up to the matron of the establishment.

"My name is Hong Meigui[1], and my dream is to become the world's best tea server!" she said with a determined yet distinctly feminine voice.

Hong Meigui's determination and natural good looks quickly won her a position in the reputed establishment. That evening, she was quizzed on her knowledge of various teas and tea-serving etiquette, as well as her skills in holding a pleasant conversation. After assuring herself that the girl's skill matched her determination, the matron arranged for two senior tea servers to give her a haircut and a makeover.

Despite their insistence in giving her a bath, Hong Meigui stubbornly refused. It was only once she emerged from the bathroom perfectly washed and scrubbed to their satisfaction that they relented. Instead, they focused on painting her nails and cutting

1 In Mandarin, Hong Meigui translates to Red Rose.

her hair so that it matched the establishment's standard style. They also arranged for appropriate clothes to be tailored to her supplied dimensions.

The next morning, they introduced her to their regular clientele. Middle-aged men showed up in droves to greet their newest darling.

"Well, have you found him?" Elder Bai asked in a stern and infuriated voice. The older man's eyes were bloodshot; it was clear he hadn't rested since the second young master's disappearance.

"I've looked all night, but I haven't found the slightest trace," Li Ming replied. "Should we be so hurried, though? I've heard the young master's survival abilities are legendary. More to the point, *that man* must have given him some sort of protective treasure he could rely on."

"You will not relax for a single second until he is found," Elder Bai said. "If you'd kept tabs on Hei Ling like you should have, we could ask him where the young master ran off to. If he doesn't come back, I'll have your head. Is that clear?"

"Crystal," Li Ming replied before returning to his search.

Elder Bai fidgeted as he read through many incoming reports. Unfortunately, quantity did not equal quality. No one had seen a trace of the young master since his disappearance the day before.

It had been a busy morning for Hong Meigui. She laughed at her patrons' not-so-clever jokes and blushed at their insinuations. Thankfully, there was no groping involved, as such behavior would result in their immediate expulsion. It was one of the many reasons she'd chosen the Violet Wind Tea House to begin with.

"Thank you for coming!" she said as she bowed to the guests she'd just served. She cleaned and stowed away the tea set with refined grace as the two gentlemen concluded their business discussion. She had no doubt that this information was how the teahouse made most of its profits. In the future, she'd consider starting her own teahouse. For now, however, she had much to learn.

"Your talent is wasted in this establishment," the middle-aged man said. "If you were to serve guests at my estate, the additional business generated would be nothing to sneeze at. Name your conditions, and I'll take you out of this place."

"My apologies, sir, but I'll have to refuse," Hong Meigui said with a sweet smile while covering her cherry lips. "Working here has always been my dream. Now that I've finally gotten past the most difficult hurdle, I really want to stay here for as long as possible. I know that I don't have much time remaining."

The man sighed. "That's true. Everyone who works here is at most twenty-seven years old. However, that doesn't mean that it's the end of the road for you. If you're ever looking for employment, remember that this old man will always have a place for you at the Cai estate."

"I'll be sure to remember your generosity," Hong Meigui said while bowing deeply. The man nodded and left the room.

"It's not often that our ladies refuse such a tempting offer," the matron said with a smile as she walked into the room. "Most take off as soon as a suitable opportunity arises."

"I was serious when I told you that this is was my dream." Hong Meigui said as she finished cleaning up. "Whom will you be requiring me to serve next? It's almost closing time, but I'm sure there are many regulars who've yet to meet me."

"Strangely enough, it was a new customer who requested you," the matron said. "Tidy yourself up for an incense time before heading into Room 43."

Hong Meigui breathed in deeply. She composed herself before donning her usual sweet smile and walking into the last guest room.

She was greeted by a cold figure in a black hooded robe. Her smile faded lightly as she gulped, then regained her composure.

Hong Meigui walked to her seat in front of the mysterious guest and kneeled down on the soft pillow reserved for the second guest. This was the teahouse's custom when serving lone guests.

"May I know what tea this esteemed sir would like to drink?" she asked.

The man paused a while before answering. Hong Meigui could feel his cold gaze scanning her thoroughly, leaving nothing unchecked.

"Pu'er tea will be fine," he said in a young voice she'd heard once before. It was the voice of the second young master of the Wang family, Wang Jun. She pushed this small detail out of her mind before opening the drawer with unsurpassed grace. She opened the container with her left hand despite being accustomed to using her right. After retrieving a single scoop of the extremely expensive tea, she poured hot water into the small brewing cup and immediately poured it over the lone cup in front of her guest. This first washing step was necessary for bringing up the temperature of the porcelain cup and disinfecting it.

"Why don't you keep this lonely man company and drink a few cups?" the man asked.

"It would be my honor," Hong Meigui said as she skillfully retrieved a second cup. This request wasn't unusual with single guests. "What might I call this esteemed elder?"

The man chuckled. "I'm hardly an elder. In fact, I'm barely over twenty. You may call me Young Master Wang."

"I'm sure that Young Master Wang is a handsome man," Hong Meigui replied. "Would you like me to stow away your cloak?"

"That won't be necessary," the man said. "You're very skillful for someone who just started this morning. Where did you learn to brew tea?"

"I haven't told any other guests this story, but for you, I'll make an exception," Hong Meigui said. "I was born in a small town called Fallowroot City. It's only a few days' walk away. My father is Hong

Hao, and he used to own a tea shop in the capital. He was a very skilled owner, but unfortunately, he had a terrible mind for business. In fact, you paid a visit to this business once two years ago."

"I recall this faintly," the man said.

"Eventually his shop closed," Hong Meigui said. "As his only child, he taught me everything he knew about tea." She let out soft sigh. "It's a pity that he passed away a year ago. That's when I decided to become the best tea server in the city and eventually own the best tea shop."

"So you've come to scout out the competition." The man chuckled. "How interesting. We have a need for ambitious minds like you. Would you like to work for the Wang family?"

Hong Meigui hesitated before ultimately shaking her head. "I still have much to learn. It's best that I wait until I'm ready before proceeding with this dream of mine."

"Don't you know you're insulting me?" the man said suddenly, releasing a stifling pressure. She hovered on the brink of consciousness before the pressure was immediately released. However, she felt a hand grasp her neck and pin her to the wall. A trickle of blood ran down the corner of her mouth.

"I don't like it when little girls disobey me," the man said as he held a black dagger up to her face. "Why don't you apologize?"
Hong Meigui could do nothing but helplessly gasp for breath as she struggled against the man's powerful grip. She tried to scream but to no avail. Her face turned red as she tried to squirm free. A pool of wetness formed at her feet as she slowly lost control of her body and eventually fell unconscious.

"Was I wrong?" the man said doubtfully.

Out of the seventy-six suspicious characters that had suddenly appeared in the city, this Hong Meigui was the most suspicious.

The guards had no record of her, but that wasn't a dead giveaway. Although her technique was different, it was similar in many ways to Wang Jun's tea-brewing method. What intrigued him the most was that the choice followed Wang Jun's thought pattern, which he had grown very familiar with in his time at the Jade Bamboo Conglomerate.

Grimacing in disgust, he tossed her to the ground away from the pool of urine. Just to be sure, he lightly groped the woman's body, both ensuring that the lady bits weren't fake and looking for any treasures that might be found on the body.

"I guess she's just an unfortunate girl who was in the wrong place at the wrong time," he said, sighing. He might be an assassin, but he wasn't unscrupulous.

He stowed his dagger before disappearing from the room. A few screams confirmed that the staff had found the woman's unconscious body. Hong Meigui would be fine. Wang Jun, on the other hand, wouldn't be so lucky. He'd left a surprise on his dagger, and even a strong-willed person like the second young master would only be able to resist for a short time before collapsing under the strain.

"I'm so sorry, my dear," the matron said soothingly. "We usually don't get characters like these. I'll make sure that this despicable Wang Jun fellow gets a lifelong ban for this."

"Thank you, Matron," Hong Meigui said. Her eyes were red from all the crying she'd done.

"Make sure you get a good rest tonight, and you'll get the day off tomorrow," the matron said. "Let me know if you need anything, and I'll take care of it personally."

Hong Meigui nodded as the woman retreated from her small bedroom. As soon as the door closed, she scampered to the small board in the floor where she held one of her most precious possessions: a small gold ring.

Wang Jun sighed in relief as the talisman finally dissipated.

Elder Bai, I'm fine, Wang Jun sent mentally once the bubble of interference dissipated. *Don't alert anyone but Protector Ren. I'm situated on the first floor of the Violet Wind Tea House.*

It wasn't long before Protector Ren arrived. The black-cloaked cultivator raised his eyebrow. Wang Jun rolled his eyes as he dismissed his disguise. He was no longer a woman but a young man with blond hair.

The next day, operations in the Jade Bamboo Auction House resumed as normal, minus one small detail—the odd rumor buzzing around the crown prince's faction that Wang Jun had physically assaulted a new waitress in the Violet Wind Tea House.

Interlude: Violet Wind Master

Gong Lan's orange kasaya fluttered as she landed on the aptly named Violet Wind Mountain. Waves of purple gas buffeted her as she walked up the remaining steps leading to the ancient monastery. Three men walked behind her—they were her senior apprentice-brothers, monks who had been carefully selected and raised by her master. While she'd originally wished to leave them behind, the bodhi seed had convinced her otherwise. The trip was dangerous, and she was here to find out why.

They remained unfazed as they climbed the enchanted steps one by one. They were different than those protecting the World Tree Monastery. Instead of reflecting one's innermost heart, they caused the climber to brood on their future. The only way to climb the steps was to focus on the present moment. It was no wonder that the Violet Wind Monastery hadn't received any visitors other than monks in the past hundred years.

"Greetings, World Tree Master," a middle-aged monk said as they reached the end of the stairs. "The master predicted your arrival. He awaits you at your earliest convenience."

"I don't dare share a title with the Violet Wind Master," Gong Lan said humbly. "I am but a junior who has taken up a heavy mantle. Please call me Gong Lan."

The man shook his bald head. "Seniority must be respected at all times. It is what keeps us united, no matter what tribulations we face." He led the way through their modestly built cloister, where each building was built from an odd purple stone. The wondrous material naturally repelled spiritual force. The monks in the Violet Wind Monastery were strongest due to the constant polishing their souls received.

They soon arrived at the Violet Wind Monastery itself. The large purple building had been built tall, and the edge that faced the constant purple wind was sharp as a blade. They climbed 999 steps before reaching the top floor, where an older monk waited. He was accompanied by six men who had all reached the resplendent soul realm, a watershed in the Buddhist soul-cultivation system.

Gong Lan sat down on the cushion directly in front of the aged master, while her followers obediently sat behind her. "I assume Violet Wind Master knows why I am here?" she said.

"The World Tree Master is wise," the old man said. "In private, Violet Wind is fine."

"Then in private, you may call me Gong Lan," she said. "Though I hardly deserve to be called wise. All master's apprentices know of your prophetic abilities."

"I call you wise, not because you know of my abilities but because you are not doing this alone," Master Zi said. "Sibi was rash and impetuous. He should have waited for one of the masters to resolve the issue in the Song Kingdom. Unfortunately, he let his pride cloud his judgment. It is good that you have not followed in his footsteps."

Gong Lan kept her head bowed. "I have come to request two things. First, I wish to borrow the Spirit-Banishing Pagoda and men capable of using it. Second, I wish to request a foretelling."

"I know of these requests," Master Zi said. He placed a small golden tower in front of Gong Lan. It was a precious core treasure, but he parted with it without batting an eyelash. "These six monks will accompany you. I have briefed them on your journey, and they are aware of the gravity of this situation. Each of them has been studying how to use the Spirit-Banishing Pagoda for the past year, and they are ready to die to fulfill this mission."

Gong Lan smiled. "Master Zi is indeed worthy of his reputation. I thank you for your timely assistance."

"As for the foretelling," Master Zi said, "I will do what I can. Unfortunately, the heavens loathe it when I share their secrets. Therefore, I can only impart scant information to you. It comes in the form of three pieces of information. The first is a warning: If you go to the tomb with your current forces, you will certainly die."

Gong Lan frowned. "You mean to say that even the equivalent of ten core-formation cultivators aren't enough to ensure success? It's only one evil spirit!"

"I can't say any more on this subject," Master Zi said. "The second piece is that you will find a friend in Songjing City. Should he accompany you to the tomb, you will stand a chance."

Gong Lan nodded slowly. "Very well, I shall seek out aid in Songjing. What is the third piece of information?"

"Another warning," Master Zi said. "You are the only one who can resolve the Song Kingdom's crisis, but you will also be responsible for a much greater battle. It is best that you give up on the Song Kingdom if you cannot salvage the situation. Even the Violet Wind Monastery can fall, but the World Tree Monastery must always remain."

Over the course of their conversation, Master Zi's face had paled and was now covered in a sheen of sweat.

"I thank Master Zi for his guidance," Gong Lan said, bowing. "I will take your words to heart." As she stood from her cushion, she sent a wisp of green qi to the old monk. To her surprise, however, he rebuffed it and sent it back.

"The bodhi seed's energy is far too precious," Master Zi said. "It's a waste to give it to a dying old man like me."

Gong Lan shot him a concerned look before leaving with the nine other men. Their next stop: Songjing City.

Chapter 15: First, Stop the Bleeding

Feng Ming winced as he held a large chunk of ice against his cheek. The blue blotch was fading quickly due to a healing salve he had applied, but the pain hurt him less than the scolding words his father had said.

It's not that I don't care about the family, Feng Ming thought, *it's that I'm a prisoner in my own home.*

"Do you really think I have enough influence in the military to change your situation?" Wang Jun said. "Your father is in the upper echelons of the military—either he or the crown prince would have to deploy you. Otherwise you'll be stuck in this city until you die of old age."

The five-fire chicken, a delicacy unique to the Song Kingdom, dripped bloody where Wang Jun had cut into it. It was the only fowl in the continent that could be eaten rare with little to no risk.

"I'm not asking you to get me deployed," Feng Ming said. "I just want you to get Marshal Yong to ask for my assistance in the south. Maybe if I misbehave enough inside the city, my father will be forced to deliver me himself."

"Fair enough," Wang Jun said. "How has the city been treating you otherwise?"

"Good enough." Feng Ming shrugged. "I've made some friends here and there. Sometimes I drink and gamble with them. Though gambling isn't exactly possible anymore, not since the underground arena was shut down. By the way, where is Cha Ming? Did you scare him away?"

"He's out on a mission," Wang Jun replied. "It's best if you don't know what it's about."

Feng Ming shrugged. "Do let him know that he has some competition on the way. I heard the crown prince's men talking about it. All I know is that it's a professional from Quicksilver."

Wang Jun frowned. "Did you happen to catch what kind of profession or his grade?" Feng Ming shook his head. "I'll keep that in mind when negotiating."

Their meal passed by uneventfully. When every dish was finished, Wang Jun created a portal on the wall. "Would you like a lift anywhere?"

"No, thanks," Feng Ming said, waving him away. "It's not like I have anything important to do anyhow."

Meanwhile, the gears in his mind were turning. *How much chaos do I have to cause to get kicked out of the city?* he thought.

Since the events at the arena, he'd conveniently found damning evidence of financial corruption by three of the crown prince's ministers. In addition, he'd found one of the crown prince's wives cheating on him. He thought that would be the straw that broke the camel's back, but instead it came back to hit him in the face. Literally.

In his boredom, Feng Ming walked around the city until he got to the palace gates. While the gardens were off-limits, the walkway beside the thin metal fences was not. Their magical formations protected the gardens while leaving the beautiful sight revealed to the public. Walking near the palace walls was the preferred activity of most couples in Songjing.

As he walked, Feng Ming saw many familiar sights. He saw

familiar gardeners tending familiar trees he had climbed as a child, and a familiar pond where he'd gone swimming without permission. By the pond, he saw a familiar princess. She sat there with a dispirited expression that was much more sullen than the pouting he'd seen as a child.

As he reached the end of the walkway and the entrance to the palace, Feng Ming saw a pale black-clothed man resting by a tree. The man looked at him lazily with piercing red pupils. While most people would give him either a favorable or unfavorable feeling, the man gave off a neutral vibe.

Is that Zhou Li? Feng Ming thought. *Why does he seem so different than how Cha Ming and Wang Jun describe him? Why does he seem so peaceful?*

The man closed his eyes, and Feng Ming continued. He passed the guards and walked down main street and back to Central Square.

Save for the odd theft or raised voice, the afternoon passed by quietly. Feng Ming spent it sipping hot baiju on an open patio. He sat there until the sun set, and a familiar tingling finally reappeared. His fingers twitched as he looked around for the source of the disturbance. He finally found it in the form of a black cloak, which disappeared around the corner of an alley.

Feng Ming paid his tab and walked toward the inconspicuous alley. As he walked into the dark passage, he noticed beggars and street urchins going to bed while burglars and thieves exited their familiar hovels. He soon turned a corner in the alley, where he caught yet another flicker of black in the distance.

Feng Ming and the mysterious individual took many turns as they walked through the winding passageways behind the businesses in Central Square. Before long, they arrived at a small restaurant. Feng Ming walked in and saw a black-cloaked man sitting at one of the six tables. The restaurant was otherwise deserted, save for its owner, who began cooking as soon as he saw them.

"He only knows how to cook one dish," the mysterious man said. "Stir-fried beef with shredded potato. It gives me a very homely feeling."

The man then pulled back his cloak, revealing a pale, black-haired man with red pupils. "Are you bored of city life yet?" Zhou Li said.

The owner arrived at their table and placed two cups in front of them. One contained red wine and the other steaming-hot baiju.

"I thought my recent activities made that quite clear," Feng Ming said as he examined the mysterious man. "I'm hoping they'll let me go after I get a few more people arrested."

"I'm afraid it's not that simple," Zhou Li said. "Your father is a very powerful figure, and very difficult to ignore. You'd need to cause a devastating amount of trouble for the crown prince for him to even consider sending you out."

"I suppose you have a suggestion?" Feng Ming said.

"As a matter a fact, I do," Zhou Li said. "Believe it or not, I want you out of this city as much as you do. You're killing my family's businesses, and I want to cut my losses. Though I doubt you would trust me. I'm sure you've heard many things about me from your friends."

"Something along the lines of being evil incarnate," Feng Ming said. "Are you going to tell me it was all a misunderstanding and that I should be careful who I make friends with?"

"Heavens, no," Zhou Li said. "They know what I did, but my motives are misunderstood. Has it ever occurred to you that I might have legitimate reasons to contract people from the Obsidian Syndicate?"

"And what might that be?" Feng Ming asked.

"The prince asked me to," Zhou Li said. "Plain and simple." Feng Ming frowned as he mulled over this statement. A steaming plate of stir-fried beef and shredded potato was placed in front of him. He hesitated slightly before taking a bite.

"This is very good," Feng Ming said. "It's much better than all those 'delicacies' in the city."

"Those have never suited my palate," Zhou Li said as he ate. "If my health was better, I'd eat here more often. In any case, it was Prince Tian who asked me to hire the Obsidian Syndicate. He's the one who footed the bill. All I did was place the order and muddle karma. Unfortunately for him, the Alabaster Group interfered once they found out, just like I'd warned him."

"A plausible explanation, but why should I care?" Feng Ming said. "I have no interest in your games."

"For your freedom, of course," Zhou Li said. "I've come here to share some information with you. If you act on it, it will damage the crown prince enough for him to send you on your way. You'll even get to choose where you go."

"Excuse me?" Feng Ming said, aghast.

"Ironic, isn't it," Zhou Li said. "To tell you the truth, I'm only supporting the crown prince for my sister. But I don't approve of his methods. The collusion with devils and evil spirits is more than I can stomach. In four weeks, there will be a secret auction in Songjing. They'll be selling sin-tainted items, Sin Crystals, and even slaves. I want you to go to the basement of this location and crash their party. If you play your cards right, you'll be able to catch at least half a dozen generals who report directly to the crown prince." Zhou Li slipped a small piece of paper on the table.

"And why exactly should I believe you?" Feng Ming asked.

"You shouldn't," Zhou Li stated. "You'll trust in your friend Wang Jun's abilities. He'll be able to confirm what I've said with his auguries. I have faith in his abilities, despite our various misunderstandings."

Feng Ming thought for a moment before pocketing the piece of paper. "You're playing a dangerous game," he said.

Zhou Li shrugged as he stood up. "And so are you. We do what we must, and the world cares little for our personal wishes. You're just like me—adrift on the river of fate, trusting that it will take you in the right direction. Unfortunately, fate only cares about the result. It doesn't care whether ants like us live or die."

Feng Ming sat at his seat brooding as Zhou Li left through the front door. The man gave off a neutral vibe, which was strange. That meant he wasn't a saint, but neither was he a devil. Sighing, he crumpled the paper without looking and tossed it at an open fireplace that was crackling by a small bar.

To his surprise, the crumpled ball shifted strangely in the air and halted just before the fire. Frowning, he picked up the paper and tried tossing it again, this time more slowly. Strangely, his hand twitched as he tried to throw it and it hit the side of the fireplace. It landed on the floor unburnt.

"Third time's the charm," he muttered. He tossed it again. This time, it rolled out of the fireplace with several small fires slowly burning the crumpled paper. The flames spread, and before long, over eight tenths of the paper had burned.

"Let me get that," a voice said beside him. The owner, who had been sitting at the bar, stamped the paper out with his foot. Most of the paper crumbled to ashes, leaving only a small piece unburnt.

Curious, Feng Ming picked up the small piece of paper. He unfolded it, revealing a small piece of white paper covered in black ink. Four characters were still intact on the sheet of paper, despite the heavy burning. They spelled out the name of an establishment, the Honey Badger Inn.

Huxian, Cha Ming, and an old doctor walked off Silverwing's large body just outside Songjing.

"Who would have thought that flying could be so fun!" Li Yin exclaimed.

Cha Ming could only admire the man's courage. The slightest mistake in the journey could have caused him to drop off the large bird and fall to his doom.

"We should get going," Cha Ming said to the group. "We lost a lot of time on this trip, and the king could die at any moment." Huxian, Silverwing, and Lei Jiang donned their beast collars while Li Yin prepared himself mentally for entering the city.

They were greeted politely at the gates. "I hope your trip was fruitful," a guard said. "No need to reregister your contract beasts, Master Du. We already have their information and only require you to update it once their realms change."

"Much obliged," Cha Ming said, laughing. "This is my senior Li Yin. He'll be entering the city with me today."

"Not a problem," the guard said, waving them through. "Any friend of yours is a friend of mine."

"They seem to respect you an awful lot," Li Yin said after they'd walked a few blocks. "Do you hold some sort of political position in the Song Kingdom?"

"Nothing so important," Cha Ming said. "I am dual formation and talisman master. It affords me a certain degree of respect. Even spirit doctors need to watch their words around me."

As they approached Central Square, Li Yin admired the local architecture while Cha Ming observed newly built structures. Several buildings owned by Prince Tian's faction had been demolished and reconstructed in a very short timeframe. They now bore a semblance to the many large buildings in Quicksilver. The buildings contained earth-based runes to bolster their strength and defense. Each of these storefronts were now veritable fortresses.

Did a geomancer arrive in the city? Cha Ming thought.

To test his hypothesis, he walked up to one of these new buildings and placed his hand on it. His resplendent force mixed with his earth qi and examined the building's structure in finer detail. Smaller runes aside, he detected 108 nodes throughout the building. There was only one possibility for such a configuration: A peak master geomancer had been brought in. This level of craftmanship wasn't something that Cha Ming could match.

"Let's go to the Jade Bamboo Conglomerate first," Cha Ming said to his companions. "Wang Jun will want to hear about this as soon as possible."

An incense time later, they were sitting in Wang Jun's office. Wang

Jun and Elder Bai were finishing up some urgent business while employees filed in with many snacks and beverages. No tea was brewed, which was a first, given Wang Jun's obsession with the beverage.

"Sorry about that," Wang Jun said, shooing Elder Bai away. "Some complications have popped up. Nothing unexpected, but they required urgent attention. Now, then, I presume that this gentleman is the Dr. Li you spoke so highly of?"

"Hardly a doctor," Li Yin said. "My license was revoked. Now I consider myself a medical researcher who happens to treat people occasionally. It ruffles less feathers."

"It's the results that matter, and conventional medicine is not affecting the king in the slightest," Wang Jun said. "Did Cha Ming brief you on his condition?"

"He did," Li Yin said. "Having one's qi restrained will undoubtedly affect health functions. I'm helpless to treat this, but delaying the inevitable... that's possible. I'll need Cha Ming's help, however. He's the only one I can trust with important matters like these."

Cha Ming's heart warmed at the recommendation.

"The king's health is a high-priority matter," Wang Jun said. "How soon can you start?"

"The sooner the better," Li Yin said. "Seconds matter."

"Unfortunately, we'll have to wait until a few hours after nightfall," Wang Jun said. "The royal physician will be done with his treatments by then and will leave the king to rest for a few hours."

"Then I'll make the necessary preparations," Li Yin said. "Is there anywhere where I can procure herbal or alchemical ingredients? And someone to blend them? Preferably not a physician's shop."

"That's easy to arrange," Wang Jun said. "Cha Ming recently recruited an alchemist. He arrived just yesterday, and he's located in this building. He brought a very large amount of alchemical supplies with him to kickstart a competing Alchemists Association. He should have what you need." Then he rang one of the many bells on his desk. A younger man entered the room immediately. "Su Ming, please take them to the alchemist and instruct their workshop that I will foot the bill for anything they need."

"Before we leave, I thought you should know that the crown prince has recruited a geomancer," Cha Ming said.

"Feng Ming hinted at that, and new buildings have been popping up all over the city," Wang Jun said wryly. "I'd be a fool if I couldn't connect the dots."

"Then did you know that it was a peak master geomancer?" Cha Ming asked.

Wang Jun frowned. "That I didn't know." He then sighed. "Then there's nothing we can do about it. We're outgunned, and it will take you at least a year to reach the peak of foundation establishment. Don't worry yourself about these things; I'll find a way to deal with it. I always do."

A shadowy door opened in the king's dimly lit chamber. Cha Ming, Wang Jun, the third prince, and Li Yin walked out from it and toward the king's bed. The dying man was much thinner than before, and his life force much dimmer.

"Who is this?" a voice said from above the king's bed.

"It's a fifth opinion," Prince Lei said. "Cha Ming found some help and has someone else working on a cure to the king's poison."

"Very well," the king's protector said. "Same rules as before, but this time, I'll have *your* head if anything happens."

Cha Ming immediately approached the bed and laid down a healing formation. Then he projected the situation to Li Yin. "See here, how the healing runes disintegrate on contact? That's the effect of the venom. I have someone else working on that issue, so you don't need to worry about it. However, as you can see, his blood toxicity is extremely high. He's being poisoned to death, and if his body hadn't been strengthened by his core-formation cultivation base, he would already be dead."

"Interesting," Li Yin said. "Can you magnify a cross section of the kidney? I want to inspect the cause of its malfunction."

Cha Ming shifted the formation's focus. The many interlinked capillaries and fibrous exchange centers were brought up on the projection screen. To Cha Ming, it looked like a perfectly normal kidney, albeit one that ran much slower than it should. It didn't appear damaged in any way.

"There is nothing medically wrong with this kidney," Li Yin concluded. "It's running slowly, but it must be due to some other reason. The qi-restraining venom you described doesn't have this power."

Cha Ming frowned. "Then how can we cure him?"

"We can only take it one step at a time," Li Yin said. "Once the venom is cured, we can inspect the situation further. For now, we need to reduce the strain on his body so that he can recover some energy." Li Yin then took out a small storage vial from his coat pocket. It was a cooled storage treasure which carried a solution Li Yin had invented, the blood-plasma solution. "Do you remember our discussion about semipermeable membranes? I want you to build one that won't let blood pass."

"Of course," Cha Ming said. "Prince Lei, we'll be purifying the king's blood, but for this, we need to take it out of his body a little at a time. Would you be so kind as to remove his bandage?"

Prince Lei frowned but did as he was told. There was no response from the king's protectors. Soon a small dripping wound appeared. Cha Ming quickly used his resplendent force to quell the bleeding. Then he took out the Clear Sky Brush and began painting a tiny but complex structure. To ensure success, he magnified it with the healing formation and precisely controlled his every brushstroke. A thin, clear membrane began to take shape.

Cha Ming flicked his finger and willed over a droplet of blood. The cells were misshapen and clearly unhealthy. He pushed it against the membrane, which gave way to it.

"Too big," he muttered. He willed his qi to contract, and the pores in the tiny matrix tightened. Then he used much broader brushstrokes to expand the existing structure.

Cha Ming produced a thin, clothlike sheet of unknown materials that spread out for fifty feet before doubling back. He rolled the one-inch sheet into a tube less than an eight of an inch wide. Then he created a much thicker clear sheet. This time, he didn't bother magnifying it. He wrapped it around the inner tube and filled the gap with baffles to compartmentalize flow.

"Now fill the membrane with the plasma," Li Yin said. He handed him the vial, which contained a clear fluid. Cha Ming filled both the inner and outer walls with the clear liquid. "You know what to do next," Li Yin said.

Cha Ming nodded and directed the inner tube, which was now full of fluid, to the tiny wound on the king's body. He used his qi to form a seal. The king's blood began displacing the clear fluid, which Cha Ming dumped into an empty vial. This continued until the entire inner tube was filled with blood. "My apologies, Prince Lei, but I'll need to create another wound on his body."

Prince Lei sighed but waved for him to continue. With so much blood having left his father's body, he was committed to this treatment method. Cha Ming went ahead and made a small incision right next to the original one. He used his resplendent force to separate the inflow and outflow of blood. Then he willed the blood in the king's body to circulate.

After the first incense time, there was very little change. However, after a half hour, the clear fluid in the outer wall began to change color. It turned more and more yellow as increasing amounts of impurities were ejected from the king's blood. Cha Ming wondered how it was even possible for Li Yin to think of dialysis, but he had rolled with it and used his own knowledge from his engineering days to suggest the counter-current extraction method.

Li Yin's original plan had also involved the use of sheep intestines and the like. Cha Ming, with his handy creation qi, would have none of this. Li Yin had readily agreed to each of his proposed improvements.

Two hours later, the tube nearest to the incoming blood was

filled with yellow and red-colored impurities, while the plasma fluid closest to where the blood returned was slightly yellow.

"That's about it for today," Li Yin said. "You can return his blood. We need to clean his blood every three days at the latest. The lack of impurities will allow his body to heal and recover some energy. With any luck, that's all we'll need to do."

Cha Ming finished squeezing the remaining blood back into the king's body. The man's unhealthy red blood cells concerned him, but there was nothing they could do for now. He speculated that Li Yin's next method involved treating the blood. Shaking his head, he used fire qi to burn the contaminated dialysis equipment.

"I'll make a few sets in the near future," Cha Ming said. "I'd hate to be responsible for an infection due to improper cleaning."

Li Yin nodded. He was a big fan of using sterile equipment.

"We should leave," said Wang Jun, who had been standing to the side. He materialized a shadowy door and ushered the small crowd out of the room. Cha Ming hastily tied the bandage before leaving.

The king's chamber door opened just as the shadowy door vanished.

Princess Guo quietly entered her father's chambers like she always did. While her siblings were out fighting each other and politicking, she spent her time keeping her father company. She wrinkled her nose as a light, ashy smell came and went.

"So strange," she muttered. Her eyes wandered to the hastily tied bandage.

Song Guo sighed. "Why does he always do such a sloppy job in tying even simple bandages? How can doctors be so lacking when it comes to such simple things?" She unwrapped the bandage and carefully wiped away the blood before refastening it.

"What's this?" she whispered as she gently touched a new wound that had appeared on her father's arm. It hadn't been there yesterday when she'd replaced the bandage. "Is the royal doctor performing extra treatments without telling me?" She looked at her father doubtfully. He looked just as sickly as before. "Well, it doesn't matter what he tries, as long as he hasn't given up."

She took out a wet cloth and carefully washed her father's face. As she washed, she couldn't help but see the shadow of a smile forming on his sickly lips.

"It must be my imagination again," she muttered.

Chapter 16: Progress

W ell, that went well," Wang Jun said cheerfully. They'd returned to the Jade Bamboo Auction House, where Li Yin locked himself up to continue his research. "What are your plans now that you're back? I'm afraid there's not much demand for your energy-gathering formations now that the geomancer has entered the equation."

"I'm not sure," Cha Ming said, massaging his brow. "I'll likely pursue body refinement. There's a fight brewing, and I need to be able to participate."

Wang Jun frowned. "I'm working on it, give me time," he yelled out suddenly. His eyes glazed over for a moment before returning to normal.

"Are you all right?" Cha Ming asked.

"Never been better," Wang Jun said. "Why?"

"You suddenly yelled 'I'm working on it, give me time,'" Cha Ming said.

Wang Jun looked at him with a puzzled expression.

"It must have been my imagination," Cha Ming muttered.

Wang Jun shrugged and returned to work.

Hours passed as Cha Ming lounged around, thinking about his next course of action. During that time, he overheard many conversations from the auction house's customers.

"I heard the Shen family was won over by the crown prince's camp this morning," a young man said to his two friends. "Six of their storefronts and their family estate were fortified to the point that even an initial-core-formation expert couldn't damage them in the slightest. In addition, various traps and functions have been added to each building. If chaos breaks out inside the city, they'll be able to remain relatively unscathed."

"Some other families might have gotten a few formations by joining Prince Lei's camp, but what use are they if their home gets reduced to rubble?" the second man said. "That's the third family in two days. It looks like the struggle for the throne is settled."

"That's nothing to complain about," the third one said. "If both sides are too even, the resulting civil war would devastate us. We'd all be drafted one way or another. Even the commoners would suffer."

"Right, it's better to have a clear winner," the first man said.

Cha Ming pulled away his resplendent force once the conversation was over. Was he really doing all he could? He was deeply worried about the people of the Song Kingdom, and despite their desire for peace, he suspected life under the crown prince would be far from ideal. As he thought, he withdrew a jade bottle from the Clear Sky Space and opened it. A faint medicinal aroma caused his qi pillars to shiver with excitement.

"They say that haste makes waste," the kindly Elder Bai said as he walked past. "You should make sure to consolidate your foundation before continuing. The young master said it hasn't been long since you broke through."

"What's the worst that could happen?" Cha Ming asked as he stowed away the pill and stood up.

"In most cases, it delays one's cultivation progress," Elder Bai explained. "In other cases, it causes irreparable damage to one's foundation, making cultivation extremely inefficient in the future. Why the rush? Only needing a year to reach the peak of foundation establishment is extremely quick. I'm envious."

"Don't worry, Elder Bai, I'm aware of my limits," Cha Ming said.

"I feel that my recent experiences have sufficiently stabilized my qi seas. I'll be attempting my breakthrough tonight, though I'll be back in time for His Majesty's treatment. Would you kindly inform Brother Jun when you see him? I want him to procure some late-grade scrolls and flags in the meantime. While a geomancer's peak-grade buildings are a desired commodity, formations are far more useful for clans and sects. While it won't win over everyone, it should stop the mass exodus of undecided families to the crown prince's faction."

Elder Bai looked at him long and hard before nodding. "Very well. You know your condition best. I'll inform the young master when it's convenient."

Cha Ming proceeded downstairs to his cultivation chamber where he activated a built-in formation to prevent intrusion. Then he directed his attention to his qi seas. Although they were mostly clear, a few dozen specks of unconverted qi remained.

"What difference will two weeks make?" he muttered. He popped a few pills in his mouth and willed his qi pillars to grow using the excess energy. They grew with little trouble, despite the turbidity that was slowly seeping into the pillars.

Once they reached their maximum height, he popped three pills into his mouth. A vast energy traveled through his stomach and into his Dantian, causing his qi pillars to creak and groan as they destabilized.

The Pillar Eruption Pills worked their magic and shattered the bindings that restrained Cha Ming's foundation. He directed the potent qi to his foundation and willed it to grow. The pillars grew until a quarter of their surface was visible above his qi seas.

"Consolidate," Cha Ming whispered. A whirlpool formed around each pillar as they rapidly sucked in each of the five viscous qi seas. He squirmed with discomfort as each drop of turbid qi entered his pillars.

He gritted his teeth as he forced his foundation to absorb every drop. His qi pathways strained under the effort, while the rumbling in his foundation threatened to tear apart the black-and-white matrix that held it together. Finally, as quickly as the rumbling started, it stopped. Every drop of qi had disappeared and was replaced with an even thicker liquid. The degree of turbidity was much greater than last time. The damage to his cultivation seemed hardly irreparable. It would likely only take him a few months reverse the effects of his rash behavior.

"It's a small price to pay to prevent the Song Kingdom from being overrun by devils like in Fairweather," Cha Ming mumbled. Although it seemed like just a half hour had passed, two days had already come and gone.

It was time for the king's next treatment.

With his new and improved cultivation base, Cha Ming continued studying formations with renewed vigor. Every three days, he stopped his studying to administer the king's treatment. The man's yellow complexion had improved drastically, and he now looked like a man in his nineties instead of someone at death's door.

In order to compete with the geomancer, Cha Ming was studying something far different than he'd experienced thus far. Seventy-two flags fluttered as they drew on the energy of heaven and earth. They were spread to each corner of the room, which was filled with hundreds of lines that moved as he willed them. Within the confines of the formation, he held absolute awareness and could attack enemies as he pleased. It would be difficult for anyone below core formation to survive the onslaught.

Before long, the formation dimmed as the ambient world energy was exhausted. Cha Ming pulled out a high-grade spirit stone, which the formation plundered mercilessly before activating once more. This time, it lasted for an incense time before dimming again.

"Can I eat it?" Huxian said as he walked into the room.

"Eat what?" Cha Ming asked.

"The formation," Huxian said nonchalantly. "For science." Seeing Cha Ming's unconvinced expression, Huxian continued with his explanation. "I need data to answer the oldest unresolved question in my inherited memories. My ancestor's lifelong companion was a great talisman artist and formation master. He could rend the heavens and sunder the earth with his arts. By accompanying him, my great ancestor devoured billions of formations. However, not all of them pleased his palate. He wasn't sure if it was the essence of formations themselves that weren't appetizing or if it was their construction that made the difference. For example, excellent ingredients can taste like garbage when prepared by a subpar chef, but a great chef can make a great dish from the most mundane ingredients."

Cha Ming looked at the small fox in disbelief. "That's very sensical, but I still don't understand why you would ever want to do such a thing."

"Because that's what being a food enthusiast is all about," Huxian huffed. "Eating isn't just a hobby; it's a way of life. It is both my pleasure and *honor* to uphold the bagua family tradition of eating everything under the sun. And above it. And heck, the sun itself if I get strong enough."

Cha Ming's curiosity was piqued. "Can you eat it without eating the flags?"

"Of course," Huxian said. "My ancestors have determined that sigil focuses and flags are fundamentally untasty. However, the verdict is still out on the formation energies themselves."

"By all means." Cha Ming gestured. Huxian's shadow distorted, and with a yip of excitement, it leaped onto the Gold Slaughtering Formation. Hundreds of mouths shot out and nibbled away at the many lines forming it. Eventually, it shattered.

Cha Ming collected the flags while Huxian's shadow collected the remaining fragments. "I gather that this one was tasty?"

"Extremely," Huxian said. "They're all much tastier than many of the others I've sampled in the city."

"Wait, which formations have you been eating in the city?"

Cha Ming said in a panic. He'd hate it if all his hard work had been undermined by his furry friend.

"Oh, I just started recently," Huxian said. "I've been taking bites out of the fortified buildings that have cropped up over the past two days. They were delicious, but nothing special. Don't worry, I made sure not to destroy them. They'll work normally—for the most part. Of course, they're faring much better than those Lei Jiang has gotten to." Noticeable amounts of drool were pooling on the floor below his mouth.

Cha Ming massaged his brow. "What damage?"

"He's been eating those new buildings like an addict," Huxian complained. "At first it was just holes in the walls. For the sake of verminkind, he said. However, I think he might have started eating into the foundations. Apparently the fancy materials they're built with are very beneficial for strengthening his body. I've been doing my best, but he's very difficult to rein in."

"And no one's caught you both thus far?" Cha Ming asked incredulously. This was his greatest concern. After all, he was liable for all damages they caused within the city.

"Those slowpokes?" Huxian snorted with contempt. "The city guard is basically useless, and those so-called experts inside those big families can't even hear us, much less see us."

Cha Ming pondered for a moment. "Let's talk to Wang Jun and think of a plan."

"A plan for what?" Huxian asked.

"I want you and Lei Jiang to eat your heart's content," Cha Ming said.

Huxian eyes brightened instantly.

Wang Jun burst out laughing when he heard the news. He rang for Elder Bai, who was brought to tears at the thought of the two little miscreants eating through the crown prince's hard-earned coin.

"And here I was wondering which guardian angel was doing my dirty work for me," Wang Jun said. "There's no need to stop them. Anything is fine if they don't get caught."

"I was thinking more in terms of which buildings you wanted to prioritize, and which ones you wanted relatively undamaged," Cha Ming said. "For example, I'd hate to have them eat away the foundations of a building you're planning on buying."

"Fair enough," Wang Jun said, quickly scribbling down three lists. "The buildings on the first list should be damaged in any way possible. I want the damage to be so severe so that fixing it will cost the crown prince a fortune.

"The second list contains buildings that should be damaged superficially but should be fully functioning," Wang Jun said. "I want the damages easy to fix. They are there for the sole purpose of undermining the geomancer's reputation and reducing the value of the properties in case their owners want to sell them at a discount.

"Finally, those on the third list should be damaged discreetly. I want their foundations destroyed and their walls weakened. It would be best if we could topple them over with a flick of our wrist. They should sustain some superficial damage to avoid suspicion but nothing serious enough to cause the geomancer to inspect them. These buildings are most likely to be used in city warfare, should the situation devolve to that level."

"Noted," Cha Ming said as he stowed away the list. "I'll instruct them as soon as possible."

"Run, sister, run!" Wang Jun suddenly shouted.

Both Cha Ming and Elder Bai looked toward him.

"There's seriously something wrong with you," Cha Ming said. "That's the second time I've seen you blurt out strange things. This time you said, 'run, sister, run.'"

"Nonsense," Wang Jun said. "Elder Bai, did I say anything?"

"I'm afraid you did," Elder Bai said. "And it's not the first time. I think you should get some sleep."

Wang Jun frowned. "I'm afraid I can't. There's too much going on.

Speaking of which, how is your progress on the Gold Slaughtering Formation?" Wang Jun asked.

"I've finished the prototype," Cha Ming said slowly. "As long as I have sufficient materials, I should be able set it up without much difficulty. The formation is eighty-five-percent efficient. I project being able to expand each grand formation to cover a square mile without any loss in efficiency. However, the materials required will scale with the surface area being covered."

Wang Jun nodded. "I'll give you supplies and a list tomorrow. Soon I'll be owing you money instead of the other way around."

"I'm not doing this for money," Cha Ming said. "I'm doing it so there isn't another Fairweather."

A few brief pulses suddenly interrupted their conversation. Wang Jun pulled out a core-formation jade, which he activated. Prince Lei's projection appeared on the corner of Wang Jun's desk.

"To what do I owe the pleasure?" Wang Jun said.

"There are complications to the original plan," Prince Lei said. "I'm afraid we'll have to come clean."

"What for?" Wang Jun asked. "Did the doctors detect something?"

"It was my sister," Prince Lei said. "I overheard her yelling at the doctors and asking for an explanation on father's sudden improvement in condition. When the doctor said he hadn't done anything differently, she brought up the wound you inflicted to circulate the blood. When he said he knew nothing about it, she swore she wouldn't leave father's side until she got an explanation from them."

"So we can't continue our treatments until we clarify the situation," Wang Jun said.

"Exactly," Prince Lei said. "But we're in a much better position than before. The doctors might scoff at Dr. Li's lack of credentials, but my sister will only care about the results. Therefore, I confessed the situation, and the royal uncles corroborated our story. She wasn't happy about our taking actions behind her back, and she was quite annoyed at the royal uncles for not telling her, but she said she'd like to meet the doctor who's succeeded where others have failed."

"It was bound to happen sooner or later," Wang Jun said. He turned to Cha Ming. "Can you speak with Dr. Li on this matter?"

"I'll explain it on the way," Cha Ming replied. "He's very good with stressful situations, but he'll lose his mind if anyone interrupts him during his research."

Cha Ming, Wang Jun, Li Yin, and Prince Lei walked into the king's chambers. This time, they walked through the front door. Princess Guo stood beside her father's bed with an annoyed expression. The chief physician was there as well, and judging by the embarrassed look on his face, the princess had brow-beaten him the entire time they waited.

"Dearest sister," Prince Lei said, "thank you for taking the time to meet with us. I realize you've been terribly busy of late, and—"

"Cut the crap," Princess Guo said coldly.

The prince shrank back, leaving Cha Ming, Wang Jun, and Li Yin at her mercy. She turned to them. "I understand that you've been treating my father in secret. Normally this would be a grave offense worthy of execution. However, my father's condition has noticeably improved. Therefore I wish to thank whoever has been treating him and ask him to continue his work under my supervision. I take it that you are Dr. Li?" Princess Guo said with a smile.

"Doctor is too noble a title for this lowly one," Li Yin replied. "I am just a medical researcher who happens to know quite a bit about treating people without qi. I am unable to cultivate, but I haven't been able to leave people dying by the wayside. Which is much more than can be said for the people bearing the title of doctor."

"That's a little unfair," the chief physician interjected. "We often treat people free of charge, but it's simply too difficult to balance the needs of the masses with the needs of the rich and affluent."

"You may speak when you're spoken to," Princess Guo said to the doctor. "As far as I'm concerned, you're useless, while this medical researcher isn't. I hope I won't have to repeat myself."

The chief physician gulped. "Understood." He stood at attention next to the king's bed and awaited his judgment.

"Please continue with your efforts," Princess Guo said. "All I ask is that I be allowed to stand by while you do your work. I am greatly worried about my father's health."

"Very well," Li Yin said. "We've just been cleaning his blood while the Quicksilver Alchemists Association tries to find a cure to the qi-binding poison that is restraining his cultivation."

"A qi-restraining poison?" the chief physician exclaimed. "No wonder none of my healing or analysis techniques worked!"

"It's also why Zhou Bei from the Quicksilver Alchemists Association couldn't identify the poison," Cha Ming said.

"Wait, how is the Zhou family suddenly involved?" Princess Guo interjected.

"Zhou Bei is not on friendly terms with the Zhou family, and he is the foremost expert on poisons on the continent," Cha Ming said. "When the chief physician suspected poison, he had initially sent a vial of blood to Zhou Bei. Is that correct?"

"Exactly so," the chief physician said. "That's why I concluded it wasn't poison. If it was a poison, that man would surely have found and identified it."

"I don't want to interrupt," Li Yin said. "But we're already late for the treatment. Would you be so kind?"

The princess and the physician quickly backed off while Cha Ming and Li Yin performed their treatment.

Chapter 17: Complications

T hat was simply amazing!" the chief physician exclaimed as Cha Ming purged the blood cleansing apparatus. "Might I keep it for study?"

Cha Ming looked to Li Yin, who nodded. He cleansed the apparatus with water qi before offering it to the man.

"Make sure not to use it on anyone, as it's not sterile," Cha Ming said.

"Of course, of course," the chief physician said. "It seems like the king's blood is now quite clean. What might Dr. Li's next plan be?"

The man had given up all pretenses of superiority. Instead, he had relegated himself to the role of an inferior student.

"This is where it gets tricky," Dr. Li said. The princess and the chief physician were listening in rapt attention. "We've cleaned his blood, which has allowed him to regain some vigor. Nutrition is not an issue, since the chief physician has been injecting him with a nutrition serum daily."

"Please, call me Dr. Dong," the chief physician said.

"Very well, Dr. Dong," Dr. Li said before continuing. "Then the next logical step is replacing his blood. His Majesty's blood cells are extremely unhealthy, and it seems like his body is incapable of producing healthy ones."

Dr. Dong frowned but didn't interrupt. The princess, seeing his expression, couldn't help but speak up.

"Is there are problem with changing out a person's blood?" Princes Guo asked. "I've taken dozens of blood multiplication potions with no ill effect."

"It's complicated because we can't use such potions," Dr. Dong said. "The only way we could proceed is to replace His Majesty's blood with another person's. However, this is a taboo in the medical community since we normally possess alternative means. It is forbidden because of the many complications that can arise."

"Such as?" Princess Guo said.

"For one, diseases can be passed through blood," Li Yin explained. "Some potentially deadly diseases cannot be passed on any other way. More importantly, there is a phenomenon called the principle of blood rejection."

"Different people's blood tends to be rejected by the one receiving the infusion," Dr. Dong clarified. "The medical community studied it at some point but eventually gave up since blood multiplication potions were far too easy and cheap to make."

"Then how could we possibly risk this with my royal father?" Princess Guo asked.

"We'll do it in two steps," Dr. Li said. "I've determined through preliminary research that incompatible bloods agglutinate, though I'm not sure of the exact mechanism. Blood tends to be most compatible within a family, so I'll need a sample of the king's blood, your blood, and your two brothers' blood. We can look externally after that."

The princess instantly retrieved her hair pin and pricked her finger, allowing blood to rapidly trickle into a crystal vial. "Is this amount sufficient?"

"More than sufficient, but could you please secure the vial, Cha Ming?" Dr. Li asked.

Cha Ming grabbed the vial and placed a special lid on it. Then he opened a plug and whisked away the remaining air in the vial. "Exposure to air degrades the blood. The blood must also be kept at a low temperature to prevent rotting."

"Disinfecting the blood shouldn't be difficult," Dr. Dong said. "It hasn't been contaminated with qi-binding venom, greatly simplifying the process. My only concern is proof of concept."

"I'm willing to personally undergo this trial," Li Yin said. "We can start gathering random blood samples in the Jade Bamboo Auction House for compatibility testing. Once I've found a suitable blood type, I'll receive a transfusion for proof of concept."

No one spoke out against this. The king's life and the kingdom were at stake. After saying their goodbyes, Cha Ming and company left the palace in high spirits. They had obtained a blood sample from Princess Guo and Prince Lei. Only Prince Tian's blood sample remained.

The wooden door to Prince Tian's study creaked opened to reveal a court eunuch. He stood as Prince Tian finished a discussion with his guest.

"What is it?" Prince Tian said, looking over.

"Your humble servant is here to inform you that Dr. Dong has requested an audience," the eunuch said. "He wishes to secure a vial of your blood to be used in finding a treatment for your royal father. What are your instructions?"

"Bring him in," Prince Tian said.

The eunuch scurried out the door, leaving only him and Zhou Li in the study. "Should I tamper with the blood?" he asked.

Zhou Li snorted. "That seems like a very easy way to expose yourself and your past misdeeds."

"Misdeeds that were committed under your instruction and coercion," Prince Tian added. "Regardless, I'm committed to this course of action. I must do this for the sake of the kingdom."

"Removing the king from the equation was the only way to tide us through these difficult times," Zhou Li said. "War will soon envelop the entire continent. Whose side do you wish the kingdom to stand with? The winning one or the losing one? In any case, it doesn't matter if they treat him. It's virtually impossible for them to find the true cause of the king's malaise. By the time they've figured it out, it will be too late." Zhou Li moved toward a bookshelf, where he revealed a secret exit.

"Is it really necessary for my father to suffer so much?" Prince Tian asked before the black-cloaked man slipped away.

"Timing is everything, my prince," Zhou Li said. "Each and every step of the process is necessary. In a sense, it's not a bad thing that the third prince is scrambling to treat your father. At least his suffering will be eased considerably before his eventual demise." He then walked out of the room.

The chief physician appeared shortly after. The prince dutifully gave him a vial of his blood and expressed his best wishes. How could he not hope for their success? The man was his father, and he hated every second of his slow and painful death.

Cha Ming returned from an appointment with a smile on his face. The Jing family, one of the most adamant neutral camps in the city, had finally given in for the high price of two mid-grade gold-gathering formations and a Gold Slaughtering Grand Formation. Unlike most families, they did not possess significant assets in the center of the city. Therefore they were less concerned with collateral damage from powerful cultivators; they were more worried about the possibility of ransacking and pillaging by local ruffians.

A middle-foundation-establishment elder could only do so much to safeguard his family. However, with a Gold Slaughtering Formation, he could easily crush anyone below core formation who dared enter his home. The deterrence alone would provide his family with a substantial degree of protection.

Cha Ming passed several Jade Bamboo office workers on his way to Li Yin's study. Each one looked haggard and sleep-deprived. Elder Bai was no different. As a foundation-establishment expert, his ability to keep working through fatigue was surpassed only by the young master himself, who was rumored to never sleep.

He soon found his way into a stone-walled laboratory, which was situated right next to a budding alchemist workshop. Li Yin was busy examining several blood-filled test tubes with a minor healing formation Cha Ming had set up before leaving. The older man shook his head as he examined each test tube with a grim expression.

"All failures," Li Yin said. "My own compatibility tests are failures as well."

"Can you show me?" Cha Ming asked as he walked closer to the magnified projection of one of the vials.

"You see this blood clumping?" Li Yin asked Cha Ming. "Incompatible blood agglutinates in this fashion. Only in rare cases of compatibility will this not happen."

"What do you think causes it?" Cha Ming asked, carefully choosing his words. "It must be something outside the blood cells that makes this happen."

"I speculate it has to do with the plasma fluid," Li Yin said. "However, the blood will be transfused into the recipient's bloodstream. There is no way to prevent interaction with blood plasma."

"Could the donor and the recipient's plasma be different?" Cha Ming asked. "What if they were separated, and we only tested with the donor's blood cells?"

"Brilliant!" Li Yin exclaimed. "Quickly, separate a portion of this blood for me."

Cha Ming hurriedly used his resplendent force to separate the thick red blood cells from the clear plasma. He repeated the process with a portion of blood from Prince Tian and Prince Lei. The doctor then dropped a portion of each blood into samples of the king's blood. Two vials agglutinated, while another didn't.

"Success!" Li Yin exclaimed, barely containing his excitement.

He then had Cha Ming repeat the process for the dozens of blood samples on his desk. It was no problem for him to find a few compatible bloods. "I'll be testing the blood transfusion on myself tonight. With any luck, we'll be able to proceed with the king's transfusion tomorrow. Please tell Wang Jun to secure four cups of Prince Tian's blood. He's a core-formation cultivator, so he can handle it." The doctor then rushed off to secure his own blood specimens.

"Should I even tell him about blood types?" Cha Ming muttered. With his intelligence, he'd figure it out in a day or two. Plus, who knew if the blood types here are the same as Earth's?

Wang Jun was hard at work when a soft knocking sound, followed by the click of his door opening, revealed Elder Bai's reassuring figure. "What is it this time?" he said, sighing as the man walked over with a bundle of paper.

"Yet another round of loans being called," Elder Bai said. "At this rate, any loan that can be called will be called. Which makes no sense, given our superior financial situation."

"It's like they're out to get us, Brother Jun. What will we do?" his sister asked.

"What was that?" Wang Jun asked.

"I said it's like they're out to get us," Elder Bai repeated. "Are you sure you're all right? It seems you've been having difficulty hearing lately."

Wang Jun shook his head. He looked past his sister's ghostly figure, who was playing on the floor, before continuing. "I'm fine. Now what's the story with the remainder of that thick pile?"

"Incident reports," Elder Bai said. "Although the cost of the goods and the trade caravan itself are insured, I'm afraid that exporting anything outside the city will be impossible in the near future. All of these high-grade weapons will need to be sold within the Song Kingdom itself."

"Were any of those goods Cha Ming's?" Wang Jun asked. Elder Bai shook his head. "I would ask where the military was when these incidents happened, but I'm sure I know the answer," Wang Jun said. "Prince Tian's stupidity knows no bounds. It's not only me that's suffering, but his kingdom's international credibility. Anything else?"

"None," Elder Bai replied.

"Good. Let's go get some good news," Wang Jun said as he walked out the door.

"Don't forget me!" the ghostly child on the floor said. Wang Jun ignored her like he always did.

It isn't a poison, and it isn't a curse, Wang Jun thought. *Just what is it that's causing me to see and hear these things? The average person would have gone insane by now.*

"Young Master, I have an important message for you," someone said suddenly. Hei Ling appeared out of nowhere and completely caught Wang Jun and Elder Bai unaware. Protector Ren appeared inside the room just in case.

Hei Ling looked at Protector Ren with what seemed like disappointment. "Here it is," he said, placing a small piece of paper in Wang Jun's open palm. "If Protector Ren was right beside you, I wouldn't have been able to breach his defenses," Hei Ling commented before walking out the door.

Wang Jun shivered but read the message. It lit up in his hands, leaving not a shred of evidence behind.

"I thought I asked to have him tailed!" Wang Jun yelled. "How the hell can he come and go as he chooses?"

The Jade Bamboo staff in the vicinity looked at him with shocked expressions. They'd never seen him lose his temper.

"Elder Bai," said Wang Jun, "I want to speak with Li Ming tonight. Protector Ren, please follow me to the alchemist workshop."

The man clung to him like his shadow—Hei Ling's breach had reminded him of his own shortcomings.

They passed through many corridors before arriving at a room bustling with customers. At Wang Jun's instructions, these customers were all in Prince Lei's camp. Such an arrangement would only change if the supply produced by this workshop far exceeded his faction's demand.

"How can I help you today?" a beautiful attendant in a green cultivation robe said.

"I need to speak with Master Ling Bai," Wang Jun said.

"Right this way," the attendant replied. Fortunately, they were inside the Jade Bamboo Auction House. Everyone here would recognize Wang Jun at a glance. He was soon brought into a small office in a remote corner of the workshop.

"How are things looking these days?" Wang Jun asked Ling Bai, who was just finishing his review of an important document.

"Things are going very well," Ling Bai replied. "One of our peak-mortal-grade alchemists broke through and became a magic-grade alchemist. Our number of apprentices has doubled, while the number of low-leveled alchemists has also doubled. Many of these people have defected from Master Alchemist Zhou's workshop. Due to his bad policies, we were able to rope them in without even offering them a pay raise."

"How about sales?" Wang Jun asked.

"As you know, it's difficult to increase margins on mortal-grade pills," Ling Bai said. "However, our market share is sitting at twenty-five percent. It won't be long before we cannibalize another fifteen percent of the market. Unfortunately, our market share on higher-level goods is quite low. This will take much time to fix. We'll have to recruit an opposing master alchemist to make any progress on this front."

"Keep up the good work," Wang Jun said.

"Thanks, brother!" his little sister's ghost replied. He ignored her and walked out of the room. His next stop was another secret meeting with the Black King. This time, he brought Protector Ren along as a precaution.

"Are you sure you want me to wait here?" Protector Ren asked doubtfully. They were in a quiet wine shop that offered private rooms.

"I can't take you with me for reasons I can't speak of," Wang Jun said. "I should be using a Void Transfer Talisman to arrive at your side directly. I don't want a repeat of last time."

"Suit yourself," Protector Ren said. "It won't be my fault if you die."

Wang Jun nodded and walked out into a dirty street. The wine shop was quiet because the street was quiet. It was the perfect place for an ambush. Wang Jun gripped the Void Transfer Talisman tightly.

A few turns later, he entered yet another dark alley. This one contained a similar door to last time. No, that wasn't it. It was the same door, but in a different location. This time, it opened for him without asking him the security question. Wang Jun proceeded down the staircase before arriving at the same room as before.

"I'm so glad you could make it here alive," the Black King said. "Was my warning helpful?"

"It bought me a fraction of a second," Wang Jun said. "I take it you weren't contractually allowed to tell me anything?"

"I don't know what you're talking about," the Black King said. "Everyone must be self-sufficient in this world, and you must never let your guard down. Now then, here are your profits from our latest transaction."

He tossed three sacks onto the table. "The first was successfully sold at two times the list price. Your profit is based on selling at 1.75 times the list price, for a total of 11,667 high-grade spirit stones. Similarly, the next batch netted you 12,500 high-grade spirit stones. Finally, I managed to sell the last batch at 2.5 times list price. This netted you 13,333 high-grade spirit stones. Are you satisfied?"

"Very," Wang Jun said, retrieving the bags and plopping two

more on the table. "Please sell these two bags of goods for me. Sell one at 2.25 times market price, and another at your discretion."

"Why all the caution?" the Black King said.

How could anyone be anything but cautious around you? Wang Jun thought.

"How can anyone be anything but cautious around you?" his sister's apparition pouted. Wang Jun ignored her.

"Each bag contains 20,000 high-grade spirit stones' worth of goods," Wang Jun said. "How can I not be cautious?"

"That's more like it." The Black King laughed, summoning the usual contracts.

Wang Jun signed them only after cautiously inspecting them. "Will that be everything today?"

"There's one more thing, but I'll require a confidentially contract," Wang Jun said.

The Black King shrugged and summoned another piece of black paper.

"I have a large quantity of immortal-jade core I wish to liquidate."

"How much are we talking?" the Black King asked with interest.

"Five hundred jin," Wang Jun said. "The estimated market value on the batch is 750,000. However, it can't be sold to a buyer from within the Song Kingdom."

The Black King thought for a while. "I can do it, but it will take some time. The Xia Dynasty has the lowest taxation rate on newly excavated products at ten percent. However, this is a restricted resource that can't be sold anonymously on normal markets. For such a huge sum, I can sell it for a twenty-percent commission over and above the tax."

"Ten percent," Wang Jun said.

"I thought I told you there was no bargaining with me?" the Black King said.

"And without me you won't be able to secure such a huge, effortless deal," Wang Jun countered.

Both sides looked at each other tensely from opposite sides of the table. Meanwhile, his sister's apparition was running around wildly chasing a rat.

"Fine," the Black King said. "Ten percent it is, but it will take six weeks to secure a buyer. You're not holding the immortal-jade core with you personally, are you?"

"That would be a gross violation of my family's policies," Wang Jun said. "There is only one place where we can store such precious resources. If you pay me, I'll even tell you where it is. I'm quite confident in its security."

The Black King grunted. "No need. Will that be everything for today?" His eyes flickered to the talisman in Wang Jun's hand. "I see that you're learning."

"I never fall for the same trick twice," Wang Jun said. "Though I'd hate to use it. Could I interest you in providing me a secret way out? For a fee, of course."

The Black King chuckled. He waved his hand, revealing a hidden staircase. "Follow this hallway, and you'll arrive just outside the wine shop where you left your precious Protector Ren. Speaking of which, it seems that he's actually taking his job seriously now."

Wang Jun frowned but moved into the tunnel.

He passed through many hallways and staircases before finally exiting into the very room where Protector Ren was sipping away at a glass of wine.

"Let's go," Wang Jun said to Protector Ren, who dropped his cup in surprise. "We have a lot of work to do."

The clock in Wang Jun's office ticked away, adding pressure to Li Ming, who had just been cross-examined.

"So you're saying that he's managed to evade you seventy-two times, and that even a core-formation cultivator would have trouble doing this?" Wang Jun said. "We'll have to change our plan of attack. I want you to go on a team mission."

"With who?" Li Ming asked.

"With Hei Ling, of course," Wang Jun said. "You'll both be framing someone, and I want you to use this opportunity to dig into his real identity and his past. Can you do it?"

"I'll try my best," Li Ming said. "Many thanks for trusting me with such an important mission."

Chapter 18: Possession

A week passed by swiftly. By the time it was over, Cha Ming had laid thirty-three formations at various locations, securing much-needed allies for the Wang family and Prince Lei. Meanwhile, the king's condition improved continuously. His bodily functions stabilized, though he remained comatose. The spirit doctors were helpless until the poison was cured. Even Li Yin could do nothing more than tailor nutritional supplements that could be injected directly into his bloodstream.

"I finally get to finish what I started," Cha Ming said as he isolated himself in a cultivation room below the Jade Bamboo Auction House. He'd put off his personal cultivation for as long as possible, and there was no need to delay any longer.

His advancement to late-foundation establishment had come with the side benefit of greatly reducing the amount of time required for cultivating the Seventy-Two Transformations Technique. Since he had already completed the gold and earth bone forging, he proceeded directly to fire bone forging.

Cha Ming's brush moved fiercely as he painted one bone after another. He started with the bones in his legs and proceeded to his ribcage, his skull, and his spine. One by one, runes of fire shot into his body, overwhelming him with searing pain as the quality of his bones, tendons, and muscles were improved. His golden spine and earthen legs gained complementary red runic lines while his skull and ribs gained a third color.

After completing the rest of his body, he painted the most complex runes—the arms. While the spine's core was gold and the leg's cores were earth, his arms were aligned with fire. The violent red runes restructured his arm bones, shifting the gold and earth runes slightly to replace them as the core component. Rather than the beating of a thousand hammers, his bones felt as though they were scorched by a thousand flames. The entire process took a single day, a large improvement over the original three.

After finishing fire bone forging, Cha Ming proceeded to wood bone forging, which focused on the ribcage, where the vital organs were located. He painted the other bones on his body first, adding green runic lines to his arms, legs, and spine, while his skull gained a fourth color. Then he completed the ribcage with calm brushstrokes.

Wooden runes became the central component of his ribcage. As the last rune entered his bones, they were forged by the whipping of a thousand willows. His ribcage resembled tough, wooden runes. Like the three stages of bone forging before, the voids in his bones drank heaven and earth energy once more, increasing their gravity-manipulating abilities to five times his fist strength. His supporting muscles and ligaments also strengthened to compensate for this ability. The process was once again completed in a single day.

Finally, Cha Ming began painting the water-bone-forging runes. He first completed the remaining bones in his body before moving on to the most dangerous and painful part of bone forging—forging the skull. The runic bone structure he painted was complex and filled with lines that reached from one part of his skull to the other. Once he completed this rune, he felt the forging of a thousand gentle waves. The most painful migraine in existence caused him to almost lose consciousness as his skull fundamentally transformed into a soft blue rune.

As the forging proceeded, the power of his senses increased exponentially. His skull, though only being forged by gentle waves, felt like it was being pummelled by one tidal wave after another.

The pain only lasted half a day before his bones and joints crackled with newfound power. While he had only reached the peak of bone forging, he could display the strength of a half-step marrow-refining cultivator. The voids in his bones changed structurally once more, making it possible to increase his weight to ten times his fist strength. His supporting muscles and tendons naturally changed accordingly. Now, should he wish to do so, Cha Ming could increase his weight to one hundred thousand jin!

Three days had passed since he began the process. Only a single step remained to break into the marrow-refining realm. After adjusting his condition, Cha Ming directed his attention to the immortal-jade core in the Clear Sky World. It melted into a puddle like the rest and was rapidly absorbed by the mystical artifact. Gray runes lit up all over the white brush. He got to work quickly, painting one intricate detail after another. The amount of "ink" available for this stage of bone forging was just as much as the previous ones. However, this ink needed to be spread out across a much larger runic diagram.

He constructed the array piece by piece, bone after bone. He used the gray ink to first paint his spine. The runes were completely different than the ones he had painted previously. Instead of providing a framework, it was filled with thousands of tiny supporting runes. The same was true for the legs, the arms, the ribcage, and the skull.

Cha Ming rested every few hours to replenish his qi and resplendent force. On the first day, he'd only completed the spine. On the second day, the arms and legs. On the third day, he finished the ribcage and skull. He was covered in sweat by the time he finished the translucent gray skeleton. It was the same gray that connected his qi pathways to his Dantian and organs. Once he drew the last connecting line, the entire gray skeleton burst apart and shot into every single bone in his body. To be more precise, they shot into the voids in his bones.

There was no pain this time. After all, he'd already completely forged his skeleton. Instead, each rune he painted crawled into a void. His senses followed a gray rune inside a single void, where he saw what seemed like a small five-colored world complete with black-and-white specks. The gray rune floated to the world and gently imprinted itself on it and underwent a fundamental change.

The moment the gray rune appeared, the world in the void rapidly shrank onto a single point and exploded into a spiraling vortex. It was like the birth of a tiny runic universe that began expanding ever so slowly.

Cha Ming felt the urge to try something. He willed the vortex to shrink, and in the blink of an eye, he felt his weight lessen. He willed it to expand, and his weight increased.

He also noticed that he could shift the miniature universe's orientation. At his command, the universe retracted its energy, and he became weightless. Then he flipped its orientation and allowed a small amount of energy to leak out. To his surprise, he felt his body outside the void float upward. Thousands of voids were operating in tandem, and with but a thought, all of them retracted their energy. He became weightless once more, but this time he was floating in the air. This flotation was fundamentally different than what a foundation-establishment cultivator could accomplish with a magic treasure. Instead it resembled the flight of a core-formation cultivator.

At the same time, Cha Ming's bones lit up with a black-and-white light as the five-colored runic diagrams combined with the glowing gray runes in each universe spiral. The runes formed two cycles—one of creation and one of destruction. Pain wracked his body as his bones were tempered by destruction qi and reformed by creation qi. With each step in the forging process, his bones became increasingly milky and translucent. The destruction and creation even seeped down into his marrow. Each wave of creation and destruction lightly brushed the marrow, greatly increasing its quality.

It wasn't long before his skeleton was fully comprised of gray jade runes. They contained hints of the original elements and creation qi that forged them as well as traces of the destruction that had tempered them. Cha Ming exhaled a breath of impure air as what used to be his bones became ashes that littered the cultivation chamber's floor. His body pulsed as his heart spread the blood created by the new marrow into his body. It flowed to his muscles, organs, and skin, nourishing them and vastly improving their functions.

By the time the process was completed, two weeks had passed. Cha Ming extended his enhanced senses to the lobby just outside the Jade Bamboo Auction House and found Feng Ming waiting there while patiently cultivating.

How unusual, Cha Ming thought. *Something must be wrong.*

As he moved to go greet his friend, he noticed that not only was the room covered in dust, but even the protective formations had been damaged by his breakthrough.

"Maybe I should clean up a bit before going," he muttered.

An hour later, Cha Ming and Feng Ming were seated in a private room at the Laughing Buddha, a famous restaurant in the city. After a brief review of the menu, Cha Ming ordered multiples of each vegetable dish. His breakthrough had left him famished. As Feng Ming slowly ate away at a few of them, Cha Ming gorged himself on whatever he could lay his hands on.

"You look like you haven't eaten in a year," Feng Ming said. "Did anything happen?"

"I broke through to marrow refining just before coming to see you," Cha Ming said before continuing to another dish.

"So fast?" Feng Ming said. "How could you skip over so many subrealms? Body refining is known to be one of the most difficult and painful cultivation methods. Advancing to marrow refining should take several decades of effort—it's why grandmaster spiritual blacksmiths and core treasures are so rare."

Cha Ming shrugged. "My body-cultivation technique requires one to be a talisman master, and it also requires five jin of elemental immortal jade and one jin of immortal-jade core, prepared with special methods to dissolve them. Tell me, is it fair that I broke through so quickly or not?"

There was a price for everything, and it would be ridiculous if there were no benefits to cultivating the exclusive technique.

"Hm…" Feng Ming said. "Maybe you can help me out with something."

"What's this something, and why are you being so secretive about it?" Cha Ming said.

Feng Ming quickly explained the information Zhou Li had shared.

"Are you kidding me? You're going to trust information given by that guy? That's a terrible idea."

"But I tried tossing the note in the fire," Feng Ming said. "I know it sounds silly, but do you remember what happened at the arena? If it was a bad idea, something or another would be stopping me from doing it. I'm lucky, remember?"

Cha Ming hesitated. "Let's at least ask Wang Jun about it. He's pretty good at this kind of thing, right?"

"But he's too averse to risk," Feng Ming said. "He'll definitely try to stop us."

"When did it become 'us'?" Cha Ming said. "Besides, if he agrees, both me, Huxian, and his two friends will come along. In my humble opinion, there aren't many forces in the city that could stop us."

He rapidly finished off the remaining dish; a healthy glow had appeared on his previously pale face.

"How could we possibly lose this much money over a short period of time?" Wang Jun exclaimed. "And where did these crappy and overvalued real-estate purchase ideas come from?"

The sudden burst of energy was all he could muster. He began coughing with no end in sight.

When did my health become so poor? More to the point, there was nothing wrong with him physically according to the best doctors he could get his hands on.

"They came directly from you," Elder Bai said. "Do you truly not remember?"

"How could I remember something that didn't happen?" Wang Jun croaked. "My memory has always been photographic. You know that."

"That's why I'm so concerned," Elder Bai said. "We know you can't be cursed, and the doctors say there is nothing physically ailing you. Having known you for all these years, however, I refuse to believe there is nothing wrong with you."

"I agree with Elder Bai's assessment," Protector Ren said. "Although I can't detect a cultivator's tampering, there is definitely something amiss. Your odd behavior started as soon as you escaped the assassination attempt. We initially thought you might be an imposter, but you knew far too much for that to be the case."

Wang Jun collapsed into his chair in a dispirited manner. "Elder Bai, do you remember our conversations from before the attempt on my life?" he said.

"I took extensive notes," Elder Bai said.

"Please use these notes and your best judgment and operate the business as per our initial plans and modify accordingly," Wang Jun said bitterly. "We shouldn't lose too much money if we follow them, but neither will we gain."

Elder Bai nodded. "I'll do what I can. Please get well soon." He swiftly exited the office and began issuing a salvo of commands.

Wang Jun looked to Protector Ren. "Would you mind letting Cha Ming inside?"

Cha Ming walked into the office with a frown. "I take it things have gotten worse?" he said to Protector Ren.

"I can no longer be trusted," Wang Jun said wistfully while throwing his hands up in the air. "At least things aren't so bad with you, seeing as you broke through to the marrow-refining realm."

Cha Ming nodded. "I now have a fist strength of 43,200 jin, among other abilities. I might not be stronger than Protector Ren, but I'm at least confident in surviving his attacks."

"Body refiners are best at survival and stamina," Wang Jun said. "They also have very keen senses. Speaking of which, I take it you are aware of my issues?"

"I am," Cha Ming said. "I also have a theory. I think you might have been possessed."

"Possession?" Wang Jun mulled that over for a bit. "Yes, that could be the case. But these cases are so rare. Why would you think evil spirits are involved?"

"Because the aid I lent to the chaplain of the Church of Justice was related to evil spirits," Cha Ming said. "I covered the entire church in a grand formation that detects evil spirits, and we found multiple cases. The chaplain believes that evil spirits are causing much of the problem in Songjing."

"The Church of Justice," Wang Jun muttered. "They can't help me."

Cha Ming frowned.

"Don't get me wrong, it's not that I'm being obstinate, but their arts are extremely ineffective against me. Not only do I cultivate shadow and fate, but I have something called a Shadow Soul Constitution. I'm practically immune to most of their methods."

"Why don't we at least give it a try?" Cha Ming said. "Perhaps the chaplain will take this case seriously in the hopes of converting a heathen."

Wang Jun chuckled wryly. "Yes, I'm sure he'll see it that way."

"So the heathen finally shows his face within these blessed halls," the chaplain said with a satisfied smile. "What can I do for you today, Second Young Master Wang?"

The pale-faced Wang Jun was sitting uncomfortably in a wooden chair.

"My friend seems to be afflicted by—" Cha Ming started.

"I want to hear it from him," the chaplain cut in. "Only he can ask for his own salvation."

Cha Ming facepalmed inwardly. It was exactly as they'd predicted.

"I'm not asking for salvation, I'm just here for an evaluation and potential treatment," Wang Jun said. "We suspect that I've been possessed by an evil spirit. However, the light-based grand formation you've set up seems to have detected nothing. I'm only speaking with you as a formality."

"You are a heretic by birth, not by choice," the chaplain said with a compassionate tone. "Therefore, I can forgive your obstinate viewpoint. As for the failure of the formation... Well, this is your unique constitution's fault. However, Heaven never seals off all exits."

He walked over to a simple cupboard in his office and withdrew a golden box. He opened the box and revealed a pill that glowed brightly with the warmest and most consoling light Cha Ming had ever seen.

"This pill is reserved for emergency situations," the chaplain said. "Some vile means are able to resist an inquisitor's powers of light. This pill completely negates any resistance to light a person has for a full twenty-four hours. It is only effective if willingly ingested.

"This is an important core-protection treasure reserved for chaplains. If I use this on you, I put my life and the lives of my believers at risk. Therefore, I can only trade it for other means which will increase the church's ability to protect the people in the upcoming conflict."

"I hardly see how this petty royal struggle will affect the great Church of Justice," Wang Jun remarked snidely.

"You know nothing," the chaplain said. "The conflict I am speaking of is much greater than the tiny Song Kingdom. Regardless of whether you understand why, I want 10,000 high-grade spirit stones in mortal-grade weapons and alchemical products and 100,000 high-grade spirit stones in magic-grade weapons and alchemical products. If you can't produce it right away, I want a certificate of obligation issued on behalf of the Wang family."

"That's absurd," Wang Jun said. "What are my other options?"

"You can find a powerful Buddhist monk," the chaplain said. "One of the three masters will do the trick, and they'll have a much easier time acting than I will. I can handle a simple possession, but if it's something else… I might not be able to do more than help you for a single day."

"Give me a moment," Wang Jun said. He withdrew his core-transmission jade and sent a message to an imprint Cha Ming couldn't see. Then a shadow appeared above the globe. It was a man or woman with completely obscured features. The words they spoke were completely distorted. Even the chaplain could do nothing but frown as the conversation continued.

Finally, Wang Jun put away the globe. "It's no use," he said. "It would take at least a month and a half to secure the Violet Wind Master's aid, and that's only if nothing more important crops up. I can't wait that long." He turned to Chaplain Chen. "You say that even your best efforts might not be able to buy me more than a day?"

The man nodded.

"It's still worth it. I can make new plans in that period of time. Cha Ming, would you mind giving me a loan?"

Cha Ming smiled and tossed a bag containing many of the weapons, talismans, and pills he'd bought in Quicksilver. He'd already given a portion of them to Wang Jun, but the market hadn't been able to absorb this remaining amount."

"Excellent!" the chaplain said. He flicked his sleeve and willed the pill into Wang Jun's hands. "Consume this pill, and we can begin straightaway."

Wang Jun ate the pill without any hesitation. As it wormed its way into his stomach, his body began to glow like a lantern from the inside. Meanwhile, the golden light suffused the entire room. It complemented the light of the grand formation and revealed a crimson cloud surrounding Wang Jun.

"It's not a possession," the chaplain said. "It's a haunting."

"What's the difference?" Cha Ming asked.

"A haunting does not directly invade the owner's body," the chaplain said. "Rather, it bewitches their mind. It will affect their mental health and constantly subject them to illusions. It's something rarely seen in the cultivation world, and I only know about it because of the sacred writings of our church."

"Can you do anything about it?" Wang Jun asked worriedly.

"I can only restrain them for as long as the pill's effects last. You'll be able to function in a mostly normal capacity for a duration of twenty-four hours. This is the best I can do for you because of your unique constitution. Evil spirits are like diseases—if they aren't destroyed, they will build an immunity to whatever ails them."

Wang Jun nodded. He was prepared for this answer.

"I think we may have even lost out on this deal," Chaplain Chen said. "Our specialty is in supressing darkness, curses, and devils. Evil spirits are difficult for us and require a tremendous amount of our accumulated faith power. Now, please follow me to the center of the church."

They followed the chaplain to the main prayer area, where the exorcism circle was still active. The pastors ushered the curious parishioners outside, while the chaplain sent out commands for the inquisitors to gather.

"Everyone," the chaplain said, "we are gathered here today to bind the evil spirits ailing this heathen. While he might be born of darkness, he has donated sufficiently to our cause to show his support and understanding. Please take your positions."

Their twelve most powerful members, peak-foundation-establishment inquisitors, assumed the twelve most important positions, while eight dozen other inquisitors took supplementary positions. Cha Ming wasn't even aware that they had so many forces at their disposal. Had they received reinforcements?

Chaplain Chen began reading from an ancient golden book. "And the Holy Mother did say, abandon not the children of the shadows, for they are cave dwellers who have not seen the light of day. However, forgive not devils and the unseen, for they have abandoned all righteousness and goodwill. They are a scourge upon this world, which should be uprooted at every opportunity.

"And if uprooting is ineffective, do not abandon hope. Bind them in shackles of light, lest they cause greater mischief if left unattended."

Countless light runes began circling around the chaplain as he chanted. Motes of light burst out from the 108 inquisitors. Each of them paled as the light left them; it was clear that the price they paid wasn't small. The chaplain's inner glow also diminished.

"Oh, Holy Mother, please lend us your aid. Transform these runes of faith into holy shackles," the chaplain intoned.

The motes of light manifested into runes, which linked together into chains. "Bind these evil spirits with your holy presence, lest they ravage your flock. We entrust this matter to you in humble appreciation of your power." The golden chain glowed brightly before shooting out toward the crimson spirits hovering over Wang Jun and wrapping them together in a tight bundle. It hovered near him and turned invisible.

"Many thanks for your help, my brothers in the light," the chaplain said.

"Our duty is to serve!" the inquisitors said before dispersing.

"I suggest you get your affairs in order before your affliction returns," the weak-looking chaplain said before leaving them near the thrumming formation.

Chapter 19: Corruption

Feng Ming took a deep breath as he launched himself off a rooftop, his spear bearing down on a late-foundation-establishment expert. The man didn't know what hit him. It took a split second for his life to end as the butt of Feng Ming's spear crashed into the back of his neck. The newly promoted general proceeded to strip the man and confiscate his bag of holding.

He easily broke the spirit mark on the storage device and scoured the man's possessions. It wasn't long before he detected an ominous black card bearing the word "invitation." Luckily, this man had hidden it in an easy-to-find location. After securing it, he donned the man's black garb and doupeng, which happened to be his size. The last one he'd killed had morphed into his devil form upon death, destroying the uniform clothes these "customers" seemed to wear.

A hot wind blew over Feng Ming's obscured features as he made his way to the Honey Badger Inn. Like many of the figures he'd seen, he approached it without making a sound. The bar was empty save for two customers. Like the ones before him, he silently placed his card on the bar, prompting the bartender to pull a hidden lever. A carefully hidden flight of stairs opened to the basement.

The spiral staircase traveled fifty feet down before splitting up into several corridors, where a beautiful lady wearing black metal collar greeted him with a smile. "Right this way, esteemed lord," she said.

They walked straight through the intersection into a wide-open hall, where many figures were already seated. Like him, they also wore black garb and doupengs to obscure their features. They didn't speak or make a sound, which was curious given the voice-concealing features of their magical garb. Feng Ming took the opportunity to spread his resplendent force into the adjacent hallways. He spotted several guards, servants, and prisoners—information he rapidly relayed to Cha Ming.

"If sir could please leave the hundred high-grade-spirit-stone deposit, I will give you your bidding paddle," the servant said.

Feng Ming grunted and placed the deposit he'd pillaged onto a silver platter she held out. He then retrieved the black paddle with the number "77," his lucky number, and took a seat beside a tall cultivator.

As a formality, Feng Ming attempted to a relay a message outside to Cha Ming, but to no avail. It seemed that his communication earlier had hit a "sweet spot" in the dampening formation.

Well, he thought, *at least they won't be able to communicate with each other. I hope.*

A figure walked onto the stage as Feng Ming took a seat. "Welcome, lords and ladies to the thirty-seventh biannual auction," the figure said in a raspy voice. "Today, we offer premium goods in preparation for the upcoming struggle in the capital. Make sure you don't miss out; failure in this mission will cost you your life and soul. First up today is a devil-barb anemone, perfect for crafting devilish infusion pills. The bidding starts at ten high-grade spirit stones."

A flurry of rough, scratchy voices laid down one bid after another before the item finally sold at thirty high-grade spirit stones.

"The second item, ten mid-grade Sin Crystals," the figure intoned. "Ideal for condensing your initial devilish form or upgrading it to foundation-establishment level." Sin Crystals, devilish pills, and devilish-cultivation manuals were snapped up one after another.

"This item is called a karmic-enhancement flower," the

auctioneer said as he procured a crystal globe containing a jade-and-ochre-colored flower.

Feng Ming's fingers itched with an urge to grab it.

"It is especially difficult to procure because it benefits both sin-based and merit-based cultivators. The starting price is ten thousand high-grade spirit stones."

"Eleven thousand!" a voice shouted.

"Thirteen thousand!" another shouted.

The bidding continued before finally stabilizing at 17,000. "Nineteen thousand!" Feng Ming shouted.

"Twenty thousand!" a new voice joined in.

"Twenty-five thousand!" Feng Ming yelled. Since the arena incident, he was practically swimming in money.

"Sold!" the auctioneer yelled after three breaths passed. The crystal ball floated to Feng Ming's seat. It was quickly followed by a collared servant that walked out with a tray. He placed his bid of twenty-five thousand high-grade spirit stones onto the tray and stowed the crystal ball into his bag of holding.

"The next item is one that my master personally refined with the anguish of ten thousand souls," the auctioneer said.

A black flag oozing a malevolent aura appeared on stage. Feng Ming was utterly repulsed by the item. He knew, however, that this was just the beginning. He clenched his teeth as he watched the auction unfold and waited for Cha Ming's signal.

"Finally, one who actually kept his invitation somewhere I could find it," Cha Ming said. He wasn't upset at having to kill and loot fifteen not-so-innocent people to secure it, but time was of the essence. He rapidly imitated the man's appearance and shifted his clothes to match the black garb everyone wore. Then he entered the bar and descended the spiraling staircase.

Right before reaching the bottom, he spotted a shadow just outside a torch's illumination.

It's your turn, Huxian, he sent mentally. Fortunately, their bond could not be disrupted by a petty dampening formation. He wreathed himself in shadows and followed Huxian into the thin world that ran along the hallway.

We need to be quick, Huxian said. *This is very draining. I can give you can hour at most.*

An hour's all I need, Cha Ming said. He jumped between the sparse islands of shadow separated by a sea of bright light and found what he was looking for: thirty-six obscured locations in the outer ring where the guards and servants walked. He rapidly threw down pairs of formations—the first was a least-grade obscuring formation, which was there for the sole purpose of hiding the second ice-based formation. Then he hopped over to the other thirty-five spots and placed down similar formations.

How long do we have left? Cha Ming said after placing the last flag.

A half hour, Huxian replied.

Cha Ming quickened his pace. He traveled through the shadows to the inner hall, where the auction was proceeding. In the shadow world, he could only make out partial conversations at best. He carefully avoided the senses of the many cultivators and laid down another thirty-six formation eyes. Many of them had even been erected right beside a foundation-establishment cultivator's foot!

Get out quick! Huxian yelled.

Cha Ming immediately hopped out of the shadows where he'd entered at the foot of the stairwell as Huxian ran out of energy. Then he activated a formation he'd carefully placed near Feng Ming's foot. Chaos would ensue shortly.

Feng Ming waited nervously as the auction proceeded. It was one thing to kill a few people, but it was an entirely different thing to catch a crowd in an inescapable dragnet. For this, they needed a distraction.

Maybe I should eat that weird flower for now, he thought. Under the curious gazes of the surrounding cultivators, he withdrew the crystal globe from his robes and shattered it. A wonderful fragrance wafted out to them, causing them to twitch nervously. Feng Ming wasn't sure if it was fear of the unknown or fear of the ten core-formation cultivators outside that kept them in check.

Ignoring their greedy looks, he popped the delicate ochre-and-jade flower into his mouth. It immediately dissolved and bypassed his body, entering his soul directly. As it did, he instinctively became aware of the function of the flower—to increase merit by twenty-five percent. For most people, this would be a piddling amount, but for Feng Ming, it was an enormous quantity. His soul was immediately surrounded by a thick jade glow, which immediately began syphoning toward his resplendent vestment. Soon, a jade rune just like the first appeared on the white garment.

Feng Ming's cultivation automatically began evolving. The qi of heaven and earth rushed toward his body unbidden as it caused his core to increase in diameter. It grew rapidly until it reached a bottleneck at one and a half times its original size.

But to his surprise, it didn't stop there. The jade glow, which had previously formed a second rune, had also condensed into a third rune. As soon as this happened, Feng Ming's Dantian let out a soft pop as it expanded to double its initial size, propelling him to early core formation.

Feng Ming's breakthrough naturally didn't go unnoticed. At first, the auctioneer was slightly annoyed that the winner of the flower had taken it out, arousing the envy of nearby cultivators. Once the current auction was completed, he walked over to a nearby guard and instructed him to pass on a message to the first through third protectors. They were to evict the man immediately, before any chaos broke out in the auction hall.

He then continued with the auction. Unfortunately, things didn't go as smoothly as expected. In the middle of a fierce bout of bidding, the heaven and earth qi in the room suddenly rushed over to the man who had taken out the flower. Who would have thought that someone could immediately break through just by consuming the flower?

He immediately halted the auction. "Everyone, please bear with me for a moment. First through ninth protectors, seize that man. I sense merit glow on him."

This was, of course, pure nonsense. He just didn't have a legitimate reason to kick the man out, so he made one up on the spot.

Nine core-formation cultivators rushed into the room. Including himself, there were ten core-formation cultivators overseeing the auction. It wasn't a large force by any means, but rather the minimum allowable for any traveling auction house in their organization.

The nine black-cloaked protectors very cautiously approached the man who was breaking through. They brandished their weapons, approaching him with a set of black chains.

But why would he break through now, of all times? the auctioneer wondered. *Isn't that just suicide? Unless... could it be a distraction?*

The auctioneer directed his resplendent force to the entrance of the hall and found it was obstructed. He pushed against the obstruction aggressively until it shattered. To his surprise, he saw a large blue circle containing ten thousand high-grade spirit stones, which were rapidly being ground to dust.

"Everyone, attack the man at the entrance, or we're all dead!" the auctioneer suddenly shouted. He pushed open the large black doors leading into the hall, revealing a blue-robed man and three small animals. The man held a pillarlike staff; he stood guard in front of the blue formation. Its energy was rapidly feeding a grid on the floor.

The blue lines were so cold that white frost covered the floor beside them.

The nine protectors immediately pounced toward the door while the other cultivators were finally coming to grips with the situation.

"I said everyone!" the infuriated auctioneer yelled. The chaotic mass of customers immediately regained their composure and assumed battle positions against the blue-robed man.

Earlier, Cha Ming had seen three of the core-formation cultivators patrolling the outside perimeter rushing into the hall. It was less than expected, but he'd have to make do. To his surprise, however, the energies of heaven and earth in his surroundings suddenly thinned and rushed to the auction hall. The six remaining protectors rushed in as well.

I have no idea what he's doing, but it's working, Cha Ming thought. He threw out thirty-six flags and rapidly painted the complex lines of a Water-Gathering Formation. It was a formation he'd grown very comfortable with in his time in Songjing.

Sixty breaths later, the formation thrummed to life. He then painted a few dozen more lines, connecting the energy-gathering formation to a nearby formation eye. He tossed out ten thousand high-grade spirit stones onto the sacrificial formation. They began crumbling to dust as their energy was rapidly converted to the purest water energy that then seeped into rapidly growing runic lines.

Cha Ming took a deep breath and summoned Huxian and his two friends. The floor crumbled as he increased his weight to a phenomenal 400,000 jin, and he increased the Clear Sky Staff's diameter to two feet and its length to twenty-four feet. Its weight grew to 40,000 jin, which was slightly lower than his fist strength.

Shortly after, the black doors to the auction hall burst open, revealing the auctioneer, nine protectors, and hundreds of enraged cultivators. To his surprise, they ignored Feng Ming, who was calmly breaking through in the center of the room.

"That lucky bastard," Cha Ming muttered as he braced himself for the onslaught.

"Go tie a few of them up," Cha Ming said to Huxian and his friends. "I'll handle whoever gets through."

"You got it, bro," Huxian said as he split into two and executed his familiar style. A domain of white light expanded from the white fox and began eroding the many cultivators in the auction hall. Unsurprisingly, the light's purifying powers affected some more than others. Many of them roared as they changed shapes to their devilish forms in a futile attempt to ward off the light's powers.

Silverwing let out a piercing cry as he flew out toward two of the nine protectors. His silver wing strikes forced them to direct all their attention on defending. Meanwhile, Lei Jiang burst out with frightening power. Lightning was the bane of evil creatures, and the nine protectors were just that. They transformed to fight off the iridescent lightning and finally supressed Lei Jiang with two of their members.

"Shoot everything you have at the man with the pillar!" one of the protectors shouted. He raised his sword and accumulated core-formation qi into a malevolent flame. The four others followed suit, activating the black runes on their bodies to push their power up to early core formation. The two hundred cultivators behind them also charged up various attacks.

Seeing that only half of the grand formation was active, Cha Ming activated two mid-grade ice-shield combat formations. Then he activated a Hardening Talisman and three Myriad Ice Shield Talismans he'd purchased from Luo Ming before swatting at them with what he now called the Clear Sky Pillar.

Fire and ice burned his body simultaneously as techniques breached his defenses. Metal cut his skin and earthen spikes bruised his muscles as they bypassed the large staff and hammered into him. His strong body ripped away any vines that managed to sneak in and wrap around his arms and legs. The pillar continued through the barrage of blows unimpeded and smashed into two of the core-formation cultivators. The lead cultivator's body wasn't weak, so he managed to survive the blow with only a little damage to his internals. The one on his right, however, wasn't so lucky; he was mostly a qi cultivator that dabbled in devil arts, so he was reduced to nothing more than a meat patty.

Seventy-five percent of the formation was activated by the time the wave of blows came to an end. Many gouges and burns on Cha Ming's body were healing rapidly. His marrow worked double time to replenish the flesh and blood required for regeneration.

"One last wave," the lead cultivator yelled. "We almost have him!"

Cha Ming gritted his teeth as he prepared to defend against their last stand. His strength was bolstered by what he'd seen as he toured the underground facility—hundreds of trained slaves, to be used as vitality farms, soul farms, and cultivation furnaces by the cultivators who purchased them. What these people did was an abomination, and only by killing them here and now could he stop them from performing more of these atrocities.

Chapter 20: Anonymous

Feng Ming awoke to a scene of chaos. A blue formation was rapidly forming behind Cha Ming as a mass of cultivators began attacking him in tandem. Huxian, Lei Jiang, and Silverwing had flown out to supress some of the core-formation cultivators and divert some attention from Cha Ming.

Why did they start fighting without me? he thought, only to realize that in retrospect, breaking through in the middle of a covert auction would definitely attract some attention. He sighed inwardly and projected his lucky aura to his companions. The attacks against Cha Ming clustered together at the last second, and his pillar smashed down and fortunately knocked most of them out from the air. Wounds still covered his body from head to toe, but he'd seen Cha Ming in worse shape.

Meanwhile, Silverwing's attacks began finding timely gaps in his opponent's defenses, while their counterattacks kept striking his thickest feathers. As for Lei Jiang, the random lightning bolts surrounding him seemed to grow a sense of purpose; they bypassed his opponents' defenses while residual sparks landed on large numbers of unfortunate cultivators.

Seeing that everything was under control, Feng Ming focused his attention on the only person who wasn't accounted for—the auctioneer. The man stood calmly, waiting for Feng Ming to attack him.

"Why didn't you kill me when I was cultivating?" Feng Ming said.

"What? And incur the wrath of heaven and get struck by a lightning bolt?" the auctioneer said sarcastically. "I recognize those four. It doesn't take a genius to figure out who you are. I wouldn't be caught dead tangling with you."

"You make a lot of sense, but I don't think you have any choice in the matter," Feng Ming said. He summoned his lucky spear and activated his Fire General's Steps. His movements were rapid and crisp, ideal for generating power in his spear strikes.

The auctioneer grunted and threw out sixteen sabers, which collided against Feng Ming's spear while the man himself stepped backward. Feng Ming could tell he was a middle-core-formation cultivator, so he was perplexed to see him retreat. The auctioneer withdrew a slip of paper from his robes and poured qi inside it. The man yelped as he dropped the talisman, which burst into a spatial crack.

"Really?" the man yelled. "A defective talisman? I even made this one myself. The odds aren't even one in a million, when most talismans won't even form with defects. This is exactly why I didn't attack you earlier!"

The man sent out another sixteen blades to complement those already attacking Feng Ming. They gathered together in a hasty formation, which was promptly pried apart by Feng Ming's lucky spear. The auctioneer took out one more talisman. This time, the runes seemed to activate properly. However, the man threw it out at the last second, and an even greater spatial crack appeared.

"Third time's the charm," the overly talkative auctioneer said. He took out a small core treasure, a brooch that formed a golden shield. It deflected Feng Ming's spear just in time for him to activate the third talisman. This time the man disappeared without a trace. Moments later, the grand formation activated.

"What terrible luck," Feng Ming muttered. Unbeknownst to

him, the auctioneer lost an arm in the teleportation process and said those exact same words.

"I never realized just how potent this luck thing can be," Cha Ming said as he batted away a fourth salvo of joint attacks. Somehow, his formation malfunctioned in just the right way, and the additional burst of energy boosted the completion from ninety-four percent to ninety-nine percent. Then, the Icy Hell Grand Formation glowed light blue. Shards of ice materialized on the edges of the circular shield, which blocked off any escape routes. This included the circular corridor—Cha Ming controlled the delicate shards to incapacitate the servants and lesser guards in the perimeter. Then, he methodically impaled one evil cultivator after another.

His opponents' movements became sluggish. With the support of the Icy Hell Grand Formation and Huxian's dual suppression, they quickly gained the upper hand. Cha Ming's Devil-Sealing Intent was mixed in with the icy formation; some of the weaker devils even perished before the shards of ice touched them.

A single slap of the Clear Sky Pillar caused dozens of men and women to perish. A single flap of Silverwing's wings decapitated a core-formation cultivator. The battle was sealed once Feng Ming joined in. His blazing spear joined wind and lightning, light and darkness, and ice and staff to put an end to the evil cultivators. An incense time later, every man and woman who had participated in the auction was dead.

"What should we do with the bodies?" Feng Ming said as he unmasked one person after another. He recognized many of them— they were from the upper echelons of society, most of them part of the crown prince's faction. Meanwhile, Huxian, Lei Jiang, and Silverwing were busy looting the corpses. After all, beast meat and medicinal ingredients were expensive, and beast monarchs had their pride.

"The bodies of those who've undergone a devilish transformation have disappeared," Cha Ming said. "As for the others… I have an idea." He explained his thoughts to Feng Ming.

"It's not that I'm against being anonymous, but how am I going to get kicked out of the city if they don't pin my name on this?" Feng Ming asked.

"You said one of them escaped?" Cha Ming asked, and Feng Ming nodded. "Then they'll know. If you take credit for this, Prince Tian won't be able to justify driving you out. It would look far too suspicious to chase you away after you've accomplished such meritorious achievements."

Feng Ming's mood brightened. "Who said Brother Jun was the only one with a head on their shoulders? Do you think we could tip the crown prince off while we're at it?"

Cha Ming nodded. "That we can."

Marshal Feng woke up at dawn like he always did. Although he was a core-formation cultivator who didn't require sleep, he felt it had some psychological benefits. As a man with substantial military achievements, he didn't have to argue against anyone about this quirk of his.

A soft knock sounded on his door as he ritually groomed his healthy beard. "Come in," he said.

His assistant, General Tang, saluted as he entered and waited beside the marshal until he finished. He was used to the marshal's morning ritual and knew full well that the man didn't like to be interrupted.

"You don't usually come see me so early in the morning unless something important has happened," Marshal Feng said. "What is it this time?"

"Reporting to the marshal: A dome of darkness was discovered surrounding a small place called the Honey Badger Inn this morning," General Tang said. "The dome is a full hundred feet in diameter."

Marshal Feng maintained his composure as he walked over to a small table near the door, where a light breakfast had been left for him. He calmly sat down and had a cup of his favorite tea before continuing their conversation. "Have you sent anyone inside for reconnaissance? And has the Church of Justice dispatched any troops?"

"We haven't been able to breach the darkness, and neither have they," General Tang said. "We thought it was a formation, but no flags, focuses, or sigils have been detected. Therefore, we speculate that it is a technique."

"A domainlike technique..." Marshal Feng said. "Very well, let's take a look." He donned his black-and-gold cape and flew outside his window, his resplendent force carrying General Tang alongside him. As they traveled, he sent his resplendent force out to probe the disturbance. To his surprise, however, it was devoured as soon as it made contact.

The dome vanished as he landed. In its place was a razed building, a pile of corpses, and several hundred unconscious men and women tied up with hempen ropes. Marshal Feng floated down to the corpses where he found a note stuck to a wall with a mortal-grade dagger. They flew to his hand, and as he read it, a smile appeared on his lips. The note read as follows:

Dear Marshal Feng,

This band of evildoers was found frequenting an establishment that bought and sold slaves. According to the laws of the kingdom, this is a capital offense. We have gone through the trouble of executing these criminals.

Please report this matter to the crown prince at your earliest convenience. I am sure this news will lighten the load

on his heavy heart.
Sincerely yours,
Anonymous

"Silly," he muttered as the note burst into flames. "If you want to be anonymous, at least hide your handwriting a little."

"This has a huge impact on our plans," Prince Tian said to Zhou Li.

They were both sitting in his guest chambers drinking wine. The large room was spartan, containing only two couches, a fireplace, and a small table. No paintings adorned the walls, and the curtains and rugs were plain but durable. While the crown prince was austere and hard on his subordinates, he was twice as hard on himself.

"We'll have to go with the backup plan, then," Zhou Li said. "It'll be messy, but I have confidence that we can unite the kingdom starting from the capital." He grimaced as he drank the inexpensive wine in his cup. The prince's austerity didn't merely extend to his decorations.

"There are too many variables," Prince Tian said. "Most importantly, that Feng Ming's luck is ungodly. How the hell did he even find the auction in the first place?"

"That is why I told you to send him out of the city," Zhou Li said. "If he stays, your forces won't even be able to put up a fight. Who knows what will happen—maybe they'll contract the plague the night before a decisive battle."

"And what about his friend, this Du Cha Ming," Prince Tian said. "It seems to me like he and his three beast companions did most of the heavy lifting."

"I have a plan to get them outside the city as well," Zhou Li replied. "Your coup won't work without both of them gone."

"Fine," Prince Tian said. "I'll find a way to relocate General Feng."

"I do have some good news, however," Zhou Li said. "Our

PATRICK G. LAPLANTE

efforts against Wang Jun are bearing fruit. This will remove the last remaining shred of uncertainty from the equation. The succession will proceed as planned."

The crown prince walked toward the window and gazed at Central Square, where the Jade Bamboo Auction House was located. Despite the late hour, it was still bustling with activity. "Just why do you pay so much attention to him? Have you ever wondered if your actions are having the opposite effect?"

"Wang Jun is inscrutable, and I'd rather remove him from the equation," Zhou Li said. "Although he is not like Cha Ming, my inability to read him concerns me. We at the Southern Alliance are trying to change the destiny of the realm. The plane's will won't sit back and relax while we go about our business."

Prince Tian sighed. "If only we weren't located in such a strategic location. Then our kingdom wouldn't have to bear the brunt of the suffering that's about to unfold."

"People can wish all they like, but they can only play with the hand they're dealt," Zhou Li said. "I've been dealt a poor hand for more lifetimes than I can remember."

A soft knock interrupted their conversation. "What is it?" Prince Tian asked.

"Your Highness, Marshal Feng has come to report important events that have transpired this morning," his guard said.

Prince Tian signaled for Zhou Li to disappear through his secret entrance before replying. "Let him in," Prince Tian said. Marshal Feng walked in with a pleased expression. "What happened?" Prince Tian asked.

"A large devilish cult was located inside the city, and their members were executed by vigilantes," Marshal Feng replied.

The crown prince's heart clenched. "That's great news," he said with a smile. "Did they leave a name?"

"It was anonymous," Marshal Feng said. "At first I was unconvinced, but all was made clear once we questioned the slaves that were freed. That is, the ones who didn't immediately commit suicide."

"Regardless, we owe this hero a favor," Prince Tian said. "On an

– 223 –

entirely unrelated note, I was wondering if I could ask *you* a favor."

"Of course, my liege," Marshal Feng said. "What can I do for you?"

"Your son, Feng Ming," Prince Tian said. "His ungodly luck is a huge asset that shouldn't be wasted. I was wondering if we could mobilize him to aid Marshal Yong in the south."

Marshal Feng frowned. "You promised he could stay here in the capital, where it's safe. You know full well how dangerous it is out there."

"But it's like he has a guardian angel protecting him," the prince pleaded. "You know how difficult it is to find good men, and your son happens to be one of them." He softened his voice when he noticed the marshal clenching his fists. "I know it's difficult for you—he's your only son. I'll tell you what, he can report directly to Marshal Yong, who requested his help recently. You're both old friends—surely you can trust him to keep your son safe?"

Marshal Feng hesitated for a moment before nodding. "Very well. I'll talk to Marshal Yong to confirm the arrangements."

"Then it's settled," Prince Tian said. "Are you still free this afternoon for our weekly meeting?"

"Of course," Marshal Feng replied.

Sending my son away as soon as he destroys a bunch of devil worshippers. Do you take me for a fool? Feng Chuan thought. *This is the last straw. You think I'm upset, but I'm happy my son is being sent outside of this devil-infested hellhole.*

He'd thought that the crown prince would win an easy victory. He knew now that he'd placed too much confidence in the normally competent man. Although his military advantage was large, his finances were in shambles. And with his strong reaction to the death of those devil worshippers, he finally figured out where all the mystery money in the prince's accounts had been coming from.

Since he's lost his finances, it's only a matter of time until he starts the war preemptively, Feng Chuan thought. *Otherwise his brother will continue to grow stronger.*

He sighed. He predicted it would happen within a month.

Interlude:
Of Mice and Men

Huxian was in his element. He slithered skillfully through the shadows of the Shen family compound, carefully avoiding the many guards that now patrolled its tall and sturdy walls. He knew they couldn't find him even if he told them where he was, but he still liked making a game of it. Sometimes, he would scurry past their legs. At other times, he would slightly nip their arms, making them scream out in pain out of nowhere, sparking a search for ghosts or other such creatures. He snickered as he watched the pitiful fools guarding their pitiful dwelling, or what was left of it.

After traveling through a crack in the wall, he ate his way to one of the few remaining geomantic cores. He carefully peeled away the rocky outer shell and slurped out the purest formation power. It might not be the most delicious one he'd tasted, but it was a cut above most. The key was to eat it in the appropriate fashion; consuming it with the coarse outer shell would leave a bitter aftertaste.

He shook as the last vestiges of stability left the wall he occupied. As the wall fell, he ate his way down a few floors to a network of tunnels where Lei Jiang was hard at work, gnawing away at the building's crumbling foundation.

"How many more tons of demon-bone concrete do you need to eat before your breakthrough?" Huxian asked.

"It's hard to say," Lei Jiang said between mouthfuls. "At least a thousand, but it could be as much as ten thousand. Most of what I eat ends up going to waste. All I'm doing is sifting through the debris to find the delicious pieces of demon bone."

"So *that's* why you're eating it," Huxian said. "And here I thought you were just being a glutton. That's good thinking on your part. You'll be able to break through to core formation very soon this way."

"How about you, boss?" Lei Jiang asked. "When will you be breaking through to core formation?"

"I'm in no rush," Huxian said as he took a casual bite out of the concrete. He spat it out immediately. "I want to wait until Cha Ming does. Although he should survive with his strong body, I don't want to take any risks this time."

"Smart," Lei Jiang said. "That's why you're the boss." The ground suddenly quaked when he took a bite that shattered a structural pillar. "Looks likes it's time to run."

"Let's do it," Huxian yelled. His fur suddenly glowed with black-and-white runes that condensed into a suit of armor. He and Lei Jiang tore through space before arriving in the sewers right below their next target. "This battle armor I had Cha Ming paint for us is awesome! We can sneak anywhere we want, and it'll reduce the damage we take in battle by quite a bit."

Lei Jiang zipped past him. He was a blur of black, white, and purple. "It also doubles our speed. How did you come up with this great idea?"

"It was my ancestor's brother who invented it," Huxian sighed. "He was an unparalleled formation master and talisman artist."

"Do you think he's still alive?" Lei Jiang asked as he began his assault on the structural pillars of the Sima family.

"I don't know," Huxian said. "My ancestor spun off these memories aeons ago when he had his first child. The trail ends there. The only way to find out is to attain immortality. He could be anywhere in the higher realms."

"What was his brother's name?" Lei Jiang asked.

"I'm not sure," Huxian said. "All I know is that he created the bagua. Before my ancestor met him, he was a normal many-tailed fox. He feared the heavens, which resented his existence. Then the man who became his brother asked him a question that changed his life: If the heavens resent you, why not fight them? Why live under the painter's rules when we can make our own?

"The bagua lineage began that day. We would no longer seek to sprout the ninth tail that would spell our demise. Instead we would search for something greater. A bagua fox will only sprout eight tails before he begins his search for perfection. He will remain this way until he finds it.

"What a deep story," Lei Jiang said. "My father once shared a story with me, and I've never told it to anyone. I think it's time I shared it."

"What's that?" Huxian said. "Is it some inherited wisdom for ages past? A forbidden legacy?"

"It's something he perfected on his own," Lei Jiang said solemnly. "Listen carefully as I share with you the perfect way to eat a geomantic boa's egg."

Chapter 21: Winds of Change

Cha Ming stood atop the Jade Bamboo Auction House's roof and watched his friend exit the city with a team of a hundred soldiers. He wasn't sure why, but he saw Feng Ming's departure as a turning point in the struggle for the crown. The Lucky General wasn't one to stand idle when he was needed somewhere, so there must surely be a reason he wanted to leave.

"At least he knows what to do," Cha Ming muttered. With the slaughtering formations in place, he didn't have much left to do but craft talismans in a feeble attempt to restabilize his foundation. Sometimes he would go teach Feng Huoshan's many students.

"Big brother, what are you thinking about?" Huxian said. He appeared beside the cross-legged Cha Ming and rubbed his muzzle against his elbow.

"It's just too strange," Cha Ming said. "The devils in the city make sense, and so does the king's poisoning. But what is it with the evil spirits? And why is Zhou Li playing both sides? He just purposefully decimated his own forces without batting an eyelash. I can't help but think that he *wants* a civil war in the kingdom, rather than the crown prince's victory."

"Isn't he a pretty despicable person?" Huxian said. "Isn't wanting many people to die only natural for someone like him?"

Cha Ming shook his head. "People do things for a reason.

Even the most atrocious devil would usually have a motive for the trouble he causes. Living beings are ultimately rational, even the psychopathic ones."

"So you're saying he's benefitting from all this chaos?" Huxian said.

"Yes, Zhou Li is a very rational person," Cha Ming said. "He's benefitting some way or another. I suspect that even Wang Jun's haunting was orchestrated by him and that evil spirits and devils are working together in this plan of his."

"What can we do, then?" Huxian said.

"We can only prepare," Cha Ming said. "I'll focus on making talismans and studying formations. In the meantime, let me know if there's anything else like the battle armor you want me to make."

"There is one thing," Huxian said. "You should know that I can break through at any time. The next tribulation is the Swamp Tribulation."

The colors on his fur faded, and he produced a small pill-like object. Cha Ming popped it in his mouth and became enlightened on a special technique—Swamp Tribulation Totem. They could be used on any creature, man or beast.

"I've been waiting until you broke through," Huxian said. "Lei Jiang is strong, so he shouldn't have any problems. You, on the other hand... Well, I don't want to take any chances like last time. But it's better to be prepared, and these totem markings can reduce the strength of the tribulation by thirty percent."

Cha Ming's heart warmed at the consideration. "I didn't know you've been putting off your advancement. Give me a week, and I'll definitely master these markings and make one for each of us."

A man was walking calmly on his way to Songjing. He had a young face, and his long black hair was covered in thin streaks of white.

As he walked, all of creation made way for him. Birds flew away, and rodents jumped; even the earthworms struggled to create some distance between them.

Despite their struggles, the man didn't harm them. Instead he spent his time enjoying the familiar scenery. "Songjing, how I have missed you," Zhou Bei said. He passed by a familiar stream, where he used to fish before his constitution was activated. He passed a peach orchard that used to produce fruit before he'd accidentally laid waste to the land. It was also where a single unmarked grave was kept. His late wife was buried there. She was the reason why he'd rebelled against the family in the first place.

"Zhou Fan, why are you here?" he said as he stared at the patch of grass beside the largest peach tree. A pale, black-robed young man with red pupils matching his own walked out.

"I think you have me mistaken for someone else, Ancestor Bei," the young man said. "My name is Zhou Li, a member of the younger generation."

Zhou Bei shook his head. "I'd recognize you anywhere. Back then, you were the one who convinced me to have the Zhou Clan defect to the Southern Alliance. And although I finally realized my foolishness with her death, the damage was already done. When I tried to expose the family, you framed me as a traitor and had me chased out of the kingdom. Regardless, you shouldn't be here, seeing that I killed you."

"This junior is fortunate enough to know some family history," Zhou Li said. "It's unfortunate that Ancestor was treated so unfairly. I'm sure that the family would welcome you with open arms."

Suddenly, Zhou Bei rushed toward Zhou Li and swiped at him with his fingers. A corrosive poison caused the air to sizzle as Zhou Li barely dodged the strike and blocked the poison with a flaming black shield. Zhou Bei twisted in midair and kicked at Zhou Li, releasing a poisonous flood dragon that wormed its way around the black flame shield.

In response, Zhou Li summoned chains of black fire that bound the poisonous flood dragon, which fell to the ground and dissipated.

"I hope Ancestor can calm his anger," Zhou Li said.

Zhou Bei chuckled and shook his head. He walked away from the orchard toward Songjing. "I knew it was you. I'd recognize that honeyed tongue from a mile away. Take care, Zhou Fan. Your plan didn't work then, and it won't work now."

Come to the main lobby immediately, Elder Bai sent mentally. Cha Ming, who was busy studying the Swamp Tribulation Totems, immediately dropped his brush and made his way over. He passed several guards and attendants with pale complexions. It was only once Cha Ming entered the lobby that he understood what had happened.

"Grandmaster Bei," Cha Ming greeted. "I take it you've made some progress in your research."

"Yes, I finalized a cure just this morning," Zhou Bei said as he glanced around at the surrounding paintings. "Whoever decorated this hall has good taste. I've always enjoyed Bai Suyan's paintings."

Cha Ming chuckled. "I'll show you around later. Let's go see the king as soon as possible."

They immediately flew out of the Jade Bamboo Auction House, where relieved customers continued their business. Truthfully, they had no understanding of what had just happened. Their reaction stemmed from their survival instinct, something that only high-leveled cultivators would gain full control over.

As they traveled through Central Square, the populace scattered in a mad panic. "Is there any way to restrain your aura?" Cha Ming asked.

"Oh, I forgot again," Zhou Bei said. He retracted his wild spiritual force, instantly calming everyone in the vicinity. "I always work in an isolated basement where I don't have to worry about this. It's so troublesome to keep myself in check, day in and day out."

Bewildered, Cha Ming led the way to the palace gates.

A short while later, Cha Ming, Zhou Bei, and Prince Lei were waiting nervously outside the king's chambers. Of the group, Zhou Bei seemed the most out of place. His clothes were ragged and torn in many places, making him look like he belonged on the street. But the three of them knew better—with a wave of his hand, he could easily cause the four of them to melt into unrecognizable pools of acid. In fact, the damage to his clothes was anything but ordinary. Cha Ming could sense that the man's robe was a core treasure, which was the only reason it didn't dissolve from the constant exposure to his skin.

The two of them flinched when the man gently lifted his white hand to brush away the white and black hairs that obstructed his black eyes with red pupils. "Must we really wait so long? Can't we just walk inside? I doubt even those unseen protectors could stop me."

"Senior Zhou, the king's situation is no longer life threatening, so there is no need to resort to such extreme measures," Cha Ming said diplomatically. "We are already so fortunate that senior rushed here as quickly as possible."

"A poison is best treated as quickly as possible," Zhou Bei said softly. "Sometimes powerful poisons are only a cover for other nefarious means. It's best to know the whole story sooner rather than later."

The door suddenly opened, revealing an anxious princess. "Is something the matter?" she said. "I expected you tomorrow night. And whom might this other guest be?"

The prince stood up to respond. "Dear sister, this man is Zhou Bei, the esteemed poison master who has been searching for a cure to the qi-binding poison. He's come all the way from Quicksilver City to see our father."

The princess bowed deeply. "Thank you so much for looking

into this a second time. We're eternally indebted to you."

"I'm only here to correct my previous failure," Zhou Bei said softly. "Let us skip the pleasantries. I wish to see your father."

"Of course," Princess Guo said. She led them to the king's chambers, where the chief physician and two others were administering some nutritional supplements. Li Yin was standing off to the side.

"These are?" Zhou Bei asked as he inspected the physicians from head to toe.

"They are the royal physicians, who have been doing their utmost to keep my father alive," Princess Guo said.

"Please dismiss them," Zhou Bei said. "I despise spirit doctors and can't stand the sight of them."

"How dare you besmirch our occupation," one of them started, only to be harshly cut off by the chief physician.

"This humble one will leave the king in Elder Zhou's care," Dr. Dong said, nodding slightly to Zhou Bei. The dumbfounded doctors quickly filed out from the room.

"It's a wonder that Dr. Dong sought me out in the first place, given my dislike for his profession," Zhou Bei whispered as he approached the king.

"May I ask what happened?" Cha Ming said.

"The usual," Zhou Bei replied. "They called my work an abomination and sought out an injunction against me." Just as he neared the king, an invisible pressure prevented him from advancing further. Zhou Bei rolled his eyes before saying, "Do you really want to do this? Here? In your king's chambers?"

The suppression lifted, and Zhou Bei placed a hand just above the king's comatose body. "They eventually gave up. Seven of their senior members died suddenly without any traces of foul play. The incident made them distraught, so they choose to drop my matter and focus on restructuring."

Cha Ming shivered at the implications.

"The poison has seeped into his bones," Zhou Bei said. "This poison requires me to use my unique constitution to devour it. It will take twenty-four hours. Please ensure that I'm not disturbed during this time."

"You mean you can cure him?" the princess asked.

Zhou Bei didn't reply. A purplish mist began leaving the king's body and entering the poison master's outstretched hands. Purplish lines began forming on the man's skin where his veins ran. They quietly left him to his work as the king's invisible guardians protected him.

Li Yin and Princess Guo chose to stay in the king's chambers and observe from a distance, leaving Cha Ming and Prince Lei to their own devices. Night soon fell. They had long since run out of things to speak of, so they began playing *Angels and Devils*. Everyone's skill level was roughly on par. This was great news for Cha Ming, who had been getting trounced in the complex game ever since his rebirth.

"It's time I told you about the second reason for my visit," Cha Ming said to Prince Lei. "Zhou Bei entrusted me with a device before we arrived. My job is to use the device to collect evidence." He revealed a clear stone the size of a thumb. A single purple drop was suspended within the stone.

"What does it do?" Prince Lei asked.

"It detects faint traces of qi-binding venom," Cha Ming explained. "It will glow bright and hot when within ten feet of a person or thing affected by the venom. The brighter the glow, the more contamination, and the greater the chances." To demonstrate this, Cha Ming withdrew a small sample of qi-binding venom, which Zhou Bei could now produce on demand. "It isn't affected by the venom's qi-binding properties, as it operates according to the laws of karma."

"Wasn't my father the only one affected?" Prince Lei asked.

"Zhou Bei speculates that it is difficult to administer the venom to food or drink without being affected by miniscule amounts of airborne venom," Cha Ming said. "Therefore trace amounts of the venom are an important clue to discovering the perpetrator. We need to bear in mind that whoever poisoned the king was greatly trusted, as he was able to bypass the keen senses of the king's guardians. The only people whom I do not suspect are Li Yin, the three physicians, the princess, and the both of us. I inspected them within the chamber." Cha Ming grinned. "Why don't you take me for a tour of the palace?"

"What an excellent idea," Prince Lei said, catching on right away. "I haven't gotten a chance to show you around. Why don't we start in my wing of the palace?"

It took them a quarter hour to reach the relatively remote wing. As they passed through the rooms, they also went out of their way to speak to any servants, eunuchs, or nobility they encountered. It wasn't long before they completed their inspection and moved on to Princess Guo's wing.

In Princess Guo's much more effeminate and well-decorated area of the palace, each room contained a unique artistic flair.

"This room was renovated by the great painter Fang Yi. It was commissioned by my great grandfather," the prince explained as they inspected the last hall. He looked around. "Could you please give us a more detailed introduction?" The staff in the room immediately fawned over them and explained everything they knew.

The crystal shows no signs of qi-binding venom, Cha Ming told Prince Lei, who acknowledged his verdict. They patiently waited for the servants to finish their explanation before proceeding to the center of the palace, where the third prince took charge of introducing Cha Ming to the many persons within. Neither the people nor the rooms showed any response to the crystal.

Their next stop was the harem. While they weren't allowed within the premises, Cha Ming recruited a tiny friend for the mission. For the small promise of an all-you-can-eat buffet, Lei Jiang readily agreed to scout out the relatively small section. Cha Ming fastened the small stone to the two-inch mouse with a piece of cloth. Before long, he returned to them with a negative.

"There are only three places left to see," Prince Lei said. "The Crown Prince Palace, the Scholar Palace and the Military Palace." While they were titled as palaces, they were, in fact, mere wings of the greater royal palace complex.

"The military palace will be tricky," Cha Ming said. "They wouldn't take too kindly to a small demon beast roaming the premises."

"Then let's hope we find the perpetrator in the other two palaces," Prince Lei said as they walked toward the Crown Prince Palace.

Cha Ming paid special attention as they wandered through it. According to Prince Lei, the decorations were plain and spartan due to his brother's disciplined temperament. As soon as he became the crown prince, he had emptied it of the lavish decorations and even auctioned off some of them to fill the royal treasury.

Black curtains were the norm. Here and there, they spotted a servant, but for the most part there was much less hustle and bustle in what should have been the most magnificent of the royal residences.

"Can I help you?" a voice asked as they approached the crown prince's chambers. Zhou Jia, Prince Tian's chief consort, approached them from a side hall where Prince Tian's other wives resided.

Prince Lei stepped up to greet her. "I was just taking Cha Ming for a tour of the palace. As I was just explaining, my brother has a spartan temperament, and he removed most of the gaudy decorations the palace had previously used to adorn the residence."

"Yes, the only luxury he left behind was in the crown prince's harem," Zhou Jia said pleasantly. "I can't show you around, but I can definitely introduce you to the various rooms and gardens in the Crown Prince Palace.

"Then we'll thank you for your hospitality," Prince Lei said.

Cha Ming had anticipated that this would happen—they could only delay a more thorough inspection to another time. Perhaps Brother Jun would be able to make something happen. As expected, their inspection of the many rooms, halls, gardens, and its various inhabitants bore no fruit.

"Sister dear, I see that we have guests in the palace," a voice said. "They even brought Ancestor Bei to treat the king. With any luck, he'll make a speedy recovery." The black-robed Zhou Li approached their group from a small hallway off to the side.

"Yes, with any luck, Royal Father will make a speedy recovery," Zhou Jia said. She was clearly uncomfortable at her brother's intrusion. "Should we go greet Ancestor Bei?"

"Only if you want to be killed on sight," Zhou Li said. "You should have paid more attention to our family history. By the way, didn't you say you had something important to take care of around this time?"

"Of course, brother," Zhou Jia said, bowing to them and heading off.

Zhou Li then walked up to them and smiled genially. "You all seem to be looking for something," Zhou Li said. "Perhaps I can help you."

"You're awfully brave, appearing before me after what you did," Cha Ming said. He immediately summoned his Clear Sky Staff, whose weight increased to the point that cracks appeared on the marble floor.

"No harm, no foul, my friend," Zhou Li said. "I just wanted you to get acquainted with the Church of Justice. Besides, I even tipped you off about the Honey Badger Inn. It was all for the greater good. But, if you wish to attack me within the royal palace, be my guest."

Cha Ming could only grit his teeth and bear with the man's annoying smile.

"It's the results that matter. Regardless of your feelings about me, I feel obligated to tell you that the crown prince is currently holding a special civil meeting. It will end in a tea time within the assembly hall, and many influential characters in our kingdom will be present."

"Many thanks for the information," the third prince said. "I think we'll pay them a visit." He grabbed Cha Ming's robe and pulled him toward the assembly hall with unusual haste.

"Don't be late," Zhou Li called out as they walked away. "It's a once-in-a-lifetime opportunity."

Chapter 22: Recovery

W hy exactly are we listening to him again?" Cha Ming asked as they hurried down the marble hallway.

"It occurred to me that this is the best way to inspect the high-ranking civil officials in the kingdom," Prince Lei replied. "Anyone with any influence on the king, at least on civil matters, will be present. If we inspect everyone in the meeting, we can skip our inspection of the Scholar Palace."

Just what game is he playing? Cha Ming wondered. They soon reached the center of the palace, then headed north toward the assembly hall, where the royal court took place every day. The large doors to the hall were shut, and solemn-looking soldiers stood guard at the entrance. In a few breaths, the doors opened, and the many officials who had just been meeting poured out. They were all discussing the results of their meeting.

Prince Lei quickly grabbed Cha Ming and brought him to the large group of officials, making a careful arc to include as many of them as possible in the crystal's ten-foot range.

"Teacher! Teacher!" Prince Lei yelled as he brought him to one of the older men, interrupting their discussion.

"What can I do for you today, Prince Lei?" Hao Bodong asked. The two other men he had been speaking with stood off to the side, impatiently awaiting the end of this rude interruption.

PATRICK G. LAPLANTE

"This is Cha Ming, the formation master I spoke of previously," Prince Lei said. "He's recently advanced to a late-stage master, making his formations a hot commodity in the capital."

"Yes, I seem to recall that," Hao Bodong said. "However, I was in the middle of an important discussion. If Your Highness could please excuse this old man…"

Prince Lei flushed with embarrassment. "How short-sighted of me. I will accept my punishment when you have more time."

"As long as you understand your mistake," Hao Bodong said with a gratified smile. He then turned to the two other ministers and completely ignored the two youngsters.

Did we find any suspects among the ministers we covered? Prince Lei asked.

We didn't, Cha Ming said. *Is there any way to bring us closer to the remaining ones?* He understood that Prince Lei had already lost quite a bit of face to cover so many people at once.

I have a way, Prince Lei said. He brought Cha Ming through the thick crowd of ministers as they made their way to the hall's entrance. The crown prince was just exiting the hall. He was engaged in an intense discussion with a cultivator who wore a silver badge on his chest.

"Second Brother, I've finally found you," Prince Lei said as they approached.

The crown prince frowned. "Whatever matter you have, could it not wait until we're finished here? The official meeting has ended, but many important discussions will take place immediately after."

"I just thought I'd introduce Master Du to you, a genius formation master from Quicksilver," Prince Lei said. "Perhaps he can lend you a hand in the future."

The crown prince's face twitched, but he nonetheless gestured for Cha Ming to come over.

A light tingling sensation appeared in Cha Ming's hand as he approached the duo. The sensation grew stronger and stronger as the crystal in his hand heated. He cursed Zhou Bei for his inaccurate description. The man had told him the crystal would heat up in proximity of the poison, but he hadn't mentioned that this heat could sear even his ridiculously strong skin.

"Master Du, I'd like to introduce Master Tu to you," Prince Tian said. "He's a famous geomancer from Quicksilver who will soon become a grandmaster. It wasn't cheap to bring him over. Now that he's here, I plan on comprehensively reinforcing the city's infrastructure."

Cha Ming's supressed the urge to scream and smiled as the stone continued to burn his rapidly regenerating flesh. "It's a pleasure to finally meet Master Tu in person. I've seen many examples of your work in the city these past two days. Geomancer structures are known to last for long periods of time without suffering so much as a crack. It's a pity that someone felt the need to sabotage your work."

Meanwhile, he sent a mental message to Prince Lei. *Is there a way to pull your brother away for a few seconds?*

Master Tu winced at the comment. "I've never had anything so shameful happen to my work in the past. These structures can even stand up to blows from early-core-formation cultivators. Judging by the marks, they were damaged by some sort of powerful demon beast of the rodent variety."

Meanwhile, Prince Lei pulled an unhappy Prince Tian back into the audience hall. Cha Ming heaved a sigh of relief as the burning sensation left his hand. Having obtained the necessary confirmation, he stowed the detection crystal into his Clear Sky Space.

"We all have bad days, Master Tu," Cha Ming said. "Perhaps you could inspect the wreckage and gain some inspiration, propelling you to the grandmaster stage in one fell swoop."

"Many thanks for the best wishes," Master Tu said. "I've been stuck at this bottleneck for fifty years, but this is the first time one of my structures has been breached so casually. Perhaps some self-reflection is in order."

Paff!

The sound of Prince Lei getting backhanded by Prince Tian and crashing into a wall alerted all the nearby ministers.

"Go back to your discussions!" Prince Tian yelled. He then

picked up Prince Lei, who was now unconscious, and walked over to Cha Ming and Master Tu.

"Master Du, would you please be some kind as to remove my unruly brother from this meeting area?" Prince Tian said, casually tossing Prince Lei's unconscious body. Cha Ming caught him single-handed.

"Not a problem, Your Highness," Cha Ming said. "I'll make sure he gets medical attention immediately."

A black eye was rapidly forming, and blood was flowing from Prince Lei's mouth. Cha Ming channeled healing runes into his body as he carried the prince back to his chambers.

"What did you tell him to upset him so much?" he asked Prince Lei when he'd regained consciousness.

"Several things that were a long time coming," Prince Lei said. "What about the test?"

Cha Ming lifted his right hand, whose palm was adorned with a crystal-shaped burn scar that was rapidly fading away. "It's as we suspected. Prince Tian is the one who poisoned your father."

Cha Ming sat meditating in the small guest room next to the king's chambers with only Prince Lei to keep him company. Meanwhile, Prince Lei was hard at work, reviewing and completing documents his aides brought to him. His black eye was mostly healed.

Tick. Tick. Tick.

They counted the seconds as the twenty-four-hour deadline approached. The door opened like clockwork, allowing them inside the king's chambers once more. Cha Ming could detect the aura of a cultivator from the king—his qi was now circulating normally through his qi pathways, nourishing his organs and meridians.

"It is done," Zhou Bei said weakly. "I have removed all the poison, but I still feel there is something amiss."

Cha Ming inspected the king's body with his Demon-Subduing Eyes. The purple traces within the king's body had disappeared and shifted over to Zhou Bei's. "I can't detect any traces, either. We'll just have to wait and see what happens."

Zhou Bei nodded. "I've done all I can for now. However, I've decided to stay within Songjing for a while. Make sure you prepare an isolated cultivation chamber for me."

The man then walked to a window and jumped through it. A sigh of relief echoed through the king's bedchamber as his protectors were finally able to relax.

Li Yin hurried over from the side of the room. His eyes were bloodshot from having not slept for an entire night. "What an interesting method," he said before sending his spiritual force into the king's body to examine it.

Dr. Dong and his two assistants soon appeared. They glanced about the room nervously before approaching the king.

"He's recovered his cultivation abilities!" one of the doctors exclaimed as the three of them began using spirit-doctor techniques to heal the king's failing body.

"His organs are rapidly healing," the other confirmed.

Only Dr. Dong frowned as the king healed at a rapid pace. "I feel there's still something amiss. Although he's recovering quickly, the speed is only a quarter of what it should be."

"Perhaps it's due to the extended qi deprivation?" Li Yin pitched in.

"Perhaps," Dr. Dong said. "We'll need to continue monitoring him closely during the next week. I hope you'll stick around to offer your guidance."

"After some sleep," Li Yin confirmed.

Cha Ming looked over to Princess Guo, who was softly crying by her father's side. He wondered how she would take it if she found out about her brother's treachery. Fortunately, that wasn't his decision to make.

Feeling out of place, he slipped out of the king's chambers and exited the palace grounds.

Central Square was far more lively than normal. And with good reason: The seemingly impregnable buildings built by Master Tu had been ravaged by mysterious creatures for the past few nights, causing many gawkers and rubberneckers to come personally inspect the damages. Many others came to enjoy the show. They stayed at various famous restaurants, bars, and teahouses in Central Square, using their enhanced senses to catch every embarrassing conversation that floated around.

As Cha Ming walked through the throngs of murmuring people, he spotted a crowd of jeering cultivators. They watched on in amusement as Master Tu carefully inspected a scar on his carefully constructed masterpiece, patching it along as he went.

On a hunch, he activated his Demon-Subduing Eyes and noticed that while Huxian and Lei Jiang had already disappeared, a new threat to the building's occupants had taken their place. The holes in the building were now chock full of demonic rats, who had already begun terrorizing the neighborhood.

Cha Ming's name came hand in hand with Master Tu's. The city's inhabitants were all excitedly discussing the two popular professionals and the advantages and disadvantages of each one. Suffice to say, Cha Ming was on the winning side of these discussions. None of his arrays had collapsed while his opponent's buildings were all in shambles.

A curtain of darkness hung over Songjing as two figures jumped from rooftop to rooftop. Their spryness exceeded their apparent cultivation realm: middle foundation establishment. While the qi they consumed for each movement and the pressure they emanated fit the bill, their movements bore a charm that could only be produced by unfathomable experts.

"You're awfully swift for a mere foundation-establishment cultivator," Li Ming commented as they landed on the wall surrounding the Sima family. He waited as Hei Ling pulled out a sharp black dagger.

"Right back at you," Hei Ling said as he twirled the black dagger in his hands. It cut into a translucent membrane a mere foot away from the wall. He moved it in a wide circle, leaving just enough room for a person to fit through. They both jumped through it consecutively, landing on the soft ground below.

"Do you normally do this sort of work?" Li Ming whispered.

"I wouldn't go around announcing it to the world if I did," Hei Ling said, chuckling. They passed three patrolling guards before jumping up to the third floor and carefully opening an unsecured window.

What did you do before working for the young master? Li Ming asked while they rummaged through the room's contents. He was the first to locate a pile of sensitive documents, which he carefully scanned with a recording globe before replacing it exactly as he'd found it—with a few added details.

I worked for the main branch in Gold Leaf, Hei Ling said. *You can tell the young master that if he has any concerns, he can speak to the family head for clarification. Or he can speak to that man. He will tell him everything he needs to know.*

Li Ming's face flushed. *I don't know what you're talking about.*

Look, Hei Ling said, walking up to Li Ming, *you and I both know that the young master suspects me of foul play. We don't have to pretend. I'm comfortable with my background. But are you comfortable about yours?*

Li Ming tried to retort, but the words stuck in the back of his throat.

Hei Ling chuckled. *We both know what your background is. So*

I'll tell you what: Stop sabotaging my efforts, and I won't expose you to the young master. I think that's a more than fair offer given your line of work.

Li Ming gulped. *Fine. You win this one. Now what about the Sin Crystals?*

We'll walk through the front door, of course, Hei Ling said. A cloak of shadows covered him as his aura rapidly changed to that of a core-formation expert. Li Ming's cultivation also increased to match his.

Their combined auras caused everyone in the residence to fall unconscious. They entered Sima Liang's bedroom without a hitch and walked over to the safe hidden in his wall. Hei Ling withdrew a small black lockpick which immediately transformed into a suitable key for the safe. He opened it and placed a small black bundle into a corner of the vault. Then it disappeared as though it had never been there in the first place.

That should be damning enough evidence, right? Li Ming said.

It's enough to make the Church of Justice suspicious of the crown prince, but not enough to convince them, Hei Ling said. *They're a big fan of the "innocent before proven guilty" rhetoric.*

After securing the room and ensuring everything was undisturbed, they floated out to the window they entered and stepped back onto the wall. This time they didn't use the black knife to tear open the membrane; they used their qi to directly supress it.

A few roofs later, their cultivation returned to normal. *How about you give that recording crystal to me?* Hei Ling said.

Li Ming chuckled. *Only if you give me yours. And your backup.*

Hei Ling shrugged. *Only if you give me your backup and your second backup. How about we sign a life-bound oath, and whoever spills the beans dies?*

As if I'd be crazy like you, Li Ming said. They soon negotiated a deal and signed a black contract.

Chapter 23: Deterioration

A week passed by without complications. Aside from the occasional conversation with Prince Lei and his daily visits with Wang Jun, Cha Ming immersed himself in talisman crafting and the mystical Swamp Tribulation Totem. He focused on supplementary or "buffing" talismans to aid his physical prowess but didn't ignore other utility talismans.

During the day, he spent some time assisting Feng Huoshan in teaching budding young talents. While Feng Huoshan and his friends were very experienced, they knew far less than Cha Ming did about runic characters. He was very rigorous in his approach. As he taught, he kept an eye out for any talents that might be worthy of accepting Fuxi's legacy.

Since Songjing was a large city, there were seven talents that possessed high innate soul force and five-element affinity. However, none of them had accrued a merit halo. He found that three of the seven had a good character. He encouraged them to focus on their heart and good conduct as they cultivated and gave them much more pointers than he did everyone else.

Among the other students, there were two with an affinity for shadow that came after hearing of his rare ability to teach them. The Church of Justice also sent three talented inquisitors to learn light-based runic arts from him. He wished these peaceful days could continue, but he knew this was only the calm before the storm.

A thrumming sound interrupted Cha Ming as he was painting a complex high-grade talisman. He frowned and sent a generic automated message to the recipient, indicating that he was busy. Moments later, however, the ringing resumed. He sighed and reabsorbed the ink from the near-perfect talisman before checking who the message was from.

"I hope this is important," Cha Ming said to Prince Lei. Their relationship had turned a lot more collegial than before.

"It's a matter of life and death," Prince Lei said in a worried voice. "Please come over as quickly as possible."

Cha Ming dropped what he was doing and hopped out his office's window. He used the power of the void to quickly fly through the city streets. He ignored the indignant guards at the palace gates and immediately flew to the king's chambers, where Prince Lei awaited him.

"It makes no sense at all," Li Yin whispered to the other doctors. "His qi is fine, but his vitals have all given up."

"I can't detect any poisons," Zhou Bei said. "No poisons should be able to escape my senses now that the qi-binding venom has been purified."

Cha Ming swiftly walked into the room. He immediately activated his Eyes of Pure Jade and his Demon-Subduing Eyes but detected nothing out of the ordinary. "Huxian?" he asked. The cute two-tailed fox jumped out of his shadow and awaited instructions. "Please fetch Wang Jun. Perhaps he can shed some light on this situation."

"But Brother Jun is…" Huxian started.

"This is just a precaution," Cha Ming said. "Please help Protector Ren escort him. I'll be fine on my own."

Huxian nodded and disappeared back into the shadows. Through their bond, Cha Ming could tell that he'd immediately arrived at Wang Jun's bedside.

Without saying a word to the three doctors, he quickly set down thirty-six array flags. His proficiency had greatly increased, so it only took him thirty breaths to install it. He immediately shared control with the three doctors and Li Yin, who scoured his organs.

"There are no traces of demonic or devil influences," Cha Ming said.

"Medically this doesn't make sense," Dr. Dong said.

"The timing is also very strange," Li Yin said. "As soon as the clock struck midnight, his condition immediately worsened."

Cha Ming glanced at the ancient clock in the room and confirmed that it was only an incense time past midnight. "At this rate, he won't last more than an hour."

Hurried footsteps sounded from across the door before Princess Guo suddenly rushed in. "What happened?" she asked worriedly.

"The king's condition has worsened," Dr. Dong snapped, "and I would greatly appreciate if everyone stopped asking me questions while we're trying to save him!" The red-faced doctor turned back and continued his conversation with the other medical experts. They were currently employing powerful healing techniques to fight for the king's rapidly failing body.

Suddenly, a black door opened into the room. Huxian and Wang Jun suddenly appeared inside the king's chambers. Wang Jun looked extremely gaunt and fatigued. "What can I do for you today, Brother Cha Ming?"

"Remember how you said you couldn't read the king's story?" Cha Ming asked. "Can you read it now?"

Wang Jun focused his gaze on the comatose king. He held his hand out and tried to grasp invisible threads, but to no avail. "I still can't do anything. It seems that the poison wasn't the only thing afflicting him."

While Cha Ming wracked his brains for a solution, heavy footsteps sounded outside the king's chambers. "We need to speak to

Prince Lei," a guard said. "It's urgent!"

"What is it now?" Prince Lei said as he left and closed the door.

Cha Ming cocked his ear to the door to catch the gist of the conversation. They'd just received a message from the southern battlefield that the south's attacks had suddenly intensified. Marshal Yong's battlefront was faring particularly badly. This was also the battlefield where Feng Ming was headed.

Suddenly, bells tolled within the palace. Cha Ming walked out and looked to Prince Lei, who frowned. "There's an intruder in the city," the prince said. "How much more bad luck could we ask for in a single hour?"

A figure in an orange kasaya walked through the streets. Wherever she walked, people shied away. Any guards who tried to stop her immediately put down their swords and renounced their violent ways. Occasionally, a foundation-establishment cultivator popped out of the woodwork and attacked her with a qi-based technique. She swiftly spoke a soothing mantra, which formed runic characters that blocked his attack and rendered him unconscious.

There's one, Gong Lan thought.

She pushed off from her location, traveling three hundred feet in the blink of an eye. An old man gasped as a blade of light cut right through him. A dying wail pierced the air as specks of crimson dissolved into nothingness. The old man kneeled with grateful tears. She didn't stop to accept his thanks, however. Time was limited.

She repeated this action many times, slaying dozens of evil spirits before arriving at the palace gates, where she was joined by nine other monks in orange kasayas. They had funneled into the city from various directions to catch as many evil spirits as possible in a dragnet.

"It looks like we have company," she said calmly as they walked toward the small army at the gates.

"In the name of the king, halt and surrender!" a figure wearing a black-and-gold cape shouted. It was Marshal Feng, and Prince Tian stood beside him. Their overwhelming battle intent combined with the soldiers beside them, forming a repulsive barrier that was impossible to pass. For most people.

Gong Lan simply sheathed her swords and whispered some reassuring words, which formed protective runes around her body. Her orange kasaya turned golden, and wherever she walked, the small cracks on the road mended and the plants breaking through them receded.

"I said halt!" Feng Chuan shouted. He waved his spear, sending fire and brimstone raining down on the bald, gold-cloaked woman. Gong Lan and the other nine sped up, expertly dodging the fire and ashes that rained down upon them. Whenever she couldn't dodge, she waved her hands, sending golden runic patterns out like shields to deflect them.

Seeing that Feng Chuan couldn't hold out, Prince Tian and a dozen generals joined him in creating a battle formation. It took the shape of a giant blue flood dragon. Their combined power pushed the dragon's might into the peak of late core formation. Most experts wouldn't dare face such a technique head on.

But Gong Lan and the nine weren't most experts. She spoke gentle words of gold that rushed toward the flood dragon, imprinting themselves on it. One character after another struck its giant frame until they accumulated into words spoken by the Buddha himself:

"Hatred will not cease by hatred, but by love alone. This is the ancient law."

As soon as these words were fully formed, the flood dragon roared and dissipated into a million motes of golden light. They shot back to the soldiers, who had created the dragon in the first place. As soon as it touched them, they dropped their swords, unable to move a single inch toward them. Even Feng Chuan and Prince Tian were affected.

Gong Lan and the monks walked past them and entered the

palace unhindered. They walked through the palace with purpose until they arrived at the door to the king's chambers.

"Who are you? What is your purpose here?" a distorted voice yelled out. Three red-cloaked figures suddenly leaped out and blocked off the bedroom door.

"I am here to treat your king's affliction," Gong Lan said. "As I come with a peaceful purpose, you cannot stop me."

She walked toward the three men unperturbed. All three of them tried drawing their swords to act against her, but to no avail. As soon as the very thought of stopping her crossed their minds, a powerful force pressed down and paralyzed them. The nine monks followed.

Gong Lan pushed open the doors and was greeted by eight shocked humans and a baby fox.

"The king isn't poisoned," she said in a deadpan voice. "He is possessed and cursed."

After briefly ruffling Huxian's fur, Gong Lan walked over to the king and placed her hand on his forehead. Those who wanted to speak out against her couldn't. Cha Ming couldn't help but gawk at her metamorphosis. He exchanged glances with Wang Jun, who was similarly affected. However, to Cha Ming's surprise, Wang Jun quickly recovered from his fatigue. In fact, a slight rosy blush blossomed on his face.

"Don't think I've forgotten about you now that you're hiding," Gong Lan said as she glanced over to Wang Jun's position. Two of her fingers shot out, sending blades of light toward the paralyzed Wang Jun. Protector Ren, who was standing right beside him, jumped in front of the blades to shield the young master with his body. However, they pierced through him unimpeded and struck Wang Jun square in the forehead.

"What have you done to my young master?" Protector Ren yelled, drawing his saber. A sanguine aura of blood and shadow pervaded to the room at this instant. Only the protective Buddhist light around Gong Lan and the nine prevented everyone from being injured.

"I banished the evil spirits haunting him," Gong Lan said nonchalantly. "He'll be back to normal in a few breaths."

Cha Ming looked to Wang Jun, who was rapidly recovering from his fatigue. He looked refreshed, as though he'd woken from a deep sleep.

"I previously inspected the king but found no indications of a curse," Wang Jun said. He patted Protector Ren on the shoulder as he passed him and joined Gong Lan at the bedside.

A small clamor was occurring outside the bedchamber.

"Tell them they may come in but must not disturb us," Gong Lan said.

Prince Lei, who was shocked by everything that had occurred over the past hour, could only shake his head and open the door. Feng Chuan, Prince Tian, and the three protectors rushed in. As soon as they tried to speak, their mouths snapped shut and refused to open.

"You inspected him, but you couldn't find the curse because he was also possessed," Gong Lan said. "He was possessed by many evil spirits simultaneously. They are tainted by corruption and karma, making it difficult for you to read his story."

Wang Jun sucked in a sharp breath. "That would do it."

Gong Lan then muttered some mantras and took out a large rosary from her robes. She went through each bead one by one. Each word she spoke lit up one of the 10,080 pearls with a blessed golden light.

The chant increased in volume as she spoke. The surrounding air congealed, revealing auras around everyone present. Most people were revealed to possess varying degrees of crimson, while Gong Lan glowed with a golden aura. Wang Jun revealed no aura, and neither did Huxian. Cha Ming was covered by a white glow.

Soon, she spoke the last word. The 10,080 beads burst apart and surrounded the king in a complex formation. Dozens of crimson shadows darted out from his body. They tried to escape but were ultimately destroyed by Gong Lan's fierce attacks. The single crimson shadow that managed to escape was cut down by a saber of light, which Gong Lan threw at the last moment.

"Now you can try," Gong Lan said to Wang Jun, who immediately pulled over a wisp of shadow. It formed many blurry words. Cha Ming could make out some but not all of them. He couldn't make out the king's true name, nor could he see most of his story. However, he recognized three of the thousands of characters: disease, terminal illness, and death.

"The story reads as follows," Wang Jun said. "On the second full moon of the year, the king will fall unconscious and gravely but not fatally ill. On the third full moon, his condition will worsen until he dies. As a note, it has been exactly one month since he's fallen ill. It is also as Gong Lan said—the king is cursed."

"I have no idea what's going on," Prince Tian said, but we're suddenly supposed to believe the words of this woman? And who *are* all these people? What are they doing inside my father's chamber?"

"These people have been saving your father's life," Princess Guo said coldly. "We've gotten along just fine without you. You should return to your post, or maybe help out the armies that are suddenly falling like flies out in the field."

Prince Tian flushed crimson. "We're working on the military situation, but I can't allow a trespasser to remain in the king's chambers," Prince Tian said.

"Don't worry, I'll be leaving soon," Gong Lan said. She turned to Wang Jun. "I have a friend who says you have a way to obscure his fate. Can you do it?"

Wang Jun hesitated. "Can't we just invite the Church of Justice to break the curse?"

Gong Lan shook her head. "This curse is far too powerful. It is tied to the destiny of the nation, and the ancient Song Dynasty's Seal of Pure Jade. We cannot break this curse. We can only buy him time until the other issue is resolved. You know that things won't go in your favor if he doesn't survive."

Wang Jun grimaced before forming multiple hand seals. Yet another strand of gold left his hair and poured into a ball of shadow, which he threw at the wall of characters forming the king's story. It shot toward the character for death, which instantly blurred. Then the story folded back and returned to the king's body.

"There. His death is no longer certain. You'd better make sure my efforts aren't wasted. I've given up ten years of my life for a king I don't even care about."

"Don't worry, I'll stake my life on it," Gong Lan said with a grim smile. "It's now time that we leave." She and the nine monks bowed to everyone present and walked out of the king's chambers. They walked out the front door and dispersed throughout the city and began exorcising evil spirits and feeding the hungry.

Chapter 24: The South

Following the events in the palace, Cha Ming sat in meditation at the Talisman Artist Guild. Huxian slept soundly on his lap as he worked hard to calm himself from the hectic hour he'd just experienced. He thought about his diminishing utility in the city and the war to the south. Should he go south and help Feng Ming fight off the invaders?

A soft knock on his door interrupted his train of thought. Cha Ming opened it to find the hardworking Feng Huoshan. "What can I do for you today?" he asked.

"A guest has come to see you," Feng Huoshan said. "I left her in a private room. I was afraid that she'd try and convert customers if left to her own devices."

Cha Ming nodded and followed the red-robed man to a small room. Gong Lan sat there cross-legged in her orange kasaya with two cups of steaming-hot tea.

Cha Ming closed the door and approached Gong Lan with Huxian in his arms. The fox yawned and hopped onto Gong Lan's lap. "You've changed a lot," Cha Ming said as he took a seat on a soft cushion. "When did you decide to become a monk?"

Gong Lan smiled. "My brother took me to a monastery to save me. Little did he know that it would change my destiny forever."

Cha Ming took a sip of the small cup of tea before placing it down again. Gong Lan immediately refilled it.

"Back in those days," she said, "I just wanted to help everyone and not be useless. I've finally found a way to do it without losing myself. Speaking of which, I'm not the only one who's changed."

"I've been through a lot," Cha Ming said. "I've learned to become a little more proactive, but this sudden change of events has taken me by surprise."

"It's not a sudden change," Gong Lan said wistfully. "This started hundreds of years ago with the fall of the Song Empire. It was a thriving kingdom that eventually collapsed. Hundreds of years passed while civil wars were fought. Territory changed hands until only this tiny Song Kingdom remained."

"I still don't understand how this could have any bearing on the current situation," Cha Ming said. "To me, it seems that the battle for the throne is a recent concern."

"Do you know anything about destiny?" Gong Lan said.

"Only a little," Cha Ming admitted.

"Let me give you brief explanation, then," Gong Lan said. She took a tea leaf and a bowl of hot water. "Let's say that this leaf is all the vengeance and resentment that is sown whenever a major conflict arises in a nation." She placed the leaf inside the bowl. A brown cloud immediately surrounded the leaf. However, it eventually diffused outward.

After several minutes, the bowl of hot water had attained a light brownish coloring. "See how all the resentment spread across the entire teacup? It's the same in a nation. Therefore, when kings supress rebellions, if each one is not quelled quickly, resentment will spread across the entire country. In turn, more rebellions will sprout all over the kingdom and tear it apart." She dropped three more leaves in, and the water turned increasingly dark. "Just a few events will cause an entire kingdom to be embroiled in perpetual bitterness.

"The Song Kingdom, however, thought of a solution to this threat long ago. To secure their nation's destiny, they tied it to the emperor's Seal of Pure Jade and stored it in the emperor's tomb, where each successive emperor was buried and subjected to a ritual to protect the nation forever. They encouraged meritorious acts to constantly refill the nation's destiny.

"Unfortunately, time has taken its toll, and the seal has accumulated too much corruption. The Song Kingdom is but a small piece of a larger entity. It has been soaked with so much warfare and corruption that the remaining kingdom could collapse at any time."

Cha Ming frowned. "But the Song Kingdom is no longer a part of the previous empire."

"That would normally be true," Gong Lan said. "However, the seal is a transcendent treasure that bound the entire empire by karma. The first emperors encouraged and rewarded righteous behavior, so that merit would cleanse the seal and providence would shine upon the kingdom as a whole. However, a scheme caused the chain of emperors to be broken. The kingdom split into twelve pieces that fought many wars over meaningless scraps of territory. But they are still bound by karma, and the hatred between the kingdoms eventually corrupted the original intent of the seal. Its guardian spirit has been convinced that the only way to protect the kingdom's inhabitants is by destroying the kingdom from the inside."

"How do you know all this?" Cha Ming asked.

"Because my teacher fought against this corruption 160 years ago," Gong Lan whispered. "He lost his prized disciple in the process and has requested that I atone for his failure. Coincidentally, the king's curse originates from the seal. I need someone to help me journey through the emperor's tomb and reach the emperor's seal and cleanse it. I need *you* to help me."

Cha Ming shook his head. "I need to stay here and do everything I can." Inwardly, he doubted his own words.

"What *can* you do here?" Gong Lan asked. "I've heard the whispers of your deeds in the city. You've strengthened the citizens and reinforced the third prince's faction, but ultimately a civil war *will* erupt. Your strength may be great, but it's a pittance compared to the might of the emperor's seal. When its corruption is completed, the remnants of the empire will fall no matter how you try to stop it."

Cha Ming sighed. "What do you need me to do?"

"I need you to do what you always do," Gong Lan said. "I need you to get to the bottom of things and tip the scales. Haven't you noticed that despite all the struggles in the city, there's a strangeness you can't put your finger on? Something that gnaws you from the inside?"

Cha Ming nodded.

"That's because much of the work is happening behind the scenes. The enemy's focus is in the emperor's tomb, which is why the third prince has been able to gain an advantage in Songjing in the first place. This is also why I need your help—us monks might be strong, but we're not invincible. We need protection, especially in those vulnerable moments when we fight the corruption. Besides, you're favored by the plane. You can make miracles happen even in hopeless situations."

"How long will it take?" Cha Ming said, closing his eyes.

"If my master's records are correct, it will take a little less than a month to reach the emperor's seal," Gong Lan said.

"Can I call a few friends?" Cha Ming asked.

"You have three days," Gong Lan said. "In the meantime, I'll join the others in destroying as many evil spirits as we can find in Songjing."

Feng Ming looked gravely upon a multitude of campfires blanketing the clear sky in a layer of smoke. They were still fifty miles away from Southhaven Fortress, where Marshal Yong stood as Songjing's vanguard, along with twenty thousand men, a fifth as many as the invading forces. The large stone castle guarded Southhaven Wall, a remnant of the ancient Song Dynasty that had protected the kingdom until this day. If Southhaven and the three other fortresses didn't fall, neither would the wall.

"What a damnable time to attack our kingdom," General Qin

said. "What kind of bastards attack a kingdom during their monarch's succession? They're despicable, rotten to the core."

Another eight generals were part their small group. Unfortunately, they were much weaker than their brawny counterpart and could only bite their tongues.

Feng Ming snorted. "Are you sure you're not an inquisitor of the Church of Justice? This is war, and it's the perfect time for them to attack." General Qin was about to retort when Feng Ming cut him off. "Don't let that muscle you call a brain convince you otherwise. Just listen to the rest of us and charge where we say charge, and *when* we say charge, and we'll do just fine."

He added in a bit of his early-core-formation pressure for good measure. The general's indignant expression was instantly replaced with one of respect.

General Qin suddenly burst out laughing. "Who said people promoted to general by reaching core formation are all meatheads like me? You're right, I'm not a thinker. I wear my heart on my sleeve, and everyone knows it. Just say the word and I'll charge into a sea of ten thousand men. That's much more than those eight cowards would be willing to do."

Seeing the eight other generals' indignant expressions, Feng Ming couldn't help but comment to smooth things out. "Truth be told, they're ten times more useful than you or me when directing our men in the battlefield. I'm like you—I'll charge when they say charge and retreat when they say retreat. We'll need to work together to fight those southern devils off."

They covered the fifty miles within the next hour, where they were greeted by Deputy Marshal Mo just outside the wall. The man was also a core-formation expert, but unlike Feng Ming or General Qin, he had a sharp mind for strategy. Recognizing his talent, Marshal Yong had immediately recruited him to his side.

"Welcome, Generals," Deputy Marshal Mo said, saluting. "As you can see, the situation is dire, and we need all the men we can muster. Marshal Yong has called an emergency meeting for all generals. Colonels and captains, please report to the barracks for duty. Make sure you familiarize yourself with the fortress's functions—it's a very advanced structure imported from a transcendent realm."

"Sir!" Everyone saluted. Feng Ming and the ten others followed Deputy Marshal Mo through a series of sturdy stone passages to a room at the core of the fortress. There, they saw thirty other generals in their red-and-gold capes surrounding a rectangular war table. Unlike those found in the capital, this one was intrinsic to the fortress—the adjustable table perfectly reflected the terrain and enemy forces outside each of the three fortresses. To his surprise, all of the enemy's forces were concentrated outside a single fortress.

"As you can all see, we're only fighting on one front, which greatly improves our defensive situation," Marshal Yong said. The grizzling man's chest was a foot wider than most men's, and coupled with his black-and-gold marshal's cape, he struck an imposing figure. "As a result, we have called back five thousand troops from each of the other fortresses. This way, we can man ten more defensive battle formations and keep men in reserve for rotation and special operations.

"What I need you all to do now is ponder over the situation and discuss the strategic options available. I want no stone left unturned. While thirty thousand men seems like more than enough to fight off these 100,000 men, remember that the Southern Alliance can employ strange means, many of which they have not yet revealed. They are far more advanced in key warfare technologies, weaponry, and alchemy than our troops. Our scouts have also reported that one thousand members of their reclusive Spirit Temple have joined the battlefield. We don't know anything about their capabilities, and they are a wildcard in this war. Our only advantage is this wall, which our ancestors paid a great price for in the realms up above. Any questions?"

There were none, and the generals got straight to work.

Only Feng Ming and General Qin felt strangely out of place. While the generals began evaluating the terrain and stratagems, the two generals began playing cards, only pausing when the occasional general requested a clarification of their combat capabilities. To Feng

Ming's surprise, General Qin was not a qi refiner but a body refiner. He didn't even use qi to refine his body—instead he used alchemical assistance and natural sources of heaven and earth energy to temper himself. Thus, while he might not be stronger than Feng Ming, his endurance and survival skills in battle were nothing to scoff at.

"Are you enjoying your game of cards?" a deep voice said from above them.

Seeing Marshal Yong, they both scrambled to their feet and saluted. The marshal walked up to the table and picked up Feng Ming's hand, which was smaller than General Qin's. "Are you so lucky that you need a two-card handicap in a five-card game?"

"And he's still winning," General Qin complained. "When they say he has the luck of a thousand men, they're not exaggerating."

Marshal Yong nodded. "Come with me, General Feng."

Feng Ming waved apologetically to General Qin, who wandered off to his second-favorite pastime: weight training. Surprisingly, he kept an assortment of training equipment in his spatial ring.

Feng Ming followed the marshal down a few hallways until they reached a secluded room with a stone door. The marshal placed his palm on a square, causing the door to open horizontally with barely a sound. The chamber was plain and simple—it contained a small bed, a desk, and a meditation mat. On the table, Feng Ming spotted an *Angels and Devils* board.

"This fortress comes with more conveniences than even a technologically advanced nation like the Quicksilver Empire," Marshal Yong said, motioning for Feng Ming to sit down. "Have you ever played *Angels and Devils*?"

"A little," Feng Ming admitted. "My father forced me to learn when I was a boy. I haven't played in ten years."

The marshal nodded and placed an open container of black stones in front of him. Then he placed five of the black stones on the board and placed his own white stone. "The average general can only defeat me with a five-stone handicap. I force them to play often—it's a useful exercise to develop and sharpen their minds."

"I'll likely embarrass myself," Feng Ming said. He still placed a stone, however. It was a career-limiting move to disobey a superior officer.

The marshal replied in turn, and before long, they'd each played twenty stones. As far as Feng Ming could tell, he was getting slaughtered. After peering at the board for a while, he shook his head and laughed inwardly. Since he couldn't will this battle, why take it seriously? He began to treat it as the game it was, and soon the game reached its middle stages. The marshal's pace slowed to a crawl while Feng Ming kept placing his stones based on gut instinct.

Marshal Yong frowned as he observed Feng Ming's latest move. Based on how the boy had played for the first twenty stones, his skill level was at least five stones worse than most of his generals. While Feng Ming was being modest when he spoke of his skills, it nevertheless fell short. Everything changed, however, when he placed the twenty-first stone. While it wasn't enough to turn the game around, it caused Marshal Yong to hesitate.

Thirty stones later, the marshal was sweating. Judging by Feng Ming's relaxed demeanor, the boy had stopped playing seriously and was just following his gut. But that alone revealed a frightening fact—while Feng Ming wasn't trying, he was supressing the 300-year-old marshal like it was child's play. Therefore, what he saw as a hundred-point lead in the beginning shrunk to fifty points, and fifty shrank to twenty. Marshal Yong soon found himself taking a teatime for every move. This lasted until the endgame, where the moves became much simpler. By then, his lead had shrunk to a mere ten points.

I can't be careless, Marshal Yong thought. *I have to fight for every point, or I might lose.* Therefore, he played cautiously, closing the existing gaps on the board and therefore reducing Feng Ming's opportunity to come back.

There, he thought as he placed one last stone. *That should do it.*

His brow was covered in sweat.

Suddenly, General Feng reached over to the other side of the board, which the marshal had overlooked as secure. He placed a single stone in the center of his existing territory, and the seemingly casual move caused the marshal to pale. He played a series of moves in his mind before realizing that he had to respond. They played one after another until neither the marshal nor Feng Ming could play anything in what used to be the marshal's territory without losing something. It was something called dual life, where a move by either player would cause his own stones to perish.

After some quick calculations, he sighed in relief when he realized that he still had a single-point lead. The game finished without any more surprises.

"Thanks for the game," Feng Ming said as they swept up the stones into their respective cups. "I guess I still fall a little short from a general's standard. Though in all fairness, I just got lucky."

His words were relaxed and modest, but his mind was actually working double time as he thought of the implications. Although he didn't know how he did it, the moment where he stopped thinking was when the losing game turned around. Didn't that mean that he might have won if he'd played that way since the beginning?

"In your case, luck is a form of strength," Marshal Yong said. "In the upcoming battle, I want you to listen to my or Deputy Marshal Mo's direct commands."

Feng Ming nodded. This was what he expected all along.

"*However,* that is only in ordinary circumstances." The man walked over to a drawer and pulled out a red cape covered in black runic symbols. While a general's cape was an enhanced piece of defensive equipment, it didn't affect his combat prowess too much.

However, Feng Ming could tell at a glance that this was a core treasure that would substantially improve his fighting strength.

"If at any point in the battle you feel there is something you should be doing, I want you to act on your instincts," Marshal Yong said. "I want you to conscript our men into your group and do what you do best—get lucky. I've seen your records, and I know how you can turn even hopeless situations into wonderful victories. You're even better at it than your father was. This is something that we need, but it's not something I or the other generals can channel. You need to act on your own terms. That is why, from now on, you're the second Deputy Marshal of the Southhaven Fortress."

Feng Ming's jaw dropped as he accepted the black cloak that resonated with his rune-covered black armor and even his lucky spear. He felt his movement speed double and his physical resilience shoot up to the point where only marrow-refining body cultivators could exceed his toughness.

He felt strong enough to fight against a demon beast monarch.

Chapter 25:
A Beast's Nightmare

T his is awesome!" Huxian yipped. "We finally get to go on a trip! We've been so bored in this city. The only bit of excitement we've had is tearing apart those shabby buildings."

Three days had passed since Cha Ming sent out the message. After confirming with Wang Jun that his help was no longer required in Songjing, he spent all his time preparing talismans and studying the Swamp Tribulation Totem.

"They should be here any moment," Cha Ming muttered. Sure enough, he soon sensed four presences approaching from afar. Two were at the peak of foundation establishment, and two were core-formation experts. All four of them wore alabaster-white cloaks.

"Sister Xuehua, Brother Hao, I'm so glad you could make it," Cha Ming said. "And these are?"

"Two elders we convinced to come along," Xuehua said. "Teacher decided to allocate some contribution points for participating in this mission. It turns especially lucrative if devils end up being involved, though he was especially intrigued by the cooperation between devils and evil spirits. Such cases are rare, even in transcendent realms."

"I'm glad he could spare some manpower," Cha Ming said. "Gong Lan should be here any minute."

"We're already here," a voice said from beside them. Gong Lan and nine other monks had appeared without anyone noticing.

"Greetings to our friends from the Alabaster Group."

"Teacher Lu sends his regards to your master," Luo Xuehua replied.

"If only he were still around," Gong Lan said wistfully. "However, I am thankful that the Alabaster Group remembers our long-term friendship. This is an important turning point for this small kingdom, and while the situation isn't as dire as in the south, the consequences for failure in this mission are far-reaching.

"Noted," Luo Xuehua said. "I've just transmitted this information to Teacher. He'll be monitoring the situation for external interference."

No wonder they agreed so quickly, Cha Ming thought. *It was just a passing suggestion, but they already have history.* He now felt much more confident about this outing. Anything Lu Tianhao was concerned about was worth investigating.

"Are you sure Silverwing is up for carrying so many people?" Cha Ming asked Huxian.

"He's actually getting quite fond of carrying people around now," Huxian said. "It's a great way to show off."

A falcon's cry suddenly pierced the skies, and a small whirlwind formed as Silverwing majestically landed before them.

"See what I mean?"

"Everyone hop on," Cha Ming said. He and Huxian jumped on Silverwing's broad back, which he had padded with a cushion of clouds. Seeing their concerned expressions, he laughed. "Don't worry, I've flown with Silverwing many times before. It's perfectly safe, and extremely quick."

"I, for one, can't wait to experience flying," Luo Xuehua said. It was usually only possible to do so at her level with the help of special artifacts, and just barely at that. After seeing that even a blind woman was willing to hop onto the beast, the remaining members hopped on to save face.

Only Gong Lan remained. Instead of hopping on, she walked up to Silverwing's large head. "A friend of mine was good friends with your ancestor, Silverwing," she said. "He asked me to pass on this blessing to you."

A tiny green bodhi seed appeared in her hand. She crushed it between her thumb and index finger, and the green dust flowed into Silverwing's open beak. Cha Ming's eyes widened as Silverwing's back suddenly doubled in size. His wingspan also doubled to 160 feet.

This is amazing! Huxian sent. *She just fed him super-concentrated life force. The bloodline he painstakingly nurtured suddenly became much stronger. I've never heard of such an impressive tonic.*

There's no point worrying about a good thing, Cha Ming sent back. *Who knows, maybe she has something for you.*

Huxian shook his head. *I wouldn't dare take something like that until you break through to core formation. We don't want a repeat of last time.*

Cha Ming agreed. As they spoke, Silverwing excitedly flew off. Each flap of his wings carried them ten miles. It only took them an incense time to reach their destination.

"There." Gong Lan pointed to an old forest that didn't stand out in the least bit. "Once you fly through the barrier, you'll understand."

Silverwing nodded and plunged down. Everyone on his back felt an incredible repulsive force before hearing a loud pop. The forest disappeared and was replaced by a large stone city. It was filled with crumbling buildings and covered in rampant greenery. The only undamaged structure was the front gate, where three characters proudly displayed the name of their location: Song Imperial Tomb.

They circled five times on their way down. Silverwing's wind gusts cleared the dust and gravel that had accumulated on a large road that led up to the tomb's opening.

"This is where the first twelve emperors of the Song Dynasty were buried, along with their famous generals and selfless protectors," Gong Lan said. "Even their first emperor, who transcended, returned to be buried with his people at the end of his lifespan. They served their country well—for a time. Now, they have been corrupted by time and conflict."

A golden aura covered Gong Lan and her nine protectors. It spread out one hundred feet before stopping and enveloping the

CORRUPTED CRIMSON

entire group. As they approached the tomb, they became aware of an ominous presence. Crimson veins covered the once-pure pathway that should have lasted for millennia. Meanwhile, crimson spirits hovered around them, wailing in resentment as they approached the entrance. Some told them to go back, while others goaded them to approach. The distance to the tomb seemed to increase one moment and decrease in another. Only one thing remained constant—the writing on the entrance: Guardian Labyrinth.

"Brother Cha Ming, what's a labyrinth?" Huxian asked.

"I'll tell you later," Cha Ming said. "Let's just get inside and discuss once we get there."

"It's important to stay together inside the labyrinth," Gong Lan said. "One misstep, and you could be trapped for all eternity. As a precaution, here is the labyrinth's map, which was discovered by my master 160 years ago."

A beam of light shot from her forehead and split into each of theirs. A clear golden picture of the maze within was etched into their minds.

"What are all these lines about?" Huxian said nervously. "And why do I suddenly feel afraid?"

"Relax," Cha Ming said. "Nothing will hurt you. I'm here."

"Let's enter the labyrinth now," Gong Lan said. As they approached the doorway, the lines of corruption grew increasingly dense. Gong Lan crossed the threshold first, while Cha Ming crossed alone. The three beasts followed, and Luo Xuehua, Dongfang Hao, and the two core-formation cultivators passed next. A crimson light shimmered once the last person passed.

"It's a spatial fluctuation!" Huxian yelled. He pulled back Silverwing and Lei Jiang and rushed toward Cha Ming. "Stay together!" he yelled.

Cha Ming rushed toward Huxian, but it was too late. A gray light enveloped him, and the next moment, he was surrounded by tall gray walls.

Brother... Brother... Where have you taken us? Huxian yelled mentally.

Cha Ming sighed. He could only hope they'd get over it. He tuned out Huxian's ranting and focused on his surroundings. The tall stone walls were inlaid with golden runes, but for all he knew, these were illusions just like the outside of the tomb. All around him, voices whispered in his ears.

He walked a few steps before a voice said, "There's a trap up ahead!" He pushed the voice out of his mind, but to his surprise, the warning was accurate. The floor crumbled, revealing sharp stakes dripping with deadly poison. He screamed as his body was impaled in three dozen places.

"And I thought things wouldn't get complicated until later," Gong Lan said wryly. "It seems that even the protective labyrinth has been corrupted. The map is now useless."

"I hope Brother Hao will be fine," Luo Xuehua said. "He's very strong, but he's not the sharpest tool in the shed."

"I believe I saw him teleport together with your two elders," Gong Lan said. "They should be fine. I take it that communication is impossible between our different parties?"

"Right," Luo Xuehua replied. "The walls seem to be covered in some sort of dampening formation."

Fortunately, Gong Lan's aura covered the walls in their vicinity. They could see a plethora of crimson lines along with the authentic appearance of the maze walls.

"Stop!" Xuehua suddenly yelled as Gong Lan was about to take a step.

Gong Lan paused in midair and allowed Luo Xuehua to send three dozen blue sigils right below her feet. The tile she was about to step on shimmered before going dull. "There seem to be traps in this labyrinth," Luo Xuehua said. "Please let me scout ahead before we proceed any farther."

"It's fortunate that we came here together," Gong Lan said as they walked. "I think Cha Ming will pull through fine, but I'm more worried about those beast friends of his."

"Why is that?" Luo Xuehua asked as she disabled yet another trap. "Their physical bodies are so strong. How could these traps possibly do anything to them?"

Gong Lan chuckled. "Beasts have an innate phobia of walls. While I'm not worried that the traps can damage their insanely strong bodies, I'm more worried about them going insane. Think about it, what is a labyrinth made of?"

"Um… walls?" Luo Xuehua said.

"Exactly," Gong Lan said. "Endless walls, up, down, and to the sides. It's literally a beast's nightmare in here."

"Don't stop running!" Huxian yelled as they stumbled across one trap after another. "It's the wall's ploy! If we stop to face the traps, they'll surround us, and then we'll be doomed!" A white aura surged around him, crushing arrows and spikes to smithereens. He'd already torn fifteen of these damnable traps to bits, but it wasn't enough. It was never enough.

"Boss, I touched one!" Lei Jiang yelled. "Am I going to die?" To avoid one of the poisonous spikes, he'd jumped off one of the tall gray abominations. In his memories, that spelled certain doom.

"We must never lose hope," Huxian said. "I'll die before letting any of them get to you."

Meanwhile, Silverwing was putting on an impressive show of aerial gymnastics. Evidently traps had been laid in such a way that even flight could not avoid them.

"There's even a wall above us!" Silverwing yelled. "What sort of damnable place is this? And where is Cha Ming? Did he betray us and abandon us?"

"I just don't know," a teary-eyed Huxian said. "I tried to speak to him, but he cut me off. Is he upset with me? Does he want to get rid of me? I swear, if he takes us out of this damnable place, I'll behave."

"Incoming!" Lei Jiang yelled. A large marble man detached from the wall and charged at them. "The walls even have servants to do their bidding. What can we do? Boss, I think we're doomed."

"Let's charge this wall servant together," Huxian said grimly.

Light and darkness overlapped as he used his strongest move to charge at full speed toward the stone monster. Silverwing sent blades of wind at him while Lei Jiang turned into an iridescent ball of lightning. The guardian didn't stand a chance. It crumbled before it could even swing its mighty hammer.

"Ha! There's hope yet," Huxian yelled. "Onward! There's only one road up ahead—it must lead to the outside."

They continued for some time before arriving at a fork.

"Um, it must be the center one," Huxian said confidently. Then they arrived at a second fork. "The center one?" Huxian said in confusion.

Before long, they arrived at a tall gray blockade. There were now four walls—one above, two to the side, and one ahead.

"This…" Huxian breathed in sharply. "This is worse than I ever imagined."

For the first time in their lives, they prayed to their ancestors.

Chapter 26: Trap

The labyrinth was eerily silent. Very few traps now sprung as Gong Lan and Luo Xuehua carefully walked from one hallway to another. Despite their superior senses and spiritual perception, the quiet felt like a prelude to a sinister attack.

Suddenly, a blade sprung out from the wall without warning. It was followed by a crimson stone hand and a muscular statue. Gong Lan's eyes narrowed as she sensed the immediate threat to her life. Golden sabers materialized and slashed out against the incoming blade. She felt a snag at her feet, however. A hand appeared from the ground below, interrupting her defense. She chanted a mantra just in time to defend herself, but the stone figure swung back again with another strike.

"Behind you!" Luo Xuehua yelled. She threw out a talisman at Gong Lan's feet, encapsulating the hand in ice. While Gong Lan defended against the new threat—a sword heading straight for her chest—Luo Xuehua sent 108 sigils out and manifested a Nine Frigid-Ice Shield. Nine lesser ice shields joined and superimposed their defensive capabilities. The blade that struck it froze over and shattered, prompting a roar from the corrupted guardian that held it.

Gong Lan ignored him and chanted a Mantra of Purification. The golden words struck the lunging guardian's spirit points, turning it into nothing more than a decrepit statue. As the force that originally propelled it forward disappeared, it crashed to the ground and became pile of rubble.

Seeing that Gong Lan was safe and sound, Luo Xuehua jumped over the frozen hands and elegantly slashed out twelve times with her two icy sabers. The strikes superimposed into something akin to a formation, amplifying the power of her techniques as they smashed into the stone guardian. The first six strikes peeled off the statue's outer layer, while the three remaining ones struck spirit points, effectively paralyzing it. She finished it off by piercing her two sabers through the heart and mind spirit points.

Meanwhile, Gong Lan flipped backward while twisting in midair. She channeled the power of righteous indignation as she summoned six sabers of light to strike down at the frozen hand's position. Layers of flooring crumbled under the assault and revealed a much smaller guardian, who succumbed to the fifth and sixth blades.

"It seems they're getting stronger and stronger," Luo Xuehua said as she wiped the dust off her blades.

"And yet I don't think we're getting closer to the source," Gong Lan said. "I think the labyrinth just requires time to mobilize its guardians."

"What makes you think that?" Luo Xuehua asked.

"Because we've been here before," Gong Lan said, pointing to a gold speck on the side. "I've been leaving markers as we go."

Luo Xuehua frowned. "Let me take a look at the walls." She cast out her sigils, which danced around the golden runes and crimson veins of corruption. She continued walking while analyzing, with Gong Lan keeping guard. Soon enough, they reached a fork in the road. Luo Xuehua spent a large amount of time inspecting the walls and ceilings.

"It seems each fork and intersection are shifting points in the maze," Luo Xuehua said. "They use strange principles to swap hallways whenever we pass them. Technically, this intersection could lead to eight different hallways instead of the three we see."

"How many are new?" Gong Lan asked.

"Only one this time," Xuehua replied. "We'll be exploring new ground, likely with traps, but at least we won't be running in circles."

Gong Lan nodded. "That's all we can ask for at this point. No wonder it took Master Zhen and Sibi so long to get through it last time. There's more to this labyrinth than meets the eye."

Cha Ming charged toward a stone guardian. He used his weight manipulation ability to propel himself forward as he swung the Clear Sky Staff in a vertical arc. He poured his resplendent force into it, increasing its weight to 40,000 jin as it became as large as a temple pillar.

Coincidentally, the floor behind the guardian also collapsed, revealing another painful spike trap that would have caused Cha Ming a great deal of pain.

"I guess that's one way to do it," he muttered, massaging the painful wound he'd suffered on his shoulder. Fortunately, his body's regenerative powers made it so healing such a flesh wound only took a few breaths. It was also impossible for these traps to break his bones. The Seventy-Two Transformations Technique had increased their hardness to the level of a mid-grade core treasure, despite his initial marrow-refining cultivation.

From then on, Cha Ming walked forward like a blind man. He used the Clear Sky Staff as an extra-long cane to "gently" tap the passageway up ahead. He dismantled one trap after another, making it increasingly easier to handle random guardians that stumbled his way.

Suddenly, he saw an unfamiliar silhouette up ahead. *Is there someone else here in the labyrinth?* he wondered. He'd discovered the peculiarity in the intersections some time ago, but he'd never seen another person until now. Cha Ming rushed forward, smashing many traps and crushing guardians as he advanced. The black-robed silhouette grew clearer and clearer in the distance.

They approached an intersection, where the robed figure turned right. Cha Ming followed, and it wasn't long before they reached an open room, something that Cha Ming hadn't seen until now in the labyrinth. Then, the figure turned around, revealing a face that Cha Ming was very familiar with—Zhou Li's.

Zhou Li sighed. "I knew you'd come here. Which is a shame. We don't have to stand on opposite ends of the spectrum, you know. That's why I'll give you a chance—you can turn back now before it's too late. Take it as a token of my good faith."

"I already experienced your good faith when you cursed me and Huxian," Cha Ming said. He summoned combat sigils in preparation for battle. The stone floor sank slightly under his increased weight but didn't shatter.

"I already told you it was a misunderstanding," Zhou Li said, shaking his head. "I was doing you a favor, but you failed to appreciate it."

"I don't think talking can resolve this," Cha Ming said. Clouds formed under his bare feet as he summoned a Stormwalker Formation. He struck forward with his Clear Sky Staff at breakneck speed, seemingly too fast for Zhou Li to react. This swift movement was only possible with his gravity-inversion ability and was the embryonic form of his Swift Staff Art. Shattered rocks flew around as Zhou Li's figure disappeared.

An illusion, Cha Ming thought.

Zhou Li immediately appeared in another corridor. Meanwhile, gold and crimson runes activated around Cha Ming in a three-layered shield. "This is a useful trap, though only thirty-three-percent effective against someone like yourself. I won't tell you how to escape, but make sure you consider all your options. It would be a shame for a talent like you to get ruined for the sake of the Song Kingdom." His figure shimmered, then disappeared.

What are these three barriers? Cha Ming thought as he inspected them with his resplendent force. He barely probed the first one before it shattered into a million pieces. However, it completely stopped as soon as it reached the second barrier.

After probing every inch of it, his hands clenched around the Clear Sky Staff, and his feet sank into the ground as his weight increased to 430,000 jin. The Clear Sky Pillar bent as he swung it at the red-and-gold barrier with all his might.

The second shield shattered on impact, but his staff couldn't penetrate the third layer. Unconvinced, Cha Ming swung against it again and again. He even crushed the rocky ground beneath him until it was nothing more than dust. Unfortunately, this only exposed the bottommost part of the shield, which formed a perfect sphere. Seeing that it was no use, he stowed the staff.

Huxian, can you hear me? Cha Ming sent.

I can hear you, but I don't have time to talk, Huxian replied. *The walls are coming. What have you done to us?*

Just calm down, Cha Ming said. *The walls aren't a big deal. They can't hurt you.*

Tell that to Lei Jiang and Silverwing, Huxian retorted. *They've both been wounded by the traps and minions the wall has sent out to attack us.*

Cha Ming sighed. It seemed it would be impossible to clarify the situation. *You're much stronger than the walls, but you just don't realize it. But enough of that, I need to pick your brains. Have you ever heard of a shield with three layers? One layer crumbles to spiritual force and another to physical force.*

A triple-restraint barrier? Huxian said. *They're common. You can't escape them unless your cultivation level exceeds the limits of the barrier. This applies to all three levels, and their limits are always the same. If you could break the soul barrier, that means the cultivation barrier will also be at initial core formation.*

Cha Ming's complexion changed. *So that's what he meant by ruining my future. Is there any other way to break it?*

You can wait, Huxian replied. *You can usually tell by the power decay rate in the formation. It could last as little as a day but as long as a year.*

Cha Ming used his spiritual force to probe the barrier, which he now noticed was weakening little by little. *It looks like this one will last a month.*

Well, I can't help you because of this wall business, Huxian said. *The barrier can be broken from the outside, but whoever does it would need a higher cultivation base by a level or two. I can't reach such a high level even if I break through to core formation. You need to make a choice. Either quickly increase your cultivation or sit this one out, brother.*

I understand, Cha Ming said, closing off their connection. He reached out to the barrier with his qi and noticed that unlike with his physical blows, his qi caused some disruption in the red and gold runes that composed the shield. After thinking for a while, he threw out seventy-two flags and summoned a Gold Slaughtering Formation. The energy of heaven and earth mobilized and struck against the barrier. Unlike his qi, however, the Gold Slaughtering Formation didn't even provoke the slightest change from the red-and-gold bubble.

Perhaps a combat formation will work, he thought. He mobilized seventy-two sigils and formed a substantially less complex array, which he used to unleash multiple blows against the shield. While these blows caused some distortions, they weren't enough to break it.

I have one more thing to try, he thought. He unleashed five groups of twelve sigils, which each formed one of the five elements. He then channeled five-element qi into the formation and poured in his destruction qi. A glistening black blade of qi formed at the center of the five-colored formation. It was an evolution to the previous one that only used five sigils. He breathed in deeply before willing the black blade to slash out against the barrier.

The slash caused a ripping sound as a tiny hairline crack formed in the red-and-gold shield. He willed it to strike again and again, but the crack only widened slightly. It wasn't long before his destruction qi was completely exhausted. He crumpled in pain as his body regenerated from the damage caused by the destruction qi. If an enemy were to attack him, he'd be completely helpless. It dawned on him that Huxian was right—there was no other way to get through without increasing his cultivation.

Now, he had a difficult choice to make. He knew his cultivation was already unstable due to his rapid ascent to late foundation establishment. Could his foundation bear the strain of breaking through to peak foundation establishment then core formation? He was nervous about risking it. Not only could he damage his Dantian, but if he was forced to recultivate, he wouldn't know how to incorporate creation and destruction qi into his Dantian as a framework. As far as he knew, it was impossible to do so without external interference. A slight misstep could cause everything he'd built up to crumble to pieces.

The stampede had finally ended. Huxian, Silverwing, and Lei Jiang collapsed on the labyrinth's stone floor, completely devoid of energy. However, they didn't dare let their guard down. They took turns glaring at the seemingly mundane but obviously murderous structures that surrounded them.

Brother Cha Ming, your plan worked, Huxian sent. *As long as we hold our position, the walls are far too cautious to act out against us. They fear our mighty power as much as we fear them. It's much like how normal beasts often fear humans due to a misperception of their size.*

Great, Cha Ming replied. *Now focus on the wall's weaknesses. What can you think of?*

Huxian pondered a little. *They might be endless, but they are immobile. Also, their attacks don't seem very strong. They at most cause flesh wounds. We were clearly overreacting earlier.*

Good, Cha Ming sent back. *You'll need to come up with something yourselves, but I believe that you have the power to conquer these walls. There's nothing to be afraid of. They're trying to scare you away because they're nothing more than paper tigers! They're being aggressive to cover their weaknesses, much like a small dog when facing a larger one.*

All right, Huxian sent back hesitantly.

A half hour later, the trio had fully recovered. "Everyone, listen up!" Huxian yelled to the other two, who sat up. "Now is not the time to be overwhelmed by fear. The wall might have advantages, but we have some too. What are they?"

"Our battle armors?" Lei Jiang said. He instantly summoned the black-and-white runic armor that covered him from head to toe.

"Sure, that's one," Huxian said. "Another one is our strong bodies. Even if the wall crumbles down on top of us, we'll barely be hurt. Lei Jiang, I order you to hit the wall with a full-force blow!"

"Are you sure, boss?" Lei Jiang said nervously. "What if this is just a ploy by the wall king? What if it *wants* us to attack it?"

"It's not a ploy," Huxian said. "Think about it: Has it attacked us yet?"

"No, but—"

"Then attack it!" Huxian barked.

"I refuse!" Lei Jiang squeaked back.

"Silverwing, hit him for his insolence," Huxian barked again.

Instinctively, the falcon lashed out lightly, propelling the mouse several hundred feet due to the difference in their realms. The mouse landed on another nearby wall, causing many cracks to propagate from the impact crater.

"It was a trap after all," Lei Jiang whispered and scampered away in fear. He ran back to the other two, who looked on fearfully as the large cracks made their way toward them.

A fierce rumbling echoed through the tunnel as it filled with dust. Huxian and Silverwing activated their strongest defenses as the dust billowed lightly against their powerful figures. It soon settled down, revealing another empty corridor. It was on the other side of the wall that had collapsed because of a light blow from Silverwing.

"Would you look at that," Huxian whispered in awe.

Chapter 27: Siege

"Just what are they doing?" General Wei wondered as they overlooked the giant battle map. Instead of attacking immediately and taking advantage of the element of surprise, the opposing army had stopped and pulled up a large wagon.

"It must be a siege engine of some kind," Marshal Yong said. "Though I've never heard of a siege engine with a ten-mile range before. Is it a new technology?"

"Even if it's a new technology, how could it ever eclipse the might of Southhaven Wall?" General Wei scoffed. They looked on as the opposing army joined several dozen pieces into what resembled a finger. Seven other such fingers were attached to a fifty-foot-by-ten-foot platform. Then they mounted an assembly that was just as large as the platform but contained several pistons and strange gems covered in runic designs.

Finally, they unveiled the last compartment of the massive wagon. Ten core-formation cultivators flew together with thick cables and lifted a large bronze barrel. They placed it gently on the mount that had just been installed. It clicked into place and was connected to a small secondary platform covered in runic designs and connected by a thick cable. They then loaded a large black sphere covered in runic designs into the bronze barrel and dumped tens of thousands of high-grade spirit stones on the platform.

"First through fifth formations, activate," Marshal Yong commanded through the fortress's voice transmission system. Five thousand cultivators poured their qi into multiple focus points along the wall. Five shields came together in formation and reinforced each other just in time to meet the cannon's first blast. The black ball exploded in a rain of shrapnel that was effortlessly repelled by the Southhaven Wall's intrinsic defenses.

"If that's all they have, we can defend against them indefinitely," General Wei remarked.

They carefully observed the aftermath of the blow and watched on in rapt attention as the opposing forces struggled to reload what Southhaven's forces now called a spider cannon.

"That's because you're blind, Old Wei," another general said. "I'm sure you noticed the nine other similar carts and the eleven munition carts carrying those large spheres. It won't be long before our forces are completely tied up by their cannon fire. Who will defend the wall then?"

"Just how were they made?" another man said. "It seems like they are magic weapons from the outside, but the explosion they create is far too potent."

"That's because the inside of the spheres contain an alchemical compound," said a general who wore cultivation robes instead of armor. "Those are alchemical flames. I'd bet my life on it." As the chief military alchemist, no one was qualified to overrule him on this assessment.

Marshal Yong, who had been listening all this time, finally spoke. "Call another five thousand men from the adjacent fortresses via transport formation while we think of a solution. With these men, we can still defend against their cannon power and stall out for reinforcements from the east. Deputy Marshal Feng?"

"Yes, sir?" Feng Ming said, standing at attention.

"You're the idlest here," the marshal said. "Go to the reception hall and receive our men."

Feng Ming bowed and scampered off, dragging General Qin

along with him. "Where's the reception hall and what does it do?" he whispered.

General Qin's eyes widened. "You don't even know about the reception hall? It was in our orientation manual, and its location is common knowledge."

"I may have ignored the manual," Feng Ming muttered. "Regardless, lead me there so I don't lose face."

General Qin went out of his way to explain many of the wall's advanced features as they walked. They crossed many troops on their way who saluted them reverently. After all, these two men were the pinnacle of martial power in the empire, their idols. The stares grew less and less frequent, however. They soon approached the location of the five active combat formations, where tired men and women were rushing in and out of focus chambers. Those rushing in were fully rested individuals while those who came out were completely drained from having powered the formation for an extended period.

"Why did the marshal assign you as a deputy anyway?" General Qin said. "It's not like you're much stronger than me. Besides, we're both goons. All we can do is fight on the battlefield like they tell us to."

Feng Ming shrugged. "Not everyone who gets a promotion deserves it. I just got lucky, that's all. Regardless of my title, I'll be trading blows in the battlefield alongside you."

They soon passed the active formations and entered a pathway that ran through a "buffer" courtyard that surrounded the reception hall. A wave of brilliance assaulted their eyes as they approached one of the most mystical buildings in the fortress. Mysterious white glyphs rapidly faded as thousands of men appeared one after another inside it.

So we can teleport people anywhere on this wall? Feng Ming asked General Qin mentally.

Not exactly, General Qin answered. *We can technically send them anywhere within ten miles, but the wall itself counts as a single entity. As such, we can teleport people safely within the three fortresses. Some time ago, the marshals experimented with teleporting troops outside the walls, but they got extremely mixed results. I'm not sure about the actual details, but a single man could be teleported with 100% success, while ten could be sent with fifty-percent success.*

Feng Ming breathed in sharply. *What happened to those who failed?*

General Qin remained silent about the obvious answer: They'd died a terrible death. Still, Feng Ming felt a familiar itchy feeling in his fingers. *Oh no you don't,* Feng Ming thought, supressing the tingling. Teleporting was far too risky.

"Greetings, generals," Feng Ming said as he received the ten thousand men in the abnormally large hall. "Thank you for making it here so quickly. The situation is dire, and we need all the help we can get."

The general frowned. "And who might you be? Why are you a deputy marshal when I've never heard of you?" The middle-aged man was a foundation-establishment cultivator. Judging by his appearance, he was over a hundred years old.

Feng Ming was a bit embarrassed about his sudden rise through the ranks. "I guess I got lucky and broke through to core formation. The marshal took a liking to me, so here I am."

The man snorted. "Just a young buck. Make sure you don't trip on that cape of yours." The man swished his own cape and walked away. In the process, however, it flew back and tangled between his legs. The grumbling general tumbled a few dozen feet before planting himself face-first into the ground.

A younger general ran up beside the older man and helped him up. He bowed to Feng Ming apologetically. "General Liang has not returned to the capital for some time. As such, he hasn't heard of the illustrious Lucky General."

Feng Ming coughed awkwardly because at that moment, another young general, along with a few other colonels and captains, pelted him with voice transmissions requesting an autograph.

"No offense taken," Feng Ming said. "Please make sure you report to Relief Barracks 11 through 20 for duty. I'll have to see you all later—we're currently taking heavy enemy fire, so you'll likely be needed to provide immediate relief to those manning our defensive formations."

Like this, the ten thousand reinforcements trickled out of the reception hall and proceeded to their appointed stations. General Qin left after an hour, while Feng Ming decided to ponder the ten spatial transmission formations in the reception hall.

Five days passed. In that time, one cannon after another rose up and joined the offensive. Defending against the spider cannons proved to be more exhausting than they'd anticipated. It wasn't long before a steady rotation of fifteen thousand men was established to maintain the barriers. These men could only tirelessly cultivate day and night to replenish the energy stolen from them with each successful defense.

On the surface, it seemed that the 40,000 troops they possessed would be enough to support against the salvo. However, this was not accounting for any other cards the enemy had yet to play. Marshal Yong refused to believe that the enemy was so stupid as to play all their cards from the get-go.

"Marshal Yong, I have some disappointing news to report," Deputy Marshal Mo said as he approached the grizzled man.

"Speak," Marshal Yong said.

"It's about the reinforcements," Deputy Marshal Mo said hesitantly. "I'm afraid that Marshal Tian has refused our request for reinforcements. Apparently a beast tide has just begun near the eastern wall, and they are already stretched thin as it is. Meanwhile, the rest of our forces are tied up in the capital."

Marshal Yong briefly sent his resplendent force into a black-and-gold medallion on his chest, confirming this information. While he noticed that Marshal Feng had not been notified, both Marshal Feng and Marshal Tian were in the capital and in constant communication.

"That damnable fool," Marshal Yong cursed. "What's more important to him, the throne or his country? If the southern wall falls, we're all doomed. You know full well how savage those southerners are."

"In their defense, it's not like we need any immediate reinforcements," Deputy Marshal Mo said. "Even with all ten cannons fully activated, we can still hold out. Besides, I've inspected some residual shrapnel. Do you know what those spheres are made of?"

Marshal Yong shook his head.

"They're made of star steel, and their runes are traced with immortal jade! That means that the cannons must be built from even more impressive materials. I refuse to believe they can take more than a few of them out at a time."

Marshal Yong sighed. "Fair enough. I just hope I'm not overthinking things." As he said this, the furniture in their small room shook. Marshal Yong immediately summoned a report from the control room and confirmed that the last volley had breached their defenses. He paled as he tallied the casualties caused by the backlash to his troops. "We've just lost ten thousand men in one fell swoop."

"Impossible," Deputy Mo cried. Then he looked at the other generals. "Tell me exactly what happened!"

A few nervous generals approached. "It seems that they suddenly changed up their munitions, substituting their previous black spheres for clear ones with different runes. We don't know how many they have, but their striking power is much higher than before. A bit less than double!"

Marshal Yong's expression turned grim. "Send out an emergency distress signal to the capital. All generals prepare to subsidize the formation where required. Bring out all our energy reserves and activate the remaining defensive formations. Meanwhile, the deputy and I will stand by and assist where required."

Various figures hurried off to relay their orders; no mistakes could be tolerated. The sudden changeup meant that the entire fortress's forces would be mobilized.

"What about Deputy Marshal Feng?" Deputy Marshal Mo asked. "He's been in the receiving hall all this time. Isn't this a waste?"

"Leave him," Marshal Yong said. "Pretend he doesn't exist. Just a single Deputy Feng is not enough to turn the tide. Not by supplementing the shields, at least."

Feng Ming was in a daze. He wasn't experiencing sudden enlightenment, nor had he reached a crucial point in his cultivation, but he was paralyzed with indecision.

"To suggest or not to suggest," Feng Ming mumbled. Fifty-percent odds of death for a group of ten was ridiculously high. "We'd need at least a hundred men to jump out at once to make a difference, including me. How low would the odds get with that many men?"

Still, his fingers itched, and he couldn't shake the feeling. It was like he was at a high-stakes table where a single roll stood between him and a massive fortune. But he knew this was fundamentally different. At a high-stakes table, he would only be gambling money. Here, he would be gambling lives.

"To suggest or not to suggest," he mumbled once more. Suddenly the fortress shook. He immediately ceased his contemplation and rushed out to the focus points, where troops were rapidly rushing to their stations. Corpses littered the floor, and large bags of spirit stones had been split open and poured into the channeling formations.

"What happened?" he asked a passing soldier.

"Reporting to Deputy Feng, the enemy's attacks have grown much stronger," the soldier said. "I can't stay and talk. The whole fortress, including the generals and the marshal, must man their posts." The man immediately ran off to a nearby focus point and began channeling his energy.

"Damn it all," Feng Ming yelled. He flew toward the war room. In the process, he crossed General Qin, who was running off to a nearby focus point. "And where are you going?" he asked the burly general.

"My qi may be weak," General Qin said, "but I can take backlash better than anyone else here. I'll do what I can to help everyone through this assault."

"No, you won't," Feng Ming said. "As a deputy marshal, I'm commandeering you." Then he threw out a red token with black lines. "I need you to find the hundred strongest fighters you know within a quarter hour. I also need you to go to the quartermaster and take all their inferno flasks, fire-based talismans, and as many frost shield or similar talismans as you can find."

"But—" General Qin started.

"No buts!" Feng Ming said. "The marshal gave me this cape for a reason, and I'm going to use it."

General Qin saluted and ran off while Feng Ming continued to the war room. When he entered, he saw that several focus points were hovering before each of the generals, who sat in meditation and channeled their qi to defend the fortress. Only Marshal Yong and Deputy Marshal Mo were still pensively looking at the map while trying to find a way out. Occasionally they would use their qi to send out probing shots at the cannons with some of the fortress's offensive formations. Unfortunately, each of the cannons was protected by a hemispherical shield that deflected any blows from their direction.

"Deputy Feng," Marshal Yong said. "Have you thought of something?" An eager glint had appeared in his eyes.

"Marshal Yong, this deputy requests your permission to mobilize one hundred troops through the teleportation array," Feng Ming said. "Our target is the spider cannons!"

"That's madness," Deputy Mo interjected. "Marshal, we've only conducted testing up to groups of ten because it was inhumane to send so many good men to their deaths. A group of ten only had fifty-percent odds of success, and it was speculated that a group of a hundred would reduce the odds to one tenth. Failure would mean the death of a hundred of our best combatants!"

Several generals who were busy funneling their qi in the formations mumbled in agreement.

Marshal Yong, on the other hand, looked at Feng Ming thoughtfully. "How confident are you in this gamble? And what's your plan when you get there?"

"I'd gamble my own life away in a heartbeat," Feng Ming said. "While I'm hesitant to gamble away the lives of our men, I don't see any better options for us. The reason I stayed at the reception hall was because it gave me a special feeling. I think this is a turning point for the battle. I've already sent General Qin to recruit the men and procure as many explosives and defensive items as he can lay his hands on. When we get there, we'll destroy those cannons and try our hardest to survive."

Marshal Yong took a deep breath before nodding. "This is why I assigned you as deputy marshal. I approve of this mission."

"Marshal, please reconsider!" Deputy Marshal Mo said.

"It's decided," Marshal Yong said decisively.

At this moment, General Qin returned with a hundred scar-covered soldiers who had fought in many battles. Many of them weren't high ranking, but Feng Ming could tell that their levels of qi and physical strength far exceeded even many of the generals here.

"Captain Tong?" one of the generals in the war room said. "When did you break through?"

"Just this morning." The man called Captain Tong grinned. "I had a lucky breakthrough. Funny enough, Sergeant Shen broke through as well."

"Wait, you just broke through this morning as well?" another man in the group of men said. They looked at each other with wide eyes.

"Can everyone who broke through this morning raise their hand?" All hundred men, and even a surprised General Qin raised his hand.

"Do you still have any objections, Deputy Mo?" Marshal Yong said dryly. Seeing Deputy Mo's confused expression, he chuckled.

"You don't need to understand, you just need to obey orders. Please bring Deputy Feng and these men to the departure hall for teleportation. Follow Deputy Feng's instructions to the letter."

Chapter 28: Surprise

As the hundred men and two generals marched to the departure hall, they set up a rough pecking order and divided the men into ten-man units. The two generals would carry the explosives while the individual men would carry the shielding talismans. They would escort and protect the generals as they did their best to destroy the cannons.

The technician looked on in confusion when they entered the departure hall. "Send them to these coordinates," Deputy Mo said as he handed the balding man a folded sheet of paper.

The old man paled when he read the sheet but nodded. "You are aware of the risks involved, correct?"

"Naturally," Deputy Mo said. "But these are the marshal's orders and are not to be questioned. I want these men gone as soon as possible."

"Very well," the technician said. "Have them ready to go. In an incense time, I'll send them out."

Meanwhile, the men were all laughing and joking as they awaited their imminent demise. They were under no illusions about their odds of survival, even if they succeeded in their mission. "Who would have thought we'd have the luck to go out on a final desperate charge with the Lucky General. How many do you think we'll kill?"

"At least twenty thousand," a man said. "Otherwise we'll be dragging his reputation through the dirt.

"That's fair," another man said. "By the way, what kind of defensive goodies did you get?"

"Me?" one of them answered. "I got an Earth Shield Talisman. What about you?"

"An Earth Shield Talisman? What shitty luck, I also got one."

"Wait, you got a few of those as well? Aren't those useless in hand-to-hand combat?" Captain Tong said. "Can everyone else who got Earth Shield Talismans raise their hand?"

Everyone did.

"I thought I told you to get Ice Shield Talismans or something like that?" Feng Ming said.

"I'm sorry, I *thought* that they said ice shield," General Qin said. "If you think about it, both characters look very similar."

"Similar, my ass!" Feng Ming said angrily. "They look nothing alike! How the hell did someone like you become a general? Deputy Mo? Cancel the teleportation, we need to get something."

"Right away!" the old technician said. As he reached toward the "abort" formation, however, he accidentally tripped. His hand ran past it and reached another formation, the "launch formation." A white glow rapidly filled the room.

"Can you stop it?" Deputy Mo asked.

"I'm afraid not," the technician said as they looked at the expanding white diagram. "In fact, I didn't get to input all the coordinates. It would be a miracle if they end up where they're supposed to."

Deputy Mo sighed. "Godspeed, General Feng!" he yelled.

Meanwhile, Feng Ming and the others readied their weapons as they prepared for their surprise teleportation. The white glow intensified, and Feng Ming gasped as he was whisked away by gray spatial light along with the 101 others. They screamed in unison as their surroundings jolted before they appeared somewhere to the south.

They rubbed their eyes as the light faded, only to realize that they were surrounded by men in red armor who looked at them with slacked jaws. Feng Ming was the first to regain his bearings. He realized they'd appeared in an empty parade ground where the opposing army ran drills. He looked around and soon located what they were looking for—the five cannons and the sixth cannon that had yet to finish being constructed. As soon as it was complete, it would join the others and break through Southhaven Fortress's defenses.

"What are you all standing around for?" Feng Ming yelled. "Charge!"

His yell was echoed by the battle-hardened veterans beside him as they realized that not only had they survived, but they'd caught their enemies flat-footed and unprepared. Feng Ming and General Qin led the charge. Feng Ming's steps were swift and his spear incisive; he covered their group in a defensive molten cloud. General Qin's 10,000-jin greatsword, which was twice as tall as him, cleaved through large swaths of men, mounts, and machinery as they advanced.

In sixty breaths, they had covered half the distance to the cannons. Feng Ming casually tossed out an explosive flask, a single-use alchemical item that would detonate upon impact. It landed on a nearby wagon that carried a spare cannon. Pieces of shrapnel flew out toward nearby enemy troops. Conveniently, the large cannon landed on one of the few obscure black tents belonging to the Spirit Temple.

"Keep at it, men!" Feng Ming shouted. None of the hundred had fallen yet. They unloaded technique after technique, strike after strike toward the tender opening in their opponents' formation. Every strike felled three or four elite troops.

"Deputy, I found a weapons shack!" a man yelled.

"Stow away any weapons you find, and destroy any combustible goods," Feng Ming shouted, tossing out three other bundles of explosives.

This time, a large wind swept them up and brought them directly to the Spirit Temple tents. Dark crimson plumes emerged and let out tens of thousands of agonized wails. The screams sent shivers through Feng Ming's spine. At the same time, he noticed a large amount of merit rushing toward him. The men in the tents were incomparably evil—it was no wonder that fate wanted them dead so badly as to push the explosives in their direction.

As time passed, however, he grew worried. He and General Qin threw one explosive flask after another, and they all landed on the Spirit Temple's forces. They soon ran out of them, having only succeeded in destroying the western portion of the Spirit Temple's camp. Now only explosive talismans remained. Feng Ming had to make a choice—would they target the munitions tents or the cannons?

"To the munitions tents," Feng Ming swiftly ordered. Their group, which had just suffered their first casualty, cut a wide arc as it circled around eleven large carts covered in black tarps. Their pace slowed as they approached, and the enemy's forces mobilized against them.

"Pick one cart per talisman," Feng Ming said. Both General Qin and Feng Ming threw out one talisman at each of the ten carts simultaneously. They could only hope that they'd gotten the one with special ammunition. Feng Ming directed their forces to the canons to use their shields to defend against the explosion.

"Charge!" the men yelled. Hundreds of red-armored men roared as they attacked the hundred-man team that was lucky beyond all reason. Blades that should have struck their necks slipped from the southern force's fingers. Arrows missed their marks and struck their own men. Axes fell off their handles and weapons broke as they tried to stop them. By all rights, all hundred men should have died ten times over, yet only five brave men had fallen. The hundred men were like gods of war who couldn't be killed no matter what was thrown at them.

Fifty more feet, Feng Ming thought as he slashed and stabbed through soldier after soldier. The tall spider cannon's legs were rooted firmly in the ground before them.

Forty more feet.

Their pace slowed to a crawl as the enemy successfully surrounded them.

Twenty more feet.

"Everyone, jump!" Feng Ming yelled. Each of the men, sensing the desperation in his voice, unleashed their secret techniques one after another. Icy flood dragons and fiery phoenixes cleared swaths of men out of their way. Earthen spikes and poisonous vines batted away enemy forces. General Qin even threw his treasured greatsword, which flew out toward one of the spider cannons and struck its leg.

The sturdy structure collapsed under the 10,000-jin object and struck three other legs, causing the cannon to fall sideways and backward, crushing a hundred troops in the process. Now the cannon was facing the south.

The startled southern soldiers collapsed under their fierce assault. As soon as Feng Ming's group passed the invisible energy shield that had previously been defending the cannon, Feng Ming realized that it wasn't enough. It couldn't protect them from the back.

"Everyone, duck and use your Earth Shield Talismans!"

It suddenly dawned on the eighty-one remaining soldiers that the resulting explosion could easily take their lives. Fortunately, they weren't stuck with mediocre Ice Shield Talismans but the extremely useful Earth Shield Talismans. The eighty-one overjoyed men activated them one by one, forming an impromptu convex wall to defend against the imminent explosion.

"Will they succeed?" Marshal Yong thought as he looked worriedly at the live battle map. A large earthen shield had appeared just in front of a collapsed cannon. The building rumbled as their men absorbed yet another strike from the four old cannons and the newly installed one. If Deputy Feng's team hadn't downed that one piece of equipment, then the marshal and deputy marshal would have been forced to intervene. Even then, many of their men would have perished under the backlash of their formation.

Deputy Marshal Mo sighed. "The original plan was for them to destroy the cannons, since the possibility of there being extra munitions was very high. But even if they destroy those munitions, can't they always mobilize more and handle us just the same?"

"Let's wait and see," Marshal Yong said. He held high hopes for Brother Feng's only son. The room was dead silent as they waited for the inevitable detonation. A small glitch appeared on the screen as the talisman went off. One after another, they detonated. Large pieces of shrapnel flew from the munition wagons. However, these pieces of shrapnel were round.

"Even that failed," Deputy Mo said, shaking his head. "The munitions likely need a large impact to detonate. All they managed to do was scatter them, buying us a few hours at most."

After inspecting for another moment, he sighed. "They didn't even get the key munitions wagon. All the spheres they spread out were black, while the last of the eleven wagons contains the clear spheres. It's over, Marshal."

Many of the generals in the room's eyes became bloodshot. They channeled even more of their qi into the formation, preparing themselves for their inevitable demise.

Marshal Yong, however, stood staring at the battlefield projection. "Deputy Mo?" he asked.

"What is it?" Deputy Mo grumbled.

"Did you notice the direction that cannon is pointed in?" Marshal Yong said.

Before Deputy Mo could comment, a deafening boom sounded. It was followed by hundreds of much smaller booms. The map distorted as the projection recalculated the battlefield. It wasn't long before a small crater was revealed in the center of the map. It was surrounded by many much smaller craters. In fact, it seemed like at least half of the opposing forces had been destroyed in the explosion, and it was all thanks to the initial spreading out of the other munitions carts.

"That lucky son of a goat," Marshal Yong whispered as he reviewed the damages. "Without spreading out the munitions carts, we would have only destroyed a tenth of their forces. Even their cannons would have been fine. Now, not only have their munitions been destroyed, but so have the cannons and half their forces. All because the one remaining wagon with potent ammunition happened to be standing in the line of fire of the crippled cannon."

The other generals had halted channeling their qi. They looked on in awe as a valiant group of eighty-one men continued their charge through enemy forces. Little by little, these forces became aware of the group that was rapidly charging outward and began circling around them. Even with their previous domineering performance, it would be difficult to escape.

"What are all you dolts waiting for?" Marshal Yong yelled. He walked toward a panel and entered some commands. Then he grabbed his own focus point. "System, activate the Life-Reaping Sword! Everyone, channel as much qi as you can. We're going to save those men!"

"That was the most exciting thing I've ever done," General Qin said as he slashed through five men with his recovered greatsword. They could no longer advance, so they huddled together and fought for as much time as they could. The more men they took down, the safer the kingdom would be. "If we die, they'll sing songs about us for the next decade."

"The next decade?" Captain Tong said. "More like the next century!"

Feng Ming chuckled. "I don't think our time is up yet, boys. We're just killing time until the cavalry arrives."

"What cavalry?" General Qin said. "We're eight miles away from the wall. What could they possibly do to help us?"

Suddenly a large blue blade appeared in the sky and slashed beside them. A hundred men fell, their bodies completely burned to ashes by its overbearing strength. Feng Ming didn't bother explaining. He and the men charged forward, but it didn't take long for their enemies to surround them once more. Three more of their men died before the sword appeared once again and cleared their enemies like wheat on harvest day.

"Press on, men!" Feng Ming yelled, not daring to be the least bit negligent. He and his men all wore grim expressions. They stood a chance, but how many of their men would die in the process?"

Sweat ran down Marshal Yong's face as he struggled to maintain the offensive formation. The Life-Reaping Sword was initially meant to attack at a mile's distance, and doubling this distance quadrupled the energy consumption. Even by gathering every last drop of energy in the fortress, half the generals had already collapsed from exhaustion.

Just two more strikes, Marshal Yong said as he channeled much of his remaining qi. The phantom sword reaped another three hundred lives with this strike, but the cost was staggering. Thousands of high-grade spirit stones were ground to dust while half of the remaining men in the fortress collapsed.

"Deputy Mo," Marshal Yong said. "We'll need you to lead the forces for a few days while I recover from this last strike." The deputy bowed and walked over to support the marshal as he popped yet another qi-recovery pill. Marshal Yong ignited his core and channeled the new thread of qi through the formation, finally clearing an exit for the forty-four remaining men. "That's all I can do for them," Marshal Yong whispered as he panted.

Suddenly he felt a sharp pain in his back just below a shoulder blade. A look of shock covered the faces of the nearby generals as blood flowed through the marshal's chest and mouth. His vision blurred as he sank down to the floor. He heard sounds of clashing armor, followed by the footsteps of generals dragging Deputy Mo from behind him.

"Why?" Marshal Yong croaked as the world turned cold. He looked at the man he'd served with for a hundred years before realizing his eyes were different than usual. Thin crimson lines he'd assumed were fatigue ran across the man's glazed eyes.

"Ah," the marshal whispered. "I'm relieved. You weren't Deputy Mo after all." He lifted his bloody hand to his face and looked out at the blurry battlefield projection. To his relief, Deputy Marshal Feng and his troops had managed to break free.

"The Spirit Temple has suffered disastrous losses this time," a man said as he stared into a crystal ball. "Wasn't this stratagem said to be foolproof? Yet we lost five hundred shamans and half of our cannon fodder in the process. Meanwhile, they destroyed ten cannons that took us five hundred years to save for and a hundred years to manufacture. We could only recover scrap metal from what was left of them. We require an explanation."

"Relax," said the soothing voice of a youth from the crystal sphere. "We have achieved two of four objectives. The marshal is dead, and one of our secondary objectives was completed. We didn't take the wall down today, but it won't last long."

"It's easy for you to relax, when your Cult of Enlightenment only lost a few lowly members," the man retorted. "You devils multiply easily, but we shamans might not see more than ten members in a single year. We'll expect compensation."

"I'll inform our lord of your grievances," the youthful voice said. "In the meantime, proceed with the next phase of the plan and let our bosses have a chat about compensation. Though I have no idea why you'd want money of all things."

"We want money because it hurts you the most," the man said. "You've sown karma by making a bad plan, so we shall reap it. We shamans always have our revenge."

Chapter 29: Upheaval

A plain-looking carriage covered in green livery arrived at the Jade Bamboo Auction House at the crack of dawn. Like the many other businesses in Central Square, the auction house was abuzz with activity. The ovens roared as the cooks baked bread. Papers flew as the clerks organized themselves for their busy day. Only two people knew that all preparations were meaningless for what was to come. One of them was inside the auction house, while the other was in the inconspicuous green carriage.

"Right this way, my friend," Wang Jun said hoarsely. He broke into a fit of coughing, only stopping to wipe away a trickle of blood. He led the man to a room in the middle of the auction house that had been prepared just for the occasion.

"I really hate wearing these hooded cloaks," the man said.

"This secrecy is necessary, Your Highness," Wang Jun said as they entered a room at the center of the auction house. As they traveled through layer upon layer of formations, Wang Jun's complexion quickly recovered. "If Prince Tian knew you were leaving the palace in these delicate times, he would undoubtedly think of a reason to stop you."

Prince Lei nodded. "It's ironic being a prisoner in one's own home. Though, can I still call it my home?"

"Not after today," Wang Jun said, shaking his head. "It will only become your home again if we win. Only death or exile awaits you if we fail."

The prince walked over to a strange golden globe in the center of the room. "And what about you?"

Wang Jun followed him to the orb and began tapping various runic characters. They glowed with golden light that traveled to delicate lines in the floor connected to a mosaic of additional runes. "If we fail, I'll lose my only chance at revenge. Then I'll refuse to serve the new family head and live in exile for the rest of my life, living in constant fear of the most powerful financial group on the continent."

Prince Lei chuckled. "And here I thought you didn't have enough skin in the game."

"We're in this together," Wang Jun said. "Are you ready?"

"As ready as I'll ever be," Prince Lei said, slightly adjusting his royal garb. "Let's begin."

"Owner, owner," Tan Zhi yelled. "Two more plates of steamed buns. You know the ones."

An older man behind the bar nodded and made his way back to the kitchen. Tan Zhi was seated with six friends. They were adventurers, men who risked their lives for fame and fortune.

"Heavens, I regret coming to this city," Geng Jian said. "Who would have thought it would be so politically complicated to buy things in the capital city? We want to buy weapons, not sell ourselves into indentured servitude." The man was in his midthirties, far older than the average adventurer. Most of them would retire before then, assuming they lived long enough.

"Would it be so bad to join the Ma family, though?" Tan Zhi asked. "They're offering a pretty good salary, far more than we can earn in even ten years of adventuring."

Two heaping plates of steamed buns were plopped onto their

table. The six men pounced on them like ravenous lions. It wasn't until the last one disappeared that they continued their conversation.

"You can all do what you want," Geng Jian said. "The only reason I've adventured until now is because I value my freedom." Seeing their perplexed looks, he elaborated. "Do you think retiring is easy for an adventurer? By fighting with others in the woods, we accumulate both large fortunes and bad blood. The only way to retire properly is to pledge your allegiance to a noble or a merchant, the type that can protect you. They rope you in because they know that soon enough, you'll find someone to start a family with and be trapped there for life. You give up your freedom for stability and a place to settle down." Geng Jian spat. "I don't want a life like that. I'll live free until the day I die."

Suddenly, the sound of a gong interrupted their conversation. "Greetings, everyone, this is Prince Lei. I have an important announcement to make. It relates to an important event in our kingdom: my father's illness and the selection of his successor.

"I regret to inform you that I have recently discovered some startling news. My brother, Prince Tian, has conspired against my royal father by poisoning him with the venom of a qi-binding serpent. As such, my father is close to death, with little hope of recovery. I realize that many of you may doubt this accusation. That is why I demand a trial by inquisitor. Should my words prove to be false, I will commit suicide on the spot.

"Now that you have been informed, it is time for me to share with you some important details regarding our united resistance against Song Tian."

The voice continued, but Geng Jian was no longer listening. He thought of multiple scenarios before coming to a reasonable conclusion.

"We have to get out of here," Geng Jian said. "Now!" He swiftly stood up and threw a pile of silver on the table, not bothering to count it. The five men swiftly followed him out of the restaurant and into a street that was becoming increasingly full. In the middle of their city district, a golden image of Prince Lei was speaking and providing instructions to the populace.

"Why do we need to get out?" Tan Zhi asked. "Isn't this a great opportunity? The noble families will be bidding for us like mad."

"You know nothing," Geng Jian snapped. "If we don't get out now, we'll have no choice but to participate in the conflict. Ours services will be steeply discounted, and as common sellswords, we'll be the first ones to die." Then he noticed that Tan Zhi's footsteps and three others stopped. Only Liu Cai, the second oldest, was still following him.

"We're staying," Tan Zhi said. "This opportunity is exactly what we've been looking for. This is where we make our fortune."

"Suit yourself," Geng Jian said. "I hope things work out for you." Then he sped off with Liu Cai in tow, hoping they weren't too late.

Lian Zexian was sweating. He had opened his store early, just like any other day, but unlike most days, it was unusually busy. He was initially overjoyed and had spent a considerable amount of time fawning over each of his customers. His hopes came crashing down once Prince Lei started his announcement.

"It is likely that this city will become chaotic, but I urge you to maintain order," Prince Lei's voice continued. "Our faction headquarters are situated in the Jade Bamboo Pavilion, likely the most secure building in this city. I advise you to join my faction and take shelter there…"

Most of his customers had filed out of the store to witness Prince's Lei's golden apparition, but four of them remained. Unlike before, they now carried large bags in which they rapidly stuffed whatever they could lay their hands on. They soon walked up to the counter.

"That'll be one thousand mid-grade spirit stones," Lian Zexian said with a shaky voice. The "customer" raised his eyebrow. "I meant five hundred mid-grade spirit stones." Seeing that the cultivator remained unmoved, Lian Zexian finally gave up. "I meant one hundred mid-grade spirit stones."

"That's more like it," the man said, grinning. "Make sure you give me a receipt making the discount official."

The merchant nodded to his clerk, who had no idea what was happening. She swiftly wrote up a bill of sale, which the merchant officiated with his red stamp.

"Let's cut the crap," the merchant said after the first one left. "I'll give you all a ninety-percent discount, but you need to get the hell out of my store within sixty breaths. Do I make myself clear?"

"Crystal clear," one of the three men said.

Sixty breaths later, the owner flipped a sign and closed his iron shutters. Then he swept up the remaining items into his bag of holding, emptied the register, and turned to the young clerk. She was a nice girl, but far too pretty for her own good.

"I'm heading to my house in the Jiangmen district," he said. "This place will soon become lawless and chaotic. I suggest you find your family and come find me to weather the storm."

"What storm? And what about the shop? Who'll watch it?" she asked. She usually slept in the shop and opened it first thing in the morning.

"There may not be a shop tomorrow," Lian Zexian said dryly. "This isn't my first civil war, and I won't be caught with my pants down this time."

"Your Highness," a soldier said as he walked into the crown prince's study. "There are no signs of Prince Lei in the palace. However, some servants say they saw an inconspicuous carriage leave in the morning. It went to the Jade Bamboo Auction House."

"You're dismissed," Prince Tian said. He turned to Minister Sima. "It seems my dear brother has lit the fuse, and it won't be long before the city is in chaos. Quickly issue men to send word to the people in our faction—they are to consolidate their followers in their geographical areas. Anyone who refuses to join our faction is a traitor to the crown and should be treated as such. Also, mobilize the city guard and announce that Song Lei is a traitorous rebel who is slandering the rightful crown prince to obtain personal power."

"Right away, my prince," Minister Sima said. "And what of his demand for a trial by inquisition?"

The prince smirked. "Announce that I will not bend to the will of traitors or to the Church of Justice, and that everything will be made clear once we arrest him and obtain his confession. Also, direct our information network to start slandering Prince Lei in taverns and restaurants. My guess is these will be the only places that won't get ransacked within the day."

"Right," Minister Sima said. "A stable food supply and shelter is the only bit of freedom the neutral forces will have left once we seal the city. They'll lay their lives down to defend them. If either you or Prince Lei dare to move against them, they would immediately join the other side out of indignation."

"Cultivators have a sense of pride that runs deep in their bones," Prince Tian said. "You have your orders."

"Yes, Your Highness," Minister Sima said. He frowned once he reached the door. "Have you seen Advisor Zhou and Protector Song? I'm afraid I haven't seen them in court for a full week."

Prince Tian's expression turned grim. "They're out on a special mission. There's no need to worry about them."

Minister Sima seemed to accept this explanation and swiftly left to perform his duties. As soon as the door closed, Prince Tian smashed his gauntleted fist into a small marble table.

"Zhou Li, you bastard," he muttered. "How dare you abandon me when I'm at my weakest."

For the hundredth time this week, and the twentieth time in the past fifteen minutes, he used his core-transmission jade to try contacting him. As usual, there was no response. "Has he betrayed me, or is he working behind the scenes like he usually does?"

Zhou Li's behavior wasn't anything unusual, but he couldn't help but worry about the timing. He hoped that Zhou Li would swoop in and save the day. Just like he always did.

"As predicted, my brother has begun suppressing dissent and consolidating his forces and resources," Prince Lei said. "They seem to be gathering their strength within the Ma, Bing, and Tian businesses, with subsidiary forces stationed within the Leng and Dong family compounds."

"Just as planned," Wang Jun said. "Let's focus on recruiting as many forces and civilians as possible and keeping them where we can defend them. Feed them and maintain some modicum of stability in their daily lives. Give them shelter and give them jobs. Their fear will only subside once they are directly involved in the conflict."

"Right," Prince Lei said. "We'll station our forces within the Jin and Huo family businesses, as well as the Jade Bamboo Conglomerate. Subsidiary forces will remain within the Ting, Jian, Meng, and Wei family buildings. Meanwhile, we'll have the others stand ready with their slaughtering formations. We have the advantage of financial resources and formations while they have stronger fortifications and military forces."

"About those fortifications," Wang Jun said. "They aren't nearly as troublesome as you think they are."

"Oh?" Prince Lei said. "The damage was your doing? I take it you left some hidden surprises?"

Wang Jun nodded. "Now that the announcement has been made, I need to head off to a meeting." He struck himself on the chest with a closed fist. His face paled as he coughed up blood. His expression also changed. He now looked weary and bedeviled. "How do I look?"

Prince Lei looked at him quizzically. "Positively deranged and worn out. I take it there's a reason for keeping up appearances?"

Wang Jun chuckled. "I'm nothing more than a cursed second young master who's struggling at death's door. I don't even have the strength to truss a chicken, much less control my own family business."

"If you say so," Prince Lei said. "Enjoy yourself. By the way, I left a folder of evidence with my sister and the Church of Justice. Hopefully they'll see the light and give us a hand."

"Only time will tell," Wang Jun said. "I sent the same folder to the last remaining wildcard. We'll see if he takes the bait."

Then he summoned a shadowy door and left the well-defended auction house.

Wang Jun entered a familiar stone chamber. The Black King was seated at the table as usual, looking patient as always. "I take it you're responsible for the chaos upstairs?" the dark figure asked.

Wang Jun erupted into a coughing fit. "How could I possibly manage such a scene when I'm in such a state?"

"I received the troubling news that you've been haunted," the Black King said. "Are you sure you won't die before we close the deal on the immortal-jade core? I've almost secured a buyer."

"Relax," Wang Jun said, sitting down weakly. "I'm still more than capable. This is a temporary situation, nothing more. I've already asked the family to send a monk to cure my affliction. It should take no longer than a month and a half."

"So long?" the Black King asked.

"There are only three monks capable enough in the entire continent," Wang Jun said helplessly. "You know how monks are. Regardless, you need not concern yourself. I have an additional business deal I would like to propose."

The Black King nodded and tossed out two bags. "The profits

from our last exchange. There is a ledger in each of the bags. Feel free to inspect them."

Wang Jun nodded and pulled out the ledgers, which he quickly memorized. Then, after thinking for a while, he pulled out another bag.

"Five hundred thousand high-grade spirit stones," Wang Jun said. "The fear in this city is at its peak. I want you offer a package deal to the citizens of Songjing: Anyone who wants out of the city can sell you their property at twenty-five percent of the market price one year prior, and you will help them out of the city with their remaining assets. I'll pay you a two-percent commission for each package deal. Of course, for every two percent you save in buying the properties, I'll give you an additional one percent in commission. Note that I don't care about the buildings, only the land they're built on."

"Deal," the Black King said, summoning another black contract. This time, he wrote golden words on the blank contract before signing it. Wang Jun followed up with his own signature.

"By the way," Wang Jun said. "Due to my poor health and the situation outside the city, I feel uncomfortable exchanging the immortal-jade core in these secretive conditions. I want to change the venue."

"Impossible," the Black King said. "It will be here or nowhere else."

"It must be at the Jade Bamboo Auction House, with some of my subordinates present," Wang Jun said. "Forgive me for being blunt, but I don't feel safe completing such a large exchange in your territory, not when I'm affected by this curse."

"We have a secrecy clause," the Black King said. "And I think you trust your subordinates far more than you should."

"Then we'll have to amend it," Wang Jun said. "That, or I'll pull out of the contract as per Section 4 Clause 12, which states that 'should a party's health greatly deteriorate to the point where the exchange cannot be completed safely, they may willingly withdraw from the contract with no penalty.'"

The Black King pondered for a moment before assenting. "Fine. But if you dare pull a fast one on me, remember that I've killed far more men than you realize. All of them powerful figures with great backgrounds."

"Noted," Wang Jun said. Then he pulled out a Spatial Transference Talisman and left the premises.

Chapter 30: Choice

The ever-shifting crimson-and-gold barrier taunted Cha Ming as he pondered his dilemma. He had risked his life for his friends and even strangers, but for the first time, he might have to risk something he prized most: a bright future.

There were three possible outcomes if he chose to break through to core formation with an unstable foundation. The best-case scenario was that he succeeded but delayed his future cultivation, a small price to pay if the fate of the Song Kingdom was at stake. The worst case was him crippling his ability to cultivate by trying to advance prematurely. In between these two extremes, he could potentially damage his foundation. This wouldn't affect his strength in the long term but might require him to dissipate his cultivation and restart from scratch. Without the starting point for the Greater Five Elements cultivation technique, he was doomed to mediocre achievements in comparison, and without strength, his choices would be limited.

The small silhouette of a fox came to mind. First and foremost, he owed Huxian. Any limits on his life and power would ultimately limit Huxian. He then thought of the time where Wang Jun gave up ten years of his life to save the small fox. He still owed his friend a large favor for his sacrifice.

Then, he thought of Sun Wukong, whose remnant soul still

slept in the Clear Sky Brush after protecting him from the heavenly tribulation. It was something he was ashamed to have forgotten; he only remembered it now during this rare moment of clarity.

"Even if I succeed in breaking through, I still might not be able to affect the overall situation," Cha Ming thought out loud. "Then again, Zhou Li wants me to give up. That must mean he believes I can affect his plans."

A funny thought occurred to Cha Ming. Hadn't he wanted these difficult decisions and the choices to begin with? He chuckled mentally at the thought of cowering away from the first one he was offered. If he couldn't even make this one, how would this life be any different than his previous one?

Katcha.

He felt a limit break, and power he didn't know existed surfaced and brightened the jade garment on his resplendent soul. His sudden insight had allowed him to break through to the early resplendent soul realm.

Cha Ming hesitated no longer. He immediately circulated his qi to achieve the best possible condition, despite his poor foundation. His qi pillars felt murky, and the countless bubbles that polluted them caused tiny vibrations to propagate as he forced out what little contamination he could.

Having made up his mind, he popped a mouthful of Pillar Expanding Pills, causing his pillars to grow once more. They creaked and groaned at the influx of impurities, which were swiftly diluted by the large amount of qi flushing through his system. Instead of the smooth growth he'd experienced before, the pillars grew in fits and bursts. He ignored this behavior and kept popping pills until he ran out of those at the appropriate grade. It wasn't long before his foundation reached a bottleneck and halted its growth. Any additional qi he absorbed polished the tarnished pillars and refilled his qi seas one final time before his breakthrough.

Once his qi reserves were completely replenished, he immediately proceeded to pop three Pillar Eruption Pills. His murky pillars destabilized, and a large amount of qi forced them to expand past the bottleneck. Instead of the clear sound of crashing glass, this breakthrough into peak foundation establishment sounded like metal scraping on a glass plate. His extremely turbid qi seas rushed into the already murky pillars, causing them to become opaque. Many different inconsistencies could now be found in their marvelous runic structure. They grew until his qi seas were completely depleted.

Finally, he took the last batch of Pillar Expanding Pills. One by one, they dissolved into viscous qi that dumped into the polluted cesspools that were now his qi seas. He forced the qi into his pillars, growing them little by little toward the invisible barrier in his Dantian. The pillars grew and grew before stopping just shy of the membrane.

Cha Ming frowned. "There's not enough energy to reach the limits of foundation establishment. What to do..."

It wasn't a surprising result. The pills Mo Tianshen had created were tailormade for ideal conditions. How could he possibly have expected Cha Ming to do something so reckless? After pondering for a moment, he recalled the five mid-grade energy-gathering formations he'd memorized.

Might as well try it out, Cha Ming thought.

He summoned seventy-two of the unaligned sigils Wang Bing had gifted him in Quicksilver. One by one, he painted five elemental sigils that he immediately condensed into Dao sigils. Creating seventy-two of them took him a full day. Then he took another day to paint a few of the necessary runes he required and incorporated them into the Dao sigils. After that, he used his 180 Dao sigils to summon five energy-gathering formations, one after another.

The five formations completed, he flicked out a pile of mid-grade spirit stones, which he rapidly converted to pure five-element energy and directly absorbed into his qi seas. As he expected, using five formations simultaneously was the only way to keep his qi in balance while cultivating. He mobilized the steady flow of energy to slowly grow each of his five pillars bit by bit. One day later, a loud thud ended his meditative trance. Just like that, he'd reached the peak of foundation establishment. The only way forward was to break through core formation.

Cha Ming took a deep breath and adjusted his condition. He reviewed the theory in his mind once more as he flushed out as many impurities as possible from his foundation and qi seas. While he didn't have the next step of the Greater Five Elements technique, he had casually browsed through other manuals at the Alabaster Group. Regardless of which cultivation method was being used, each one instructed the cultivator to "melt" their qi pillars. In doing so, they could combine each one into a solid core, which they would then repeatedly compress to one ninth of its original size. However, his pillars were sigil pillars—how could he possibly melt them? This would destroy their inherent runic structure, which was what granted him such potent qi in the foundation-establishment stage in the first place.

A day passed as he finished his final preparations. Much of the turbidity in his qi seas had faded. Due to the diminishing returns, Cha Ming proceeded to the first step in forming his core: assimilation. He forcibly absorbed the liquid qi in his Dantian into each of his five pillars. They struggled to take in the excess amount, but under his fierce willpower, they remained stable in the arduous process. Then he swallowed three core-formation pills, which not only provided him with great energy and resplendent force, but also slightly destabilized the firm structure of his qi pillars.

Cha Ming used this change of firmness to slightly modify the runic pillars. He increased their width to roughly double the original while slowly shrinking their length to a quarter of what they had been. He did this slowly, leaving enough time for the runes to shift. Meanwhile, the black-and-white lattice joining the pillars also adjusted. Its thickness doubled while its internal runes condensed into a more energy-efficient form.

It took a full day to fully adjust the runic structure. Cha Ming let out a sigh of relief.

The first part of my plan is a success. I did it before, so I can do it again. After checking his foundation once more, he slowly rotated the pillars, shifting them to the side while simultaneously adjusting the black-and-white lattice. It wasn't long before the five pillars were all pointed toward the center. He then started the next step—twisting his foundation.

Using the Dao sigils as his basis, he speculated that it was possible to compress his own foundation into a core in the very same way. As he shifted the pillars and brought them increasingly close together, he made sure to shift the black-and-white lattice while simultaneously thickening it. The originally cylindrical lattice now resembled five white slices of pie and a single black sphere in the center. As they shifted, they became two helixes, a large white one and a smaller black one. Cha Ming continuously shortened and thickened, shortened and thickened.

Soon, the diameter of his would-be core shrank down a quarter of the width of his Dantian, half of its original size. The originally smooth process became tiring and tedious, and every single compression caused great strain on Cha Ming's energy and soul. It wasn't long before Cha Ming realized that his foundation had run out of energy, despite his extremely energy-dense core-formation pills.

The development wasn't the least bit surprising to Cha Ming, who calmly threw out the hundred thousand high-grade spirit stones he hadn't lent to Wang Jun onto the five energy-gathering formations and slowly absorbed them. Three days passed, and slowly but surely, what was originally one half a Dantian in diameter became a quarter, then a fifth, then a tenth. After reaching a tenth, it still hadn't stabilized. This was expected, since Cha Ming's Dao sigils only occupied one tenth of their original size. Cha Ming continued. One tenth soon became a twelfth.

Suddenly, a creaking sound like metal on metal rang through his mind as the shifting runes hit a snag. He used his willpower to shove through the obstruction, and the compression continued. He hit another snag at one fifteenth, and another at one sixteenth. Cha Ming's expression turned grim as he realized what was happening: The instabilities due to the impurities in his pillars were making it difficult to shift their internal structure as he compressed. It was becoming increasingly difficult to proceed, and the process required more and more energy.

It took Cha Ming one day to go from one twelfth to one fifteenth, and one more day to go from one fifteenth to one seventeenth. It took three more days before he reached a bottleneck at one nineteenth.

Cha Ming's complexion was pale. When he had originally condensed his Dao sigils, they had snapped together smoothly like it was the only natural structure to begin with. But the runes in his Dantian were different—they were impure and difficult to shift.

Every single compression now caused great friction in the runic structure of his pseudo-core. He also realized that there was no retreating from the path he had chosen. Should he take away the pressure his resplendent force was exerting on his Dantian, it would quickly unwind, releasing the massive energy he'd absorbed into his Dantian and body. Death would be an ideal case.

Cha Ming pounded away at the spherical structure that had almost reached completion. Every blow of his resplendent force caused the pseudo-core to creak, while every surge of qi caused it to shudder. He watched as every spirit stone he possessed disappeared, one after another. Once these had vanished, he emptied out most of his liquified elemental essence. Fortunately, he only needed nine tenths of it before his core reached a saturated state.

Bang. Bang. Bang.

He continued to impact the pseudo-core with his resplendent force for an entire day. At this point, it had been almost nine days since he began his breakthrough. His mental strength was at its limits—even converting the last of his liquified elemental essence wouldn't help. It wasn't long before his blows weakened. Nine tenths, eight tenths, seven tenths… The strikes weakened gradually until finally, he could barely use one hundredth of his original strength. Despite his exhausted state, he continued giving the pseudo-core one light tap after another. This continued for an hour until he gave it one last desperate blow.

He heard a soft click. The weak blow was the straw that broke the camel's back. Cha Ming's sigil foundation suddenly snapped into place, and the voids within were immediately filled by the sudden surge of energy that accompanied his breakthrough. The five energy-gathering formations shattered as the incoming energy overwhelmed them and directly entered his body. The energy was a gift of heaven and earth for breaking through the next level and wouldn't stop until his core was formed.

The voids in his core's runic structure rapidly filled with a gaseous qi that was completely different from the initial gaseous qi he'd condensed into liquid. Instead, it was a higher-quality core qi. In his joy, he hadn't realized that his core qi was four times more potent than the average core qi due to his sigil core. As the five-element qi was replenished, so was the peaceful creation-qi helix and the frightening destruction-qi helix. The gas remained within the black-and-white structures without causing a fuss.

Once the five-element qi, creation qi, and destruction-qi reservoirs were full, Cha Ming looked on with joy as the remaining voids on his core were filled with a grayish substance. It felt soothing and frightening at the same time, and when he probed it with his resplendent force, he detected nothing. Although he couldn't evaluate its function, his instincts told him that the gray substance stabilized the entire core and was what made it possible in the first place. In fact, it reminded him of the substance in the voids in his bones.

Gray qi filled the voids in his core little by little. Yet another day passed until finally, his core was fully saturated. At this point, Cha Ming's expression grew dark as he sensed a calamity approaching him. His core, which was now almost full, suddenly began to shake. The shaking emanated from each of the five elemental sigils that composed his Dao core. It intensified with each wisp of gray qi that entered it. As much as he wished to stop the absorption process, he couldn't. In fact, the rate of accumulation increased. Before long, it reached a peak that caused crunching and screeching throughout his body and soul. A large amount of stress had accumulated during its formation and had to be relieved.

Regrettably, Cha Ming's core had already entered the final

polishing stage. While the inside of his core had a runic structure, the outside was becoming more and more like polished jade. The smooth surface contained five colors as well as black, white, and gray. The shaking increased until finally, something gave way. A heartrending snap shook him to the very core. The smooth surface of his core cracked, causing a large amount of the accumulated qi to suddenly dissipate. The cracks crossed each of the five colored surfaces.

Cha Ming waited as the remnant quakes in his core faded. Once they stabilized, he again began absorbing the energy of heaven and earth through normal cultivation. It entered the small core normally, but he sensed that one third of the qi he absorbed dissipated back into his surroundings. He sighed in relief as he concluded that he was in no danger of dying or being crippled. At worst, he could always dissipate his cultivation and start from scratch.

After completing his inspection, Cha Ming opened his eyes. His frightening core qi swept across the shifting red-and-gold barrier, which shattered instantly. He then walked forward, his powerful body and surging qi smashing any traps or enemies that stood in his way.

Not far away, many core-formation devil cultivators and corrupted guardians stood ready to receive him. Cha Ming ignored the swords, sabers, and magical techniques that flew toward him and expanded the Clear Sky Pillar to enormous proportions. His thick qi and powerful body absorbed the blows of dozens of techniques as he smashed into them with raw physical strength. The devils shrank back as his Devil-Sealing Intent ate away at their very souls.

Soon, the room was deathly quiet. Only the sound of gently settling dust and debris could be heard in the silent labyrinth. That, and a soft rumbling that grew louder and louder as Huxian's trio smashed their way toward Cha Ming's position.

Chapter 31: Swamp Tribulation

Brother succeeded!" Huxian said as he smashed yet another labyrinth guardian. His pseudo-core began rampantly absorbing surrounding energy as it transformed into an actual core instead of just a hollow structure.

"Does that mean we'll have to face the tribulation?" Lei Jiang said worriedly as he smashed into a trap.

"It can't be avoided," Huxian said. "The plane hates me and resents anyone who helps me. Don't worry, though. I'll protect you."

"These wall creatures are really weak," Silverwing commented as he smashed one after another. "Why were we even scared of this thing in the first place?" He unleashed a gust of wind that crashed through five consecutive walls as they charged over to Cha Ming's position.

"Perhaps it's just a baby," Lei Jiang said as he turned into a ball of lightning and smashed yet another wall. "Maybe it can grow stronger with time."

"Regardless, it's helpless against us," Huxian said as he joined his friends in smashing the colossal structure. His true form was now 160 feet in length, but he kept it compact for the sake of convenience. A third tail sprouted near the other two, and the three beasts were struck by a foreboding sensation.

The Swamp Tribulation would be there soon, and there was no running from it.

Cha Ming changed his direction abruptly as the position between him and Huxian became increasingly clear. The rumbling intensified as not only Silverwing but also Cha Ming smashed down wall after all. Corrupted guardians and devil cultivators guarding the maze were caught unaware by Cha Ming's sudden change in behavior. They didn't have a chance to react as he smashed through all obstacles to reunite with his brother.

One last wall finally crumbled to dust before Cha Ming and the three demon beasts stood face to face. The trio wore a victorious expression when they realized that they had triumphed over the wall.

"You were right, brother," Huxian said. "The wall was just putting on airs—it couldn't do anything against Silverwing's mighty strength."

"Good," Cha Ming said, shrinking the Clear Sky Pillar down to its larger brush form. "Huxian, you first. With my increased strength, drawing out the Swamp Tribulation Totem should be a piece of cake."

"What's cake?" Huxian asked curiously.

"It's a delicious sweet desert," Cha Ming said as he swiftly painted blue, green, and brown totem lines over the fox's fur. "They don't make it in the Song Kingdom or the Quicksilver Empire, but I'll find some for you one day."

Huxian's eyes shone brightly as he patiently waited for Cha Ming to finish. After a few hours, the murky lines on his fur glowed brightly and condensed into a tight runic structure that protected him like an armor.

Cha Ming proceeded to work on Lei Jiang and Silverwing next. Finally, he shrank the Clear Sky Brush into its talisman brush form. He used it to paint one small rune after another, which shot into various places on his body. Little by little, Cha Ming's bare skin was covered in so many tattoos that he now resembled a cave-dwelling tribesman.

"How much longer do we have?" Cha Ming asked.

"Two days, but I can call it forward," Huxian said.

Cha Ming nodded, and the surroundings immediately darkened. A peculiar smell filled the air as an ominous presence snuck into the labyrinth completely unimpeded. After all, the labyrinth was a creation of this world—how could it possibly resist the will of the cosmos?

"The first stage," Cha Ming whispered. "Corrosion." A swirling maelstrom of viscous heaven and earth energy appeared around them. It attacked their bodies constantly, threatening to burn away their skin and bones with their terrifying power. Cha Ming could have resisted this with a combination of his body and his core-formation qi, but as the greenish-blue energy invaded his body, the Swamp Tribulation Runes on his body activated and reduced its effectiveness by nine tenths. The remainder of the energy was easily handled by his fierce body, and the three demons did the same.

"You call that a calamity?" Lei Jiang yelled. The small mouse had grown arrogant since its breakthrough to core formation. "That barely tickles. I dare you to do better!"

The surrounding energy suddenly concentrated on the small rodent. "I apologize, I apologize!" the small purple mouse said, and the tribulation returned to normal.

Seeing that its corrosive abilities were ineffective, the malestream halted, and the energy in the air thickened. Cha Ming discovered that the armor could only do so much against this second stage, the poison calamity. The mist condensed into a liquid, which then began seeping through the cracks in his armor and slowly but surely dripping onto his skin. At first it felt like nothing but a tickle, but soon it felt like bee stings all over his body.

Lei Jiang was the first to howl in pain. As the weakest member of the group, and the one with the poorest defenses, small pinholes began to appear all over his hide. The purple fur he prided himself in was quickly dissolving as the green and blue qi pierced his skin like daggers and spread into his bloodstream. Cha Ming succumbed next, followed by Huxian, and finally Silverwing.

The pain was unbearable. It wormed its way through his blood vessels like liquid lava as Cha Ming mustered his qi and vital energy to fight against it. When the two energies clashed, the pain doubled. This was a small price to pay for halting the damage it caused all over his body. His flesh struggled to regenerate as his refined marrow pumped increasing amounts of blood into his veins. The only part of his body not threatened by the poison were his bones.

"Bodhi seed, what's happening?" Gong Lan asked as a small piece of stone crumbled off the increasingly frail labyrinth walls. "The corruption might have modified the wall's functioning, but it shouldn't be so fragile that a few large men with hammers could completely destroy it."

As she said this, she stretched out her hand and scratched it with her soft fingers. The nearby Luo Xuehua gasped as the wall crumbled to dust under Gong Lan's weak movement.

"I'm not sure," the bodhi seed said. "I feel the Plane Will's wrath. It has unleashed a calamity, but one that is far different than I've ever seen in my lifetime. It's much weaker than a transcendence calamity, and its elemental composition is completely off. A typical tribulation would be composed of wind, fire, and lightning, while this one bears the elements of water, earth, and wood. The name 'Swamp Tribulation' comes to mind, but I have no idea why it was summoned."

"Regardless, the walls are weakening," Gong Lan said. "We should use this opportunity to move further into the labyrinth."

The bodhi seed bobbed up and down. "The tribulation is damaging the labyrinth's walls, forcing it to divert a large amount of energy to defend and repair itself." It looked toward the center of the labyrinth. "Whatever you do, don't head in that direction. The calamity is converging there, and anything that walks within its range will experience its wrath."

Cha Ming's mind relaxed as the agony in his body receded. The first two phases of the Swamp Tribulation could not be fought, only passively endured. Having resisted the corrosion and poisoning portions of the calamity, all four of their bodies swiftly recovered as they prepared for the third stage: smothering. The totems on their bodies had completely faded while defending them previously, and they could only depend on their own power to prevail.

The swamp energy around them thickened once more until it became a slurry that weighed down on them like fifty feet of swampy debris. Cha Ming quickly realized that he couldn't breathe, and the surrounding bog was now rapidly draining away at both his qi and vitality. The remaining challenge was to escape the swamp. If they didn't, their bones would remain here for all eternity.

"I'll help Lei Jiang," Huxian yelled. The small mouse was not as powerful as the other three, and its impressive speed couldn't help it. Conversely, Huxian was the least affected. His three tails glowed with three lights that whizzed around him like three shooting stars. One glowed purple like Lei Jiang's lightning, while another was a dull azure. The third color was a murky greenish blue, much like the swamp they were currently experiencing. While it didn't glow brightly like the purple star, it wasn't dull like the azure one. In fact, it seemed to be glowing brighter by the second, as though the tribulation's energy was slowly seeping into it and reinforcing it.

A circle of light purification and dark swallowing surrounded Huxian and Lei Jiang. This move by Huxian immediately provoked the tribulation's energy to double; a tribulation could be transcended with help, but only at a great price. Nevertheless, the purple star strengthened the small mouse, and the black-and-white aura around them weakened the pressure they felt substantially. They inched out toward the outside, leaving Silverwing and Cha Ming to fend for themselves. The fox and the mouse summoned black-and-white battle armors, and Silverwing followed.

"I'm out," Silverwing said. The falcon activated its roc bloodline and grew until its wingspan reached eighty feet. Its silver wings cut through the Swamp Tribulation as though it was wind. Then Silverwing flapped his mighty wings and flew twenty feet in a single go. After ten more flaps, he forced his way out of the range of the tribulation, which ceased choking him and absorbing his vitality.

"Looks like I'm the only one left," Cha Ming mumbled. He thought for a bit before summoning his own battle armor. Black-and-white tattoos revealed themselves on his skin and formed a suit of shadow and light. The armor linked up to his five-element qi and functioned as a replacement to his normal qi shields.

Then Cha Ming summoned a high-grade Blade Barrier combat formation. Seventy-two sigils swirled around him and cut away at the bog, weakening it ever so slightly. On a whim, he summoned thirty-six other sigils and rearranged the combat-formation structure. He used his accumulated knowledge of formations and his extremely dense core qi to force them together into an impromptu peak combat formation. The blades slashed the surrounding bog and eased their pressure. He gritted his teeth and took his first step forward in the swamp's strangling field.

He paled as he realized that, despite all his efforts, that single step was more difficult than wielding a 40,000-jin Clear Sky Pillar. After substantial effort, he used his qi and fierce body strength to urge his foot forward. To his amazement, not only was he fighting against the swamp, he was fighting against himself. The voids in his bones had actually activated involuntarily and increased his body's weight to 430,000 jin. He had no way to retract it.

"What a frightening swamp tribulation," Cha Ming whispered.

Both his increased weight and the restrictive energy of the

tribulation made each step a ridiculous ordeal. The first step carried him a single foot forward but drained one percent of his total energy. After ten steps, he'd consumed a little more than eleven percent. To his amazement, the energy being consumed increased the farther from the center he was. After fifty steps, he'd consumed sixty percent of his energy reserves, meaning that he couldn't possibly transcend the tribulation with his current strategy.

Cha Ming's eyes flickered to Huxian, who was also at the same distance and panting under the pressure of supporting Lei Jiang. He didn't dare ask his brother for help—after all, the small fox couldn't possibly resist yet another portion of the tribulation. Cha Ming wracked his mind as he thought of every talisman in his possession. The offensive and defensive talismans he possessed would not have much effect, and neither would the shielding ones. This disqualified the standard ones and most of his poetic talismans. Only two talismans came to mind: the Sharp Talisman and the Momentum Talisman.

He activated the Sharp Talisman without any hesitation. His movements became concise and aggressive, like sharp blades that cut through the bog that surrounded him. It greatly decreased his energy consumption, but he could tell it was hardly enough. Therefore, Cha Ming recalled the many feelings he'd experienced when painting the Momentum Talisman. He dwelled on the unstoppable forward movement he'd experienced since bouncing back in Crystal Falls. His progression as a talisman artist and formation artist had been swift and his cultivation speed even more so.

My momentum is unstoppable, Cha Ming thought as he activated the Momentum Talisman. His speed increased gradually, and the swamp's restrictions became increasingly thin against his movements.

Still not enough. His increased speed caused him to feel the nature of the swamp's resistance; his every movement caused the bog to shift and create turbulent eddies. Then it hit him—his poetic talismans were a matter of interpretation.

He felt a boundary between the two talismans, momentum and resistance, fade. Momentum and resistance were two sides of the same coin, and as something moved faster, its resistance would increase. But the viscosity of the fluid affected its impedance, which was how the Resistance Talisman affected it in the first place. If he could increase it, could he not decrease it? The sudden inspiration struck him like a bolt of lightning. He suddenly stopped traveling through the murky waters and withdrew a sheet of paper and the Clear Sky Brush.

The drain on his strength decreased substantially, but it didn't stop. He diverted a portion of his core qi and resplendent force to isolate a small area just in front of him, where he put out a small sheet of talisman paper. He used a little of his remaining water essence to quickly put his epiphany into words.

> *The ocean cares not for drowning children;*
> *Man is a slave to the sea of fate.*
> *Flowing down from high to low;*
> *Never questioning his direction.*

Like the resistance in water, life's many challenges could be faced not only by struggling against them, but by acting upon the resistance itself. Struggling against a thick swamp was difficult, while struggling against a calm pool of water was much less challenging. Air was also a fluid—its resistance was so miniscule that people didn't even know it existed.

Conversely, momentum involved not only forward movement but lack thereof. An object at rest was difficult to move, just like a person who'd lost all hope and will to go forward. The lack of movement was another form of resistance, an impedance to both himself and the people around him. This was the nature of flow, and he called the new combined talisman the Flow Talisman. Dark- and light-blue ink swirled as the poetic talisman's color became uniform. It now looked like the purest water from a pristine glacier.

Cha Ming activated the newly created paper, which was evidently an early core talisman. The paper didn't burn but dissolved into his surroundings, thinning the nearby tribulation swamp in the surrounding fifty feet.

The thinned location intersected with Huxian's, who was still struggling to exit the swamp. He looked at Cha Ming in shock as the core talisman directly suppressed their three tribulations simultaneously. The swamp struggled to reinforce itself, but Cha Ming, Huxian, and Lei Jiang had already left its sphere of influence. Once they escaped, the Swamp Tribulation disappeared as swiftly as it had come. Heaven and earth energy rushed into them as soon as the tribulation left, like a weak apology after a fierce beating. Their wounds and qi rapidly recovered. They then gazed at their surroundings, which were nothing more than shattered remnants of a once-expansive labyrinth.

They could now see two locations: the entrance and the exit. Cha Ming saw three groups in the distance: Gong Lan and Luo Xuehua, who were nearest to the exit; Dongfang Hao and the two core-formation protectors from the Alabaster Group; and three monks from Gong Lan's original entourage.

The others were nowhere to be found.

Chapter 32: Motive

"Kill!" the Jin family's leader yelled as he led a large number of allied troops toward exposed Ma family protectors. The useless sellswords broke down as soon as a tenth of them were killed. They swiftly retreated from the gate they were guarding, bypassing the courtyard and running straight back into the Ma family complex.

"Useless," the Ma family leader muttered. "Remind me again who made the decision to hire these useless thugs?"

"Your son is incompetent," said Ma Yong, a younger version of the Ma family leader. "Shall we leave them outside to die?"

"No, we must let them in," the Ma family leader said. "If we don't shelter them, we'll affect the morale of all the mercenaries in the crown prince's faction. We simply can't bear that responsibility."

The young master nodded, and they both looked on grimly as their troops retreated and abandoned the outer courtyard. "At least this building has been fortified by the geomancer. It's one of the few buildings that weren't damaged during those mysterious attacks."

Ma Yong chuckled. "It's a good thing we paid him a bonus to establish a firmer structure. All those fools in the other households are probably pissing their pants worrying about whether their building is defective. We're the only ones who don't have such worries."

"Indeed, with these fortifications, we can hold out until the succession is over," the Ma family leader said. "By then, we'll either have contributed greatly or we'll beg for forgiveness. However, with the way things are going, I refuse to believe that we'll lose."

Suddenly, the ground shook slightly. "What was that?" Ma Yong asked. The shaking didn't subside. Instead it was accompanied by a few stronger tremors. A crack appeared on a wall that shouldn't have broken in a hundred years.

"What's going on?" the Ma family leader said. He walked up to the newly formed crack and lightly touched it. It collapsed, and pieces of wall fell down a dark gap that ran down the entire length of the wall. He paled.

"We've been tricked!" the Ma family leader said. "I'll have that geomancer's head!"

He didn't know the damage had been caused by two little miscreants on their rampage throughout the city. And he never would.

Soon after, the building crumbled as it was attacked by the Jin family's troops. Eventually the heavy roof collapsed and killed everyone in the building.

"The operation was a success," Prince Lei said to Wang Jun, who was casually leafing through a book he'd read a dozen times. "A third of the crown prince's forces were annihilated instantly. In addition, several pieces of real estate have become available."

"Don't forget your faithful helper when you appropriate them," Wang Jun said, chuckling. "I would buy them, but it seems they no longer have an owner."

While he looked calm on the surface, he was actually worried. The crown prince had yet to muster the full force of the military against them, and he wasn't sure how they would withstand it. Without external aid, they had a thirty-percent chance at best to pull through.

One message after another trickled into their makeshift command room. News of victories and defeats throughout the city were filtered and summarized to Prince Lei, who gave out orders to their field commanders under Wang Jun's discreet advice.

A half day later, Prince Lei's previously relaxed expression had turned grim. "The situation's turned around. Our attack on the Alchemists Association headquarters has failed. The geomancer, seeing the problems in the other buildings, thoroughly inspected their last few holdouts and fixed and reinforced them. It won't be easy to take them. Also, there's another piece of bad news."

"What's that?" Wang Jun asked.

He didn't have to wonder for long. Their building shook, and screams rang out from outside. His eyes narrowed. "It seems they've decided to cut right to the chase. Unfortunately, a substantial portion of our forces are in other districts." Wang Jun struck himself in the chest, regaining his sickly complexion. "Let's go supervise the situation."

Prince Lei led Wang Jun out of the room. He was soon joined by Protector Ren, who supported him as they flew to their destination. They soon arrived at a vantage point that overlooked the chaotic city.

In Central Square, two sides were facing off. Prince Lei's faction wore green livery and was composed mostly of upper-tier sellswords and Wang family employees. Prince Tian's forces wore blue. A large number of military troops meshed awkwardly with scattered cultivators and noblemen. They outnumbered Prince Lei's troops two to one.

Prince Tian himself took the lead. He flew up with Marshal Feng and twenty-four other core-formation cultivators. In response, Prince Lei jumped off the vantage point and floated out with fourteen core-formation experts. Five were Wang family employees, while the other nine were men from his own faction. They stared daggers at each other from across the battlefield, neither side daring to back down.

"You should have known your limits before committing treachery," Prince Tian said. "As much as I loathe to kill my own brother, you leave me with very little choice."

"Cut the crap," Prince Lei said. "You and I both know who's caused this situation. If you hadn't poisoned Father, and if you hadn't killed First Brother and Fourth Brother, I would have gladly let you take the throne."

Prince Tian's eyes narrowed as murmurs ran through both sides. These were fresh accusations. "After committing treason, it's easy to casually slander the other party. I personally won't bother to respond to such deceitful tricks. I'll make you submit through force."

The twenty-four cultivators erupted with core-formation might. Prince Lei's fourteen experts released theirs in response, but it was clear who was on the losing end.

"Kill them all!" Prince Tian shouted.

"Kill!" Prince Tian's men yelled. Their fighting intent flooded the battlefield, invigorating the forces beneath them, who charged with all they had.

"Fight to the last!" Prince Lei's men shouted. Their forces recovered from their opponents' battle cries just in time to defend themselves against the initial impact.

Wang Jun, who was watching from the vantage point, held out his hand. He coughed up blood as wave after wave of dark energy weaved through their forces and obscured their movements and attacks. The situation stabilized rapidly, but it was only a matter of time until they lost.

Blood filled the streets as the masses of cultivators were cut down by blades and spears. After a half hour of fierce fighting, a quarter of Prince Lei's forces had fallen, as had two of their core-formation cultivators.

Meanwhile, only one of Prince Tian's experts had fallen. Sighing, Wang Jun sent a signal to his people inside the auction house. Six slaughtering formations immediately activated and slayed a third of Prince Tian's unsuspecting men.

The instant these formations erupted, six core-formation experts broke off from Prince Tian's battle formation and began taking countermeasures. They directed their attacks to the formations, which could only retreat and match them blow for blow. High-grade spirit stones evaporated by the thousands. Despite the great blow they dealt to the crown prince's forces, the situation in the battlefield had hardly changed.

Suddenly a flash of red plunged toward the fierce melee, instantly suppressing both sides. Wang Jun's eyes narrowed as he recognized the figure—it was one of the king's guardians, a peak-core-formation cultivator. His lips curved into a smile as he pondered the implications. After all, Princess Guo was one of the people he'd sent a folio to, and the king's guardians were always in the same room as her. As the battle between the core-formation experts in the air came to a standstill, the battle below also died down.

Both Prince Tian and Prince Lei floated up to the figure. "Why has Esteemed Uncle interfered in this battle?" Prince Tian said. "Shouldn't you be guarding the king?"

"Has Esteemed Father..." Prince Lei said, his eyes tearing up.

"The king is in a dire situation," the red-cloaked figure said. "I have naturally come for an important matter. You are all to cease fighting until this matter is resolved, and I will kill anyone who dares interfere."

The crown prince's eyes narrowed. "Everyone, stand down," he shouted.

Prince Lei did the same to his own forces. Each side separated, leaving a large unoccupied gap stained with blood. A palanquin appeared in the distance just outside the palace, floating freely between two other red-cloaked figures. The palanquin was also red and adorned with a golden dragon with five claws. Everyone bowed when they saw it, for only the emperor could use it.

As the palanquin approached their groups, Prince Tian was the first to speak. "Why has Royal Father come all this way to the battlefield? Has he awakened?"

"He hasn't," the red-cloaked man said coldly. "However, the royal treasury's medicinal supplies have dried up. We require the services of a high-tiered alchemist to prolong his life."

Prince Tian's eyes lit up. "We'll be happy to provide such services."

The red-cloaked man snorted and looked up to Wang Jun's black figure. "Would the Wang family be so kind as to supply an alchemist and the necessary medicinal ingredients? We may also need your vast connections to secure additional rarer materials. I'm sure the crown prince won't interfere in this matter."

Wang Jun, who was still feigning illness, bowed weakly. "I'll be happy to assist in any way possible. Is there anything else I can help you with?"

"There is," the red-cloaked man said. "The king's condition is dire, and we wish to save as much time as possible. We understand that you cannot send your alchemists to the palace during this fierce political struggle. We don't wish to hamper your efforts, so we'll have to thicken our skin and ask you to provide your best accommodations for the king and us three old geezers. And the princess, of course. She worries deeply for her father and refuses to leave his side."

The faint silhouette of a woman could be seen through the palanquin's thin curtains.

Wang Jun naturally understood the implications of this move: The three "royal uncles" that could cause even Prince Tian to bow down were expressing favor for Prince Lei. They'd even chosen the Wang family's less-competent alchemist over the Zhou family's. The princess was also willing to accompany their father to stay in the Wang family's compound. This meant that even she, who usually sided with her eldest brother, believed Prince Lei's accusations.

"We'll naturally provide our best courtyards," Wang Jun said. "In fact, we'll demolish some walls and stick accommodations together to make them more comfortable for our five esteemed guests."

Prince Tian paled as the red palanquin turned and headed straight into the Jade Bamboo Auction House. Now that the king himself was situated there, it would be utterly disrespectful to continue with his attack. This meant that, despite their superior forces, they could no longer take the initiative.

"Fall back!" Prince Tian said venomously, signaling for his forces to retreat. The large crowd that was initially going to crush the third prince's rebellion funneled back into the Alchemists Association, their last remaining stronghold.

That night, word of what had transpired spread throughout the city like a wildfire. Many people who had already joined the crown prince's faction secretly defected. His troops' morale reached an all-time low, but fortunately for Prince Tian, he still held the upper hand in official combat prowess.

And with that, the civil war came to an awkward standstill.

Feng Chuan sighed as he looked through the information in the dossier once more, the evidence that incriminated Prince Tian. He'd originally chosen to dismiss it after reading it, but the royal uncles' decision had caused him to reconsider. These men were the king's most ardent supporters, brothers who had fought for him during his rise on the battlefield. Naturally this meant that they saw the king's children much like their own—they would never choose sides unless they had a legitimate reason.

As to how they could confirm this information, he guessed it had something to do with their residual marshal's authority. All three of the powerful protectors had been marshals in the king's time and had only retired to become his personal guards once the war against the south had calmed down. Feng Chuan had taken up one of their places following their retirement.

Feng Chuan sat cross-legged and accessed the marshal's medallion on his chest. It glowed with the same soft light as Southhaven Fortress. As a vestige of the ancient Song Empire obtained from a transcendent realm, it possessed a unique function: It held a detailed record of military activities within the Song Kingdom. This vital tool had been created to prevent treachery. While no direct military evidence could be attributed to the first prince's death, the many supporting details provided by Prince Lei could be validated.

Not only was he using it to review the information in the folio, but he was anxiously supervising the battle at Southhaven Fortress. He now realized that he should have fought back and forcibly mobilized troops to the wall. Now it was too late. The hopes of the kingdom now rested on a small squad of a hundred men who had daringly teleported into the core of their opponent's army. His son was one of them.

At this moment, a large explosion rattled the battlefield in Southhaven. Deputy Marshal Feng's military contributions shot through the roof, to the point where the system recommended his promotion to marshal. After pondering for a moment, Feng Chuan suggested Feng Ming's promotion. One other active marshal would need to support his decision.

Feng Chuan then moved on to inspect the battlefield, and his heart clenched when he noticed that Feng Ming and a squad of crack troops were struggling to escape the enemy's surrounding troops. He looked on in awe as Marshal Yong took one swipe after another with Southhaven's Life-Reaping Blade. The man was the backbone of their country's defense, and even he himself couldn't hold a candle to this man's willpower and cultivation.

One swipe, two swipes, three swipes. Before long, the enemies were all cleared away, leaving an opening for Feng Ming's retreat. Just as he sighed in relief, however, the system notified him of an important matter—Marshal Yong had been fatally wounded by Deputy Marshal Mo.

"I must report this to the crown prince," he muttered.

Suddenly he felt a sharp pain in his back. He exited the system and noticed a dagger protruding from his heart. He tried to circulate his qi and noticed that it was firmly sealed in place. A purple substance on the blade confirmed his guess.

"So it's true," Marshal Feng gasped and spurted out blood. "You used qi-binding venom on your own father, you monstrous son of a bitch."

"All for the sake of the kingdom," Prince Tian said as he walked away. He wore a mournful, tired expression. "We can't win against the Southern Alliance. We can only join them. A leader must make difficult choices for the sake of his people."

Feng Chuan coughed up more blood. "The Southern Alliance is filled with monsters," he said. "Better that every man, woman, and child in this kingdom perish than to let them live under their oppression."

"A difference in perspective," Prince Tian said. "You choose honor, but I choose life. Everyone in this kingdom deserves a chance at life. The people will realize this in time."

In Southhaven Fortress, Marshal Yong lay dying. A system notification appeared in every battle map in the room.

"Marshal Feng has been mortally wounded by Marshal Tian," the system said. "Would Marshal Yong like to pass a motion to strip Marshal Tian of his authority?"

"Yes!" Marshal Yong gasped.

"Marshal Tian has rejected the motion, while Marshal Yong has supported it," the system intoned. "Marshal Feng is incapacitated and is counted as abstaining. The motion has failed."

"Dammit," Marshal Yong said with bared teeth. "What a great crown prince you are, selling us out to the Southern Alliance like cattle for slaughter."

The generals in the room were all pale with fright. Who could have possibly expected the simultaneous assassination of two marshals?

"A matter is pending that Marshal Yong has yet to review," the system said. "Requesting the marshal to approve or reject the system-recommended promotion of Deputy Marshal Feng to marshal."

"Approve!" Marshal Yong yelled.

"Motion approved," the system said. "Authority will be transferred to Marshal Feng Ming immediately." Another alarm sounded.

"Marshal Feng Chuan has passed away. Marshal Feng Chuan's status has been toggled to deceased, and his marshal's authority can no longer be used."

Looking around at the room of wide-eyed generals, Marshal Yong could only despair. "When Marshal Feng comes in, I'll already be dead," he said, his eyes red with rage. "You are to follow him without question, defend the wall, and take down that ungrateful bastard that calls himself a prince. Is that clear?"

"Yes, sir!" the generals in the room acknowledged.

Satisfied, Marshal Yong closed his eyes and sent a mental message to the system.

Please send this private message to Marshal Feng along with his marshal's medallion and my marshal's cloak. I know we don't have any more cloaks in storage, but I won't be needing it where I'm going.

Chapter 33: Converging

Feng Ming knew something was wrong as soon as he stepped into the fortress. The soldiers looked sullen and exhausted, and he was greeted by three pale-faced generals who looked like death itself. The looks everyone gave him were not those of celebration after a hard-earned victory but rather the looks of defeated men on the brink of collapse.

"What's the situation, General Tang?" Feng Ming asked the mustached man in the lead. He bore a small black-and-gold bundle in his hands, as well as a black-and-gold medallion.

"Reporting to Marshal Feng, Deputy Marshal Mo betrayed and killed Marshal Yong," General Tang said.

The news struck Feng Ming like a bolt of lightning. "Marshal Yong is *dead*?" Feng Ming said. "How is this possible? Marshal Yong is the strongest in the army. And what's this about me being a marshal?"

"Please take things one step at a time, Marshal Feng," General Tang said. "The treacherous Deputy Marshal Mo took advantage of Marshal Yong's exhausted state when he single-handedly activated the offensive formation to carve out a path for your retreat. Please bind the medallion as soon as possible to receive his dying message."

Feng Ming frowned when he saw the man avert his eyes and

hesitate to say something else. "What else is there that I should know about? Look at me!"

General Tang swallowed. "Marshal Feng... your father. He's also dead." The man choked back tears as he said these words. "I served with your father for many decades. I'm sorry, but he was killed... by Prince Tian. Prince Tian has betrayed our kingdom. This has been confirmed by Southhaven Fortress's system. Please be strong for us."

Feng Ming's eyes turned red, but seeing the men around him, he refused to cry. He simply took General Tang's package and swiftly bound the marshal's medallion with a drop of blood.

"Pull yourselves together, men," Feng Ming said, turning around to the soldiers who were all looking at him. "Recover as quickly as possible and ready yourselves to defend the wall. General Tang, take me to Marshal Yong's body."

"Yes, sir!" the men said at once. A flurry of emotions vied for supremacy in Feng Ming's mind as he followed General Tang through the hallways and into the war room. The floor was still slick with blood where Marshal Yong's cold body lay. Feng Ming realized that the cloak in his arms was none other than the deceased marshal's.

Feng Ming kneeled beside the man who had served his country for centuries. He pushed the man's grizzled hair out of his face and gently wiped the blood out of his beard with a cloth. Despite his demise, the man had the peaceful smile filled with satisfaction.

When I die, I want to be wearing a smile just like that one, Feng Ming decided.

"Where is Mo Shen?" Feng Ming asked General Tang. Calling him by a military rank was an insult to the men around him, and an insult to Marshal Yong, so he refused to do so.

Four generals brought forward a manacled man. They tore off his red, black-runed cloak.

"Strip his armor as well," Feng Ming said. Feng Ming looked calmly at the man, who looked at him a crazed expression.

"Why did you do it?" Feng Ming asked.

"For the kingdom," Mo Shen said.

Feng Ming struck the man across the face with his qi from thirty feet away. He walked over calmly and asked again.

"Don't give me that crap," Feng Ming said. "How could crippling the defensive wall and killing two marshals while starting a civil war possibly be good for the kingdom?" He walked up to the man until they were face to face. "Why did you do it?" he asked again.

"I did it for the kingd— ARGH!" He screamed as Feng Ming plunged a dagger into his shoulder. He stared at Feng Ming and grinned like a madman. "You don't have to believe me. I just wanted to tell you personally that you are doomed, and the wall will fall. Without Marshal Yong, you're nothing. Luck can only get you so far in life."

Feng Ming sighed before giving instructions to the generals. "Confiscate his treasures, dismember his corpse, and toss it outside the wall. He doesn't deserve a proper burial."

"What will be the method of his execution?" General Tang asked.

"Execution?" Feng Ming said, looking perplexed. "Look at him, General. He's already dead."

The man's maniacal grin was frozen in place, but a trickle of black blood was leaking out of the corner of his mouth.

"I don't know what they're up to, but I refuse to let these savage southerners win. I want a tally of our strategic situation in one hour. Come find me if anything urgent arises."

Feng Ming walked through a corridor to the marshal's room, which he entered with no difficulty. The bedding and furniture were all immaculate and tidy, with not a thing out of place. He didn't touch any of them, however. He simply found a nearby wall and slumped against it in exhaustion. Then he looked at the black cloak the marshal had left him and ran his fingers along its silky surface.

"System, please retrieve Marshal Yong's dying words," Feng Ming said.

"Acknowledged," the system said. "Please approve or reject the pending proposal by Marshal Tian to appoint General Ma as marshal."

"Denied," Feng Ming said.

"Very well," the system said. "Replaying the last mental communication by Marshal Yong."

Feng Ming kept quiet for fear of missing something.

"Feng Ming," Marshal Yong's voice said, "I'm dying, and if you're hearing this, you likely know that your father has also passed on. I'm sorry. He was a good man, and he and I served in the army together for a long time. We were brothers. We saved each other's lives so many times we stopped keeping track.

"I don't have a lot of time left, so I won't bore you with my speculations on this. Cut and dry, Prince Tian must be stopped. But before that, I'm worried about the wall. A general never relies on a single tactic in war, so I doubt they'll give up with this defeat. If I were to guess what their next move is, it would likely involve the Spirit Temple. You might not know this, but all our estimates indicate that they have, at most, a few thousand members. For a thousand members to be present here all at once, it must be for something big. You should have seen how happy I was when I saw you blow up half their members. Their leaders must be coughing up blood and losing some serious sleep."

Marshal Yong paused. "My last bit of advice is to keep an eye on the other two fortresses. I was forced to weaken them, so it stands to reason that their secondary ploy will target them next. Don't take anything for granted—I want you to personally visit them.

"Even though I was betrayed, remember to trust your men. That's the curse of being a leader—you need to rely on the people around you, and it's your fault if they let you down. Don't let what happened to me stop you from having confidence in your people.

"Lastly, trust in your gut. You're the luckiest man I've ever seen, but as you can see, that won't necessarily make you happy. What *will* make you happy is doing your best. I might be dying, but I'm dying a happy man. Your father died happy as well—he approved your promotion to marshal only a few seconds before he passed away. He knows everything you did out there, and he was proud of you. Remember that."

Tears ran down Feng Ming's face as he let his bottled-up emotions pour out. He had less than an hour to grieve, less than an hour to show his respects to the man who had raised him and a marshal who had supported him.

Feng Ming walked into the war room at the appointed time. The black-and-gold marshal's cloak felt heavy on his shoulders, but he wore it all the same. Its coloring was a symbol of hope for the generals around him, an encouragement to the otherwise dispirited men.

"Reporting to the marshal, the enemy has begun mobilizing its troops," General Tang said. "Shortly after their defeat, they quickly packed up the scraps of their cannons and began collecting corpses and weapons. They should be ready to leave within the day."

Feng Ming nodded. "Retreat would be wise at this point, but be ready for eventualities and keep an eye on them. Our stores of spirit stones were depleted, so they'll consider us especially vulnerable to a follow-up attack." He casually tossed out a small mountain of 500,000 high-grade spirit stones he should have given them earlier. "Don't let that stop us from defending this place. What news is there from Easthaven and Westhaven?"

"Nothing to report," the general shrugged. "There haven't been any enemy movements within a hundred miles of their walls."

"I want you to lead things here while I conduct an inspection at Easthaven," Feng Ming said. "You are now Deputy Marshal of Southhaven." He handed the man a black-and-red cloak along with a black-and-red token. "General Qin!"

"Sir!" The large man stood up. As a fierce body cultivator, he'd already recovered from their battle.

"General Qin, you will be the second deputy marshal," Feng Ming said. "I want you to take two generals here and ten of our remaining elites to Westhaven Fortress."

General Qin saluted him and quickly selected two generals,

and Feng Ming was relieved to see that they were two of the more observant and intelligent ones. Feng Ming looked around and chose two others, General Long and General Jin. He immediately recruited ten of their elites, half of which were body cultivators, and proceeded to the departure hall.

"Please don't make me do it again," the old technician said. "It'll stop my heart if I have to send you out like that again."

"I don't want you to send us to the battlefield," Feng Ming said. "I want you to send us to Easthaven."

The technician sighed in relief. It only took a few breaths before the white-and-gray glow of teleportation materialized.

"As I said many times, Marshal, there is nothing to report," General Liu said. "Nothing has happened here. In fact, you can take more men if you want. Just be sure to send them back if we need them."

Feng Ming nodded as he inspected a large screen in the war room. Small red dots were displayed on a map of the fortress. He wasn't sure why, but something felt off about them. They were too... orderly. Which was ironic, given that order was considered a good thing in military circles.

"I'm going to go for a walk," Feng Ming said to the two generals and ten elites. "Why don't the both of you stay here for the time being?" He left them to relax in the room as he randomly roamed about throughout Easthaven Fortress.

His resplendent force picked up whispers and mental messages as he passed by soldiers who looked at him reverently. Many of them were discussing the events in Southhaven and Feng Ming's rapid promotion to marshal. Some were envious, but most of them respected him. Only a minority of the men were quiet. Among the five thousand men in the fortress, perhaps one in ten didn't speak much.

One in ten, one in ten, Feng Ming thought. *Why does that ring a bell?* As he thought this, he caught the silhouettes of two sergeants walking down the corridor with serious expressions. They walked with ordered steps toward the north end of the fortress.

Where could they be going? Feng Ming wondered. *And why would they head toward the north? The only thing there is the storeroom.*

Since he needed to stop there anyway to reallocate military supplies, he quietly followed the men, using his resplendent force to probe any potential mental conversations. He was surprised to discover that they weren't talking. They were part of the one in ten.

"What can I do for you today?" a man's voice said from within the store room when the two men arrived.

"My sword was dented during training," one of the men said. "I need a replacement."

"I've come to collect my monthly spirit-stone quota," the other man said.

"Just one moment," the man in the storeroom said. "I need to go to the back."

"Take your time," one of the men said. They began speaking about mundane topics. This concerned Feng Ming—as far as he knew, soldiers gossiped more than any other profession. That was why every general in history emphasized morale. The slightest rumor could decimate an army quicker than any enemy tactic.

Unusual soldiers and one in ten, Feng Ming thought. *Why does that bother me so much?* As he thought of this, he made his way to the storeroom, where he planned on retrieving half of their spirit-stone supply.

Suddenly his hair stood on end. Instead of ducking for cover, he rushed over to the room where the two men had previously been talking and was surprised to see that the door was shut. Unfortunately, it was built from a material that isolated his resplendent force. He moved to open it but discovered that it was not only shut but locked. Frowning, he took two steps back and kicked the door down.

"What in the world?" he whispered. The two men who had previously been chatting were now standing beside the quartermaster, who had dropped both the sword and the spirit stones. The quartermaster's eyes were white, while to his side, wisps of crimson gas left the soldiers' eyes and seeped into the quartermaster's.

Feng Ming wasted no time. He quickly summoned his lucky spear and threw it at the nearest man, who dropped dead instantly. He then darted to the next man and slashed with a short sword, swiftly separating his head from his body. To his surprise, the body dropped to the floor, but the head didn't. It continued emanating the crimson vapor in which he now saw a ghastly face. Feng Ming quickly retrieved his spear and hacked the head in two. The red vapor let out a wail of frustration and vanished into thin air.

"What happened to me?" the quartermaster said as he suddenly woke from his daze.

"They were doing something to you," Feng Ming said. "What happened to you? This is important."

"Marshal!" the quartermaster said, his eyes widening. "Of course. When I'd returned with the sword and spirit stones, those two men dashed right up to me. I thought they were attacking me, but to my surprise, their eyes suddenly turned crimson, and I blacked out. I came to just now."

Feng Ming frowned. *System*, he sent mentally, *can you identify what happened?*

Reporting to the marshal, the symptoms are consistent with possession, the system said. *Recommended countermeasures include inspecting and purifying all soldiers in the fortress using the Unfettered Gold Formation. Would you like me to lock down the fortress?*

Only the main gate, Feng Ming said. *Keep this information confidential, and only alert those I brought with me from Southhaven Fortress. Instruct them to keep quiet and watch those generals.*

Affirmative, the system replied.

He rushed out silently to the most key location in the entire fortress: the gate. As he walked, he noticed that the personnel map had shifted. One in ten men were swiftly walking toward the gate.

Up ahead, he spotted some soldiers who were calmly walking without talking. He swiftly jabbed with the butt of his spear, instantly rendering both men unconscious. As he approached the gates, he was forced to incapacitate more and more men.

One in ten, one in ten, Feng Ming thought.

Suddenly, it clicked. One in ten was five hundred men, the same number of men that remained from the Spirit Temple. He paled when he realized that the five hundred men rushing toward the gates weren't imposters but their own men, possessed by the five hundred men on the outside.

System, is there a way to stop these men without killing them? Feng Ming asked.

Reporting to the marshal, the fortress can use eighty-percent of its current energy reserves to activate the Spiritual Lockdown Formation and the Unfettered Gold Defensive Formations for ten seconds," the system said. *This amount of energy will not be sufficient to eliminate the evil spirits. The possessing spirits are unlikely to self-destruct under normal circumstances due to the backlash to the spirit's controller. However, they may use desperate means to achieve their objectives once the formations are activated.*

Feng Ming rapidly found an energy-transfer point and tossed in a hundred thousand high-grade spirit stones to supplement the fortress before approving the activation of the formations.

Before he could even sigh in relief, a pulse from his core-formation jade alerted him to a message from Southhaven.

Marshal Feng, the enemy troops have finished packing up and are headed east toward your position, Deputy Marshal Tang sent. *Their advanced forces will arrive in a quarter hour. What are your instructions?*

Have Deputy Marshal Qin keep an eye on Westhaven's gates, Feng Ming said. *Meanwhile, mobilize ten thousand men from Southhaven as soon as possible.*

Feng Ming disconnected and ran down the hall. He incapacitated any soldiers he passed, and as he ran, golden runes activated on the walls and began pouring shimmering light into the hallways. Howls of pain sounded from the gate room up ahead. He breathed deeply and rushed into the room.

"Quickly, manually open the gates and destroy the locking

mechanism," one of the men said. Ten men turned to a crystal on the wall and began channeling their qi. Despite ordering the system to lock down the gates, Feng Ming had forgotten about the manual mechanism. Given enough energy, they could force the gate to open and close, and the process would only take ten breaths.

"We don't have much time," one of the crimson-eyed men said. The golden light shining from the walls was causing a red mist to evaporate from him and combust. "Let's combine our efforts to kill this supposed lucky general. Ignore the backlash—the lowest ranked novices go first!"

Fifty apparitions emerged from their respective hosts while the men they had possessed slumped over, unconscious. The fifty spirits ignored the blinding gold light and jumped toward him. They passed through his body and directly entered his spiritual sea. His resplendent soul suddenly became aware of fifty intruders in his mind. They dove toward the miniature version of himself, and just before reaching it, they self-detonated.

The jade runes on his resplendent garment glowed and deflected the spiritual explosion. He wasn't harmed in the least. In fact, his soul had grown stronger during the exchange by accumulating merit from defeating evil spirits.

Although a few breaths had passed in his spiritual sea, three seconds had passed in the outside world. The hundreds of men looked at him in shock.

"Send out a hundred more," the man ordered calmly. The process repeated itself, and Feng Ming opened his eyes three seconds later.

"Why don't you just fight me the old-fashioned way?" Feng Ming said as he rushed at them with his spear. He knew full well that the hundreds of men were no match for him in a frontal battle.

"I refuse to believe that his soul is strong enough to resist indefinitely," the man said. "The rest of you go at him at once. Some sacrifices are necessary for victory."

The hundreds of men simultaneously fell unconscious. Feng Ming laughed as he ignored the onslaught of evil spirits and charged forward. As the hundreds of evil spirits invaded his soul, his merit skyrocketed until he formed a fourth jade rune. In fact, he accumulated enough to get him halfway to completing the next one.

The remaining soldier and the ten behind him paled. "The ten of you adepts will sacrifice yourselves to buy me time to open the gate."

The ten men stepped up, but unlike before, a dozen souls poured out from each of them. These souls were much larger than the ones before. Feng Ming shuddered as they entered his spiritual sea and surrounded him in a swirling formation of crimson. Their wails caused his soul to shudder, leaving his body to act on instinct. The remaining soldier didn't dare provoke him in this passive state—instead he inched the gate up until Feng Ming heard a soft click.

Get out of here! Feng Ming yelled inside his spiritual sea. The crimson formation of souls instantly collapsed and dissipated, causing his cultivation to shoot up to middle core formation. He ignored the influx of heaven and earth energy and swung his spear at the soldier, who had just pierced through the manual gate mechanism and ruined it.

The man grinned like a maniac, and a large apparition appeared behind him. Feng Ming stopped his spear barely an inch away from the unconscious man's head.

"You sealed this ghost in this fortress, forcing me to either give it up or use it one last time," a voice said inside Feng Ming's spiritual sea. A black-cloaked man surrounded by a crimson aura appeared before Feng Ming's resplendent soul. "Unfortunately for you, I'm not one to back down from a challenge. You've killed too many of our ghost slaves, and we shamans will always have our revenge."

The figure released a malevolent presence, and crimson tendrils of corruption expanded from where he stood and traveled through the golden floor in Feng Ming's spiritual sea.

Despite the severity of the situation, Feng Ming felt incomparably relaxed. He didn't reply to the man's goading but focused in the current problem: sealing the gates. He diverted nine tenths of his attention to his body, which rapidly inspected the gate mechanism. He quickly concluded that the mechanism was irreparable.

"What to do, what to do," Feng Ming muttered as he wracked his brains for a solution. The system had no suggestions but simply sent him a blueprint of the fortress gate. The massive star-steel gate was two feet thick and supported by a large cable, which was protected from tampering via a large enclosure.

"You think you can divide your attention?" the ghost in his spiritual sea said mockingly. "Fine, have it your way."

The growth of the tendrils intensified. Meanwhile, Feng Ming flew up to the cable-guarding mechanism. He struck the cover without a hint of hesitation, but to his dismay, he only created a small dent.

At this moment, ten thousand soldiers began rushing into the fortress through its reception hall. Five thousand men from Southhaven fortress quickly arranged themselves into groups and activated defensive formations. The generals gave out hasty instructions as the troops readied themselves to welcome the incoming charge of enemy forces.

As Feng Ming slashed away at the cover, thousands of troops rushed in and clashed with the Song Kingdom's soldiers. Although they easily repelled this first wave, more and more troops were rushing in with every passing second.

"Come on!" Feng Ming said as he struck with Ash Annihilation. A small hole appeared in the protective cover, a hole just large enough to accommodate his spear. Despite the opening, the cover cut off his spiritual force. He only had a single chance to sever the cable.

"You've already lost," the ghost in his head taunted. "Just give up and surrender. We could always use the help of a strong soul like you. If you pledge your allegiance, I can promise you a position equal to mine in the Spirit Temple!"

Feng Ming shook his head. "Sorry, not interested." He held his spear and poured all his remaining fire and earth qi into the lucky spear. He ignored the clashing in the courtyard below as he directed every ounce of his spiritual force into his weapon. White runes lit up on the black spear that clearly exceeded the might of a core treasure.

"You think I'll let you do as you like?" the ghost in his spiritual sea said. "Thousand-soul spirit, detonate!"

The black-robed man suddenly split into a thousand crimson ghosts that shot toward his resplendent soul simultaneously. Feng Ming ignored them as he struck with his spear with all his strength. The ghosts collided with his soul just as the spear left his hand. His consciousness wavered as the powerful ghost in his spiritual sea realized its mistake.

"Good Fortune Scripture? Wasn't it lost? Why is it here of all places?"

Jade runes struck the ghost one after another and caused it to explode into a thousand nourishing motes of merit.

Simultaneously, the lucky spear pierced through the cable holding up the massive gate, which crashed down onto the few unlucky Southern Alliance troops beneath. The spear then continued and struck the other side of the protective covering, piercing through to the other side of the wall, where it flew across half of the fifty-thousand-man army crushing against the Easthaven Fortress.

The spear passed over hundreds of generals and thousands of normal troops before finally shooting downward.

It cleverly bypassed dozens of hastily summoned shields and plunged straight into the enemy marshal's chest.

Chapter 34: Corrupted Crimson

"Gong Lan!" Cha Ming yelled as his group approached the two women. "It looks like you didn't even need our help to get through the labyrinth. We're starting to feel a little useless."

Gong Lan raised her eyebrow. "If summoning four variant tribulations in the middle of the labyrinth and destroying it counts as useless, I'm not sure what to say."

Dongfang Hao and the remaining Alabaster Group members caught up. The three remaining monks were slightly slower, their orange kasayas torn, their bodies bleeding from several places. Seeing their bedraggled appearance, Gong Lan sent out a wisp of green energy to the protectors, whose pale complexions immediately flushed with a healthy glow.

Cha Ming and the three demon beasts led their group through the maze's exit. The walls were black and covered in golden runes that suppressed an intense crimson glow in the distance. They passed by several dozen broken jade slabs. The corpses that used to lay on them had disappeared without a trace.

Finally, they entered a black room covered in crimson lines. The golden runes that had once adorned the walls were shattered, and only small pieces remained of them.

"Why weren't these corrupted like the rest?" he said while motioning to twelve sarcophaguses surrounding a broken dais holding up a small jade seal. He noticed a golden formation was built into these coffins and joined together with them to suppress the corruption. He frowned when he noticed a crimson formation containing runes he couldn't identify that overlaid the original gold one. The corruption found in the labyrinth clearly originated from it.

"I don't know," Gong Lan said. "Regardless, we must activate the Spirit-Banishing Pagoda and neutralize the corruption as quickly as possible. Unfortunately, six of our monks have perished, and the pagoda won't be nearly as effective."

"Can we help in any way?" Cha Ming asked.

Gong Lan shook her head. "You can only act as protectors for us. Only Buddhist soul energy can be used to activate this holy treasure."

She led the three other monks to the seal and immediately began chanting. Golden characters imbued themselves into the small glowing pagoda in Gong Lan's hands, one after the other. Before long, a beautiful golden sphere covered in holy Buddhist scriptures appeared and locked them off from the outside world.

"Let us begin," Gong Lan said.

The pagoda's glow intensified and resonated with the three monks who began chanting incessantly. As they chanted, Cha Ming activated his Eyes of Pure Jade and inspected ochre formations that overlaid the crimson ones. He only stopped once his vision blurred and his eyes began to bleed.

A light formation thrummed to life, greedily absorbing a hundred thousand spirit stones in the process. A golden mist filled the room as the spirit stones evaporated. The formation was a peak formation called Evil-Sealing Circle, one of the five formations gifted to him by the Church of Justice. He had used the gray flags gifted by Wang Bing to erect the formation and spirit stones he'd borrowed from Luo Xuehua and the Alabaster Group.

"The voices are finally gone," the blind Luo Xuehua said as she walked up beside him.

"The voices?" Cha Ming asked.

"The humming of the souls of the dead," Luo Xuehua said. "They were calling out to us, warning us. They said we were too late and that we should run away."

"What else did they say?" Cha Ming said. He hadn't known that Luo Xuehua possessed such a strange ability. If so, it explained her quiet and reserved demeanor.

"Their voices changed an hour ago," she said softly. "At first, they were warning us. Then they began saying murderous words. They told us to kill and fight. They told us to slaughter our friends and slay our family members. We're strong, so it didn't affect us. But what would it do to weaker souls?"

A cold shiver ran through Cha Ming's spine as he glanced to the formation on the floor. He activated his Eyes of Pure Jade once more and inspected the hidden characters under the light of the Evil-Sealing Circle. The golden light of the formation revealed several hidden characters that Cha Ming hadn't seen before. "Kill," "betray," and "slay" formed twisted lines that weaved in with the formation. Furthermore, he detected twelve more hidden formations he hadn't seen before. They were written in sinister runes that he couldn't understand, but they resembled several formations that Cha Ming was very familiar with: energy-gathering formations.

Suddenly, Cha Ming saw a flash of gray spatial light, and a pile of ochre crystals appeared out of nowhere and fell onto the formations. They roared to life as soon as the crystals landed and instantly began feeding the crimson formation on the floor. Its runes shifted and weaved chaotically as it drank in the negativity. The twelve sarcophaguses vibrated. As a last-ditch effort, Cha Ming summoned the Clear Sky Pillar and smashed down with every once of strength he could muster. He aimed for the weakest point in the newly revealed formation.

The floor crumbled beneath it, but the formation continued as though nothing had happened. A crimson glow left the twelve golden sarcophaguses, taking the form of twelve howling ghosts that shot into the previously inactive formation. Cha Ming rapidly summoned a peak lightning-based combat formation. The crimson lines distorted under the iridescent lightning but were ultimately unaffected.

"It won't work," a voice said from the hallway.

It was a familiar voice that Cha Ming loathed. Zhou Li walked out from the labyrinth; Protector Song and a dozen core-formation devils marched in behind him while an army of hundreds of foundation-establishment devils followed.

"The formation uses the corruption in the imperial seal to bewitch those in the kingdom and turn them against one another. The fighting causes the corruption to deepen and increase the bewitchment. It's an ingenious plan if I do say so myself. Before long, the kingdom will be in shambles and ripe for the taking.

"But do you know what the best part about all this is? The World Tree Master is here, and you delivered her right to us."

He flicked out a small needle, which shattered Cha Ming's Evil-Sealing Circle and struck the Spirit-Sealing Pagoda's barrier. The bright-red needle slipped through the shield without breaking it, and a crimson gas transformed into a red-clothed monk.

"Sibi!" Gong Lan shouted.

"Do you think you brought enough men?" Cha Ming asked as he summoned the massive Clear Sky Pillar and a peak Icy Hell Grand Formation. His Stormchaser Boots dissipated into storm clouds beneath his feet, and an armor of light and darkness covered him. The tomb's rocky floor crumbled under his bare feet as he increased his weight to ten times his fist strength.

Huxian's, Lei Jiang's, and Silverwing's forms increased in size. Huxian grew to 160 feet long while Silverwing expanded to 160 feet wide. Only Lei Jiang remained small, his height only reaching Cha Ming's. They too summoned their black-and-white battle armor. Meanwhile, the Alabaster Group duo each summoned an array of flying swords—one earth aligned and one wind aligned. Luo Xuehua summoned hundreds of talismans, and Dongfang Hao brandished a heavy blade while nine metal pillars floated around him.

"I brought everyone I could spare," Zhou Li said. "How's your foundation doing, by the way? Is this second life all that you imagined it would be? Will it be filled with choices like you imagined? Even if we don't gain anything out of this exchange, I've already crippled a game-changing piece like you."

He then looked to Huxian. "Little fox, did you know that your brother's core is crippled and can't reach rune carving? How do you feel, knowing that you'll die young and never reach the peak like your father?"

As he spoke, the core-formation and foundation-establishment devils drew their weapons and unleashed their devilish forms. Even Protector Song transformed. They let out a communal roar; their ochre auras combined into a cloud of malevolence that rushed out toward their tight-knit group. Their emotions became chaotic as their bodies lost strength, their souls felt drained, their weapons dulled, and their movements faltered. Even their defenses didn't feel as strong as before. Although Cha Ming had fought against a few scattered devils before, he had never faced so many at once; their combined auras were a truly frightening phenomenon.

Cha Ming's expression turned cold. He widened his combat formation until it encapsulated the crowd of devils. He imbued it with his Devil-Sealing Intent, which rapidly eroded the malevolent aura around them. Meanwhile, Huxian's aura of purification and devouring superimposed with a new aura released from the three stars shining on each of his three tails. The stars summoned a domain of Judgmental Lightning and Smothering Swamp, which was mediated by a gentle wind.

As the domains clashed, the devils charged as they used their consumption abilities. The core-formation devils activated black tattoos that burned and propelled their cultivations up to early core formation. They clashed with the demon beasts and the Alabaster Group's forces. Silverwing, Huxian, and Lei Jiang tied up several core-formation devils each while Luo Xuehua and the Alabaster Group's forces clashed against the lesser devils.

Blades of wind and iridescent lightning fought against devouring vortexes and ice lotuses. Earthen spikes assaulted Huxian as he batted away scores of devilish minions. Meanwhile, the Alabaster Group was a flurry of wind, earth, ice, and metal. Their superior strength evenly matched the veritable salvo of devilish attacks.

"Do you think you can hurt me as you are now?" Zhou Li said as he walked toward Cha Ming. His aura surged, and Cha Ming's eyes narrowed as he realized that Zhou Li was a middle-core-formation cultivator. In addition, he didn't reek of evil like the devils did; his Eyes of Pure Jade detected not a trace of merit or sin on the mysterious man's body.

Zhou Li suddenly summoned black flames, which formed two black dragons that dove toward Cha Ming. He sent out six flying swords that slashed at Cha Ming as he dodged using his superior speed.

Cha Ming used his battle armor to avoid the multiple attacks and shrank the Clear Sky Staff as he attacked with his Swift Staff Art. He became a blur of black and white as he struck at Zhou Li with dozens of staff strikes per second. These blows were deflected by seven black flame shields that easily predicted his movements. Before long, Cha Ming was forced to withdraw from the two black flame dragons and the six black flying swords.

"You're nothing but a cripple, and you'll never amount to anything in life," Zhou Li said. "It's too bad you didn't take my advice to heart."

He held his hands out and summoned another four black flame dragons. They charged at Cha Ming, who was already breathing heavily.

"Sibi, you dare to throw yourself into the Spirit-Sealing Pagoda?"

Gong Lan said as she slashed at the crimson-robed monk with a saber of light.

Sibi snorted and whispered a distorted mantra. Crimson characters shot out from his lips and instantly destroyed the saber. "I'm honored that the new World Tree Master knows my name," Sibi said.

He took out a small rosary filled with crimson beads. He muttered in a distorted voice, causing the prayer beads to shoot out and surround Gong Lan, suppressing her Buddhist powers.

Gong Lan summoned her own rosary. Ten thousand and eighty blessed pearls burst apart and quickly fought back against Sibi's attack.

The distracting shower of crimson and gold caused Sibi to disappear. Gong Lan frowned as a shiver ran down her spine. She summoned three blades of light behind her, which warded off a sharp crimson claw that was headed her way. Seeing that his attack was rebuffed, Sibi summoned a long scroll covered in cryptic crimson characters. Gong Lan decisively summoned back the 10,080-pearl rosary, which orbited around her like an impenetrable shield and fought back the crimson scripture.

"I am indeed no match for you in the outside world," Sibi said, calling back his vestment. "But our true battlefield is different. Our true battlefield is the place where I was born. Do you dare to follow?"

His figure turned into a crimson mist, which surged toward the jade seal. Although ten percent of the seal had previously been unfettered by the three monks, the ground they had gained began rapidly receding.

"It's your move now, World Tree Master," Sibi's voice said from inside the seal. "You can't save the Song Kingdom without fighting the corruption. Will you run, like your master wanted to, or will you do what I did and face the corruption head on?"

Gong Lan gritted her teeth and stepped forward.

"You can't!" the bodhi seed said as it appeared in front of her. "It's exactly what they want you to do. It's too difficult to kill you in the outside world, but they know I can't protect you inside the seal."

"Even if it's what they want me to do, how can I possibly back down?" Gong Lan argued. She looked over to the three monks, who were doing their best to restrain the expanding corruption. She knew they wouldn't last long. They had already staked their lives on this mission—shouldn't she do the same?

"As this plane's guardian, you're much more important than the mortals in this kingdom," the bodhi seed said. "It's better that ten Song Kingdoms fall instead of you."

"And why did you choose me in the first place?" Gong Lan shot back.

"I chose you because of the purity of your soul," the bodhi seed said. "It's too difficult to find someone with your spirit and character. If you fall, I won't be able to find anyone else to take your place."

Gong Lan shook her head. "If I can't even defend the Song Kingdom, how can I possibly protect the plane? This is part of who I am. Don't try and stop me."

She walked over to the crimson-colored seal and whispered the Mantra of Faith. Beautiful golden characters shot out from her mouth and floated in midair. She continued speaking until 108 characters came together like a small rosary. Then she sent out the 10,080 pearls. They joined together with the 108 characters and danced around the seal, whose rate of corruption rapidly slowed.

Sighing, Gong Lan sat down before the seal. Her golden soul left her body and followed Sibi's.

"It's your move," she whispered. She was surrounded by an endless field of crimson and millions of vengeful souls. They licked their lips and pounced toward her.

"Do you know why I do what I do?" Zhou Li said as he threw tendrils of black flame over to Cha Ming. They bypassed his defenses and assaulted the resplendent jade vestment on his soul, which was protected by a white barrier.

Meanwhile, Cha Ming's Icy Hell Grand Formation slightly restricted Zhou Li's movements. He tried to capitalize on this and swung out with alternating Swift Strikes and Heavy Quaking Strikes.

The superimposed benefits of his Stormchaser formation, his black-and-white armor, and his natural flight abilities as a core-formation cultivator and marrow-refining cultivator gave him unsurpassed speed within his realm. Despite this enormous advantage, Zhou Li still managed to defend against one blow after another. Cha Ming had sorely underestimated the man's prophetic abilities.

"It's all because of revenge, you see," Zhou Li said. "My people lived happy lives on this plane, doing whatever they pleased and working hard to improve their lot in life. The pursuit of happiness was the maxim of the plane, and despite being ruled by devils, the world was a peaceful place filled with millions of good-aligned cultivators."

His movements were relaxed and exact. Each one of his footsteps carried him out of harm's way as he predicted Cha Ming's movements one after another. Where he couldn't, he swung out a flaming black sword and deflected the Clear Sky Pillar. The half dozen black flame dragons pursued Cha Ming and sealed his movements.

"It was all destroyed overnight by the jade emperor's minions," Zhou Li said. His hands rapidly formed seals, and black flames congregated and assembled into a script Cha Ming's recognized as the fragment of someone's story. It shot out at him and struck his resplendent soul, which fought hard to defend against what he now recognized as a curse. A soothing white light from the Clear Sky Brush burst out and banished the darkness.

Cha Ming used the opening granted by his defense to land a direct blow. Zhou Li coughed up blood as the residual force of Cha Ming's staff bypassed his qi shields and ravaged his internal organs.

"And now I know why the higher-ups put such a large bounty on you," Zhou Li said. "The destiny surrounding you is ridiculous. You even have a soul-bound treasure? How unfair can fate be?"

While Cha Ming grew increasingly surprised by what Zhou Li knew, he didn't speak for fear of getting lured into whatever mental game the man was playing.

How are things going on your end? Cha Ming asked Huxian.

It's going well, Huxian said. *Give us an incense time, and we should be able to mop them up.* The three-tailed fox and his friend were dominating the battlefield. Huxian's five suppressions, combined with his and Cha Ming's Devil-Sealing Intent, had given them an absolute advantage. Scores of lesser devils had already fallen while a few core-formation devils were severely wounded.

"If you weren't so lukewarm about everything, if you had *passion*, you'd probably be able to accomplish something in life," Zhou Li said. "It's a pity, really." He formed hand seals again, preparing to send another curse.

Cha Ming ignored his taunts and sent another staff strike at the defenseless Zhou Li.

The man dodged in his usual pattern. He predicted Cha Ming's Swift Staff Art, blocking it with a Black Flame Shield. He narrowly avoided a Quake Staff by pushing himself to the side with a black flame dragon. After half the hand seals were formed, he switched up his movements.

Sensing an opportunity, Cha Ming shrank the Clear Sky Pillar and slashed out with a Rapid Sword Staff. Seven Black Flame Shields superimposed as Zhou Li rushed toward Cha Ming, who was forced to sidestep and bat the pale man toward the crowd of devilish cultivators. Zhou Li grinned as he turned around and unleashed the curse on another target: Huxian.

Cha Ming felt the effects of the curse almost immediately. His bodily strength lowered by a full sub-realm while his qi began leaking out at a rapid rate and his black-and-white armor crumbled to nothing. Meanwhile, Huxian's three stars disappeared along with their corresponding suppressions. The large fox shrank down to half his size while his physical strength was cut in half.

Due to their soul contract, he and Huxian shared karma. He

instantly understood that this extended to curses and that Zhou Li had targeted his one weakness—Huxian's soul. Zhou Li didn't stand still after landing the curse, and neither did he keep talking. He instantly lunged at Cha Ming with a sword of black flame and began a fierce counterattack. The six black flame dragons joined in a circle and suppressed Cha Ming's Icy Hell Grand Formation while his Black Flame Shields transformed into chains of black flames.

"You're such a nice guy, Cha Ming," Zhou Li said. "It's a pity you chose the wrong side."

His biting sword attacks rapidly made progress and finally found a crack in Cha Ming's defenses. A large black gash appeared on Cha Ming's chest.

Chapter 35: Exposing the Plot

"Prince Tian, the final preparations have been made," a man said. The vicious-looking man had a hooked nose and short black hair. He wore the black cloak and black medallion of the Obsidian Syndicate. "When will you be requiring our services?"

"In one hour," Prince Tian said. "Be at your positions by the appointed time. And be sure not to miss."

The man grunted and disappeared into the shadows. A superior cultivator like him wasn't cheap—it was fortunate that someone else was footing the bill.

Prince Tian carefully ran his thumb along the black-and-gold medallion around his chest. The system had notified him that his petition to appoint a marshal had been rejected by Marshal Feng. Seeing as he had killed the original Marshal Feng, there was only one possibility—his son had somehow become the second marshal, one who could veto all his commands.

Seeing as it was now impossible to play a safe game, today was the day he would put all his cards on the table. While the new marshal was busy fighting fires in the south, he would consolidate the capital in one fell swoop.

A soft knocking sound roused him from his thoughts. "Come in," Prince Tian said. Three men wearing red-and-gold cloaks walked in and saluted him. "Has everything been arranged?"

"Yes," General Zhang said hesitantly. "However, there have been murmurs among the troops. General Tang, Marshal Feng's second-in-command, has been especially vocal. He claims that his brother was promoted to deputy marshal, and that Marshal Feng was assassinated by none other than yourself. A fifth of our troops have defected and holed themselves up in the north of the city."

Prince Tian sighed. "Why is the capital filled with traitors and madmen? It's good that he defected—it saves me the trouble of uprooting him later. The truth of the matter is that I sent Marshal Feng to the southern wall to shore up our defenses. General Tang has simply inverted black and white and hidden his lies in a grain of truth."

As he spoke, the three generals' eyes reddened slightly, and they became especially docile and obedient.

"I knew it was preposterous that General Feng could get promoted to marshal so quickly," General Dong said. "The boy might be good, but not *that* good."

"It won't be long," General Si said. "Thank you for alleviating our concerns, Prince Tian. We'll disseminate the news momentarily and quell the rumors."

"Thank you for your hard work, generals," Prince Tian said.

The generals soon left, leaving Prince Tian to his brooding. The next step was the most important in his quest to conquer the Song Kingdom. It was a gamble that would either make or break his efforts over the past two decades.

"Prince Lei, urgent news to report!" a soldier said as he rushed through the battlefield. "Following Marshal Feng's disappearance, a rumor has spread that his son was promoted to marshal in the south. Furthermore, Marshal Yong's disappearance was confirmed. In a more recent announcement, the crown prince has declared that he sent Marshal Feng to the south to defend the border, thus the confusion."

Prince Lei was covered in soot and grime. "What of the recent troop movements?" he said as they repelled the last of an enemy invasion.

"They are going as planned," the soldier said. "Unfortunately, our movements have become increasingly difficult. Prince Tian has consolidated his power over the military in the city. There is no longer the indecision that was there back when Marshal Feng was in Songjing or Marshal Yong was in the south. Only General Tang's small group of military troops to the north remain undecided."

As Prince Lei overlooked the battlefield from above, he noticed large troop movements near Central Square. "Double back!" he yelled.

Their troops abandoned their pursuit of enemy stragglers and narrowly avoided enemy troop movements, which tried to cut them off from their headquarters. However, this interception was also part of a much larger movement—their enemies had bypassed their patrols and completely surrounded the Jade Bamboo Auction House.

"How is this possible?" Prince Lei exclaimed. "Our royal father and his protectors are here. Attacking the auction house is tantamount to treason." He rushed into the auction house and summoned his generals. "Rally the troops, mercenaries, and nobles," Prince Lei ordered. "Even if this is a false alarm, we can't risk it. My brother wouldn't act like this unless he has a plan." He then entered the war room, where Wang Jun sat nursing a cup of hot tea.

"What are your thoughts?" Prince Lei said to Wang Jun.

"I'm not sure," Wang Jun said. "It's better to be safe than sorry, and I have a bad feeling about this. It might be prudent to alert the royal uncles. Unfortunately, I have something to take care of that requires my undivided attention. You may use my forces as you see fit, save for Protector Ren, Elder Bai, Hei Ling, and Li Ming."

Prince Lei shook his head. "What could possibly be more important than defending our headquarters?"

"You know me," Wang Jun said, smiling grimly. "If I'm

preoccupied, it definitely involves a large amount of money."

Core-formation cultivators from both forces met in midair just outside the Jade Bamboo Auction House. The slaughtering formations were fully active, ready to strike at any moment. Meanwhile, the mercenaries and Prince Lei's allies stood guard just outside the large building.

"You have a lot of nerve attacking this place when our royal father is sleeping inside," Prince Lei said to his somber-looking brother. "Have you decided to accelerate your succession by killing him as well? Do you think the war to the south is a sufficient justification?"

"You've always had a way with words, brother," Prince Tian said. "Times are turbulent, and we need firm leadership. Your treacherous behavior undermines the stability of the kingdom, and for that, you must die."

"Attack if you will," Prince Tian shrugged. "I'm sure the royal uncles will make their stances clear once you make your move."

"As you wish," Prince Tian said. "Soldiers, assemble the formations!"

"Sir!" the troops replied.

Several groups of nine hundred men joined together under the guidance of several core-formation generals. Massive red flood dragons appeared above them, ready to strike at Prince Lei's forces at any moment.

"Activate the formations!" Prince Lei yelled. The six slaughtering formations in the Jade Bamboo Auction House activated. "Ready your weapons!" he shouted.

The mercenaries, nobles, and private forces readied their combat techniques.

"Attack!" Prince Tian yelled. The red flood dragons rushed, crashing into Prince Lei's forces. Core-formation cultivators defended with the support of hundreds of unorganized foundation-establishment cultivators. Tiny elemental phantoms and weapon projections clashed against the dragons and repelled them.

"Again!" Prince Tian shouted.

"Hold your fire," a voice boomed. Three red-cloaked figures appeared in the skies above them. Their peak-core-formation cultivation thoroughly supressed the entire crowd. "We didn't act against you personally as you are the king's son, but that doesn't mean we'll stand by as you attack the very building he rests in. I suggest you retreat immediately. Once the king passes away, we'll not care about this petty struggle for power."

"I'm sorry, uncles, but I can only press onward for the sake of the kingdom," Prince Tian said. "Men, direct your attacks to the royal uncles. Since they choose to interfere, we will fight against them for the sake of the kingdom."

Many murmurs of dissent ran through the troops. The generals, seeing their morale plummeting, grasped their wild qi and subdued it like a wild horse.

The three red-cloaked men's eyes narrowed. "Now that you've revealed your true colors, we'll teach you a lesson you won't forget," their leader said. Boundless qi surged forth from the three apex cultivators. As Prince Tian's nine flood dragons joined together into the Nine Dragons Battle Formation, which could only be controlled by a marshal, the three uncles summoned three bloody spears. The spears and dragons collided, throwing clouds of dust into the air in the process. The dust slowly settled, revealing thousands of men kneeling with blood trickling from their mouths.

"You're still too young to face off against these uncles," their leader said. "It's time to teach you a lesson you'll never forget."

Suddenly, three clicks sounded from different directions. The three men simultaneously threw up barriers to deflect three ominous black crossbow bolts. To their surprise, however, they continued unimpeded. "Core-breaking crossbows?" The three men gasped.

The three bolts pierced into each of the men. If one observed closely, they would have seen that the bolts were covered in a purple sheen. The three men fell like flies and were rescued by Prince Lei's men just moments before they hit the ground.

"Men," Prince Tian yelled. "Today is our moment of triumph. To victory!"

Just outside Songjing, four men were fighting intensely. Two of them were poisoned while a fourth man was bleeding. The bleeding man had a young face and black and white hair.

"Your poison has improved, Zhou Bei," the unwounded man said. "It's a pity you betrayed the family. You would have been a great asset."

"And sell out my country to the southern devils?" Zhou Bei spat. "Not a hope in hell. You and your cronies chose poorly, and you'll get what's coming to you in the end."

"It's your life." The man shrugged before continuing their intense struggle.

Hong Chen let out a puff of smoke as he faced off against his fellow guards. "What's gotten into you all?" he asked.

"We've had enough of your bullshit," one of the guards said. "You're too by-the-book, and it's time for a change. We need a new guard captain."

They rushed toward him with pathetic qi techniques. Hong Chen summoned smoke around him as he struck one man after another with a thin wooden stick. They slumped to the floor, unconscious. He tied them up and locked them inside the guard shack.

What in the world is going on? he thought as he made his way back home. The entire city was going mad—the only thing he could do now was keep his family safe as best he could.

In Green Leaf City, the normally peaceful academy was abuzz with activity. Elder Chen, one of Green Leaf Academy's teachers, was rapidly being overwhelmed by a crowd of angry students. They had lost their sanity after a student was accidentally killed in a teaching match. He wasn't the only one in such a pitiful situation.

A few hundred feet away, a similar situation was occurring. A student had killed a teacher in a fit of rage, causing a half dozen teachers to band together to pacify the students. A female teacher unleashed an icy prison to restrain the students. Unfortunately, their response defied all common sense. They rushed toward their teachers with utter disregard for their lives. Dozens of students perished as the teachers watched on mournfully.

"What's come over them?" a young female teacher asked.

In Green Leaf City, cultivators fought with cultivators in the streets while mortals fought mortals. Even domesticated animals fought each other as Green Leaf City descended into madness. Unbeknownst to them, this resentment was rapidly being syphoned away and fed to a crimson formation out in the distance. In turn, it intensified their irrational behavior.

"What the hell is going on?" the owner of the auction house mumbled as he surveyed Fairweather from his balcony. The modicum of peace that had returned to their daily lives had disappeared, and people were now fighting in the streets.

He could only sigh and send out his flying sword to incapacitate a random civilian who was inches away from ending another's life. As a foundation-establishment cultivator, he could only do so much. It wouldn't be long before blood filled the city's streets.

"What a disaster," Deputy Marshal Qin muttered as he reviewed the battle reports. Despite his external appearance, he was far more intelligent than he let on. He always reviewed briefings and incorporated them into his brave but reasonable actions.

"Deputy Marshal, something's happened," a soldier suddenly said. "The whole fortress is rioting. Something about pensions and salaries being insufficient. At first they were just arguing, but now they've taken out their swords!"

Deputy Marshal Qin frowned. "Order everyone to stand down. And get me the biggest piece of soft wood you can find."

"What for?" the soldier asked.

"Well, I can't be out clubbing people with my greatsword, can I?" Deputy Marshal Qin said.

If brute force wasn't solving all your problems, you just weren't using enough of it.

Wang Jun calmly noted the thousands of alerts as they appeared on his core-transmission jade. Chaos had erupted throughout the kingdom for no apparent reason. Unfortunately, he couldn't pay attention to such things. He had a deal to secure.

He paced about the chamber nervously, inspecting every nook and cranny to ensure that the necessary precautions were in place.

"Elder Bai?" Wang Jun said. "Bring me Li Ming. I'd like to have a word with him."

Feng Ming flew as quickly as he could. His spear cut through the air but not as much as he'd have liked—his lucky spear was never recovered from the battlefield. He was now using a shabby magic-grade substitute. As for the black spear, the enemy troops had taken it with them when they'd left. It was a shame, really—the spear would get to have fun in the south without him.

"Those guys are crazy if they think my spear will cooperate with them," he muttered.

Songjing was growing in the distance, and above it, a gray cloud was forming. Smoke, Feng Ming realized.

Songjing was burning.

Chapter 36:
The Truth

Cha Ming felt himself weakening. Every slash of Zhou Li's sword chipped away at his abundant vitality while leaving an ominous black mark on his body. Each one slowed his movements and ate away at his qi. He had long since banished his combat formations, keeping only a healing formation to sustain him as he looked for an opportunity.

Huxian wasn't faring any better. The many-tailed fox's black-and-white fur was covered in slick blood from heaven knew how many wounds. They knew that if the fox died, Cha Ming would as well. By then, the battle would be sealed. To make matters worse, both Silverwing and Lei Jiang had been hit by weaker curses as well. Their previously dominating performance was being repelled by the devilish generals and their minions. Without Huxian's support, the Alabaster Group's forces had also fallen into a disadvantaged position.

"You might as well just give up," Zhou Li said as he took another vicious hack at him. "How many breaths do you have left in you? Is it worth it to go through all that pain and suffering, only to die in the end?"

As Zhou Li spoke, Cha Ming had his sights set elsewhere; he was focused on the black threads that bound him and Huxian to Zhou Li.

Those string are immune to whatever I've thrown at them, Cha

Ming thought. *Even Lei Jiang's lightning and Huxian's purification are ineffective. It's like they operate on an entirely different plane of existence.* The five elements and wind, lightning, light, and shadow couldn't damage them in the slightest.

Cha Ming knew that nothing in the universe was without weakness. In fact, he had already determined a likely weakness of fate qi, but using it would likely put him out of commission for the remainder of the battle, and he wasn't keen on reliving the unpleasant experience.

It's now or never, Cha Ming thought. He quickly withdrew a hard talisman, which he slapped on his chest while simultaneously directing his qi into sixty sigils. A blade hacked into his shoulder as he formed a fire formation and into his thigh when he formed a gold formation. The pace of Zhou Li's attacks had increased since he'd begun laying out the formations. He also noticed another peculiarity—Zhou Li wasn't talking.

Cha Ming blocked with his body as Zhou Li tried to interrupt the next combat formation as it was being formed. After the wood formation came the earth formation.

Zhou Li sent out sword strikes and flaming black dragons of qi but to no avail. "Stop him!" he yelled anxiously. Protector Song, who had been fighting against Huxian, rapidly darted toward Cha Ming.

"Too late," Cha Ming whispered. As the water formation formed, he channeled the destruction qi through his qi pathways. They burned as black qi poured into a black star, which shielded him from Protector Song's attack.

He increased the flow, forming a thin blade of destruction qi that struck out toward the black threads in the air. They disintegrated as the blade passed through them, instantly relieving their hold on Cha Ming and Huxian. Seeing that it was effective, Cha Ming rushed out and severed more black threads that led to Silverwing and Lei Jiang.

Having been freed from the curse, Huxian instantly grew to 160 feet in length and released his five auras simultaneously. Cha Ming's Devil-Sealing Intent suffused the battlefield and killed one devil after another. With every devil that fell, the suppression against them grew. This granted respite to Luo Xuehua and the Alabaster Group, who continued their struggle against the mass of lesser devils.

Cha Ming's formation, although effective against the fate qi, shattered under Protector Song and Zhou Li's combined attacks. He was thrown back as the five formations exploded. As he picked himself up, he realized that the debilitating pain that usually followed the use of destruction qi wasn't as bad as usual. In fact, the damage to his meridians was very light. His body had become strong enough to bear it, and entering the marrow-refining realm had increased his regenerative capabilities enough to keep up with the destruction qi's light damage to his body.

"Yes!" Cha Ming yelled. The Clear Sky Pillar shrank down into its staff form. Then Cha Ming poured his remaining destruction qi into the Clear Sky Staff, which glowed with a frightening black color. Meanwhile, Zhou Li had just finished casting a second curse on Huxian. Cha Ming summoned his Stormwalker Formation and destroyed the black threads before they had a chance to affect the three-tailed fox. Zhou Li paled as the curse was destroyed.

Cha Ming took advantage of his momentum and smashed into Protector Song, whose shield of qi disintegrated under the assault of his heavy destruction-laced staff. It tore through the man's armored body. Protector Song burst into flames as his life left him.

Following the death of Protector Song, the tides of battle shifted. Huxian's aura grew more and more powerful as he swallowed and burned lesser devil souls one after another. Silverwing flicked around the room and lopped off one head after another—his victims were unable to resist his attacks because they were restrained by Huxian's five auras.

Meanwhile, Lei Jiang bounced from target to target as a ball of iridescent lightning. They couldn't keep up with his swift movements and couldn't target his tiny body.

"Look, we can talk," Zhou Li said.

Cha Ming ignored him as he had all battle. Cha Ming rushed at Zhou Li with all the speed he could muster and struck him with the

Clear Sky Staff. It sheared through Zhou Li's qi shield and amputated the pale man's right arm.

"Save me!" Zhou Li shrieked.

Cha Ming's eyes narrowed as an ominous chill ran through his spine. He struck out at the defenseless Zhou Li, but his staff struck an invisible wall. A man in a dark cloak suddenly appeared among them. Lightning crackled in the skies as the plane fought to supress him.

The man was a transcendent.

The battlefield fell silent, as everyone couldn't help but tremble under his imposing presence.

"Kill him!" Zhou Li yelled. "It's worth it!"

The black-robed man glanced at Cha Ming, his eyes boring into his very soul. "Soul-bound treasure?" the man whispered. "You're right. It *is* worth it." The man raised his hand slightly, and the void began to shatter around Cha Ming. One lightning bolt after another struck the robed man while Cha Ming felt one piercing pain after another. Countless shards of shattered space sliced through his muscles and bones alike.

"That's enough!" a voice said from up above.

A figure in white robes and jade wings flew down from the skies. It was none other than Lu Tianhao. The space around Cha Ming stopped shattering and returned to its normal state. Meanwhile, lightning crackled in the skies as the heavens roared in anger. Bolt after bolt of lightning struck down on the two men, who didn't dare resist.

"I can't kill him," the black-robed man said. "The plane would destroy us both, and I'm still needed for the final plan."

Zhou Li shook his head in disappointment. "I suppose it doesn't matter. His cultivation path has been crippled. He'll be no threat to the upper realms, which have promised us a great reward for this good deed."

The black-robed man nodded. Then a gray fluctuation enveloped them. Before Cha Ming knew it, Zhou Li and the black-robed man had disappeared.

The battle with the remaining devils was finished without any suspense.

The golden barrier surrounding Gong Lan and the jade seal dimmed as one of the monks' energy ran out and his life left him. This was the second one in a single incense time. With his demise, the corruption rate of the seal increased. It wouldn't be long before it overtook the seal completely.

"To set up such an elaborate trap to lure in a plane guardian," Lu Tianhao muttered as he inspected the formation. He moved his hands along the pagoda's barrier as he sought for a way to supplement it.

"Can I do anything to help?" Luo Xuehua asked.

"Not yet," Lu Tianhao muttered. "I can't do anything directly, but I may be able to set the stage for you all to contribute. If only we had a Buddhist monk. That way we could delay the corruption for a little while longer. The one in there won't last more than ten breaths." Then he looked at Huxian. "Little pup, come over here and help me out."

Huxian leaped over obediently. Demon beasts respected power, and that man was someone who could tear him apart with a mere thought.

Lu Tianhao worked feverishly as he laid down hundreds of formation flags. As soon as the last flag dropped into place, the formation thrummed to life and yet another bolt of lightning struck down on him.

"The punishment of the plane is difficult to resist," he explained. "It despises the actions of transcendents and attacks our very souls. I can only do so much to help you." He swished his sleeve, sweeping Huxian onto the formation he'd just installed. The demonic-light qi within Huxian began to circulate automatically, and the formation converted it into a purer golden light that resembled the light inside the dome. To Cha Ming's surprise, the energy Huxian supplemented was more effective than the three monks combined.

"That's the first step," Lu Tianhao said. "I now need all who are willing to enter the pagoda. I'll use my limited knowledge to allocate corruption equal to your capacity so that you might support her. I'll warn you, however, that you will all die if she fails."

Those from the Alabaster Group immediately stepped up to the barrier.

"How confident are you in this method?" Cha Ming asked.

"Without you?" Lu Tianhao asked. "Five percent. With you and your soul-bound treasure, as much as fifty percent."

"It's very important that she succeeds," a small voice piped up.

To Cha Ming's surprise, it was the small seed that always danced around Gong Lan.

"I can consume this avatar's life force to increase your chances to sixty percent."

"How generous of you, Lord World Tree," Lu Tianhao said subserviently.

"Huxian," Cha Ming said. "I want to try." He had to ask—it wasn't only his life.

"Let's save Sister Gong Lan," Huxian yipped.

Cha Ming, Lei Jiang, and Silverwing all walked up to the barrier. Then Lu Tianhao tore a hole in the golden shell surrounding the seal. The four individuals sat cross-legged while the beasts lay down.

"Sit down and relax," Lu Tianhao said. "Close your eyes. In a moment, you'll sink into a dream. You'll experience many people's lives—both their joys and sorrows. Attachment to the world is what creates an evil spirit. Only by experiencing it and remembering your own lives in the current moment can you unfetter it."

After this brief instruction, Lu Tianhao waved his sleeve. Six thin lines of crimson corruption left the seal and entered the four cultivators and two demon beasts. A seventh, thicker line of karma attached itself to Lu Tianhao, who was immediately assaulted by multiple strokes of lightning.

Finally, a thick line of karma left the seal and attached itself to

Cha Ming. He screamed in pain as he was suddenly thrust into a dying man's worst memories.

I am Gong Lan, and I am unfettered, she thought as she ran through the woods. Her limbs moved without her permission as she relived a painful memory. She scampered down a ravine to escape a fierce spirit beast. It had been sent by the man she trusted most.

Whether I live or die, I'll live on as a ghost and haunt him, she vowed as the spirit beast pounced on her and devoured her flesh.

I am Gong Lan, and I am unfettered, she repeated to herself.

"This is the happiest moment of my life," said the woman whose body she'd inhabited this time, tears in her eyes. She held her newborn baby in her arms and swore, "I might be dying soon, but I swear to keep you safe for the rest of your life."

I am Gong Lan, and I am unfettered, she repeated. This time, she relived an oath of vengeance. It was memories like these that she understood the most as she stepped closer and closer to her greatest enemy in this endeavor—her previous self.

Chapter 37:
Fetters

Wang Jun stared at Li Ming as he drank a cup of medicinal tea. The report the man had written sat on his desk between them. Protector Ren sat beside him.

"Hei Ling has disappeared for quite some time," Wang Jun said. "Is there something you'd like to share with me? Truth be told, I don't find your report very convincing. There are far too many holes in your obvious lies."

The man's eyes shifted. "Unfortunately, I'm not at liberty to disclose this. The repercussions would be quite severe."

"If this is a soul contract, I'll compensate you for the inconvenience," Wang Jun said.

"I don't think you can afford it," Li Ming said. "But I'll do it for fifty thousand high-grade spirit stones."

"That's ludicrous," Wang Jun said.

Li Ming shrugged indifferently.

"Fine, fifty thousand high-grade spirit stones it is, but if you've cheated me, you're not leaving the room alive." He tossed a small pouch on the desk.

Li Ming sighed. "Hei Ling is not who you think he is—argh!" The man let out a soul-rending scream that continued for thirty breaths. Neither Protector Ren nor Elder Bai flinched at the expected response. They simply waited for the punishment to end and the pale man to compose himself.

"Hei Ling is not who you think he is," Li Ming said. "And neither am I. Just now, my realm dropped down to middle core formation. Hei Ling, whom you had me tail, is a late-core-formation expert. Furthermore, he has an additional secret identity—he is the Black King who you've been dealing with all along."

Wang Jun was stunned. "I haven't been dealing with any Black King," Wang Jun immediately denied, lest he accidentally trigger their contract. "My family sent Hei Ling because he specializes in certain market connections. And why in the heavens are you, a late-core-formation expert, serving as an office worker in my Jade Bamboo Auction House?"

"It's a long story," Li Ming said, sighing. "In brief, I was once an assassin. They called me Three-Strike Killer, after my signature move that killed countless men." He swished out a dagger in a casual fashion, sending out a triple blow that made the three of them shiver.

"One day, I'd had enough of that life. I wanted to retire, so I faked my cultivation and found myself a cushy position at the Jade Bamboo Conglomerate." He chuckled. "Who could have predicted that during this retirement, I'd meet an old acquaintance of mine, an assassin called Black Death? The man had retired as well, but unlike me, he'd retreated to Songjing's underground without anyone noticing. We only recognized each other once we went on the joint mission together, and he forced me to sign a confidentiality contract. Fortunately, I was too strong, so he couldn't force a life-binding oath."

Wang Jun massaged his brow. "I'm confused. Why would any of this concern me? Isn't it beneficial to have such a man as my ally?"

"Would your family really do that?" Li Ming said with a chuckle. "I'd have thought the opposite. From what I gauged back in the Wang family headquarters, they'd rather have him kill you than anything else." Li Ming paused. "I speculate that the only reason you're still alive is that Black Death is a greedy and risk-averse man. You likely have something he wants, so he's letting you live for a while longer.

But mark my words, that man finishes a job when he accepts it. After all, he has a peculiar habit."

"Which is?" Wang Jun said.

"Every commission he takes is sworn to a time limit via life-bound oath," Li Ming explained.

The gears in Wang Jun's mind turned as he processed this new information. What Li Ming said was consistent with his own experience. The Black King's mannerisms, the inconsistences in the report. He made a mental note to confirm all the information Li Ming had disclosed. If the Black King's strength was as high as Li Ming said, that meant that his original preparations could hardly defend him should the man choose to assassinate him after completing their exchange.

"Li Ming, I'd like to hire you for a job," Wang Jun said. "It's a dangerous one, but I'll make it worth your while."

"Do tell," Li Ming said.

"We'll call it Operation Black Death," Wang Jun said.

Regardless of whether the Black King was plotting against him, killing the man after completing the exchange would instantly solve his financial problems. As for the life of a wanted assassin? It was an easy decision to make.

It was a cool spring day, and the scent of freshly sprouted willows was a soothing complement to the wonderful hot spring bath Bei Guan was currently enjoying. He relaxed as the cold wind danced on his hot skin like soft, painless pinpricks. A splash of warm water reminded him that he was bathing with someone else—the love of his life, Li Er.

"What were you thinking about?" she asked him playfully as she advanced toward him with a mischievous expression.

"I was thinking about how beautiful you are and how perfect life is," Bei Guan said. "Li Er, will you be my Dao companion and stay with me for as long as we both live?"

The woman's face flushed deeply before she nodded and floated up to him. Her dry hair clung to his wet face as she rested her head on his chest. A warm feeling appeared in his heart; the warmth spread through his chest to his whole body and triggered something inside Cha Ming. In this moment of clarity, he suddenly remembered Yu Wen, whom he had met in Fuxi's Library. The memory reminded Cha Ming of who he was.

That was a close call, he thought. Which memory was this again? The tenth? The hundredth? The thousandth? Each passing memory dragged him deeper and deeper. Gentle memories and innocent promises like these touched him deepest; they reminded him of what he lacked most in life: a loving partner to share his life with.

As quickly as it had come, the landscape shifted. This time, he was a soldier in the middle of battle. He had lost everything to the invaders and had sworn never to rest until his enemies fell. Coincidentally, these enemies were also part of the dying Song Kingdom, whose unstable borders were shifting violently during the Song Empire's fall from grace.

This was one of the more common memories. The resentment from war was both plentiful and intense, and while Cha Ming could most easily separate himself from these feelings, they wore away at him like a millstone. The soldiers who had perished on the battlefield were tiny pieces of grit that scratched away at his soul one small scuff at a time.

I am Gong Lan, and I am unfettered, she repeated once more as yet another battlefield appeared before her. This time, she was a conscript. The man cursed both his enemies and his country. He had been a tailor before the war began, and now he was nothing but a common foot soldier, an expendable meat shield for the cultivators behind him.

If they hadn't recruited me, I could have owned my own shop and married, the man thought. *I could have had children and grown old with a loving wife.* The sounds of his dying comrades and the stench of blood was overwhelming. He didn't have to endure it for long, however. His last thought was the realization that a spear had just pierced him in the chest. In his dying moments, he cursed the enemy and cursed his king.

I am Gong Lan, and I am unfettered, she said again. This time, she was surprised to see a familiar memory. She slowly entered a burning village in the distance where corpses were piled high and mutilated bodies were strewn everywhere. She faintly remembered finding a bloody doll and a bloody message warning her about a bloody moon.

Her blood boiled as she recalled the atrocities that she'd vowed to end. She smiled in satisfaction as she recalled each one of the devils and bandits she killed in the subsequent struggle.

I am Gong Lan, but am I unfettered? she thought. Although the Bodhi Tree had aided her and cleansed her soul, was she truly rid of her previous self?

She saw one scene after another of her blood-crazed self reveling in the death of her enemies. With every kill, she relived the man's resentful dying moments. She realized that this Gong Lan was a part of her, and that they were inseparable.

In the outside world, the crimson tendrils surrounding her grew. They extended into her spiritual sea where the golden resplendent soul defended itself against the intensifying attacks one after another.

I've just been running away, she realized. *I've cloaked myself in a mantle of righteousness to atone, but in the process, I've shackled myself to my own resentment. I am Gong Lan, but I am hardly unfettered.*

Crimson chains burst around the soul in her spiritual sea as the last remaining corruption she'd absorbed attacked her all at once. They formed a total of eighty-one fetters, representing eighty-one major regrets in her life. Seeing this development, she forced herself to calm down. This was her true challenge: facing her past self without the aid of the Bodhi Tree.

"There's only one way to save the world," her soul mumbled. "One soul at a time, starting with my own." She stopped resisting the corruption and took the initiative, sending her consciousness into the first of the eighty-one chains. It was the weakest one, but it covered the others in a protective film.

She found herself in a training yard. It was a hot summer day, and she and her brother were training like their life depended on it. As they performed one grueling exercise after another, a harsh figure reprimanded her.

"Look at your brother, Gong Lan," her father said. "He's very talented, but he doesn't try hard enough. You're just like me. You need to try harder than anyone else to succeed. But don't aim to be like him. You need to set your sights farther than that."

These were words that had shaped her entire personality as a child. Because of her late father's words, she'd pushed herself harder than anyone else her age. Whenever she failed to catch up, she blamed herself for her failure.

Surprisingly, however, her new frame of mind gave her a different perspective on the incident.

He was just telling me not to resent my brother's talent, Gong Lan thought. *He was telling me to aim past him because he didn't want me to set my brother as a goal in the first place. Instead I ignored his advice. I forged ahead and aimed to surpass him.*

This simple revelation brought her a great amount of relief. She reflected on this memory and many other connected memories and let them wash past her. Little by little, the thread of corruption unraveled. After what could have been seconds, days, or years, the smallest of the eighty-one chains faded away, leaving only eighty attachments.

I am Gong Lan, she thought. *And I am* not *unfettered. Not yet.*

"Prince Lei, Song Tian's forces have breached the defenses of the outer families," a soldier reported. "They are currently grouping their forces for a final push against the Jade Bamboo Auction House."

Prince Lei's face was covered in sweat and grime. He was the core of their forces, jumping from fire to fire as Prince Tian consumed them one piece at a time. "What about the royal uncles? How is their condition?"

"This… it's better if you see for yourself," the soldier replied hesitantly. Prince Lei nodded and followed the man to the largest courtyard in the Jade Bamboo Auction House. They walked inside the largest accommodation, where they were greeted by three doctors and Li Yin.

"How fares my royal father?" Prince Lei asked the three doctors who were busy tending to one of four comatose men.

"He's still at death's door," the doctors said. "We're doing everything in our power to help him. Not that we're very useful in the other three cases." He shook his head ruefully. "Li Yin is the only one who can help them."

Prince Lei noticed that Li Yin and three other elderly men were tending to the three royal uncles. Their wounds were covered in bloody bandages, something that was hardly ever seen in treating such high-level cultivators. "It's a good thing they had the sense to dabble in body refining," Li Yin said as he applied an ointment to one of the men's crossbow wounds. The shaft had been cut but not removed, indicating that the bleeding couldn't be stopped.

"The others say they can't treat the royal uncles," Prince Lei said. "Does that mean that they were poisoned like my father?"

"Yes," Li Yin said. "Two of the three are fading fast, and they won't last another half hour even under my care. The youngest of the bunch might live if Zhou Bei makes an appearance to cure the poison."

Prince Lei finally noticed the absence of the frightening man. "Where has Zhou Bei gone to?"

Li Yin shrugged. "He said something about settling a feud outside the city. Who knows when he'll be back."

Zhou Bei panted harshly. His vision was blurry from the amount of blood he had lost. Fortunately, it wasn't all for naught. The patriarch and an elder of the Zhou family had perished under his poison, and their grand elder would be crippled for the remainder of his short life.

"Was it worth it?" the man with wispy long gray hair asked. "Was it worth throwing your life away, only to die while I still live?"

"You won't live for long," Zhou Bei said in a raspy voice. "You might as well kill me now. I can't do much to you now that my poison has been depleted."

"As you wish," the grand elder said coldly. He lifted a gleaming black sword and hacked down with all his might. Zhou Bei closed his eyes as he waited for death.

However, it didn't come. Instead, he heard a clank and a stab, and a spay of hot blood splashed all over him as the man he had poisoned collapsed on top of him.

"What an idiot," a voice said casually from behind the grand elder. "Who wears his family emblem so openly in a civil war? He was asking to be killed."

Zhou Bei opened his eyes and saw the blurry figure of a young man whose black-and-gold cloak fluttered in the wind. The man held a long gold spear, but most importantly, he had the aura of a core-formation cultivator.

"My name is Feng Ming," the man said as he tossed a bottle of pills to Zhou Bei, who didn't hesitate to swallow them. A soothing sensation permeated his body as his wounds rapidly stitched together and his qi quickly replenished itself.

"My name is Zhou Bei," he replied. Seeing Feng Ming's eyes flicker to the corpse on the ground, he chuckled. "No relation to the Zhou family. Not anymore." His eyes lingered on the black-and-gold cloak the man was wearing. "Will you be going to the city, Marshal Feng?"

Feng Ming nodded.

"Then do you mind doing this old man a favor? I need to get back to the Jade Bamboo Auction House."

Chapter 38: Father

Feng Ming and Zhou Bei entered Songjing through a corroded hole in the city wall. Although he'd only brought along the odd-looking man on a whim, he'd proven to be extremely useful almost immediately. As soon as they got to the other side of the wall, he sent a quick transmission to the forces that were following from Southhaven. With such an opening, they'd have no problem participating in the final battle.

Looking around, Feng Ming quickly used his spear to carve out a section of a nearby building and place it over the entrance. Such a crude disguise would do for a short period of time, especially given the chaotic situation in the rest of the city. Feng Ming was shocked to discover that not only were the princes warring, but so were the common people. Fist fights and deadly altercations were breaking out over the pettiest things.

"They can't all be possessed," Feng Ming said.

"Agreed," Zhou Bei said. "Perhaps it's a poison applied on a massive scale." The man swished his sleeve and spread purple dust all over a group of squabbling commoners. They all fell asleep with weapons in hand.

"Perhaps," Feng Ming said. "I've been away from the city for some time. Do you know of anything that would help us cross the forces surrounding the Jade Bamboo Auction House?"

"There's one thing," Zhou Bei said. "I've heard that since your father's fall, the troops have been plagued with doubt. Your appearance might devastate their morale to the point that the crown prince will have to retreat."

Feng Ming contemplated this issue as they approached. He confirmed this information by probing nearby conversations with his resplendent soul. Accordingly, they cut a large arc and headed toward the north of the city.

"Halt!" a man cried out as they entered a run-down neighborhood. Feng Ming glanced up and saw a soldier in black armor. "Wait, is that Marshal Feng?"

Dozens of soldiers scrambled to the top of a sturdy building. General Tang, who greatly resembled his twin brother, appeared along with them.

"Is it true?" General Tang asked. "Was Marshal Feng killed by the crown prince?"

Feng Ming nodded. "That bastard Song Tian crossed the line. I'm joining Prince Lei's faction to overthrow him."

General Tang peered out from his vantage point. "Come up here, Marshal," he said.

Feng Ming and Zhou Bei flew up and saw a large mass of troops crushing around the Jade Bamboo Auction House. "If you can figure out a way to get through those troops, we'll come along with you."

Feng Ming sighed. "It's possible, but we'd have to kill many good men in the process."

"Yes," General Tang said. "And that's why I'm here in the north instead of alongside the third prince."

"I might have a way," Zhou Bei said. Feng Ming and General Tang glanced at him in surprise. "It's just tricky—whoever we bring along would have to go conditioning for at least an hour."

"What do you mean by conditioning?" Feng Ming asked. Suddenly he felt like a pail of ice water had been poured over him. The nearby men cowered and ran, while one even peed his pants. General Tang could barely hold on. He had drawn his sword, which he held against Zhou Bei in self-defense.

"I don't usually let my aura out inside the city," Zhou Bei said. "But most people find it extremely unpleasant. What do you think? Will it work?"

"There's only one last holdout," Prince Tian said as he surveyed the battlefield. "They'll fall within the hour."

Red flood dragons traded blows with the cultivators who were now holed up in the Jade Bamboo Auction House. Their forces had completely encircled the structure.

"Sir, there's a disturbance among the troops," General Zhang said.

Prince Tian looked toward where the general pointed and frowned when he saw a man wearing black armor and a black-and-gold cloak. A large group of military forces was following him in a tight, disciplined formation. He recognized the man as the new Marshal Feng, and the other man as Zhou Bei, who he'd seen in his father's chambers.

"Cut them down," Prince Tian said.

"But one of them is a marshal," General Zhang protested.

"I don't care," Prince Tian said. "Give the order."

As General Zhang rapidly gave instructions, Marshal Feng's small army arrived. To Tian's surprise, however, the troops beside them parted and ran away as he advanced. "Just what is going on?" he muttered.

Feng Ming and Zhou Bei advanced slowly but firmly as their small army struggled along. Only two things kept them moving—firstly,

Feng Ming's and General Tang's imposing manner intimidated them. Second, they'd put their strongest men on the outside. The reason for their tight formation was practical—it didn't allow any of their weaker men in the middle to cower or retreat as they advanced.

Nine red flood-dragon formations turned toward them as they cut three hundred feet into the enemy lines. Prince Tian flew up beside them. "You have a lot of nerve, coming here after killing your father and stealing his cloak," Prince Tian said.

The troops around them murmured. Half of them agreed, while half of them doubted.

"Shut up, you treacherous bastard," Feng Ming said. "First you kill my father, then you kill Marshal Yong, and finally, you have the nerve to accuse *me* of treachery?"

His words rattled the heart of Prince Tian's troops. Three of the red flood dragons disappeared as the generals lost control of their men.

"How could I kill my own marshals?" Prince Tian retorted. "I served by them in the military for decades. They were like fathers to me."

"Then let me ask you, how could you poison your own father?" Feng Ming pressed as his troops advanced. As their momentum mounted, Zhou Bei increased his pressure. "You killed your fellow marshals and poisoned your father. And now you want to kill your brother. If you're not a traitor, who is?" Feng Ming's words caused three more flood-dragon formations to collapse.

"Further, I heard that you murdered your younger and older brothers," Feng Ming said. "And while Southhaven Wall was falling to enemy forces, you didn't send a single man over to reinforce it. Tell me, do the men here even know that we lost over ten thousand good men in the south over the past day?"

Two more formations faded. For good measure, Zhou Bei completely unleashed his life-threatening aura. Soldiers around them cried and cowered in fear. Even the generals beside Prince Tian could only stand there, shaking uncomfortably.

Feng Ming walked up to Song Tian, who had landed beside his

troops. They stood six feet apart—at this distance, it was possible for either of them to lunge at each other in the hopes of landing a deadly blow.

"Get the hell out of my face," Feng Ming said. "I'm here to see His Highness. Try and stop me if you dare."

They stared daggers at each other, but neither man dared to retreat. As Feng Ming gripped his golden spear, Song Tian gripped the handle of the royal treasure, Dragon Claw. It was a peak-core-treasure sword that had been passed down from generation to generation. Feng Ming could hear his heart beating as he waited for the prince's reply. Feng Ming, despite being a middle-core-formation cultivator, could tell that Song Tian was much stronger than he was. He was also better armed.

"Like father, like son," Song Tian said. He shot out toward Feng Ming and slashed at him with Dragon Claw. Feng Ming blocked with his spear, barely deflecting the blow; his marshal's cloak allowed him to survive the impact, but his spear wasn't so lucky. It had broken in two.

Prince Tian continued the assault. As a powerful core-formation cultivator, he was immune to Zhou Bei's aura. The two men flew up into the skies. Feng Ming used his two spear halves to parry Prince Tian's sword strikes, but it was clear who was on the losing end.

Is this it? Feng Ming thought. *Is this how it ends?* He had been hoping that the prince would back down after all the accusations. He didn't think that Song Tian would abandon all reason and attack him. The troops down below had descended into chaos. They'd split up into squads that fought each other with bare fists, but it was only a matter of time until they decided to use deadly force.

Suddenly a bright light shone from just outside the military encroachment. The chaotic troops parted as a third force made its way toward the center. One hundred men in shining armor bearing golden blades marched in tandem toward Feng Ming. A man in golden robes flew out beside Feng Ming, who was in a sorry state. A shield of light covered the retreating marshal.

"I suggest you retreat," Chaplain Chen said to Song Tian.

"Chaplain Chen," Song Tian said. "To what do I owe the pleasure?"

"Are you sure you want to be asking me, of all people, that question?" Chaplain Chen said. "I suggest you leave now while I get to the bottom of this matter. I'm still granting you the benefit of the doubt—for now."

Prince Tian gritted his teeth. He looked out at his army, which was now in disarray. "Retreat!" he called. Feng Ming looked on in amazement as two thirds of the troops followed Prince Tian, and another third stayed beside him and joined General Tang's group.

"The only reason he left was to consolidate their morale," Chaplain Chen said. "He has somehow bewitched these men into following him. I only stopped this battle to save many innocents."

Feng Ming suddenly noticed that the men who had stayed were all closest to the golden inquisitors. Each of the men held on to a luminescent globe, which caused tiny tendrils of crimson corruption to evaporate from them.

"Unfortunately, my men can only treat so many people at once. Now tell me, was your father killed by Prince Tian, and do you have good reason to believe that Marshal Yong died for the same reasons?"

"Yes," Feng Ming said.

"Good," Chaplain Chen said. "Then we're temporary allies. The Church of Justice doesn't care about power struggles, but we care very much about the war against the Southern Alliance."

Zhou Bei swiftly pulled his overpowering aura back as they entered the Jade Bamboo Auction House. Prince Lei's men quickly welcomed them into the compound, and they quickly made way for Feng Ming and Zhou Bei, who directly proceeded to the courtyard where the king and the three uncles were resting.

"There goes the second uncle," a voice said. "Unless Zhou Bei comes back, the third one is doomed."

Feng Ming and Zhou Bei hurried inside the room.

"Zhou Bei, come here quick!" Li Yin said just as they walked through the door. "He wasn't poisoned so long ago, so you should be able to cure him faster."

Zhou Bei instantly assumed the role of an expert. "Give me one hour, and I'll have him cured." He glanced at the three doctors. "No need to see them out. The king needs them."

Feng Ming knew little of what was going on. He walked over to Prince Lei, an old acquaintance of his. Beside him, a familiar-looking young woman was crying as she looked at the four men's beds. Two of the men were covered in white cloths.

"Thank you for coming, Marshal Feng," Prince Lei said. "I heard your announcement outside. How goes the southern wall?"

"We were able to pull through," Feng Ming said. "The southern wall is safe, and some reinforcements are headed toward the city. They'll be here within the hour." He glanced at the comatose king. "How long has he been this way?"

Prince Lei sighed. "My royal father has been unconscious for months. The doctors say it will take a miracle to awaken him." He paused before continuing. "He'd be happy to see how you turned out, you know. You might not remember, but your father used to bring you to the palace when you were a little kid. He and the king were good friends, not just sovereign and subject."

"I remember a little," Feng Ming chuckled. "I once stole a princess's toys and got the beating of a lifetime. My father never brought me back after that."

A teary-eyed Princess Guo sat beside her father's bed and snickered softly.

"I told my father I never wanted to see you again," Princess Guo said. "Uncle Feng never had the face to bring you back after that. Ironically, the man I practically banished from the palace is back to save the day."

"It's funny how life works," Feng Ming said as he walked up to the king's side. He remembered the man's gentle expression from almost twenty years ago. Although his face was gaunt and pale, he'd remember it anywhere.

As though sensing his approach, the king's hand stirred. Then his eyes fluttered open. He looked at Feng Ming in confusion. "Brother Chuan?" he mumbled. "How did you get so young again? Are we dead?"

Feng Ming choked up as he heard these words. This was his father's friend, a life-and-death brother.

"And what happened to your spear? Why are you using that piece of scrap metal?"

Feng Ming composed himself as he thought up a soothing answer. "I lost my spear outside of Southhaven Wall," he said. "I chucked it and was lucky enough to stab an enemy marshal in the chest. I'd call that a fair trade."

The king chuckled softly. "If only I had half your luck, Brother Chuan. I hope your son inherits that luck of yours." His eyes wandered around the room. "I am having trouble seeing. Who's there? Is that you, Mei Er?"

Princess Guo's eyes teared up as she walked up. "Yes, it's me," she said.

"How's little Guo Er?" he whispered. "Is she growing fast?" Princess Guo nodded. "Good, good. Brother Chuan lost his spear again. Can you lend him my Magma God's Spear once more?"

"Of course, dear," Princess Guo said.

"Thank you. I don't know why, but I'm tired. Please take care of Brother Chuan. I'm going back to sleep." The king closed his eyes, and Princess Guo burst into tears.

Prince Lei walked up to them. "Your father was one of his best friends. Mei Er was one of his favorite wives, Princess Guo's mother. Guo Mei and Feng Chuan were childhood friends, and they would always spend time together.

"Your father had a knack for battle, but he had a notorious reputation," Prince Lei continued. "He always used to carry a black spear around with him. He called it his lucky spear. Contrary to what you might think, he always lost it when he fought. What made it lucky was that it would always come back to him in the end. Whenever he lost it, he'd go drinking with my father, who would lend him his own spear, the peak core treasure, Magma God's Spear. He would always ask aunt-mother Mei to go fetch it for him."

Princess Guo laughed and wiped away her tears before looking at Feng Ming. "Thank you for playing along. At least now if he dies, he'll die happy."

Feng Ming shook his head. "I didn't have the heart to tell him otherwise."

"Is it true, what you said about your spear?" Princess Guo asked, looking at the flimsy broken spear in his hands.

"Unfortunately, my lucky spear is indeed on the other side of the wall," Feng Ming said, laughing. "The enemy took it with them, but they're in for a rude awakening if they think it'll cooperate."

All three of them laughed.

Princess Guo hesitated before taking out a golden ring inlaid with jade. She bit her finger and dribbled a drop of blood on it, which the ring greedily absorbed. After a moment, she took out a red spear, whose presence immediately increased the temperature of the room. "As per father's wishes, I'll lend you this spear until you find yours again," she said.

Feng Ming hesitated before reluctantly accepting it. "I'll keep it well. I promise not to lose it."

Song Guo smiled. "That's what your father always said, too."

Chapter 39: Unraveling

Lin Dong had been an impoverished farmer before the war. He'd heard the army was a great opportunity to enrich himself and save his family from the drought that plagued them. Therefore, he'd signed up without any hesitation. It was only after the death of his many countrymen that he'd realized his folly. The money wasn't worth it, and neither was the war; there would be no benefit for anyone from all this fighting, not even for the victors.

Cha Ming regained a modicum of lucidity as he traveled to the next memory. In this moment, he realized a funny fact: that Lin was the most common surname in the Song Dynasty, or at least it had been in recent history.

Memory after memory, his spirit dulled. Memory after memory, he lost his sense of self. There came a time where the moments between karmic threads were nothing more than a boring interlude between the many exciting lives that came to visit him.

As he thought this, a soft green glow enveloped his tired soul. He became increasingly aware of his own self as a tiny seed entered his spiritual sea and melted within it. The short burst of life force was enough to make him realize his predicament and the near-corrupted state of his soul.

The gears in his mind turned slowly but surely as he discovered the crux of the problem—that compared to these many intense memories, his life was rather dull in comparison. He felt unpracticed and unrehearsed. If he were to fight someone at this moment, he wouldn't even have the chance to react before losing in a single exchange. If he were to try painting a talisman, he wouldn't even know where to begin.

Yet his soul reached out instinctively and summoned a white brush. The slow and steady shielding energy from the brush intensified as it contacted his clumsy fingers.

How can I paint a talisman if I've forgotten everything? he thought as he caressed the familiar object. He felt that his skill had diminished to a nonexistent level. *But can I use this? I faintly remember the characters, and I faintly remember a feeling. I can paint talismans with emotions. What better emotion to paint with than this dullness of life?*

The sharp sword that used to be his talisman artistry had grown rusty with time. Yet didn't this apply to all skills and all metals? Metals could either be sharp or dull. When they were dull, you could sharpen them, and when they were sharp, you would use them and cause them to dull once more. Sharpness and dullness were intertwined, and they came together in metal through something called shape.

Cha Ming held out his trembling fingers and began painting out these ethereal emotions. His clumsy brushstrokes created what could barely be called characters, but despite his sloppy brushwork, they held profound meaning and power.

Countless swords leave not a mark;
Man's edge is dulled by the passing of ages.

What he called the Dull Talisman poured into the imaginary ink within his soul, and inside it he poured the fatigue and corruption he had accumulated during the intense session. Little by little, the sharpness within his eyes returned. He regained the sense of self he had lost within the endless memories and karmic attachments. With this sharpness came the awareness of how to fuse the concepts of sharp and dull into shape. He painted out the remaining passages with sharp and incisive brushstrokes.

Honing his worth through endless practice;

Never questioning his skill.

The four lines fused into one, creating the outline of the Shape Talisman within his mind. He felt fully confident in being able to reproduce it in the outside world, even without the gray candle.

After finishing the talisman, he turned his attention to the last remaining traces of corruption. He snorted and swept them away with a spiritual palm, and in the process of purifying this karma, a great amount of merit imbued itself into his resplendent garment. Meanwhile, the merit halo on his body congealed and liquified, attaining a qualitative transformation. It was a protective layer of good fortune that would aid him in his most troubled times.

Slowly but surely, he cast his awareness into the outside world, where his friends were impatiently waiting.

The meaning of being unfettered became increasingly clear to Gong Lan as each chain of karmic corruption on her soul was resolved. She breathed a sigh of relief as the eightieth chain dissipated, leaving only the last and most difficult chain to take care of. This was the chain that would make it or break it for her, the one that would determine whether she would live out the rest of her life as an evil spirit or as a buddha. She slowly imbued her mind into the chain, but to her surprise, she returned to her current state.

Confused, she pondered the problem. *This last attachment is that of my desire for victory,* Gong Lan thought as she inspected her innermost feelings. *This feeling is most active in the present. I've sworn to resolve this issue for the Song Kingdom, and ironically it has shackled me with massive resentment.*

This philosophical issue was not a new one to Gong Lan, but it was one that she'd never resolved within the depths of her heart. How could one truly be unfettered? Without attachment, wouldn't a person simply waste away and die? Likewise, how would one ever achieve anything or save anyone without some level of attachment to the result?

The more she thought about it, the more she felt the chains bite into her soul. The more she struggled against the thought, the deeper it hooked onto her spirit. The pain grew increasingly intense; the contradiction kept echoing through her mind as she struggled to break free.

Suddenly it struck her. *I'm attached to consistency. This shackle isn't about my desire for victory but rather my struggle with the concept of non-attachment.*

The more she thought about it, the more it made sense. This was only a contradiction if she attached herself too strongly to the concept of non-attachment. It was a concept that should be lightly grasped at best, or it would forever evade her.

A relaxed feeling ran through her body as she realized that being an unattached monk yet serving the people was a logical contradiction. In the same sense, becoming a buddha or a bodhisattva was also a contradiction. But by following the path of non-attachment, this was a reasonable result if one learned to let go. In this way, people who followed the path of non-violence could continue to live, despite their existence being a detriment to others. It was why tolerance and righteous indignation could coexist, and why her existence was not an inconsistency like she once thought.

The last chain unraveled, and she opened her eyes. What used to be the emperor's pure jade seal was now a lifeless green color without a trace of corruption. It shattered into countless grains of dust upon her awakening and released Sibi's pale figure.

"How is this possible?" Sibi said hoarsely as his figure distorted and weakened. "How could you have succeeded where I failed?"

Gong Lan shook her head. "You just cared too much about success, and that was your downfall. Now behave while I send you off."

Sibi's ghost was silent as she released the 10,080 prayer beads. They glowed with unfettered gold light as one pearl after another shattered the remnants of corruption surrounding his soul. The remaining phantom smiled and bowed deeply to Gong Lan before being whisked away by the Yellow River.

"Thank you, my friends," Gong Lan said to her companions before collapsing in exhaustion.

A red-robed man walked out of the king's chamber with a mournful expression. His two brothers hadn't made it.

"Let's go teach those bastards a lesson," he said to Feng Ming, who nodded and hefted his Magma God's Spear.

A crowd of troops funneled out and followed Feng Ming as he walked through Central Square toward the Alchemists Association. General Tang led thousands of troops to join them as they walked. Likewise, Chaplain Chen also joined them. His inquisitors all held luminous pearls that banished away the nearby corruption.

Enemy troops filled with madness launched themselves at them desperately as they approached. They tried their best to incapacitate them, but many good men died as they advanced and entered the Alchemists Association.

The Magma God's Spear glowed with a searing light that blinded his enemies and guided his allies forward. Every step he took caused enemy forces to tumble and techniques to fail. Equipment shattered on impact while his own force's swords and sabers struck non-vital points. Still, it was an imperfect process.

If only we didn't have to kill each other like this, Feng Ming thought. *If only everyone could come to their senses and end this needless bloodshed.* As he thought this, a gentle wind blew across the kingdom. It started from Southhaven Wall, where vicious fighting had broken out. Men who had gone crazy somehow regained their lucidity and surrendered their arms. General Qin clubbed them just to be sure.

As Feng Ming's forces breached the Alchemists Association's

walls, the wind swept over Green Leaf City. The fighting amongst teachers and students was rapidly quelled, as was the fighting between the city's mortal residents.

As the butt of Feng Ming's spear struck a general's head and knocked him unconscious, the wind spread throughout the outskirts of Songjing. People who had been fighting in the streets suddenly realized their mistakes. They knelt on the ground and cried to their ancestors, begging for forgiveness.

As Feng Ming's troops arrived outside the crown prince's final holdout, the three generals regained their mental clarity.

"What have we done?" General Zhang whispered. The many details that had eluded them finally snapped into place. They suddenly realized the crown prince's atrocities and their fervent support.

"This is the final moment," Prince Tian said with a crazed expression. "If we kill this Marshal Feng, we will win!"

The three generals looked at the demented crown prince with pity. It was clear to them that they had lost, and that there was no longer a benefit to fighting.

"My prince, we should surrender," one of the generals suggested.

"We can never surrender," Prince Tian said. "I've seen the future, a future where our people are enslaved and raised like cattle. We must fight for our survival by uniting with the south. It's the only way for our people to survive!"

Sighing, the three generals drew their weapons and approached the mad prince. "Then as citizens of the kingdom, we must perform our duty and defend it to the last." They nodded to each other and simultaneously ignited their potential. The energy from their cores suddenly poured into their bodies all at once.

"It'll all be over soon, my prince," one of the generals said.

These three generals, in their delusion, had done unthinkable things. For them, there was no forgiveness.

"What are you doing?" Prince Tian exclaimed as he noticed their sudden increase in power. He drew his sword and lashed out against them like a cornered badger. They ignored their wounds and joined in a three-man formation to trap and suppress him.

"There is no future for us, but that doesn't mean there isn't one for the kingdom," General Zhang said. "We will atone for our crimes in the next life."

A massive boom filled the air, destroying the three generals along with Prince Tian. The doors to their room burst outward and allowed the invading troops inside. All that remained of the four were a few high-grade treasures and what remained of Prince Tian—a black-and-gold cloak and a marshal's medallion.

An eerie quiet pervaded the Jade Bamboo Auction House. The fighting had died down within the hour, with Prince Lei's forces claiming victory. Everyone, including Wang Jun's own staff, were busy tallying losses and damages while evaluating their path forward. Only the sickly looking Wang Jun, Protector Ren, Elder Bai, and Li Ming were otherwise preoccupied. They waited for a special guest in a building not far from the auction house, where they had agreed to meet.

As per their contract, Wang Jun had brought only three people, to which he could only disclose minimal information.

"Do you think he'll come?" Li Ming asked. He had removed his disguise and revealed his full cultivation base. After all, the Black King already knew who he was.

"He will," Wang Jun said confidently. "This is a rather large exchange, even for him."

A half hour trickled by. During this time, Wang Jun performed some routine inspections over their ample preparations. At midnight exactly, a black mist congregated into a lone figure, and the man confidently waltzed into the warehouse with not a care in the world.

"I see that Li Ming broke his contract," the Black King said nonchalantly. "Did you enjoy his story?"

"It was an interesting story," Wang Jun said. "Though I was more interested in securing his services for protection. I'm wounded, after all."

The Black King seemed to smirk from within his cloak. "Of course, of course," he said. "Have you brought the immortal-jade core? I've brought the payment." He removed a simple-looking ring from his finger. Wang Jun could tell it was a spatial artifact with a simple glance.

"I did," Wang Jun said, pulling out a bag of holding. "Pardon my frugality on the bag of holding. Money has been rather tight of late. Let's get this exchange over with." He began walking forward.

"You know, it's too bad you don't trust me more," the Black King said. "Even Daoist Obscurus places a certain amount of trust in my abilities."

Wang Jun's heart skipped a beat when he heard this name. What was his relationship with Daoist Obscurus? How could he possibly know him? His palms began to sweat as he readied himself to activate the formations as per their plan. Both he and the Black King simultaneously flicked their spatial artifacts toward each other. They caught them simultaneously, bringing their contract to an end.

As soon as their karmic ties dissipated, the Black King released a vast amount of killing intent. Behind Wang Jun, his three protectors unleashed their cultivation bases and killing intent and prepared to act. Wang Jun's mind was in turmoil, but he activated the many formations Cha Ming had prepared beforehand under his direction. While he might not be able to harm someone like the Black King, he could at least restrain him.

But what to do? Wang Jun thought. *Since he knows that man, it can't be a coincidence.*

After firming up his resolve, Wang Jun burst out with chains of shadow and fate. They surrounded him, but instead of binding the Black King, they bound Protector Ren, Elder Bai, and Li Ming. Fortunately, this prompting was all his two staunchest allies needed to stand down. Most of the restraining power was directed toward Li Ming, whose cultivation base had increased from what he'd originally revealed. Wang Jun also directed five layers of formations to further hinder Li Ming.

The Black King, seeing this development, continued rushing toward Wang Jun with his black dagger in hand. The air distorted, and he passed straight through the second young master of the Wang family and directly stabbed at the surprised Li Ming. The black dagger pierced his heart, but to Wang Jun's surprise, the man was still alive.

"How did you know?" Li Ming said hoarsely as he tumbled to the ground, mortally wounded. "My planning was flawless, my cover and my ruse without blemishes. You should have believed me and not him!"

Wang Jun sighed. "I almost didn't realize it. Not until he mentioned Daoist Obscurus."

"Who?" Li Ming asked. Black blood was trickling out of his mouth, his eyes begging for one final answer before he stepped into the grave.

Wang Jun shook his head. "Only those my master trusts can remember his name. It's wreathed in shadows, unspeakable by those who aren't his followers. If the Black King knows his name, that meant he was surely a junior brother of mine. Isn't that right?" He glanced at the cloaked figure.

The Black King chuckled and pulled down his hood. His hair was black, and his skin was pale. The man looked to be in his fifties. "This lowly one is lucky to be one of your master's inner disciples. Unfortunately, I am only skilled in shadows. One can only become a core disciple with diligence and luck."

"I see," Li Ming said, sighing in relief. "So my plan was flawless after all. Now tell me, were you the girl I caught in the teahouse?"

"The matron, actually," Wang Jun said. "The girl was an excellent smokescreen."

Li Ming nodded.

"Black Death has his own quirks, and I have mine," Li Ming said. "Since you've defeated me, you deserve a reward."

"Oh?" Wang Jun said.

"In my ring, you'll find some damning evidence," Li Ming said. "It might be useful if you return to the capital."

"But why would you give it to me?" Wang Jun said.

"Black Death has his life-bound oaths, and I have my reward," Li Ming said with a light smile on his face. "You don't reach the top without being a little odd." Then he slumped down as his last breath left him.

"I take it Master sent you to help me?" Wang Jun said, turning to Hei Ling.

Hei Ling nodded. "As discreetly as possible. He knew that the first young master had sent Li Ming to kill you, and he didn't want you to be at a disadvantage. However, he left strict instructions that I couldn't give you anything for free—only services."

Wang Jun looked at the man on the floor. "Do you mind if I confiscate your spoils of war? As a top-ranking assassin, his net worth is nothing to sneeze at."

"Sure," Hei Ling said. He tossed a silver bracelet onto Li Ming's corpse. "Who would have thought that his net worth would be so high, though?"

Wang Jun inspected the silver bracelet and frowned.

"You don't need to be worried," Hei Ling said, laughing. "These are the deeds I acquired and the commission I charged for selling your goods on the black market. I was planning on giving them to you later, but this provides me with a convenient excuse. You can use this as an opportunity to launder any money you've acquired illegally through me, including that from selling the immortal jade. After all, the family can't fault you for confiscating the wealth of a high-tier assassin who happened to be dabbling in the black market."

Wang Jun smiled. "Thank you for everything, Junior Brother

Ling. I likely would have died without you."

"As Master's only core disciple, we can't have you losing face." Hei Ling shrugged. "If there isn't anything else, I'll be off." Then he disappeared in a puff of smoke.

Later, Wang Jun discovered that any traces of Hei Ling in the city had disappeared as though he had never existed. Even the records in the Jade Bamboo Auction House had been altered. No one would ever suspect a thing.

Epilogue

Two weeks later, Cha Ming was seated at a red table near a newly wedded couple.

"Who would have thought that Feng Ming would get married so quickly," he said to Wang Jun, who was seated in front of him. Huxian, Lei Jiang, and Silverwing were in a secluded area where one roast beast after another was brought to sate their voracious appetites.

"I suppose that's one way of getting lucky," Wang Jun said. "Though I heard a funny story." He sipped on a glass of wine, the first one Cha Ming had ever seen him drink. "When the king awoke from his coma, he mildly remembered waking up for a brief moment and exchanging a conversation with Feng Ming and his daughter. In a fit of rage, he beat Feng Ming and told him, 'How dare you impersonate your father! You should be punished!' Then he turned to his daughter and said, 'Very good, very good. You wanted to help him out so much and lent him my spear? Fine. Only a family member may borrow my spear. If that's what you want, I'll act as your matchmaker. You're getting married in two weeks' time, grieving period be damned!'"

Cha Ming burst out laughing. "Is that really true? I heard the king and Marshal Feng were on very good terms."

"They were like brothers," Wang Jun said. "I figure that, in his grief over Feng Chuan's passing, he resolved to help out his nephew and arrange a marriage for him. He didn't even give them time to consider, he just forced it on them and told them to accept."

"Still, they look happy," Cha Ming said as he looked at the newly married couple. "Someday I'll find someone that's right for me." The image of Yu Wen, whom he'd met in Fuxi's Library, came to mind.

Wang Jun sighed. "I can't think of such matters until I get my revenge."

Cha Ming didn't press him. He was very aware of his heartache over Hong Xin.

"Give me a second," Cha Ming said as he saw some familiar figures in the distance. "I need to go say goodbye to some friends." He left Wang Jun to his brooding and greeted Luo Xuehua, Dongfang Hao, and the two core-formation elders at the edge of the celebration grounds. They had mostly recovered from their wounds.

"Are you sure you don't want to stay longer?" Cha Ming asked.

Luo Xuehua shook her head. "Brother Hao and I will be breaking through to core formation soon. After that, we need to rush to the southern frontier. You might not know this, but the Song Kingdom's civil war was nothing but a petty skirmish. Every day, thousands of cultivators die in the fight against the south's aggression."

"I'll be back in Quicksilver soon," Cha Ming said. "But before then, I'll be helping out Feng Huoshan for a while by teaching some juniors. Can you do me a favor and deliver this Shape Talisman to Jun Xiezi. I still owe him a favor, and I'm sure he'll be happy to see that his investment is bearing dividends."

"Sure," Luo Xuehua said. "It was nice fighting alongside you again, Brother Cha Ming. Don't be a stranger." The gentle blind woman then flew off with the aid of the two core-formation protectors. She reminded Cha Ming of a fragile snowflake being taken by the wind.

"We'll fight together again, Brother Cha Ming." Dongfang Hao laughed and flew off as well.

Cha Ming sighed and looked over to a nearby tree. "Where will you go now?" he asked Gong Lan, who walked out from behind it. Her bald head and orange kasaya remained unchanged, but her demeanor had improved drastically. She no longer seemed so subdued; a hint of wildness emanated from her relaxed eyes.

"There's only one place for the World Tree Master," Gong Lan said. "I will return to the World Tree Monastery and prepare for the upcoming battle. The Southern Alliance's ambition is far greater than you might realize. A great war will emerge in our lifetime, and it will threaten the very foundation of the plane."

"Then I'll work hard and improve as quickly as possible," Cha Ming said.

"Improvement is important, but remember to stay true to yourself," Gong Lan said. "You made a difficult choice in the labyrinth, and you gained far more than you know in the process. Don't be dispirited by a simple setback to your cultivation. Heaven never bars all exits."

"I've been through worse," Cha Ming said. Gong Lan smiled and bowed lightly. Then, motes of light left her body one by one until she disappeared along with them. He didn't know when he would see her again.

Cha Ming returned to the table where Wang Jun was seated. "How long will you be staying in Songjing?"

"Two years or so," Wang Jun said. "By then, I'll have completed my family's task. After that, I'll return to Gold Leaf City."

The frosty ground crunched beneath Hong Xin's feet as she approached a red building in the distance. It was surrounded by a forest of golden trees. According to Hong Yinyue, it would only allow those with an invitation to enter.

"The leaves are strange," Hong Xin whispered as she nabbed one off a nearby tree. Instead of the constant gold coloring that should have persisted across the seasons, it was covered in thin red lines. They increased in number until the trees near the Red Dust Pavilion had completely changed in color.

"Only two years," Hong Xin said. "After two years in this place, I'll finally be ready to help him. I won't be a burden, and I won't leave his side no matter what happens."

She strengthened her resolve and walked toward the red building in the woods. She passed by the golden trees before arriving at a small clearing surrounded by red ones. As she stood there, the red leaves fell around her. The wind blew and whipped up thousands of leaves until her figure was completely obscured by corrupted crimson.

– End Book 5 –

A Note to Readers

If you've enjoyed this book, I would greatly appreciate it if you left a rating on the site where you purchased it. Ratings lead to credibility in this competitive marketplace, and by leaving one, you signal to the world that this book is worth reading.

As some of you might know, I release each book as I write it. It wasn't necessary for you to buy this book, but your support is greatly appreciated. If you are so inclined, you can continue reading as I write at:

https://royalroadl.com/fiction/16320/painting-the-mists

I can't promise fully edited or proofread content, but I will do my best to continue maintaining frequent and high-quality releases.

If you would like to receive bimonthly updates on writing progress, releases, and the life of Patrick Laplante, subscribe to the Painting the Mists newsletter at:

http://eepurl.com/dymvO1

You can also find a link to the newsletter at www.paintingthemists. com. As a bonus for subscribing, you'll receive exclusive biography sketches for each of the key characters, starting with Huxian!

Other ways to contact me or keep in touch:
Facebook: https://www.facebook.com/RedMiragePtM/
Twitter: @RedMirage_PtM

The Cultivation Systems

Qi Cultivation

- Qi Condensation – condense the qi of heaven and earth into a liquid in your dantian
  o Stages 1-3: form a qi pool
  o Stages 4-6: form a qi lake
  o Stages 7-9: form a qi ocean
- Foundation Establishment – form pillars from your qi, setting a firm foundation for your future cultivation.
  o Traditionally, a cultivator forms between one and nine pillars, which are affixed to the bottom of the qi oceans.
  o The liquid qi in this stage is more viscous, its quantity and quality is dependent on the number of pillars.
  o Pillars are grown from the bottom up, gradually forming the foundation with which to form your core
- Core Formation – condense your foundation into a core, the basis of your future growth
- Rune Carving – ???

Body Cultivation

- Body Strengthening – basic body strengthening and purification. Typically, the body is fed with qi and then refined with an opposing qi, removing any impurities
- Bone Forging – bones are the basis of strength and durability. The strongest body is nothing without strong bones supporting it.
- ???

Soul Cultivation

- Innate Soul – cultivators are born with an innate soul, and it grows as the cultivator advances in qi condensation. Eventually, the soul will make a rapid breakthrough into incandescence.
- Incandescent Soul – the soul begins to shine with incandescent light. Advanced soul manipulation of objects and mental communication is now possible.
- Resplendent Soul – wrap the soul in a resplendent vestment

Acknowledgments

As I continue to write, I find that this list of acknowledgments grows. There are far too many people to thank—if I missed you, I'm sorry. It wasn't intentional.

First of all, thank you for the beta readers, Denis Laplante (my brother), Dave Yeung (who has been providing feedback since the start of the series), Sarah, Psiioniic (RR), Astrael (RR), and Savane (RR).

Just like before, I would like to acknowledge my parents, who continue to encourage me on my journey in writing this novel series. Special thanks go to my father this time, who started reading and caught up to the end of Book 4 in 3 weeks. Thank you to my two brothers and my sister.

Thank you to all my friends once again. I recently took some time off work to focus on writing, and after talking to them, I'm convinced that I've made the right decision.

Thank you to my girlfriend, Xing Wen, who continues to support me as I write this series.

Many thanks to Crystal Watanabe for her excellent support while editing my novel. My writing continues to improve with her help, so I'm glad to have her on board.

Thank you to Petros Stefanidis for the excellent cover and the new look.

Finally, thank you to my readers. I write to tell stories to people, and a story is worth nothing if it isn't shared.

About the Author

Patrick Georges Laplante was born in a small town in the Canadian prairies in 1987. He began publishing *Painting the Mists* online under the pseudonym RedMirage in January 2018.

An engineer by trade, he graduated from the University of Alberta in 2009 and completed his master's degree in 2011. While writing and engineering have little in common, he actively utilizes his experiences and attention to detail in fleshing out a vivid world and answering the "whys," which are often left unanswered in Xianxia fiction.

As an avid vegan, he aims to prompt internal reflection in his readers through various themes like non-violence, choice, and begging the question: Is personhood restricted to humanity? And what is proper conduct, morality, and love?

His work is inspired by a combination of Western fiction, *Dungeons and Dragons*, Chinese web novels, and various Japanese, Korean, and Chinese comics and illustrated novels.